It must have been days since his cheeks had met a razor, and the effect shouldn't have been so appealing. The fire below her navel flared, sending sparks flying through her blood in a familiar sensation. The fizzy pop of attraction acted like embers against a night sky spelling out *that's not disgust you're feeling*. Damn him.

"The more I think about it, the more I'm convinced this is your fault. Even if it weren't, you're the only person I could think to ask for help."

The pull of attraction lessened somewhat, though it didn't dissipate entirely. Her brows pinched together. "I am not sure if that's an accusation or a compliment."

"Both, I think," the impossible earl said in that same bland tone he'd used when calling the cat hell spawn. At least, that's what she assumed he was talking to a moment ago.

"For what am I being blamed?"

"Lucifer. Hell spawn. Or possibly George, in honor of our destructive and unlikable regent. I haven't decided yet."

Ah, so she was correct. If this room was any indication, it seemed their plan to wreak havoc on his orderly existence was working swimmingly.

"This is about the cat, is it?"

Praise for Bethany Bennett

"As emotional as it is steamy, this promises good things for the series to come."
—*Publishers Weekly*, on *Good Duke Gone Wild*

"This series starter shows strong promise for the next entry."
—*Library Journal*, on *Good Duke Gone Wild*

"This is a gem." —*Publishers Weekly* on *Dukes Do It Better*

"Emma's and Mal's journey more than lived up to my expectations." —The Romance Dish on *Dukes Do It Better*

"Packed with disguises, debts, and debutantes, this delightful Regency does not disappoint."
—*Publishers Weekly*, starred review on *West End Earl*

"Delicious, sexy fun."
—*BookPage*, starred review on *West End Earl*

"Filled with gripping drama, strong characters, and steamy seduction, this tantalizing story is sure to win the hearts of Regency fans."
—*Publishers Weekly,* starred review on *Any Rogue Will Do*

"Everything I adore in a Regency—wit, steam, and heart!"
—Grace Burrowes, *New York Times* bestselling author, on *Any Rogue Will Do*

My
Best Friend's
Earl

My Best Friend's Earl

BETHANY BENNETT

FOREVER

New York   Boston

Forever
Hachette Book Group
1290 Avenue of the Americas, New York, NY 10104
read-forever.com
@readforeverpub

First Mass Market Edition: August 2025

Forever is an imprint of Grand Central Publishing. The Forever name and logo are registered trademarks of Hachette Book Group, Inc.

The publisher is not responsible for websites (or their content) that are not owned by the publisher.

The Hachette Speakers Bureau provides a wide range of authors for speaking events. To find out more, go to hachettespeakersbureau.com or email HachetteSpeakers@hbgusa.com.

Forever books may be purchased in bulk for business, educational, or promotional use. For information, please contact your local bookseller or the Hachette Book Group Special Markets Department at special.markets@hbgusa.com.

ISBNs: 978-1-5387-4050-7 (Mass Market); 978-1-5387-4051-4 (Ebook)

Printed in the United States of America

BVGM

10 9 8 7 6 5 4 3 2 1

For Mama Sher, my kick-ass librarian aunt. Thank you for always making time for my teenage phone calls, and for shamelessly nurturing my love of romance novels. Every girl should be lucky enough to have someone like you in their corner. I love you.

And for Court, for saving my ass yet again when I lit the bestie bat signal. The last fifty pages of this book don't suck, thanks to you.

My
Best Friend's
Earl

Chapter One

Brush teeth
Eat something (remember
Monday's dizzy spells?)
Mend apron strap
Contact publisher regarding latest order of
Blanche Clementine books

London, Spring 1816

If her father had been a baron—or, God forbid, a duke—she'd have been ruined. However, as the youngest daughter of a modest bookshop owner, Constance Martin was merely notorious in a certain area of London.

Most days, she rather liked it. Being notorious was the opposite of invisible, after all. Invisibility was an all-too-familiar sensation after a lifetime spent in the shadow of a damn near perfect sister. It didn't take long for her to learn that if you gave people something to talk about, they'd remember your name. Your actual name, not just Betsy Martin's twin sister, who, despite being nearly identical in looks, could not be more different in ability and temperament. The implication being, that Betsy was a joy to her family, while Constance was...not.

"Inconstant Constance," a woman in the map section of the bookshop whispered to her friend. Their giggles inspired an eye roll at her cousin, Hattie. Unfortunately, since Constance's trip down the aisle—in the opposite direction from her groom—comments like these were common. At least the women weren't mocking her to her face.

A week ago, her cousin Caro asked if Constance would have made the same decision if she'd foreseen the damage her reputation would suffer after leaving Walter at the altar.

There'd been no hesitation in her answer. *Yes.*

Even if she'd known about the name-calling, obnoxious men in the neighborhood, and the whispering customers, Constance wouldn't have gone through with the wedding. The alternative simply felt wrong.

Constance slipped the missive to Blanche Clementine's publisher—or rather, Caro's publisher, since their cousin had finally announced to the world that she was the famous writer—into the pile of outgoing mail, while avoiding looking at Hattie. Hattie's expressive face spoke volumes without words, and her eyes surely had things to say about the gossiping shoppers. An inexplicable snort of laughter from Connie would only draw more attention.

Blowing a blond curl out of her eye, Constance searched for something else to do. The ever-present stack of account books with their fine layer of dust silently mocked her, a clear reminder of everything she seemed unable to make time for. With a grimace, she looked away. *Something interesting to do*, she amended.

"If you will stay out front, I'll put on the kettle for tea," Hattie said. "The damp is settling into my bones today."

"You sound like an old crone," she teased. "Go on, then. A cup sounds lovely if you don't mind making me one as well."

Saved from the account books once again. Relief and guilt

warred for a brief moment before Constance abandoned them to fiddle with the stack of bookmarks she'd embroidered last month. Perhaps the literary quotes she'd chosen were too esoteric. Silly little posies of violets, or something else equally insipid might have been a better choice. Or perhaps customers didn't appreciate the colors of embroidery thread she'd used. Regardless, they hadn't sold as well as she'd hoped.

As she arranged the bookmarks, the gossipy ladies moved toward the shelves of romantic novels, occasionally casting glances her way and whispering too low for Constance to hear. Even though she knew better, the urge to defend herself to strangers pulled at her. Given context, the women might understand the reasoning behind her most public social failure. Going through with the marriage would have ensured a life that was…boring. Days, then years, of the predictable, logical progression from one utterly monotonous life event to another.

A customer set his purchases on the counter, and she welcomed the distraction. When he paid his gaze raked over her bosom, as if he could somehow see through her gown's modest neckline, work apron, and linen fichu. She clenched her teeth, then blew out a relieved breath when he left the store without additional comment. Men were, on the whole, such ridiculous creatures. Some more than others.

Married life with Walter Hornsby would have been hell. Especially because Walter didn't lead an uneventful life. They'd even postponed the wedding once because he'd been off mucking about with smugglers to avoid the Crown's taxes on the goods he sold. Did he include her in his adventures? No. And when pressed, he'd made it clear she never would be welcome on his moonlit illegal jaunts.

The rat.

Also, despite a thriving merchant business built through routine, if illegal, acquisitions of fine French muslin, silks, and lace, Walter offered only a few scant yards of trimmings for her wedding gown. Her. Wedding. Gown. And expected *thanks*.

A rat, indeed.

Hattie appeared from the office, wiping her hands on her apron. "It will be a few minutes. Perhaps one of us should run to the shops for pasties and make a proper meal of it."

Before Constance could answer, the two women approached the register. Pasting on a wide smile, Constance asked, "Did you find everything you were looking for?"

Beside her, Hattie stood stiffly, and Constance suspected she was fighting the urge to comment on what they'd overheard. "Hattie, would you mind checking the kettle?"

The water wouldn't be boiling yet, but Hattie embraced the excuse to retreat until the ladies left the store. Once the shop was free of customers, Hattie returned with two cups in hand and a folded scandal sheet tucked under her arm.

"Extra sweet, " Hattie said, handing one cup to Constance. "To combat the bitterness I feel on your behalf. And"—she held up the paper—"the latest society high jinks for entertainment."

"Excellent. Let's see if we recognize anyone." Blowing on the dark brew, she pulled the day's to-do list from her apron pocket, and examined the remaining items while Hattie perused the scandal sheet. Her stomach growled, causing a fleeting thought that perhaps they really should run out for meat pies. However, she didn't voice it before returning her attention to the list.

"Ooh, here's one. 'Lord H——recently examined by his peers and found wanting after being discovered reeking of spirits while *sans* breeches in the dark walk at Vauxhall.'

Goodness. There's a gentleman who could have used the aid of Lord Bixby to snuff that story."

Constance smirked. "That piece of gossip would be worth a pretty penny to the likes of Bixby. Maybe this Lord H doesn't have anything London's friendly neighborhood blackmailer needs."

Lord Bixby's barony suffered notoriously from generational debt, which led him to find—*ahem*—alternative means with which to secure his unwed sisters a place at the finest tables.

Blackmail.

The Duke of Holland, now married to their cousin Caro, had needed the man's help to find his first wife's lover. The lover was Bixby's cousin. Since there'd been no love lost between the two, the baron had happily shared every bit of damning information he'd held on the man. And there'd been a lot.

Although they'd never laid eyes on Bixby, Constance and Hattie had been fascinated by him ever since learning of his existence.

"No matter how difficult the day, we didn't begin it by waking up half naked in a public place," Connie mused.

Hattie clinked their mugs in a silent toast. "Hear, hear. Offers perspective, I suppose, when I've been pouting over having finicky customers this morning, and no one to fob them off on because you were busy with your own. I realize it's not the same as 'waking up to people laughing at your penis,' but in the last hour I've endured impertinent questions about Caro's career and marriage, disposed of a dead mouse your cat left us by the window, and gone on a wild goose chase for a man who saw a book last week, couldn't recall the title, and now desperately needed to buy it."

"Let me guess, the book was blue?" Constance grinned,

then stifled a moan of pleasure when she finally sipped her tea.

Thank God she hadn't seen the mouse first. She and Hattie had a strict "you see it, you deal with it" policy when it came to Gingersnap's gifts.

"Red, actually. You have the right idea."

"Did you find it?"

"Of course not. He bought a sketch pad for his niece's birthday though, so he didn't entirely waste my time."

Caro wrote salacious erotic novels and had the audacity to not only be a lowly clergyman's daughter, but also be married to a duke in a rather public love match. People were going to talk, no matter what. Especially after everyone pieced together the clues and realized the Duke of Holland was her hero inspiration. Aristocrats nattered on about one cousin, while the laborers fed on stories of another. You couldn't say the women in their family didn't provide conversational fodder for the masses.

With the Duke and Duchess of Holland recently returned to London, the gossips were greedy for fresh information. Especially once it became known that the duchess was due to give birth to their first child very soon.

The bell over the shop door signaled another customer's arrival, and the cousins turned to greet them. A familiar blonde shook droplets of rain from her cloak and sent them a smile. Miss Althea Thompson craned her neck as she looked around, as if expecting danger to spring out from behind a bookcase. "Good morning. Connie, may we speak privately?" That was when Constance noticed that despite the welcoming smile, Althea stood stiffly, with her fingers knit together at her waist.

"I'll go chip away at the stack of paperwork on the desk," Hattie said to the room at large. "I really miss Caro," she muttered to herself. Caro had kept the office in pristine order when she'd worked at Martin House. The cluttered desk with its pile of ledgers and papers was proof enough that things weren't the same these days.

"Althea, the kettle should still be warm if you'd like some tea," Constance offered.

Her friend shook her head, then blew out a breath and flexed her fingers as if pushing blood back into them as she sat in front of the window. Constance rounded the counter to join her, taking the other chair. "You seem out of sorts. Has something happened?"

"We're friends, aren't we?"

"I would say so. Granted, we haven't known each other for long, but I think of you as a dear friend." When they'd met in Caro's drawing room a month prior, Connie had liked the young woman immediately. Althea was engaged to the best friend of Caro's husband, so in the weeks since their initial meeting, Connie and Althea had ample opportunity to deepen their acquaintance.

"And I can trust you."

Constance nodded, concern mounting by the second. "Of course. You're worrying me, darling. Whatever is on your mind, I'd like to help."

Taking in another gulp of air, Althea released it with a gush of syllables that ran together so quickly, Constance needed a moment to decipher what she'd heard. Surely, she'd misunderstood.

"I beg your pardon. Could you repeat that?"

"I need you to help me break my engagement. There's no one else I can ask. Connie, you were brave enough to run away from your wedding—literally from the altar." Color rose in her cheeks as she spoke. "If people can hire matchmakers, why can't I hire a matchbreaker? That would be you. I trust you. Please say you'll help me. If I have to marry Oliver, I'll just die, I know it."

For once, the loud clutter in Constance's mind quieted, leaving few rational thoughts. No words. She had no words for this situation. Her mouth opened and closed around silent questions that simply wouldn't form.

"I see you may require some time to think about my proposal." Humor crept into Althea's voice for the first time. "It's unusual, I admit."

Finally, one word pushed through. "Why?"

"Why do I want to break my engagement, or why am I asking you specifically?"

"Yes."

"I know our acquaintance has been brief. Regardless, I trust your discretion. No one else can know or would understand why I'd want to end my engagement…" Althea trailed off, while her fingers twirled and stroked the tassels on her reticule.

Constance reached to pet the silky fringe as well. "This is lovely. Is it new?" Jerking her hand back, she winced and felt her cheeks heat. "I apologize. Easily distracted. I am paying attention, I swear it."

Althea waved away the momentary lapse in focus. It was one of the things Connie appreciated about her. She never appeared annoyed by Constance's quirks. Unlike Althea's fiancé, who grew more tense and tight-lipped each time they found themselves in one another's presence.

She and the handsome earl first met when Caro invited them to join her and Dorian in their search for the man who'd had an affair with the late Duchess of Holland. To Connie's recollection, Lord Southwyn spent most of the day watching her as if she were an unknown species of animal. His regard hadn't warmed since.

Constance said the only thing that felt vaguely appropriate. "When I saw you with Lord Southwyn, I thought you made a lovely couple." Stiff, formal, and everything she expected of the ton, but lovely as they sat, untouching, side by side. Like attractive bookends awaiting their moment to be useful.

Miss Thompson snorted at that, and Constance grinned at the indelicate sound. However, all traces of humor disappeared when a suspicion gripped her. "Is Lord Southwyn unkind to you? Has he given you reason to fear him? Is that why you need help?"

Althea's face went slack. "Oliver? Heavens, no. He wouldn't hurt a fly. Except perhaps through neglect, supercilious lectures, or general disinterest. He's not unkind, exactly. However, he's clearly not romantically inclined toward me either. As a gentleman, he can't cry off, but my father would make life unbearable if I ended the engagement."

"Thus, the need to force his hand." Clarity began to make itself known.

"Exactly. I must either give him a disgust of me so he will have no choice but to look elsewhere for a bride, or somehow muster the courage to run away from my own wedding, like you did. If at all possible, I'd rather the former. My attempts before now at being intolerable have had little impact, I'm afraid. That's why I need your assistance."

"I have to ask. Have you told him in plain terms you aren't interested in the match? Perhaps you could work together to deal with your father."

Althea's laugh didn't resemble the tinkling trill she'd used in Caro's drawing room the week before. "I've tried. He dismissed it as nerves and suggested a long engagement so I could acclimate to the idea. Since then, I've misbehaved at events, thrown fits in private, and generally acted like the furthest thing from a loving fiancée. He ignores all of it. My parents are at their wits' end. After three years of being engaged, it's time to pay the piper, as they say. My mother is planning the wedding of the Season. Father is over the moon because he will get the connection to an earldom he's coveted for two decades. Not one person has asked me if I am ready to walk down the aisle. It's as if they all agreed my time is up, and they expect me to meekly go along." She rubbed her forehead and winced. Come to think of it, Constance's temple was beginning to throb in sympathy. "I'm not an unreasonable woman. Every time I imagine making vows to Oliver, my stomach turns and I feel faint. This is more than nerves, and it's not going away. I *need* a matchbreaker."

Constance sighed. "There's no way you can force him to listen? To see reason? Lord Southwyn and I may not see eye to eye on... well, anything. However, he doesn't strike me as the sort to marry an unwilling woman."

"I've known him my whole life. We grew up together as neighbors. There is no one more rigid and duty-bound than Oliver Vincent. Our fathers drew up the betrothal contract when we were children. In his mind, it's done. I'm running out of time. Please, Constance."

"If I do this—" Althea's crow of triumph ended abruptly when Constance shot her a stern look. "If I do this, we will need a plan. The world is not kind to women who defy powerful men, especially when weddings are involved. We must try to protect your reputation."

How she'd do it, she had no idea. Finding a way to give the Earl of Southwyn a disgust of this perfectly charming, attractive woman whom he'd already waited years to marry, would be... Well. Not boring.

Chapter Two

Matchbreaker meeting—make a plan
Find a book on military tactics. Maybe it will help?

When Oliver Vincent's mother, the late Countess of Southwyn, had been in residence, his father had referred to their ancestral seat as Bitchwood Court instead of Birchwood Court.

Suffolk was normally a lush, verdant landscape by this time of year. Today, as a freezing drizzle spit down with a relentless sort of inevitability that soaked him layer by layer until his very bones ached with the cold, his surroundings were brown and gray. Mud and fog dominated everything he'd seen since rising with the sun—such as it was—in his childhood bedchamber that morning. Pitifully few scraggly plant shoots dotted the fields.

As the Earl of Southwyn, he owned acres upon acres of muck. If anything, his estate manager had understated the situation in the last letter. Oliver stood on the bank of the river dividing his property from Sir William's and lifted his mount's foot to inspect her hoof. Using a stick, he pried out clumps of dirt and a decent-size stone. No wonder the mare had been limping. Unfortunately, she was still limping as he led her along the riverbank to test her gait.

"At least you waited to get a bruise until we'd finished our rounds. Thank you for that." The mare whuffled in his face with warm, hay-scented breath, and he chuckled.

Wandering along the bank, he nudged a rock into the water with the toe of his boot to ensure the horse didn't step on it.

For years, he'd envisioned a locks and transportation system in this spot. After the wedding this summer, ownership of this river would revert back to the earldom, and Oliver could monetize this narrow strip of land in a way that would eventually support the entire estate, and help farmers and artisans in the surrounding area.

Much of England teemed with canals full of narrow boats transporting goods to market. Thanks to his father's fiscal mismanagement and lack of caring about anyone other than himself, this part of Suffolk remained underserved. Soon, that would change.

To fulfill the original agreement between Sir William and the late earl, Oliver would marry a Thompson daughter and get the land back. Unfortunately, Althea Thompson wasn't eager to become a countess, which meant the plans he'd been meticulously laboring over for years might never see fruition.

More than once, the subject of purchasing the river outright had been set before Sir William, and each of those conversations had been nothing short of disastrous. So, in light of Althea's reluctance, the logical and most direct solution was out of the question. As was simply scrapping the whole endeavor and walking away, because given what he knew of Sir William's character, Oliver refused to end his engagement without some assurance that Althea's future would be taken care of. Her father was likely to refuse her a dowry out of spite.

What an awful muddle.

Plunk. Another rock kicked into the river. Stuffing his hands deeper into the pockets of his greatcoat, he let the reins hang loosely from his fingers as he meandered toward his favorite tree. It boasted a thick branch that jutted out over the deepest part of the water, making it the perfect place to launch oneself into the river on summer days.

A frayed length of rope dangled, bedraggled by time, from the ancient oak on the Thompsons' side of the bank. In the distance, he could just make out the orchard. Branches struck up at the sky, alarmingly gray and nearly bare of foliage, despite the time of year.

Worry gnawed at him, as it had for weeks. Staring at the reality of barren trees and empty fields made his concern grow exponentially.

This afternoon he'd visited the estate storerooms and tenants to glean an idea of what they'd need to make ends meet. He hoped that looking the farmers in the eye would soothe their rising panic. Oliver might not have the power to make the weather cooperate, but he could reassure them that no one would starve. It didn't matter if it cost him dearly. Their welfare was his responsibility.

Please, God. Don't let it come to that. The weather has to turn soon.

Many families working the Southwyn estates remembered the erratic, unreliable late earl, and still viewed Oliver with distrust. Or, if not outright distrust, they treated him the way his mother had taught him to interact with the animals housed in the menageries she'd loved. Cautious, careful, aware of his ability to hurt them.

"No one is ever truly tamed," he remembered her saying as she held his hand in hers, gliding over the leathery hide of a young rhinoceros. "Our wild nature lingers under the surface, relying on instincts rather than logic. Humans are no more than animals that have declared ourselves in charge. Be cautious, my love. Even though we treat this beast with respect, and although he's accustomed to people, we aren't safe from instinctual urges." As a grown man, Oliver wondered if she'd referred only to the rhino or was subtly speaking her piece about his father.

In the distance, the house loomed from the fog like some kind of legendary castle. His childhood home looked exactly as it always had. Imposing and solid. It gave the impression of something that had been standing since the beginning of time and would remain in place until the end. Birchwood Court had once been an abbey. During the Reformation, Queen Elizabeth gifted it to the first Earl of Southwyn—after stealing it from the Catholic church, of course.

Oliver's earliest memories were of playing hide-and-seek with nurses, nannies, and occasionally his mother in the many priest holes built into the place. They hadn't been able to find him on one occasion, and he'd fallen asleep in the narrow space, only to wake hours later hungry and disgruntled. Apparently, after some time had passed, the nurse tried to raise the alarm, but the earl declared that if his "boy was stupid enough to get himself lost, he deserved whatever he got."

The mare snorted in his ear, pulling Oliver back to the present.

Every negative feeling about his home involved his father in some way. The rest of his memories—and there were many, because the late earl was rarely in residence during those early years—painted the picture of a privileged and happy childhood.

Unfortunately, that childhood had been too short. The games and laughter stopped when his mother died. After that, the only play he found was with the girls next door.

Dorcas, the older Thompson girl, whom he'd expected to marry, and Althea, the blond pigtailed little sister who followed them everywhere. It would have been nice to simply enjoy them as playmates, free of the ever-present duty that damned betrothal agreement brought. None of it seemed real back then. More a reoccurring topic of make-believe they created as children were wont to do.

"Pretend you're a knight, and you have to rescue me from the dragon."

"Pretend we are exploring ancient ruins and this tree is a doorway to the land of the fairy folk."

Pretend our fathers bet our futures in a card game and we have to live with the consequences.

Many important life decisions stemmed from hating the old earl. When a comely barmaid had given Oliver his first kiss, his father had been drinking with friends on the other side of the pub. He could still feel his shame and humiliation when the earl lumbered over, drunk off his arse, and slapped a coin on the table.

"Here. Your first time is on me. She's a sweet one, Oliver. You'll enjoy her." Like he'd been recommending a bottle of wine, rather than a woman.

Oliver had run, ignoring the riotous laughter from the table full of his father's drinking partners. He'd vowed not to be like his sire. He would be reliable. Honorable. Honest. Steadfast. Responsible. Loyal.

The cold bit at his extremities, urging Oliver to return to the house. Saying a silent farewell to the river and depressing orchard, he led his mount away from the bank. With each step, his boots squelched in the muddy turf.

Birchwood Court sent memories—good and bad—flitting through his mind like ghosts. They didn't lessen the trepidation he felt about Althea's continued resistance to their engagement. Once upon a time, he and Althea had been friends. Perhaps that old relationship would help them create a peaceful marriage. Provided, of course, Althea ever stopped hating him for going through with the wedding.

His parents had been ill-suited and never had a chance at happiness. They'd had no prior friendship upon which to build. By the end, they'd despised one another, and the earl never forgave Oliver for his devotion to the late countess. She'd been intelligent and kind, deserving of devotion. Loving his mother so deeply had been the easiest part of his life.

This mare, in fact, was the offspring of her favorite mount. Oliver ran a hand down the wide flat of the horse's cheek, then patted her thick neck. "What do you think about going home with me to London? If your hoof is fine by morning, I'll bring you along." And bring a piece of his mother with him.

The advice she'd given that day with the rhinoceros lingered as he made the uphill trek to the house.

Mother had been wrong about one thing. Unlike that rhinoceros, there was no wilder nature lurking beneath Oliver's calm facade. Any baser instincts had been well and truly ground to dust long ago.

"All right. What have you tried so far?" Connie settled a writing box on her lap and smoothed a fresh piece of paper on the scarred wood. It had been three days since Althea enlisted her help as a matchbreaker, but this was the first opportunity they'd had to sit and plan.

Althea plucked a ginger biscuit from the tin Connie brought with them to the darkened bookshop's sales floor. With only a lamp sitting on a small table by their side, the quiet store felt cozy. Meeting at Martin House had been ideal, as it offered privacy and a place out of the weather.

"Well, when he agreed to the engagement and didn't listen to my protestations, I immediately stopped considering him a friend, obviously. Since then, I've griped and complained at every opportunity and tried to be as unlikable as possible. Honestly, Connie, I sometimes fear I am genuinely becoming the shrew I pretend to be with him. The longer this engagement goes on, the deeper the bitterness burrows into me. I hate it. And I hate who I'm becoming." She bit into the treat and offered a sad shrug. "There's only so far I can go in public, though."

Constance rolled a short pencil between her fingers and tried to determine the best line of attack for their task. "May I ask why he offered for your hand at all when you were so opposed to the match?"

Althea leaned forward. "Don't you know? I thought for sure the duchess would have told you." At Constance's blank look, she gave a rueful laugh. "He never offered for me. I'm the consolation prize, because his last fiancée, my sister, eloped with someone else."

A gentle breeze could have knocked Constance on her rear, she was so shocked at that. Not taking her eyes off her friend, she reached into the biscuit tin and took two. "Your explanation only bred more questions. Talk."

Althea smirked as she settled back in her chair. "Your shock makes me feel better about the whole thing, to be honest. Like maybe I'm not utterly mad for thinking this whole situation is rubbish. The story goes like this. Something happened when we were children—I don't think I'd even been born yet—and our fathers drew up a betrothal. Oliver's father was a rather notorious rogue, and their estate was always halfway up the River Tick. The earl needed funds.

There was some sort of card game, and a wager, I think. Father gave the earl enough money to keep him from debtor's prison. In exchange, he got a bit of land and a countess for a daughter."

Constance cocked her head in thought and licked crumbs from her thumb. "Lord Southwyn was engaged to your sister? Because you weren't born when they wrote the contract."

Nodding, Althea took a moment to chew and swallow her own biscuit. "Yes. However, Dorcas fell in love with someone else and eloped with him three years ago. I'm thrilled she's happy. Less thrilled that I'm expected to fulfill the marriage contract in her stead."

As enlightening as all of this was, more questions whirled through Connie's brain. Had Lord Southwyn loved Althea's sister? If so, was the man utterly heartbroken and shuffling through his days in a gray, emotionless fog—thus explaining his lack of reaction to Althea's previous attempts at raising a fuss? Or, was the idea of reclaiming a lost portion of his ancestral estate so important, he'd marry anyone to get his hands on it? Constance ground her teeth in frustration. How maddening to not understand his reasons for insisting on this marriage.

"No wonder you aren't thrilled with the match. Especially if he hasn't made an effort to woo you. He's had years to do so." Putting pencil to paper, Constance wrote *How to Be a Matchbreaker* across the top of the page. "Now, what things does the Earl of Southwyn hate? What gets him riled and annoyed?"

Althea rested a cheek on her fist. "Gambling. Philanderers. Liars. Scandal. All because of his father, I'm sure. Um . . . messes. Impulsivity. Unpredictability. Emotions."

"He sounds exceedingly dull," Constance muttered. "Except

for abhorring philanderers and liars, of course. I agree with him on that point." *Messes and impulsivity. No wonder he seems so appalled whenever he sees me. He hates everything about me.* An off sensation bloomed in her belly, but she didn't have time to examine it right then. Althea's footman could knock on the window at any moment, giving the signal that their time was up and she needed to return home.

A snicker caught her attention.

"Did you know he wears his waistcoats in rotation? The dark blue on Monday. Hunter green on Tuesday. Maroon on Wednesday, and so on. And they're all so *boring*. No patterns allowed beyond a subtle stripe in a slightly different sheen."

Constance stared out the window as ideas came in bits and pieces. On the street, London teemed with the usual congestion of carriages, hackney cabs, horses, carts, and people from all walks of life. Muted voices filtered through the wavy glass panes to where they sat. She could nearly make out the shapes of Althea's servants inside her coach, keeping dry. Sir William would have a fit of the vapors if he saw his servants acting thus, but Althea was made of different stuff—namely, compassion. Althea cared about others. She would make a good wife one day. Countess, if it came to it.

The plan solidified. Constance's cheeks stretched into a wide smile. "I think we need to change tactics. You've been trying to be unappealing as a fiancée. You say he doesn't like messes or big emotions? You're going to show him exactly how chaotic and smothering a wife can be."

"What do you have in mind?" Althea leaned forward.

"Rather than avoiding all marriage talk, let's turn you into a wife out of his worst nightmares. Can you get into his home? Talk to his servants?"

Althea shrugged. "Of course. Everyone knows I'm going to

be mistress there by the end of the summer, and Mother would be thrilled if I took more of an interest in his household."

"Excellent." Excitement thrummed under Connie's skin, and she bounced a little in her seat. "Is he affectionate? Does he like to be touched?"

Althea curled her lip. "God, no."

"Brilliant." *Touch him constantly*, she wrote on the paper. "Is he meticulous and organized in addition to being generally stuffy? Items on his desk arranged just so?"

"Yes. It's annoying."

"Next time you're in his home, I want you to go into his study, or wherever he works, and move everything from one side of his desk to the other. If he sees you, tell him you like it better that way, because it looks more appealing. In every room you enter, move the things on his shelves and tables out of place by several inches. Rearrange his books." That hurt her heart to suggest, but it was a great idea. "And every chance you get, touch him." At Althea's distressed sound, Constance rushed to reassure her. "I don't mean for you to throw yourself naked at his feet, darling. Fuss over him like a clingy wife would. Straighten his cravat when it doesn't need it. Brush imaginary lint from his sleeve and tut over his valet not meeting your standards. Muss his hair. Not romantic touches—try to be deliberately annoying while adjusting his person. If he protests at any point, tell him you're simply being a good wife now that the wedding is around the corner."

Althea laughed, then abruptly straightened, eyes wide. "His waistcoats. They're all solid colors, no bold patterns. What if I replace them with garish ones? I have the pin money to buy one or two, I think."

"It's well within a countess's purview to ensure her

husband isn't appearing drab in public," Constance said primly, then dissolved into giggles and wrote *Dress him up like an ugly, stuffy doll*.

A low *meow* came from the doorway to the office, and her giant orange cat, Gingersnap, sauntered past a shadow she suspected was Hattie. Her cousin wouldn't tell a soul, but Constance wished she wasn't listening in. As for her cat, he appeared to be on the hunt. Rodents were hell on the paper and leather binding of books, so Gingersnap roamed free between the shop and their apartment upstairs during the night. "Does Southwyn have any pets?"

"No. His mother loved animals, so I'm surprised he's never had one. Probably hates the mess."

"What do you think would be more chaotic—a squirrel, a dog, or a feral cat?"

"Dogs are easy to come by, but it would have to be an ugly one. A cat could work, and I'd prefer it to a dog. Squirrels would escape out the nearest window."

Grinning, she wrote *Give him a pet*. "Be sure you speak to it like a baby. Men hate that."

A short while later, they'd added *Spend his money* and *Flirt with other men* to the list. They must remember Althea's reputation, so some things required circumspection.

Examining the sheet of paper, Connie grinned. "And just like that, we have created the bride of his nightmares. We can add to this, of course. If we manage every item on this list and he still wants you, he's touched in the head."

Althea beamed, then sobered. "You truly are the best friend. I know you're on good terms with the Duke of Holland, and he's Oliver's closest confidant. I hope helping me with this won't affect your relationship with His Grace."

Constance considered that for a moment, then shook her head. "Dorian is a good man. He'll understand why I'm choosing girl friends before his earl friend."

Althea cackled. "Girls before earls!"

Connie added a note to the top of the list. *How to Be a Matchbreaker: rule #1 girls before earls.*

Chapter Three

~

Determine if cats make him ill. If yes, get a dog
If no, find a feral cat

Bloody hell. Her. That damned woman was everywhere. The only places Oliver could successfully avoid the bookseller were ballrooms and society matrons' drawing rooms during calling hours. Of course, it seemed everyone in London was in the park today, celebrating a rare sunny day with temperatures that hovered near warm. Almost.

Hope for more days like this one sprouted. Much like he prayed the plants in his fields would grow under this sunshine. Despite the clear day, and that it was early May, people still wore their winter cloaks and fur muffs. Miss Constance Martin's red cloak stood out in the sea of dark wool.

Oliver of all people was achingly aware that one could not choose their family. So, he did not hold it against his best friend, the Duke of Holland, for marrying a woman whose cousin was nothing short of a nuisance. From the moment Oliver met Caro's cousin, he'd recognized her for the problem she was. Chaos incarnate. A distraction. And God, he hated both of those things. They caused ripples in schedules and moods in those around him that he could neither predict nor control.

She was beyond anyone's control, and that was obvious. In fact, if Miss Martin heard someone discussing ways to control her, she would likely laugh in their face, flaunt that annoyingly insistent dimple, then flounce off to do whatever the hell she chose. Which seemed to be her entire life. Doing whatever the hell she chose.

And for reasons beyond his comprehension, what she'd chosen to do for the last week was cross his path every time he was with his fiancée.

Never mind that Constance was not highborn enough to be part of the parade of aristocrats through Hyde Park. Commoners gawked from the sidelines, no doubt appalled at the excess shown by the fashions, horseflesh, and flashy carriages of the ton. However, those commoners knew to stay out of the way—not make themselves known by waving merrily while shouting Althea's name.

Which in turn meant Althea, normally a very level-headed miss aware of her place in society and the expectations that came with it, grinned broadly and demanded he stop his carriage to greet her friend.

Why had they become friends? They'd met in Holland's drawing room, and for some inexplicable reason, found a kindred spirit in one another. God help him. It didn't make sense to his way of thinking. Althea was usually rather quiet. Uncomplicated. If she was in a poor mood, she could be a termagant, so he knew she had it in her to make his life difficult. She'd been a scamp as a child, but until their engagement, it had been years since he'd seen any sign of that sort of behavior.

Perhaps that's what she had in common with Miss Martin. Unpredictable emotions. Which might explain Althea's recent behavior. She'd been acting strangely during the last few days. Not just smiling, but simpering. Touching his arm when they spoke. Laughing at things he said, when they weren't terribly amusing. This afternoon, she'd adjusted his cravat and picked at something in his hair while he drove. It was unnerving.

"Pull over the carriage, Oliver."

He sent his fiancée a look he hoped showed every bit of his indignation. "I most certainly will not. I am responsible for driving these horses; thus, I'll stay exactly where I am. You may greet your friend while we are at a standstill. However, I won't veer off the path or hold up traffic."

She huffed. He gaped. "Did you just roll your eyes? Good God, Althea. Are you still in the schoolroom? This friendship with Miss Martin is a bad influence, if you ask me."

A mulish angle tilted her chin. "I didn't ask you, Lord Southwyn." Lovely, now she was in a mood. Having known her for her entire life, they'd long ago passed formalities. She only used his title when annoyed with him. "Until I say my vows, you may not dictate whom I allow into my social circle."

A headache brewed at the base of his skull, threatening an afternoon of pain instead of productivity. Taking a deep breath, Oliver searched for a thread of calm within himself. She was right. They were not married—because he couldn't convince the woman to walk down the damn aisle. That would change.

Thanks to Sir William putting his foot down, wedding plans were unavoidable. Oliver had winced when Sir William claimed his daughter required a firm, authoritarian hand. Sure, Althea might act a little spoiled. Spoiled, but otherwise a decent person with whom he couldn't find fault beyond her flappy emotional bits.

Despite his current mood, Oliver was not the kind of man who would limit her social circle. Not as a fiancé, or a husband. The late earl had been overbearing like that, and his mother suffered as a result.

Lowering his voice while keeping one eye on the unruly blond curls weaving through the crowd toward them, Oliver said, "I apologize. Of course, I am not going to dictate who you may befriend. That would make me a brute. I may be many things, but I'm not a brute."

Althea's stubborn expression softened. "I know you're not a brute. Thank you for apologizing. Won't you please consider giving Constance a chance to win you over? I'm sure you'd like her if you tried. She's become very dear to me, and I fully intend to deepen my acquaintance with her in the years to come."

Grow accustomed to the interfering woman, in other words. He could try. Tolerance might be the best he could hope to achieve. Oliver forced a tight-lipped smile as his unwelcome guest stopped beside their carriage and swung a large wicker basket onto the seat beside him.

"Miss Thompson, Lord Southwyn. Well met!"

"A pleasure to see you again, Miss Martin." It wasn't. He detested liars, and he'd just become one. Blast it all.

"What do you have there?" Althea leaned over Oliver to peer into the basket. In the process, the carved wooden bird and white feather on her bonnet whacked him in the face, then settled halfway up his nose.

Blowing out a huff of air, he jerked away, trying to remove the feather from his nostrils. "Althea, would you mind…"

"Gingersnap! Oh, precious kitty. How are you, my love?" Althea didn't heed him at all.

"He's missed you," Miss Martin said, a second before Althea lifted an animal into her lap, cooing all the while.

"You brought your cat to Hyde Park?" Oliver was hard-pressed to do more than blink at the creature.

"Of course. Gingersnap walks with me on his lead all the time." A pinch between Miss Martin's brows signaled a crack in her cheerful demeanor. "Bringing him during such a busy time was a miscalculation on my part, I'm afraid. He's been stuck in the basket for his own safety ever since we entered the park." Like storm clouds blowing by, her smile returned, and that pinch disappeared. "The rats and mice of Hyde Park are safe for today, I suppose."

"Poor Gingersnap, no little mousey-wousey snacks for you," Althea sang in a high-pitched voice he'd never heard her use before and would pay money to never hear from her again.

For his part, Gingersnap lounged with front paws curled over a round belly, and back legs splayed open to show male parts the size of large marbles. Only the swish of a fluffy orange tail hinted at annoyance with the situation. That, and the dead-eyed stare he fastened on Oliver.

Truly unsettling. Oliver caught himself curling his lip before he forced a bland countenance on his face. "Does he always stare like that?"

"Like what?" Miss Martin craned onto her toes to see the cat.

"Like a fish, unable to blink. Does it blink? Is there something wrong with it?"

Althea gasped, clutching the giant cat closer to her chest, thereby shoving those oversized hairy marbles closer to Oliver's face. "Gingersnap is a handsome boy, not an 'it.'" She cooed in that same tone, "And there's not a thing wrong with you, is there? No there's not. Gingersnap is perfect in every way."

"Are you feeling all right, Lord Southwyn?" Miss Martin asked. "Do you need to sneeze, or itch at your eyes?"

Oliver shook his head, batting the cat's tail out of his face.

To his horror, his gaze landed once more on those fluffy testicles, and he had to look away. "I am perfectly fine, aside from a general feeling of annoyance and confusion. Perhaps in the future, you might consider a more logical hour during which to walk your pet."

The women exchanged a look he'd swear held disappointment. Probably commiserating over what Althea called his "rigid disposition."

To his relief, the carriage in front of them moved. "Off we go, then. Retrieve your cat and watch your toes, Miss Martin. We mustn't tarry."

The damned woman grinned too widely for his comfort. "He's enjoying the view, I think. Why don't you take him home with you, Althea, and I'll call later this afternoon. His ribbon complements that bonnet to perfection."

"Do you really think that's a good—"

"Excellent! We will wave our paws at all our friends in the park, won't we, pretty boy?" Althea tightened her grip on the cat, who'd settled in her arms, fully resigned to his fate. Reverting to her normal tone, Althea said, "The carriages are moving, Oliver. You're making the Warrens wait behind us, and you know how Lord Warren yells if inconvenienced."

Last week Lord Warren made a spectacle of himself on Bond Street when he'd ranted to the footman parked across the street over a delay in bringing his carriage around. The man could have crossed the road and climbed into his phaeton. But no. He'd opted to stand on the corner and berate a servant over a situation entirely out of their control—namely, the congestions of shoppers and traffic—until onlookers had cleared a path out of sheer pity for the footman.

That kind of man would enjoy railing at Miss Martin.

"You're correct. If the cat is staying with us, please maintain a hold on his lead. Miss Martin, again, I must ask you to step away from the wheels of the carriage." Tightening his grip on the reins, Oliver surveyed the area around the horses to ensure there were no other obstacles in their path.

"I'll take the basket with me. Be a good boy, Gingersnap! Mummy will see you soon." And with that, Miss Martin melted into the crowd and became no more than wild curls atop a red bobbing dot in the throng. The woman was a menace. Disarmingly beautiful, but a menace nonetheless.

Oliver peered at Althea as the horses moved forward. "I didn't know you liked cats."

"I love them. Far more than dogs, although I tolerate them well enough too. Father never let me have a cat, so we shall own several." She stared adoringly down at the orange lump of fur in her lap, who had rolled to a sitting position. Back legs sticking straight out, front legs supporting his impressive size into an upright stance as he surveyed the world around him, Gingersnap appeared perfectly content now that they were moving.

"How many cats are you imagining in this scenario?"

"As many as I like." She sent him a wild grin, full of challenge.

Oliver swallowed roughly. An uncomfortable image formed in his mind of his home entirely overrun with felines. The current tidy order of his life devolving into rooms of shredded priceless tapestries. Cat hair floating in his morning tea. Malodorous stains on furniture and bedding.

Wait. Where did cats relieve themselves? Would the back garden be sufficient?

He had so many questions.

"This would have been so much easier if cats made him sneeze," Constance grumbled, tiptoeing through wet piles of refuse in the alley behind a tavern. This particular alley also served as access to the back doors of a butcher shop and a number of other businesses. Chances were good she'd find the perfect candidate for their plan. Knowing that didn't make the search any less disgusting. Her lip curled in revulsion when something squished under her walking boot.

"No," she sneered. "His greatness, the Earl of Southwyn, couldn't muster so much as a sniffle. A sneeze is probably entirely out of the question. Losing control long enough to sneeze would be unthinkably improper."

She'd lost a beau once—although calling it a loss might be overstating the matter—because he'd spent the entire evening wiping red eyes as a result of the hairpiece she'd made to give her coiffeur more volume. The hairpiece in question had been a rather ingenious idea she'd had, after noticing how closely her hair matched Gingersnap's. It had only taken a month of brushing the cat and collecting fur to create her hair pad.

She and her cousins had laughed until tears ran down their faces when she told them about the incident. Then Caro declared in no uncertain terms that a hair pad made of cat fur was disgusting and made her promise to throw it away.

Since Constance hadn't promised not to make another, she'd created a larger pad a few months later. The first had been too small anyway.

Had the earl reacted to Gingersnap with watery eyes, or even a gratifying itch, as she'd hoped, Constance would have bought a dog from the local rat catcher. Althea might prefer a cat, but a dog was much easier to find. Instead, Southwyn had the nerve to be perfectly healthy, thus eliminating her excuses and forcing Connie to find a cat—the more feral, the better.

A rag shifted to her left and she paused, eyeing it speculatively until the rag opened its eyes, revealing two mirror-shine reflections of yellow, and a tiny mouth full of sharp teeth, open in a silent hiss.

"Hello, my beauty. Would you like to live in a fine house in Mayfair?" The cat spat again but didn't move away when she crouched to study it. The poor thing appeared to be nothing more than skin and bones, with patches of dark fur attempting to grow back over sections of bare skin. Despite the relatively warm day, a near-constant shiver rippled over its gray body. Given the layer of grime covering the animal, she wouldn't be surprised to discover it wasn't gray at all beneath the soot and dirt.

Moving slowly, she reached into her basket and felt around for the oilskin bag she'd filled with food scraps before leaving the house. Gingersnap vastly preferred a walk on his leash, rather than bouncing along in the basket, and bribes were the easiest way to convince the contrary feline to stay put.

Tearing off a bit of gristly rabbit from last night's meal, she tossed it toward the kitten. In a flash, it darted toward the food, gobbling it so quickly, she doubted it even tasted the treat. "You are hungry, aren't you, little one? I can fix that. I can give you all the food your little heart desires. You just have to annoy an aristocrat into seeing that life with my friend would be intolerable. Do we have a bargain?"

She threw another piece of meat and the cat scooted closer, without another wary look her direction. "You aren't entirely feral, are you? Pity. Although that does make my job easier." Carefully, she dropped the next piece of meat near her feet.

"As long as you promise to scratch his furniture, sleep in inconvenient places, and shred at least one pair of stockings, I think you'll do nicely." The cat didn't dart away after eating this last offering, instead sniffing the toes of her boots and hem.

"I'm going to pet you now. Please don't bite me." Moving cautiously, she reached out, allowing the animal to sniff her hand. "I realize my fingers smell like your treat. That doesn't make them edible."

The cat rubbed its cheek on her fingertips, and she smiled. "Perhaps this plan of ours will serve us both. You seem eager for human companionship." Another piece of meat, this one directly from her hand. No, this cat was not entirely unused to human interaction. Likely someone had dumped it in the alley. Such appalling behavior was repugnant, yet all too common. Not everyone appreciated felines as she did.

She set the basket down, keeping her movements slow and steady. Dumping half of the remaining meat slivers inside, Constance held open the lid for the kitty to see.

"If this feels like a trick, it's because it is. But I promise, life will be better for you where we're going."

It jumped into the basket, began eating, and didn't look up when Constance closed the top and latched it.

Althea lived a short walk away. Hopefully, the cat would continue to cooperate. As she backed out of the alley and onto the busy street, Constance tried to keep a low prattle of conversation directed toward the animal.

"That's a good kitty. I promise, nothing bad is going to happen to you. If that nasty earl dares to even glare at you sideways, I will rescue you. We can piss in his boots together before I bring you home with me."

It was so tiny and trusting, probably due to desperation for a meal. "Gingersnap will have to welcome you if the earl turns into a beast."

If the earl proved himself to be anything of the sort, she'd dress all in black and burgle the cat from his fancy Mayfair home.

It was unlikely she'd need such drastic measures. Southwyn had been so patient a few moments before when she'd ambushed him in the park. Althea knew to look for her, but Lord Stuffy Pants had been taken unawares. And yet, he'd been polite, even while taken off guard, with Gingersnap's tail-end in his face.

A plaintive mew rose from the basket. Even as they wove through the crowded street, occasionally jostled by fellow pedestrians, he didn't claw or throw himself against the walls of the wicker container, despite the lack of treats. Connie had shoved the oilskin bag with the rest of the meat into her pocket for Althea to bribe him later.

The animal had a lot of changes coming in the next hours and beyond. While she hoped an unexpected pet would ruin Southwyn's peace, this was also a rescue mission. The kitten must recognize that.

Not that cats were known for being the most reasonable of creatures. But then, neither were earls—otherwise she wouldn't be doing this.

"Althea told you she didn't want to marry you, Lord Stuffy Pants." The moniker made her smile. All of this coming upset could have been easily avoided. Instead, he'd chosen to be an aloof, stubborn arse, leaving his fiancée no choice except to find a matchbreaker. Any consequences befalling him were entirely his fault.

Chapter Four

~~Deliver feral animal to Althea~~
~~Have a minor crisis of identity in her kitchen~~

At Althea's house, Constance went down the stairs by the front door, to the servants' entrance. Over the course of their friendship, she'd called several times, although never with an animal in tow. Especially a probably-flea-ridden animal in desperate need of a bath.

A kitchen maid opened the door. "Yes, miss?"

"I am Constance Martin, a friend of Miss Thompson's. I come bearing gifts." Constance held up the basket. Right on cue, the cat meowed from the basket, making the maid's eyes widen to the size of saucers. "I'm afraid the poor animal has had a difficult life before today, and isn't ready for polite society yet. Perhaps we could call Miss Thompson down to the kitchen? Or, I can wait outside, if you'd prefer."

"Is the basket latched?" The maid eyed the lid warily.

"Yes, it's quite secure." The cat meowed again, slightly more insistent than last time. Its cooperation might be coming to an end.

"Come inside then. If you'll wait here, I'll send for my lady."

Constance took a seat on a rough wooden bench near the

door. Though she sat on the outer edge of the kitchen, she felt stiflingly hot. With every second that passed, perspiration pooled between her breasts and at the base of her spine. How did the staff work in these conditions every day? It would be unbearable during warm weather.

The bookstore could be stuffy and the fireplace in the office made that room hot in the summer. However, after five minutes in this kitchen with its huge oven, she vowed to never again complain about the office.

Loaves of bread and what she suspected were rolls for the evening meal happily rose on a shelf a few feet away. They thrived in the heat, as puffs of dough pillowed above the rims of metal pans. Their yeasty smell mixed with the scents of roasting meat from the spit on the other side of the room.

Her stomach growled, and Constance placed a hand over her belly to muffle the sound. She'd eaten today, yes? Surely she'd had something with her morning tea. A hazy memory of scraping the last dregs of plum jam from the jar surfaced, and she felt a moment of satisfaction that she hadn't forgotten to take care of herself. Another gurgle served to remind her that a slice of toast wasn't enough to sustain a body for an entire day. Blast. Perhaps one of the servants would provide something small to tide her over.

She hated to ask, though. *Pardon me, I realize I'm a woman fully grown, but I can't seem to remember the most basic of tasks to sustain my existence. Might I have one of those currant scones, so my stomach doesn't gnaw on my spine? Thanks ever so much.*

Despite the servants being complete strangers who'd never given offense, Constance felt every drop of disdain they'd have for her in this imagined scenario, so she held her tongue. Instead, she dug in her pocket for today's list and stub of pencil. *Eat something.* There. Things lingered in her brain longer if she wrote them down. Besides, her favorite pie shop was on the way home.

Rather than ruminate on her empty belly, she hugged the basket in her lap and watched the activity around her. She'd never taken the opportunity to sit in Caro and Dorian's kitchens, so seeing the way a staff of this size operated was fascinating. Maids and footmen darted about with purpose, each intent on their own mission. While they occasionally gave her curious glances, no one bothered her. The cook directed her workers like a general giving orders to an army. How did they keep track of it all?

On first glance, the kitchen was unfettered chaos. However, the longer she watched, patterns emerged to explain the inner workings of the space. One maid was responsible for slicing vegetables. The sharp tang of onions rose in the air, then mingled with the earthy crispness of herbs as her knife flew across the counter mincing and dicing. One maid washed dishes, while another dunked those dishes into a bin of water, then passed to another who stacked them on a drying rack.

Pots and pans clanged. A man, probably the butler, wearing a black tailcoat seemed utterly absorbed in his task of decanting liquor into crystal bottles. Constance grinned when he stole a nip and smacked his lips in satisfaction. There had to be some benefits to his job, she supposed.

A younger boy moved past her, carrying an armload of wood, then placed the stack next to the oven before darting out the door again and sending a welcome blast of cool air toward her bench.

The room reminded her of the beehives she'd read about in nature books; everyone had their own job to do. The perfectly orchestrated nature of it enthralled her until the maid she'd spoken with returned with Althea.

Her friend carried Gingersnap in her arms, his ribbon leash trailing behind them. When Althea entered the room, there was an abrupt pause, then everyone snapped to attention. Although Althea smiled graciously at the servants, the overall air of awkwardness made Constance uncomfortable.

"Goodness, this room is smaller than I expected. Cook, you're to be commended for what you create from such a snug space."

The cook curtsied, while Constance gaped.

"Carry on. I'm just here to see my friend and the gift she's brought." Althea addressed the room. Without another word, everyone returned to their previous roles and the bustle resumed.

"You've never been inside your own kitchen?" At the sound of Constance's voice, Gingersnap greeted her with the special chirp he reserved just for her.

"I've never had reason to before now." Althea shrugged.

Connie shook her head. "You've never baked with your mum, or helped your father pluck a bird for a special meal? Could you boil water if you had to?" When Althea grimaced in answer, Constance gave up that line of questioning and spoke to Gingersnap. "Did you have a nice ride in the park? Was everyone kind to you?"

With a sigh that hinted at her relief over returning to familiar territory, Althea handed over the orange cat. "He was marvelous. Very interested in the goings-on of the park. Several people stopped to inquire about him. By the time we returned, I suspect Oliver's composure was in tatters over everyone in the ton thinking he's the odd sort who takes his cat for a drive. It was perfect." Her grin was wicked.

Constance gently patted the basket with the kitten on her lap. "Since your fiancé didn't cooperate by sneezing his way through our meeting, I've enacted the next phase."

Gingersnap sniffed at the wicker when a small mew sounded from within. "Would you like to assure our new friend that they're safe? If you vouch for us, the kitten might believe you."

"Every time someone refers to Oliver as my fiancé, my stomach clenches in knots." Althea sat on the bench beside Connie. Her voice was low, likely to keep the servants from overhearing their conversation…because Althea's place wasn't below stairs. Even the small motion of taking a seat was done with grace and poise. Althea appeared entirely foreign in her own kitchen.

Constance winced with an uncomfortable stab of self-awareness. Tucking her muck-covered boots under an equally filthy skirt hem, she smoothed a hand over her riotous curls. In her haste to get to the park at the agreed-upon time, she'd left home without her bonnet. Again.

The fabric of her gown was thick and serviceable, although a little faded. Her red cloak had begun to fray at the edges over the winter and had a fine layer of cat hair on it. Gingersnap liked to sleep on her cloak when she forgot to put it away. As if sensing the downward turn of his mistress's thoughts, the furry beast bumped her chin, then sat atop the basket. A wry chuckle escaped. She petted his head until he offered a deep purr in thanks.

Except for the cats on her lap, the only thing keeping Constance from blending in down in the servants' domain was her lack of participation in the well-orchestrated busyness. Like so many areas of life outside Martin House's sales floor, Connie didn't have a clearly defined role in which she obviously fit. No wonder the servants gave her curious looks. Nothing about her appearance or demeanor declared "close friend of a wealthy family."

For years she'd known she could exist anywhere in

relative comfort. Be it a bookshop, or the drawing room of her cousin, the duchess, Constance whittled out a place. But she'd never simply *belonged* without trying.

Althea's movements showed her to be a lady—as if her pedigree was such an intrinsic part of her that it glowed brightly—even while conspiring to terrorize her husband-to-be in front of a sweltering oven. Constance feared the myriad odd things about her were just as deeply ingrained and apparent to the world.

Taking a bracing breath, Constance forced herself to answer the last thing Althea had said. Because, she thought, she did have a role to fulfill right now. Even if that purpose wasn't clear to everyone else in the room. "For the time being, Lord Southwyn is your fiancé, I'm afraid. Although I've taken to calling him Lord Stuffy Pants in my head. I could refer to him as that instead of fiancé if it would help."

Althea laughed aloud, drawing the attention of several nearby servants.

Constance leaned close, lowering her voice. "Darling, stuffy or not, he was gracious this morning. Even though I intruded on your drive, he handled the situation with aplomb. The man isn't an ogre. In fact, he's quite good-looking—"

"You think he's good-looking?"

Constance blinked, nonplussed. "Of course. I have a pulse, and he's objectively handsome. As I was saying, he's attractive. And it's not his fault you're both bound by that bloody contract, or that Dorcas eloped. Before we check off more items from our list, especially as it now involves another living creature," she added, when the kitten meowed from the basket, "I have to ask you again. Is it possible you could find happiness together?"

The way Althea glanced around made Constance's neck

prickle with the certainty that her friend hadn't been entirely honest before that moment.

"My family's status in society is not noble enough to warrant a merger of lands, or so significant that I need to marry a man whom I think of as a brother. Not when..." She drew in a lungful of air before forging on. "Not when my affections lie elsewhere."

Understanding dawned. "You're in love with someone else. Why didn't you tell me before now?"

Pink bloomed over Althea's cheeks. "I'm not entirely certain he feels as strongly as I do. Even if he doesn't, I cannot stomach marrying Oliver, when the only real motivating reason to honor the engagement is to avoid another irate tirade from my father."

That certainly didn't bode well. "Will your father make life *that* miserable if you cry off?" Other questions wanted to follow. Was Althea in danger? Would Sir William cause her physical harm, or do something drastic and worthy of one of Caro's villains? Because if the man was likely to lock Althea in her room and starve her until she agreed to walk down the aisle, then this little project of theirs needed to have contingency plans in place.

Althea nodded. The posture that had been so straight and proper moments before wilted. "I see the worry on your face. It's not as if he will drag me before a clergyman, kicking and screaming, but he would not be above threats and manipulation. No doubt he'd pack me off to the country or take away my pin money. There wouldn't be violence."

Pity made Constance's eyes burn. "Violence does not always involve fists."

"Yes, I suppose you're right. Then the best I can promise is Father won't leave me with bruises. More than anything, I think he fears society's opinion if Oliver ended things. However, his overblown sense of self-importance is not worth my long-term happiness." She forced a bright smile. "Which is why I am eager to meet what I don't doubt will be an entirely perfect and feral beast. I hope he or she is ideally suited to wreak havoc on Oliver's life. May I see?"

Gently nudging Gingersnap off the basket with a murmured apology, Constance unlatched the lid. "Alas, I suspect our beastie is not entirely feral." Her cat met the tiny pink nose poking from the basket with his own, and the whiskers of the two felines tangled as they commenced a thorough inspection. "However, the poor thing is starving. Also, he or she is filthy, so there's that to deal with as well. I'd thought to bathe it before bringing the cat to Lord Stuffy Pants, but perhaps gifting him the animal in this condition works toward our goals of creating maximum discomfort." The tiny gray kitten poked its scraggly head from the basket, eyes wide as it took in the room and people.

"Oh, it's so small…" Althea whispered, reaching out a finger for the cat to sniff. Her gesture was met with a low growl, so she snatched her hand away.

"He accepts bribes." Constance handed over the bag of meaty bits she'd saved for exactly this reason.

Hesitantly, Althea offered a treat to the kitten. Instead of a growl, it nipped the meat from her hand, then began to purr.

Althea grinned. "Not so hard to win over after all, I see. You're brilliant, Constance. Perhaps this scamp will be what convinces Oliver that I'll make his life hell. I told him today that I intend to have a whole herd of cats. I've been doing as you suggested and fussing over him. Not only did I adjust his cravat when we were in the carriage, I also spent more than a full minute brushing off his coat. The poor man played statue through all of it. Like I was a wild animal and would lose interest and leave if he simply held very still."

Constance laughed, startling the kitten into retreating back to the safety of the basket. Worry made her bite her lip at the idea of letting an innocent creature into the unknown environment of the earl's home. "You're certain he won't mistreat our tiny friend? It's already so skittish."

Althea nodded. "Oliver would never be cruel to an animal. It's not in him."

"I insist on taking it home with me if the earl shows any sign that he will take out his frustrations on this kitten. Am I clear on that point?"

"Of course. If I suffer even a moment of doubt when I offer our gift, I'll turn it into an opportunity for a dramatic scene over his unsuitability as a pet owner. Truly, I wouldn't do this if I thought he'd harm the kitten."

Comforted by that, Constance relaxed. "I'll leave you with the basket, since the little one seems rather settled in here. Gingersnap and I will let you get on with the work of further ruining his lordship's day."

As she stood, the familiar heft of her cat was a soothing weight in her arms. Burying her nose in his fluffy neck, Constance sighed. The kitten would be fine. Anything the tiny creature encountered in a London townhome had to be kinder than the alleyway in which she'd found it. The gray head poked out of the basket and stared up at her with enormous eyes. "You'll be fine, pet. I promise." It didn't growl when she stroked a finger between the disproportionately large ears that swiveled toward the noises of the kitchen.

"I'd best be getting back to the shop. Hattie has been working alone today, while my father tries to catch up on the bookkeeping."

Althea gave her a light hug, kissed Gingersnap on his head, then picked up the basket and escorted Constance out the door.

As Constance climbed the steps to street level, her stomach growled.

Right. Pie shop first, then home. Good thing she wrote that down, so she didn't forget again.

Chapter Five

Oliver was marrying a madwoman. Well, if not actually mad, then certainly determined to drive *him* to madness. The scene before him was one he'd never imagined, yet somehow should have expected.

Perhaps not this exact scenario. But something equally ludicrous. In his defense, when listing the many ways Althea annoyed, nagged, and generally made a nuisance of herself since Dorcas eloped and left them stuck with each other, he'd never expected a feral cat. This was also the girl who'd once released chickens into his bedroom as a prank when she was ten years old.

So yes, he should have known. Believing she'd grown past such things was his first mistake.

"I've brought us our first pet. Every home should have at least one." She held a familiar basket with a distinctly feline, if patchy face, poking out the top.

"Have you suffered a knock on the head? That is not a pet. That"—he pointed at the tiny, rather battered-looking gray lump—"is a hodgepodge of fur, fleas, and teeth."

Althea hugged the basket to her chest. "Don't speak to

our first child in that tone. You'll scare the wee mite, and he's had a rather trying day."

"It's a boy?" Against his will, Oliver found himself stepping closer to peek at the animal. Hell, it was so small. Was it old enough to be away from its mother?

"I'm not sure, actually. Being so recently acquainted, I didn't think it seemly to check under the tail. However, since it is determined to be temperamental except when offered food, I think it safe to assume it's male."

Damn, she was funny when she wanted to be. Oliver covered a budding smile with his palm and left it there until the urge to laugh passed, lest he encourage her antics. This whole situation reeked of the meddlesome Miss Martin and her giant, unblinking cat. "May I ask what brought on this idea?"

Overly wide eyes, full of faux innocence, gazed up at him. "I told you I want cats in my home. Surely your memory isn't faulty already? Obviously, you are quite a few years older than I, but I didn't expect to address your decline so soon." Slowly, like talking to a child, she said, "Today in the park. Remember?"

Lord, she was a brat. Shaking his head, he said, "Forgive my confusion at your drastic change in attitude. Last month you refused to keep the appointment with the modiste to discuss your wedding gown. Yet here you are, filling my home with cats and referring to it as our first child."

Alarm bells sounded in his head when she raised her chin in an increasingly familiar gesture. "It's only one cat. For now. And I wasn't feeling well enough to attend that appointment."

"Hogwash. You were dancing and drinking champagne hours later at the Highford ball." Oliver crossed his arms and rocked back on his heels as he kept an equal eye on the color rising in her cheeks, and the mongrel kitten's increasing curiosity with the room beyond its basket. Huge, shiny eyes seemed to take in everything at once, and he couldn't tell if the creature was terrified or intrigued.

"The malady was blessedly short-lived. I'd have hated to disappoint Lady Highford."

"Am I to believe you've changed your mind about the wedding? You won't fight your parents at every turn, or treat me like a villain for fulfilling my part of the betrothal contract?"

Althea tightened her jaw, making the muscle near her ear jump as she ground her teeth. Oliver recognized it for what it was. Despite her talk of being married and trying on the role of wife in small ways, she hadn't changed her mind about the marriage. The dishonesty of it, her saying one thing while feeling another, grated.

"What is really going on here, Althea? You've been fairly honest about what you want until now."

He waited, letting his disbelief speak for itself in the ensuing quiet. It was a trick he'd learned from his father. When faced with minimal response, a liar would often tell on themselves to fill a silence. However, this was Althea, not the late Earl of Southwyn.

"Honesty hasn't provided success so far, has it? I've told you what I want. I've been telling you for three years." Her words were no less fierce, despite their hushed volume as she lightly stroked the kitten's ears.

Oliver rubbed a palm over his face and gave a heavy sigh. "Wants and needs are two different things, Althea. Our position and responsibilities mean we must prioritize needs over our own desires."

"Is that the same speech you gave my sister? That you didn't want to marry her, but would? Or did you actually love Dorcas, and she didn't want a stuffed-shirt like you?"

This entire conversation was exhausting. "Althea, what are you going on about? I was fond of Dorcas, as I am you." When the news of Dorcas's hasty marriage over a Scottish anvil reached him, he'd been just as surprised as everyone else.

"From my earliest memory you were engaged to my sister. I think of you as a brother, not a husband." She pursed her lips and continued to stroke the kitten's head. A low grumble sounded from the animal. Growl or purr, he didn't know, but it didn't shy from the touch. "Now that Dorcas is Cyrus's wife, I've inherited the burden of the family promise."

"Please remember that I am also bound by that promise. Your sister's elopement impacted my marriage plans as well. We both are doing what we must." Oliver brought his finger up to smooth the fur between the cat's ears. The resulting sound from the animal was less than friendly. To ensure there was no miscommunication, the kitten curled its lip in a hiss, showing tiny, needle-like teeth.

"So, you admit you're settling for the younger sister."

That was not the answer he'd expected. Oliver shot her a questioning look. "No one is settling, Althea. Marriage to Dorcas, or marriage to you, it makes little difference to me. Our families made a contract with impacts far beyond just us. Although my father's vows weren't worth the paper they were written on, I am a different man. When I give my word, I keep it. My honor is the one thing this world can't take away. I said I'd marry you, and I will."

A white line appeared around her lips and he knew she was biting back words. Frustration pushed against the barrier of his calm. Yes, their situation was less than ideal. However, without him, she'd be at the mercy of her father, who would likely punish her for going against his wishes. Why couldn't she recognize that he was trying to do the right thing here?

"I'll do my best to make you happy. You'll have my title, a fortune, several houses to decorate however you like. Fill them with cats, or dogs, or monkeys for all I care. Your parents won't wait. They've decided this Season will see us wed."

Oliver eyed the kitten. It had pushed back the wicker lid entirely and stood with its tiny paws on the rim of the basket as it surveyed the room. If one small kitten was what it took to secure a better future for the Southwyn estate and surrounding county, then so be it. Should the coming years bring another disastrous growing season like this one, having a locks system in place, and the income from it, might make all the difference.

All right. So, he had a cat to worry about, along with everything else.

"If this fellow is the way to get you excited about your new life, then I will happily accept our first family member... even if I am confused about why you brought me a cat."

"I saw how you were with Gingersnap. And I was telling the truth when I said I intend to have animals." Althea set the basket on the floor. Oliver bit back a comment about the expensive carpet. "Here you go, little one. Your new home," she murmured. Then she whispered something that sounded suspiciously like *do your worst*.

The cat perched at the edge of the basket, content for the moment to look around. Its ears were impossibly large compared to the rest of the body, which appeared in desperate need of a good meal or five. In the hall beyond the study door, Roberts, the butler, conversed with a footman. The cat's fur twitched with the cadence of the low tones from the men's voices, as if it were preparing to bolt.

"Do you think a man mistreated it? You can pet it, but it growled at me," Oliver hypothesized aloud.

Althea straightened, that defiant chin lift in place once more. "Then you'd best win its trust. And win mine as well while you're at it. If you want a willing bride, I am going to need more from you than your heartfelt declaration of apathy about not caring if you marry me or my sister." Althea pointed to the kitten as it leapt from the basket and began creeping across the carpet, staying low to the ground, ready to run scared. "Show me you're capable of affection and caring. Start with him." She shook her head. "Or her. You should probably begin with a name."

This rapid turn into pet ownership made more sense now. Althea wasn't enthusiastic about their marriage, and she'd been honest about that. The cat was a test of sorts. It was the only thing about this damnable situation that aligned with the future she wanted for herself—a house full of pets. And she was entrusting him with it.

The kitten disappeared into the shadows under a carved wooden table. Oliver glanced at the window above the table, and the view of the garden beyond. "It will need to relieve itself outside. If it doesn't trust men, how am I to make sure the damned thing doesn't run away when I let it out?"

Althea blinked, then bit her lip, as if holding back a smile. "I suppose you have your first challenge. A man of logic like you should be up to the task." She bent down to peek under the table and cooed, "Be a good kitty. I'll see you soon." Rising, she gave Oliver a hard look. "Don't lose our cat."

And with that, she left the room, closing the door behind her.

"Well, fuck," he said to the empty room.

A growl sounded from under the table.

"If that's a commentary on my language, you and I are not going to get along at all."

* * *

Owen Martin wasn't a tall or imposing sort of man. He was kind, bookish, usually soft-spoken except for the bark of laughter that often took people by surprise. He and Constance's mum were a perfectly patched pair, complementing the other's strengths and weaknesses. Constance frequently thanked fate, or the gods, or whoever was responsible for handing out parents, that she had been lucky enough to get these two.

Especially when, from an early age, she spent so much time comparing herself to Betsy. The first person to explicitly point out Connie's strengths, rather than her failings, was her father. And the one she could rely on to come to her rescue when she found herself in a scrape, or to finish her abandoned projects, was her mum.

That didn't mean they were oblivious to her faults. Of course not. Anyone with eyes and ears would notice the many ways Constance was different—and not in a good way—from her twin. Her mum used to say it was a blessing that one of their children was easy and uncomplicated. What went unsaid was that Betsy's way of sailing through life, smooth as butter, allowed them to be on hand to deal with Constance.

It wasn't until she turned twelve that she realized boredom was the enemy, making impulsiveness her default ally. Before then, her oddities had been frequent, if benign, things like forgetting tasks, having to write everything down (then lose the list, find the list, and promptly lose it again), and being physically incapable of keeping her dress clean, or her body unbruised. Betsy frolicked and danced around the shop. Constance ran into stationary objects and corners, be they walls or counters.

After a while, Connie accepted that whatever was

different about her wasn't temporary. Since her strangeness was permanent, she could choose to castigate herself constantly, or smile through the pain of being different. Usually, she chose to smile. People appreciated her sunny disposition, and they came to expect it.

Which led to the men. Once she was old enough to begin courting, her parents grew accustomed to Constance's busy social life.

Betsy fell in love with the first man who courted her, married him, moved to his home village in nearby Kent, and settled into a peaceful existence as the wife of a barrister.

Constance, on the other hand, endured heartbreak after heartbreak—either as the breaker or broken. Things came to a head when she finally agreed to marry someone, then ran from her wedding. After the abandoned nuptials, Constance's decision to stay home rather than go out in the evenings shocked her family.

Leaving Walter in that church put so many things in perspective for her. On that day, she'd embarrassed not only herself, but also her long-suffering, loving parents. Not only that, her actions cost them dearly financially, since she'd insisted on a huge wedding breakfast for the entire neighborhood.

So, she'd stayed home. Lived quietly. Tried her best to learn the inner workings of the business.

After two years of such behavior, her parents believed that Constance had turned over a new leaf. Owen taught her about things like paying taxes, inventory control, and how best to negotiate with publishers and printers. Mary stopped asking if Constance had met any interesting young men lately.

Her father poured himself a cup of tea, then joined her at the kitchen table, snapping Constance from woolgathering.

"Poppet, do you have a moment to talk?"

She raised her cup to her lips, only to find it empty. "Yes, of course. Let me just refill my cup."

The pot was still hot, and soon the dark brew was ready to work its magic. By the time she resumed her seat, her mind had returned to the present rather than mulling over her disastrous life choices. Constance frowned, then tucked her hand into her pocket. In addition to her ever-present list was another piece of paper.

Without opening it, she recalled the contents. A chatty missive from a friend down the street full of gossip about Walter marrying last week.

Constance hadn't heard about the match before today. Which in itself was both a mercy and a miracle. Gossip was practically currency, and the fact that not one person in her life knew about Walter's engagement struck her as highly suspect.

Fixing a neutral countenance, she studied her father. Had he known and kept it from her? If so, he must believe he acted in her best interests. But that kind of coddling suggested he thought her fragile.

Honestly, Walter getting married came as a relief. Maybe now that he'd found happiness, the universe would remove the guilt she carried for hurting him. Even if he had acted like a horse's arse during their last argument, he hadn't deserved the humiliation of being left at the altar. She ran her finger over the outline of the letter in her pocket and silently wished him well.

"You seem awfully deep in thought," Owen said.

Constance blew on her tea before answering. "Walter has married. I suppose it made me contemplative."

"Does this news upset you?"

No surprise on his part. He'd known and stayed silent on the matter. "Not the way you're probably thinking. There's no jealousy or anything like that. I feel bad over how I ended things, not because I ended them."

He remained quiet and a pulse of irritation made her push. "You knew about it, didn't you? Why didn't you say anything?"

Her father cleared his throat, staring into his mug. "Your mother and I... After Walter, you didn't want to meet anyone else. We thought it would hurt too much to hear he'd moved on."

Constance shook her head, amazed her reasons for changing her behavior could be so different from why her parents believed she made those changes. "Everything that happened with Walter was difficult. I won't deny that. Just because he wasn't the right man for me, that doesn't mean I can't genuinely wish him well."

"You aren't hurt?"

She shrugged one shoulder and sipped her tea. "No. And that just proves I was right to end it. I thought I loved him at the time. Once I realized I didn't love him more than everyone else in my life, I knew it would be wrong to marry him."

"Love can grow and deepen over the years, you know. Not that I'm saying you should have married him. But if you're waiting for some grand romance like the ones in Caro's novels, you're destined for heartbreak."

Hearing that made the milk she'd splashed in her tea curdle in her belly. "Then I suppose I'm destined for heartbreak. In that case, I'm grateful to already have all I need. My wonderful family is close by, and I have the bookshop."

Her father cleared his throat again, and a wave of trepidation washed over her. She had Martin House, right?

Chapter Six

That is what I wished to discuss with you. Your mother and I have been considering what we want to do with the rest of our lives. Martin House is successful, and that's such a gift. It allows us to dream and have conversations like this, when so many others will have no choice but to work until the day they die. Your mum misses Betsy. With Georgia growing so fast, we want to live closer to them. Not tomorrow, but relatively soon. In the meantime, we'd like to start spending more time in Kent with Betsy's family."

When her arm cramped, Constance realized she'd grown very still. Slowly, she set her cup on the table. "What will happen to the shop? Are you going to sell?"

What will happen to me, she wanted to yell. *I don't belong anywhere else. Martin House is my home.*

Pity strained her father's smile. That look, she decided, was her least favorite of all his expressions. "You're brilliant with customers, and you've a knack for displays. But paperwork and the office side of business ownership don't come easily to you."

"I finished last quarter's accounts two nights ago," Constance protested, even though he had the right of it.

"And I'm grateful for the help. But relying on erratic bouts of insomnia where you spread the account books and receipts on the floor at three in the morning isn't a feasible long-term business plan."

She had no defense for that, since he described exactly what had happened this week and six months ago. "Even you don't enjoy doing the accounts." If she sounded petulant, it was because after two years of effort, of learning all she could about the business, she still hadn't inspired confidence in her parents.

"You're correct. The accounting side of the business has never been something I enjoy," he agreed readily enough. "I still do it. You don't, Connie. It's as if those stacks of receipts become invisible."

He rested a hand on hers, but Constance didn't derive comfort from the touch. She was too numb.

Those receipts did disappear. Most days it didn't cross her mind to sit down and handle them. And when she remembered, she felt guilty for letting them pile up for her father to handle. Then the enormity of the task overwhelmed her until she backed away from it, and the cycle began again.

If there was a way to predict or harness those late-night periods of focus, when the world fell away and she magically completed a month's worth of work in a few hours, she'd be fine. Since she hadn't determined how to do that, and establishing a regular habit of office work seemed impossible, she couldn't blame her father for where this conversation would inevitably end.

If Betsy were here and wanted the store, Constance would understand her parents leaving Martin House in her sister's capable hands. Betsy enjoyed all kinds of things Connie thought were boring, including maths. And her twin never struggled with handling tasks, even those she didn't enjoy. She simply did whatever it was, like the responsible adult they were both supposed to be.

"What about Hattie? She's smart as a whip. Not as good with numbers as Caro, but far more organized than I am." She already knew the answer, though.

"I'd happily give the store to Hattie, but she doesn't want the responsibility of ownership. You know her. Having ties to anything makes her feel trapped."

Hattie had lived at Martin House for ten years and never spoke of leaving. But her dear cousin hadn't had a peaceful childhood, and a painful incident she refused to discuss cemented her desire to remain unmarried. Even after a decade, Hattie kept a carpetbag under the bed, packed with essentials, ready to flee at a moment's notice. Constance pretended not to know it was there, although she occasionally stuffed extra pin money in the bag, just in case Hattie ever felt the need to run.

"If I can't convince Hattie to stay, then what? You'll sell the store?"

Her father nodded. "I believe so, yes. Unless you've been having a secret romance with a businessman and keeping it to yourself, then I don't see any other way for Martin House to continue."

Constance attempted a smile. "No. I have no marital prospects on the horizon." Something Past Constance wouldn't have believed possible. "Is there enough in the budget to hire a bookkeeper?"

"It's a possibility we can discuss as the time grows closer for your mother and me to make a decision. Right now, we have higher profits because part of your and Hattie's wages is room and board. I'm not sure if paying a full-time book-keeper would exceed those profits."

"I see." Constance drained the last of her tea, then stood. "Thank you for telling me."

Her father rose as well. "Nothing is set in stone. I wanted to include you in the discussion so talk of selling didn't take you unawares."

"I appreciate that." Constance sent him a tight smile. "I'm going to bed. Good night." She kissed his cheek.

"I love you, poppet."

"I love you too."

The bedroom she shared with Hattie was empty, and she stood at the threshold for a moment, puzzled. "Right. She's tutoring the Widow Fellsworth's children." The hour was later than Hattie usually stayed out. When she arrived home, she'd be tense from walking in the dark.

Constance turned around and went downstairs to the shop.

In the office, she lit a lamp, then walked to the front window and set the light close to the glass. The glow from the lamp would shine through to the street, and she knew from experience her cousin would appreciate the gesture.

With a grumble, Connie fetched the receipts from the day and the ledger, then curled up in the chair beside the window. Might as well work on the damned paperwork while she waited for Hattie to come home.

"I look like a camel when I have a lie-down," Caro commented from between Constance and Hattie the following evening.

That the three of them shared this bed for years was hard

to believe, after the luxury of only having a single bedmate since Caro married. Constance shifted on the mattress, trying to find a comfortable place on the pillow. Since the duke and duchess's return to London for the birth of their first child, Caro made a habit of visiting Martin House to see the family. The cousins usually ended up like this, side by side in the manner in which they'd once slept, as they caught up on the events of their day.

"My ankles are swollen, my wedding ring doesn't fit, and today I cried over cheese," Caro lamented.

"Cheese?" Hattie asked. "Cheese as a general topic, or one particular cheese?"

Constance snorted a laugh. Pregnancy had played havoc on poor Caro's emotions, so Hattie's query wasn't outside the realm of possibility.

"Our neighbors in Kent make an apricot honey goat cheese that I've been craving for days. This morning, I finally collapsed into sobs because I wanted it so fiercely, I could almost taste it. My poor husband."

"I have a tuppence that says Dorian sends someone to Kent to get your cheese within the week," Hattie said.

Constance lifted her head from the pillow and reached a hand across Caro's giant belly to Hattie. "My tuppence says he will have it by the time she returns home tonight." Because if there was one thing worth placing money on, it was the Duke of Holland's absolute devotion to his wife. That man would empty the channel with a teacup if it made his duchess happy.

Hattie considered Connie's hand, then shook. "Too many variables are at play for him to acquire it that quickly. The roads, weather, and their neighbors having some on hand. I'll take that bet."

"Oh God, now I want cheese again!" Caro wailed,

although there was obvious humor in it. "Quick, one of you distract me."

It was on the tip of Connie's tongue to tell her cousins about the conversation she'd had with her father the night before, and the worries for her future and the shop. Before she could open her mouth, Hattie said, "Constance is conspiring with Althea to make Southwyn break their engagement."

Connie's air froze in her lungs as she jerked upright. "Hattie McCrae, that is not something you're supposed to know."

"You *saw* me eavesdropping!" Hattie protested, sitting up as well.

"That is not the point. If we don't speak of it, it never happened."

"Could one of you please help me? If we're going to sit up in bed, I need assistance." Caro held out her hands, like a child asking for someone to pick her up. Each of her cousins took an arm and were kind enough not to comment on the grunt the Duchess of Holland made when she moved.

"How do you function with that belly?" Hattie wondered aloud. Silently, Constance seconded the question, even as she panicked over what to tell her closest friends about the matchbreaking plan.

"I usually have some kind of furniture to use as leverage, or can roll over and get into a better position. Has this bed always been so tiny?"

"Yes," Hattie and Constance answered in unison— Constance from behind her hands, covering her face.

Huffing and slightly out of air from the simple act of sitting, Caro said, "Now. What is this about Althea and Oliver?"

Constance groaned, letting her hands fall to her lap.

These two women were more than family to her. While they kept few secrets from each other, information never strayed beyond their trio. Their discretion was sacrosanct. "Althea doesn't want people to know about this."

"I see you're conflicted, Connie. You don't have to explain. I will. Our dear cousin and Althea concocted a plan to convince Lord Southwyn to cry off. Their ideas are deliciously devious. I'm proud that Connie hasn't said a word about it."

Connie shot Hattie a mocking glare. Really? She could keep a secret. Her cousin simply laughed at the look and carried on speaking. "They found a kitten in an alleyway, and Althea has given it to Southwyn in hopes of the thing terrorizing his peace. Today, Althea visited the store and had a bundle of cloth with her. Was that the swap of waistcoats you two planned?"

Nodding, Constance gave up on the idea of protecting Althea's secrets from her meddlesome cousins. "When she gave him the kitten, she sneaked up to his rooms and stole two waistcoats. Thursday's and Sunday's, I believe." At their obvious confusion, she explained, "He wears the same waistcoat on certain days. Blue on Monday. Green on Tuesday. Anyway, Hattie generously let me slip out for an hour and we visited a tailor to have replacements made."

Caro's eyes were bright with amusement. "Will they be hideous?"

Constance chuckled, recalling the fabrics they'd chosen. "Oh, they're atrocious. He's going to hate them with the passion of a thousand suns. Assuming he has the capacity for larger emotions, of course. I didn't realize fabrics that ugly existed. Who makes them? Who designs them? Althea is practicing what she will say when he's faced with wearing them. Right now, we are emphasizing how horrible a wife she will be. This will support her claim that she expects to be a leader in fashion once she's a countess."

A wrinkle pinched between Caro's eyebrows. "She doesn't really have plans to be that sort of wife, though. Correct?"

Constance waved away her concern. "Of course not. It's all designed to make his life unbearable, so he will back out of the betrothal."

"What else have you planned? Is there anything I can do? Please let me help," Caro begged.

Constance stood and went to her apron, where it hung by the bedroom door, and dug out the matchbreaker list. "Most of this is specific to Althea. But if you call on him, you could move his things around. She says Lord Stuffy Pants is rather particular and orderly." Her cousins laughed, and she looked up.

"Lord Stuffy Pants?" Caro giggled. "I can't wait to tell Dorian." Noticing Connie's expression, she hastened to add, "Only Oliver's nickname. I won't mention the rest of it."

The reassurance loosened some of the tension in Constance's shoulders. "We discussed rearranging the items on his desk and shifting everything on his shelves a few inches. Just enough to make him feel like everything in his life is… off somehow." An idea occurred to her. Althea had suggested a few things they'd ultimately rejected, out of concern for her reputation. "There is something else you can do. Would you mind hosting a small gathering? Just us, Althea, and Southwyn."

"You mean Lord Stuffy Pants?" Hattie said.

Constance ignored her. "Althea could attempt a few of the items we left off the list. A private setting would help with some of the more daring tactics."

Caro grinned. "Host a party where at least one guest will misbehave? I'd love to. These last few weeks of pregnancy are boring me to tears. The distraction will help me endure until the baby arrives."

"Perfect." Constance made a note on the list to tell Althea of this development.

"When will the waistcoats be ready?" Hattie asked. "And is there any word on how he handled the kitten? Southwyn has always reminded me of an overwound watch. Your particular style of chaos might be good for him."

Resuming her place on the bed, Constance shrugged. "Althea said the kitten sparked a good conversation between them. Hopefully he will see reason soon. In the meantime, he's prepared to care for the cat. As to the tailor, he claimed the new clothes will be ready in a couple days. It helps that we gave him the other waistcoats to use as patterns."

Which meant they could expect some kind of reaction or movement on Lord Southwyn's stance regarding the engagement within the week. If he truly was as rigid as Althea claimed, the destruction of his routines might make their pending future together seem bleak indeed.

One could only hope.

A knock at the bedroom door interrupted the conversation, and Constance's mother peeked around the doorjamb. "Caro, dear? Dorian is here with the carriage."

"Thank you, Aunt Mary," Caro said, and swung her legs over the edge of the bed once Constance moved out of her way.

The cousins followed the sound of voices down the hall, to the kitchen. Caro's husband, the Duke of Holland, sat with Owen, looking entirely at home in the tidy, simple room. On the table in front of him sat a small, paper-wrapped lump. Constance suspected she already knew the contents of that lump and grinned when Caro's shriek echoed through the room.

"Is that what I think it is?" Caro dived for the parcel, sniffed it, and let out a sound that was nearly sexual. "Dorian, I didn't think I could love you more. You just proved otherwise." She placed an enthusiastic kiss on his smiling lips.

"Did he really manage—" Hattie hissed from behind Connie.

Constance snickered and held out her hand. "Pay up, darling."

Caro perched on her husband's lap, unwrapping her precious goat cheese. "I would marry you again, any second of any day. You glorious man."

Dorian's smile pressed against her temple as he kissed her. "Anything for you, love."

Unexpected tears burned at Constance's eyes as she watched them. Crossing her arms, she tried to cover the ache under her breastbone.

That. That's what she wanted someday. That bone-deep sense of knowing she'd found the one person she loved above everyone else. Someone who would care for her as fiercely as she cared for him.

Over her shoulder, Hattie handed her a coin, and Constance took it. Yes, betting on the Duke of Holland's love for Caro was always going to pay in her favor. Someday, she hoped someone would say the same thing about a man who loved her like that.

Chapter Seven

~~Ignore the fizzy feeling in your belly. It's not attraction~~
Embroidery: make one new bookmark
~~Lecture an earl~~

*Y*es?"

One word couldn't melt her spine to jelly, although that tone might. Constance clenched her teeth into a semblance of a smile and stood straighter—just in case she wilted against her will, then slunk down the steps and scurried out of Mayfair. "If there's a school for butlers, I'll bet you took top marks, didn't you?"

Nothing. Not so much as an eye twitch. The frosty butler might be immune to her charms, but she was here on official business. And frankly, Constance was just as surprised by that as anyone. In the three days since Althea gave Lord Southwyn the kitten, she hadn't anticipated a scenario in which he contacted Constance directly. Because why would he?

In lieu of a calling card, she held out the missive she'd received that morning. "The earl summoned me. Please tell him Miss Martin is here."

The butler offered a single nod, then stepped aside to allow entry.

A few years ago, Constance would have gawked at the foyer. Thanks to repeated exposure to Caro and Dorian's ducal home, when she took in the carved marble and gilded details of the high ceiling and finely decorated walls around her, she merely caught her breath for a moment.

The table beside her wouldn't fit through the door to her bedroom, much less in the room itself. What an appalling waste of space. And all to hold a vase of flowers, a salver with a collection of calling cards and post, and one gentleman's hat.

Meanwhile, her bedroom slept at least two people, and more often, three. Betsy moving out had given Connie and Hattie a brief reprieve before Caro arrived. It was everything she could do to not shake her head and make a disparaging comment about wealthy people.

Since the butler stood nearby, silently watching her instead of sending for Lord Stuffy Pants, Constance raised an eyebrow in his direction. "Please inform his lordship that my time is just as valuable as his. I came quickly, as requested. I expect his prompt attention in kind."

Finally, the butler cracked enough to blink twice. Good, she'd taken him off guard. It served him right when he'd opened the door looking at her as if she were something one scraped off a shoe.

"Please wait here, miss."

Left to cool her heels in the echoing entry hall, Constance did her best to maintain a neutral mien. Servants passed as they went about their duties, casting the occasional curious or pitying glance at the woman the butler abandoned in the foyer rather than showed to a drawing room. It was on the tip of her tongue to defend herself to each of them.

I'm here by invitation.

I'm related to a duchess. In fact, the duke sat at my kitchen table last night and fed her cheese until she cried from happiness.

Really, I belong here.

Instead, Constance stared at the table, with its single hat and collection of items. She'd seen beds smaller than that table. Hell, if she had to wait much longer, she might just lie down on the thing and nap until the earl deigned to see her. Oh, how the servants would stare then. The butler would likely keel over clutching his chest in shock.

Several minutes passed before he returned, considerably friendlier than when he'd left. "He will see you right away. Anything you need, don't hesitate to ask. This way, Miss Martin."

She had to trot to keep up with his long strides. Tempting as it was to ask the man what this was about, Connie held her tongue rather than admit she didn't know why she was here.

They stopped before a heavy wooden door. He gave her a grave frown and repeated, "Anything you need. Anything at all. Just ask." As if on cue, a deep yelp came from somewhere inside the room, followed by a crash.

Good God, what was happening behind that door?

There was only one way to find out. After a nervous look at the butler, Constance entered absolute chaos. The servant closed the door behind her so quickly, a breeze ruffled her hair.

At some point, this room had been equally grand as the foyer. Drapes framed large windows that allowed in enough light to make out the baffling scene before her. A wood desk held a stack of ledgers teetering askew at one corner. Several bowls, cups, saucers, and three brandy snifters cluttered the surface. Why hadn't the servants cleared any of this away?

Upon closer inspection, she noted areas of the drapes with shredded threads and pilled fabric. The crash from moments ago was probably from the plant falling to the floor. Broken shards of what used to be a rather nice white ceramic pot poked from dark earth scattered across the wood plank floor and a rug. Given the obvious quality of the rest of the furnishings, that rug probably cost more than her bookshop made in sales per quarter.

Someone had made a bed on the chaise beneath the window. A thick blanket draped off the cushion, pooling onto the floor at one end, and a pillow lay at the other. The pillow still held the imprint of a head. An intimate thing, that. Especially when the head in question likely belonged to the Earl of Southwyn.

Who...knelt in the corner peering under a cabinet, cursing in a mild tone. She cocked her head and stepped closer to hear him.

"And damn you too, hell spawn. If you hadn't bitten me, I wouldn't have bellowed. Apologies for startling you, but you'll need to set aside your taste for human flesh if you don't like your prey to make noises like that. Also, you owe me a plant."

The sight of him in his shirtsleeves and breeches captured her attention more than the absurd scene. Instead of focusing on the mess or the questionable odor wafting from somewhere, Constance couldn't look away from the plane of the earl's back under the fabric of his shirt. Even more engrossing was the way his buckskin breeches stretched over slim, defined muscles in his legs. The temperature in the room rose several degrees as she observed him, so she untied her cloak and slung it over her arm.

Southwyn was slightly taller than average, and she'd have described him as handsome, if a bit lanky before now. Seeing him like this, disheveled and half dressed, it was a revelation to realize his body was long and lean, rather than skinny. Even his bare feet showed lines of muscle and sinew she wouldn't have expected, had she ever given thought to a man's feet before.

But those toes, curling into the carpet to balance his position, crouched and bent over as he was, caught her off guard.

Constance removed her bonnet as well, then set it and the cloak on the nearest surface—the desk chair, piled with books and several pieces of cutlery.

The earl shifted, still seemingly unaware of her presence, and the lines of his back actually rippled with the movement. A low whimper escaped before she turned the sound into a polite cough. "Milord?"

The heat building in her belly had to be discomfort or surprise, she told herself firmly. Any other emotion would be wildly inconvenient, all things considered.

He jerked his head around. "Oh good, you're here."

It must have been days since his cheeks had met a razor, and the effect shouldn't have been so appealing. The fire below her navel flared, sending sparks flying through her blood in a familiar sensation. The fizzy pop of attraction acted like embers against a night sky spelling out *that's not disgust you're feeling*. Damn him.

"The more I think about it, the more I'm convinced this is your fault. Even if it weren't, you're the only person I could think to ask for help."

The pull of attraction lessened somewhat, though it didn't dissipate entirely. Her brows pinched together. "I am not sure if that's an accusation or a compliment."

"Both, I think," the impossible earl said in that same

bland tone he'd used when calling the cat hell spawn. At least, that's what she assumed he was talking to a moment ago.

"For what am I being blamed?"

"Lucifer. Hell spawn. Or possibly George, in honor of our destructive and unlikable regent. I haven't decided yet."

Ah, so she was correct. If this room was any indication, it seemed their plan to wreak havoc on his orderly existence was working swimmingly.

"This is about the cat, is it?" Constance crossed to where he sprawled on the carpet, looking more casual than she'd imagined him capable of being. The toes that had caused such a ruckus a moment before wiggled like a child's playing in grass, and she wondered if he realized he'd done it. She took a seat on the floor beside him, then peered under the cabinet. "Hello, my darling. Are you giving him fits? Psss, psss." Holding out her fingers, she fluttered them in greeting.

"If that thing comes right to you—bloody hell." When the gray cat pranced out to Constance and climbed into her lap, Southwyn rolled onto his back and closed his eyes. "I give up." A deep sigh rattled from his chest. His distractingly defined chest, given the way the thin shirt draped over him.

The kitten released a low rumbly purr, making Constance grin and earning a scratch under its chin. "Are some of those dishes yours? Have they been feeding you?"

"Yes," Southwyn answered.

"I was speaking to the cat."

"I assumed as much. As he has yet to master the King's English, he can't assure you that he hasn't been starved, beaten, or abused in any manner. Well, except exposure to some strong language. My staff has kept us both fed and watered while my life spiraled out of control in this room."

She glanced around, absently petting the cat. The animal

was slightly less bony than the last time she'd seen it, despite not warming to its new master. And given the rough appearance of Southwyn, she suspected the reluctance was mutual.

An entirely different, softer feeling grew as she took in the mess in a new light. The chaos told the story of a man who had tried.

And that...that melted her heart in a way that was dangerously close to spawning affection.

"When is the last time you left this study?"

He didn't open his eyes and took long enough to answer that she almost thought he'd fallen asleep. "What day is it?"

"Thursday." No wonder he hadn't noticed his waistcoat was missing. The man was barely dressed. Without meaning to, her eyes lingered over his loose-limbed pose beside her.

"Ah." A matched pair of deep lines appeared between his closed eyes. "When did you meet us in the park? Monday?"

"You've been in this room for three days?" She gaped in shock, not that he could see it.

Not only had he neglected shaving for the last three days, but with his eyes closed and lying so still, she couldn't miss the purple shadows under his eyes, and the way his hair stood on end every which way, as if he'd run his fingers through it countless times.

"Althea gave me orders. Not only am I forbidden from losing this beast, I am to win over its affections as well. I thought I could do it, but the monster resists all efforts. You're my last resort. You have a cat that clearly tolerates you and is thriving if its sheer size is anything to go by." Those eyes—a rather surprising hazel—opened. Perversely, the bloodshot nature of them actually increased their green flecks, making them more attractive. Damn and double damn. "Teach me your ways, Miss Martin. Teach me how to get this thing to love me."

Her incredulous laughter took them both by surprise. Southwyn's eyes—still green hazel, exhausted, and far too direct for comfort—flared with what she'd think was admiration on anyone else, and she had to look away. This whole situation was so far beyond what she'd expected when plotting to upend his life. Had she wanted him uncomfortable? Yes. Inconvenienced? Of course. Had she anticipated being acutely aware of him, and his scruffy beard, and those blasted eyes? Or sitting beside him on the floor of an untidy study in which he'd locked himself while attempting to woo a mostly feral cat?

Never. Not in a million years.

Constance peered down at the kitten, now contentedly curled in a spiral of fur on her lap, sneaking a snooze. "Why is it so important to win its affections?"

He seemed to give that genuine consideration, and part of her was surprised he didn't merely brush off the question. Perhaps he was too exhausted to operate at his usual level of aloofness. Which was a pity, because she liked him better this way.

"If I give my word, I do everything I can to keep it. I told Althea I'd take care of her furry little hell spawn, so I will. But also…he's so scared. Of everything. Of me. Loud noises. A cart tipped over outside in the mews sometime last night, and I thought he was going to fly out of his skin. No one should be that scared all the time. So, if I make him love me, it solves both problems."

Her teeth clamped so firmly on her lower lip, she was in danger of breaking skin, as she bit back a smile. "Of course. Several problems, one solution. Very efficient."

"Quite. Two birds, one stone, and all that." Southwyn watched her out of the corner of his eye. A twitch at the edge of his mouth resembled a budding smile.

Clearing her throat, Constance stared down at the cat instead of the man who suddenly felt as if he took up all the space in the room. "You might begin by giving him a name. Perhaps something princely and a touch exotic, to give him something to aspire to."

"Exotic? Do you know a word in another language that sounds nice, but means 'shits on the rug at two in the morning'? If so, we will name him that."

A laugh escaped as she shook her head. "You need to let the poor thing outside to relieve himself. What did you expect?"

"If I let it out, it will run away. If it runs away, Althea will throw a tantrum. If Althea throws a tantrum, my life will become uncomfortable. Do you see the problem? The maids brought a large pan in for it to use. We lined it with newspapers. He's used it twice, although he isn't happy about the situation, and isn't using it exclusively."

"I suppose a collar and lead was out of the question for some reason?"

"He'd have to let me catch him first, and you can see for yourself how well that's going."

Lord Stuffy Pants didn't seem like such a fitting name anymore. Not seeing him like this. Guilt over the way she'd mocked him tried to rear its head and she batted it away. For one thing, Southwyn hadn't known about the moniker. Also, she hadn't known he was capable of being anything besides tightly controlled and vaguely annoyed all the time.

Constance wrinkled her nose. "That explains the smell."

"In all fairness, the smell might also be me. But yes, most of it is from Carpet Pisser over there."

A snort escaped, and she tried not to let it turn into another full laugh.

Besides, he was wrong. While he didn't smell particularly

fresh, she could detect the complex notes of his cologne or soap lingering faintly on his skin. Lemons, rosemary, and perhaps a trace of sandalwood, she thought. A combination she'd smelled before, though it had never affected her like this.

Constance closed her eyes and tried to hone in on the other scents—cat odors, sweat, dust—to combat this unwelcome awareness of him. "First things first. The pan is a good idea until he will accept a leash and lead. Cats like to bury their waste. It keeps them safe from predators if they hide their smells, you see. Bring in dirt from the garden and fill the pan with that."

He rolled his head to look at her directly. "That's rather ingenious. Thank you. Luckily, I happen to have soil from the plant he just murdered. What about the rest of it?"

"The rest of what? Handling him? Has he let you touch him at all?"

"Once, this morning."

"That's progress." As she stroked the furry body in her lap, a vibration began in an answering purr. "He's fine with me and Althea, so I suspect the issue is you're a man. A man probably hurt him."

Southwyn glanced at her lap and, she assumed, the sleeping cat. "I arrived at the same conclusion. However, if my maleness is the issue, that may be an insurmountable problem."

Constance shrugged one shoulder. "Nothing is truly insurmountable. After all, you aren't the one who hurt him. Given enough time, he will learn you aren't a threat. He will simply love you for yourself. For whoever you are at your core." She risked a glance and saw him staring at her with an intense expression she couldn't decipher. "As long as who you really are is a good person, Prince Puddles here will eventually trust you."

A crooked smile tilted his mouth, and the fact that it wasn't straight and perfect did something to her insides. Oh, this feeling was *not* helpful. "Prince Puddles?"

"He needs a name, and given the state of this room, it seems fitting."

"Prince Puddles it is. Making him feline royalty might restore a bit of his dignity." Southwyn lolled his head back to stare at the ceiling, and within moments his eyes closed again.

"Dignity, eh? I thought he was hell spawn."

"Everyone is allowed dignity, even demons from the pit of hell."

Tiny hairs stuck up along the edge of Prince's ear. When she brushed her finger over them, the entire ear twitched. "Althea gifted you with quite the challenge, didn't she?"

"I think she's trying to make a point, but I'll be damned if I know what it is. She gave a whole speech about proving I was capable of caring, et cetera. I've known her for too long to believe that's all this is."

"Have you considered simply asking her?"

"I tried, but I don't think she's being truthful. If she doesn't want to tell me, then so be it."

Constance rolled her eyes. Althea had mentioned his disinterest and emotional detachment. This attitude certainly supported that. If he knew his fiancée wasn't being frank, shouldn't that inspire a deeper concern or curiosity to understand the woman he intended to marry? Whether it was the result of deliberate disinterest or an asinine level of male obtuseness, she didn't know.

However, when essentially trapped with a semiferal kitten, he'd reached out to Connie rather than ask Althea for help. Stubborn, obstinate man. "I'm beginning to see why she isn't looking forward to marrying you."

"What is that supposed to mean?"

Gently shifting the kitten to the carpet next to her, Constance rose to her feet and brushed the fur from her skirts. "Dignity goes hand in hand with respect, wouldn't you agree?" She didn't wait for his answer. "You honor the dignity of a feral cat, yet can't extend the same respect to the woman you're planning to marry. How hard you're trying to win over Prince is your saving grace right now. Otherwise, I'd let this kitten claw your eyes out and leave you to your fate."

Southwyn watched her with a wary, albeit confused, expression. Even if he didn't know what brought on her current emotion, he was paying attention.

"Cats are carnivores, you know. Like little tigers or lions. If you died in your sleep, he would eat your corpse before anyone was the wiser." Despite the macabre statement, Connie bent and stroked the kitten one more time. "Lord Southwyn, if I may, I'd like to offer some advice. Whether it applies to your fiancée, or a woman sometime in the future after you wake up and realize how ill-suited you and Althea are, I suggest you exert the same effort in understanding her that you've shown for Prince. We are not the unknowable mystery poets make us out to be. Ask a woman what she needs, then *listen* to her. I know Althea has told you what she needs, yet you're more concerned with this kitten's comfort than with that of the woman you've promised to marry. If you respected Althea as much as this animal, you'd help her retain her dignity as well."

Constance gathered her bonnet and cloak from the chair. Feeling extra combative in the face of this unwelcome, yet familiar, awareness, along with a healthy portion of frustration toward men in general, she held Southwyn's gaze and deliberately moved the inkwell on his desk six inches to the left. Then, lifting her chin defiantly, she plucked the stack of papers from beside the inkwell, threw them into the air, and made her exit as they fluttered to the floor.

As expected from a well-trained butler, the unsmiling man met her in the foyer and waited by the door. However, even an excellent servant of his ilk couldn't have guessed at the way she silently chastised herself while she donned her things.

You know better than to lecture a powerful man like that. It is asking for trouble of the sort you don't need right now. And yes, making a dramatic exit and leaving a mess behind you felt wonderful. But don't think I didn't notice how completely alive you felt in there. The way her pulse rabbited at her throat was exhilarating, even though half of it came from the way his eyes had followed her with rapt attention. Drawing in a sense of calm, Constance willed her first response into extinction.

Her role today was to help him win over a cat and advance Althea's agenda. That was all. Perhaps he would take her advice, listen to his fiancée, cry off, and everything would sort itself. Then she'd never need tell her friend that she'd momentarily forgotten her place and told the earl he should care more—when the ultimate goal was to make him care even less. Enough to run away and set Althea free.

Tugging on her gloves, Constance shook away the thoughts and addressed the butler. "Give his lordship bits of meat to offer the cat, and tell him to feed the kitten by hand. No more bowls or saucers unless it is water or cream. Have someone fill the cat's pan with soil from the garden, if not the dirt from the plant he knocked over. Also, bring used linens from the earl's bed into the study for the kitten to sleep on. The faster Prince Puddles adjusts to his lordship's scent, the faster they can make peace with one another. Once they're on better terms, I suggest leaving the cat in that room for a few more days before allowing him to roam in the house. Such a large space will be overwhelming to a small animal."

"I beg your pardon, but... Prince Puddles?"

Constance stopped before a large mirror and tied the ribbon of her bonnet in a jaunty bow, even though the bleak weather outside would make her efforts moot within minutes. "I think it appropriate. Whether the earl realizes it or not, that tiny bundle of fur outranks him." She offered the butler a sunny, albeit forced smile. "Are my instructions clear? Do we need to write down anything for your staff?"

The butler somehow managed to straighten his spine further, until he resembled a soldier standing at attention. "No doubt we shall manage. I will send you a missive should we need elaboration. Thank you, Miss Martin." His demeanor softened. "I hope if you have reason to visit again, you'll see his lordship in a state more appropriate to his position. He's not himself right now."

In her mind she saw the image of Lord Southwyn lounging half-dressed on the floor of his study as he swore at a cat, and it made her smile. That might not have been reflective of the earl's grand status, but she'd never found him more appealing than when he'd smiled at her with those bloodshot hazel eyes.

"I'm sure he will be feeling more like himself soon," she said, believing every word, and hating the twist of disappointment in her gut.

Chapter Eight

Try to ask the right questions. Is there a way to wiggle out of this commitment?

Sir William Thompson's study had an air of disuse to it. As if the maids swept through the room, opening drapes and windows to relieve months of stuffiness right when Oliver arrived. Few personal items were strewn about. Nothing like Oliver's own study. Which, at the moment, was one part workspace and three parts feral cat sanctuary.

Thankfully, the instructions Miss Martin left with his staff were working, albeit slowly. He and Prince may not be the picture of domestic bliss yet, but the cat was eating from his hand and allowing the occasional pat, even without bribery. Not bad progress for a few days' effort.

Althea dropped by every day, ostensibly to check on Prince. That morning, he'd realized visiting the cat wasn't all his fiancée did when she called.

Oliver smoothed a hand self-consciously over his waistcoat. Navy blue, the one he wore on Mondays. Except it was Sunday. However, his Sunday waistcoat seemed to have disappeared, replaced by a pink and lime-green floral monstrosity shot through with gold thread. The garishness of it threatened to make his eyes bleed.

Pinned to the hideous fabric had been a note:

Dear future husband,

The Earl of Southwyn should shine just as brightly as his countess, don't you think?

> *Happy Sunday,*
> *Althea*

He hadn't the stomach to wear it, so he'd grabbed the first waistcoat at hand. Now, the entire week's wardrobe was topsy-turvy and he was wearing blue. At the moment, he had to wonder if he should have just worn the bloody thing, if only to restore order to the rest of the week.

Unfortunately, Althea wasn't the only woman haunting him. Miss Martin's little tantrum at the end of her visit continued to intrigue and baffle him in equal measures. Moving the inkwell? Tossing his papers? What had that been about? Unless of course she simply loved creating chaos everywhere she went. The woman was a whirling dervish. Maybe that's why her words circled round and round, mingling with Althea's until a continual chorus of female displeasure accompanied him wherever he went.

I've told you what I want. I've been telling you for three years.

I think of you as a brother, not a husband.

I'm beginning to see why she isn't looking forward to marrying you.

We are not the unknowable mystery poets make us out to be.

Meeting with Althea's father seemed a reasonable course of action to escape the chastisements in his head. If he could examine the actual agreement their fathers wrote all those years ago, Oliver might find a way to honor his word and the spirit of the promises made, while avoiding marriage to a woman who didn't want him.

Sir William entered the study wearing a wide grin. "Oliver! Good to see you, lad. To what do I owe the pleasure? My little Althea isn't causing you grief already, is she? Women and weddings, am I right?" His chuckle grated on Oliver's nerves.

Sir William tended to put him on edge, even when he wasn't being a condescending nodcock. That he'd so easily maintained a close friendship with Oliver's father—a man of dubious worth as a human, and low value in general as a companion—always seemed like a mark against his neighbor. Besides the knight's questionable friendships, he refused to see Oliver or his own children as grown adults.

That he couldn't foist them onto nurses and governesses these days was likely a great annoyance. That thought cheered Oliver somewhat. However, he'd rather eat glass than tell Sir William about the various challenges he faced in his relationship with Althea. He wouldn't risk making her a target for the man's wrath.

"Althea is her usual charming self." Absolute truth. Althea was as lovely as ever—just not toward him. Her moments of acting like a brat were alarmingly frequent these days. Yet, when she wasn't trying to annoy him, he caught glimpses of the young lady he'd once considered a friend.

"Happy to hear it. I'd hate to think of you carrying tales of cold feet now that we've set a date. Her mother and I are eager to see this whole thing done after so long. Anyone would agree I've been more than patient."

As if the delays had been Oliver's idea, and not the product of both of Sir William's daughters stalling or outright running away. It was enough to make a man doubt his appeal to the fairer sex. Oliver bit his tongue and laced his fingers behind his back.

"Now that we've set a date, I thought it time you and I looked over the specifics."

Sir William's jovial expression froze. "Meaning?"

Instincts went on alert, like a hound scenting prey—the same feeling Oliver experienced when a problem was a hairsbreadth away from unraveling to show its core issue. The smile he offered Althea's father felt more natural this time, albeit a bit wolfish. Sir William's reaction to a perfectly reasonable question struck him as wrong. Was there an obvious weakness in the contract, and Althea's father knew of it?

After all, Sir William couldn't have been friends with Oliver's spendthrift, dishonest father without having something in common with the blackguard beyond also being something of a bully. Oliver considered himself more than qualified to recognize that particular trait.

Which raised the question—what if he wouldn't actually benefit from a match with Althea's family, beyond restoring the entirety of his ancestral lands? He'd hoped the dowry would help finance the eye-watering expense of building a canal system. Counted on it, to be honest. Especially given the unexpected expenses of maintaining the estates this year.

If her dowry was a pittance, would owning the river be enough incentive to push forward? However, if he backed out, what would happen to Althea?

Taking a step closer, Oliver tried for a casual, friendly air. "The marriage contracts, Sir William. I've yet to see them, or the agreement you made with my father. Given it's my future at stake, anyone would agree *I've* been more than patient."

Hearing his words repeated back at him made Sir William curl his lip. Within seconds the forced jolliness returned, as if the sneer hadn't existed. "You've always been a good boy, seeing to the obligations Lord Southwyn made."

Ah, there was the defensive patronization again. Oliver took another step toward Sir William's desk, that feeling of anticipation thickening his blood. "If you need a moment to gather the documents, that's understandable. I'll wait."

"Well, I don't have the contracts, you see?" the man blustered. "They're still with my solicitors."

Oliver took a seat and made a show of getting comfortable. "I imagine they won't be that different from the contracts you drew up for Dorcas a few years ago—which, come to think of it, I never saw before she eloped. Surely you have those lying around." Placing his hat on one thigh, Oliver smoothed his soft leather gloves over the top, admiring the contrast of camel leather against black felt.

In his peripheral vision, Sir William moved around the desk, then took his seat. "I burned those contracts. When Dorcas abandoned her duty, she brought shame on the family. I haven't spoken to her since."

Thompson family holidays during these last few years must have been brimming with joy and good cheer, Oliver mused wryly. "Then let us take a look at the agreement you made with my father. I'm sure you can recall details of the marriage contract from memory. I'll have my solicitor assess the final papers before I sign them, of course." Dorian had sponsored the private practice of Caro's solicitor friend, Gerard Bellmore. With that man's sharp eyes and keen mind, Oliver was confident the contract would be ironclad by the time they'd hashed out the specifics.

Assuming there was a marriage at all.

"Of course. Yes, of course." Sir William opened and closed one desk drawer, then a second, muttering under his breath. "It's here somewhere."

After several minutes of more of the same, Sir William placed a piece of paper no larger than the palm of Oliver's hand on the desk. "Here it is. See, told you it was here." Sir William pushed the paper across the desk with one finger.

It took a moment for Oliver to comprehend what he was seeing.

For the entirety of his life, he'd known it was his duty to marry the neighbor's daughter, combine the families, reclaim the ancestral land, and bring prosperity to both estates. His father always said Sir William would do his part in making Oliver's effort to uphold the family honor—laughable when you consider the source of such a statement—worth his while.

The conversations, if one could call them that, were never open to Oliver questioning the plan. After enough years of everyone presenting the situation as written in stone, he'd accepted it as such.

Two fathers concocted a complex plot, planned their children's lives, then sold the idea as the only way forward to secure their futures. Perhaps it was naive, but he'd imagined the men deliberating over the details at length before reaching an agreement.

Oliver tilted his head, reading the scrawled penmanship upside down. Silly of him. After all, he'd met his father and should therefore know better.

It wasn't really a piece of paper at all. It was a playing card. An ace of spades to be exact, with a few words written around the black pip in the center and both men's signatures at the bottom.

On this twelfth day of March, 1787, Lord Southwyn promises his son, Oliver Vincent, in marriage to Dorcas Thompson, daughter of Sir William Thompson.

"This is the extent of the agreement? What about specifics? Dowry, investments, land…" Oliver's voice trailed off. He didn't know what to think. His entire reality had just shifted on its axis, in a way much larger than simply wearing the wrong color waistcoat on a Sunday.

"All of that is implied, surely."

A deep groove pinched between Oliver's eyebrows as he shook his head. "No, I can't say there is much to work with to imply, infer, or assume a damned thing. Besides, this specifies a marriage to Dorcas. Dorcas is already married, and happily so, to another man. That makes this agreement—if we can call it that—null and void."

The knight opened his mouth, surely to bluster some more, and Oliver cut him off with a wave of his hand. "In light of this, I need to ask what your expectations are regarding the joining of our two families beyond a marriage license. Not to be crass, but what are you getting from this union beyond a title for your daughter? And what do I get from honoring this"—he picked up the ace and flicked it with a finger, making a satisfying *thwack* noise—"besides a reluctant bride? Wouldn't it make more sense for Althea to choose a husband she can be happy with? I'm sure her dowry is ample enough to tempt the right suitor, especially since you didn't have to dower Dorcas."

After all, Sir William's knighthood had resulted from him aiding the king's coffers a few decades earlier. When he'd bought the estate neighboring theirs, he'd been Mr. William Thompson, shipping tycoon. Eventually, the new knight sold his fleet and retired, content to enjoy his piles of money. The only thing keeping fortune hunters from mowing down the man's door had been this long-standing betrothal.

However, at the mention of dowries, Sir William shifted in his seat. Alarm bells sounded in Oliver's head. He leveled Althea's father with a look and raised his brows expectantly.

"Not every dowry comes in the form of cash and gold. Some are investments, or properties." Again, Sir William blathered on without saying anything specific.

"And Althea's dowry is comprised of which of those things?"

"I have several minor properties I will hand over upon the marriage, in addition to the orchard and river separating our estates."

Oliver cocked his head. His father always said the river would be part of the marriage settlement. In that, at least, Sir William appeared to be keeping his word. However, the rest of this conversation wasn't going as expected.

Behind the desk, Sir William refused to meet his gaze, while wearing a wide, frozen smile. His fingers tapped atop the desk. The man must be a terrible gambler, because he couldn't bluff to save his life. A blind man could see that Sir William hid something, but the full picture of this debacle in which Oliver found himself lay just out of reach. One thing seemed certain—if Sir William was prevaricating, there must be a catch.

"So, you will be letting go of several smaller properties and the parcel of land by the river." Oliver didn't want to show too much enthusiasm and give away that he had plans for the river. "Are the smaller properties of significant value? I ask, because if Althea found a suitor she preferred over me, a loving father would ensure her dowry would attract such a match."

Not to put too fine a point on it, but Oliver did not trust the man to take care of Althea's future without putting it in writing. More writing than was on this damned playing card, of that he was certain.

Sir William shrugged, still wearing that jester's smile. "Doesn't really matter in the end, and we won't have time to find out."

Oliver's sense of foreboding deepened. "Is there a rush for her to marry that I'm not aware of?"

He didn't think she was the type, but if Althea found herself in the family way and hoped to marry him before she started showing, Oliver deserved to know. Even as the thought crossed his mind, he dismissed it. Most women did not walk into a scenario in which they needed an honorable man to step in like that, with open antagonism and feral cats. There had to be another reason for her parents' rush, despite Althea's reluctance.

Finally, like a puppet who'd had his strings cut, Sir William's shoulders slumped and the near manic grin he'd been sporting since walking into the room fell from his face.

Oliver braced, already knowing that whatever the man had to say would complicate everything further.

"I can't afford the taxes. Even with Parliament abolishing the income tax, which will certainly help things, it does nothing for the land taxes, window taxes, house taxes, and all the other myriad ways our king claims his share of our so-called luxuries. As if it's any of his business if my family buys wine, or silk—especially when the palace drips with those very things," he grumbled. "I borrowed money to pay this year's taxes, and the lenders aren't the friendly sort, if you catch my meaning. I need those properties to go to Althea's husband this year to avoid further debt. Her mother won't be satisfied with less than a society wedding, so you two will wed by the end of the Season." A shimmer of tears welled in the older man's eyes as he spread his hands—either begging for understanding or preparing to catch gold coins should Oliver feel so inclined to throw any across the desk. "And you, my boy, can afford it. You're a good lad. You won't allow your father's oldest friend, much less your father-in-law, to sail up the River Tick."

Oliver bit the inside of his cheek to hold back the instinctive ire that swelled at such blatant manipulation. "What did you use as collateral to these less-than-friendly moneylenders?"

"The, ah, properties themselves, of course."

So not only were the dowry lands of low value, they were also mired in debt and came complete with cent-per-centers who'd eat their own mother's liver if she owed them a tuppence. Lovely. "If this all comes down to money, why not sell me my ancestral lands, as I've repeatedly asked you to do? Then pay back your loan, let Althea marry whomever she wants, and we all go our separate ways. We can be neighbors who wave at one another in the village, and nothing more." Oliver held up the playing card. "This is worthless as a legally binding document, and you know it."

All signs of tears vanished, and in a flash, Sir William's face took on a purple hue. "When the earl was up to his neck in debt, I bought that land on the condition that you'd make my daughter a countess." White spittle collected at the corners of Sir William's mouth as he spoke.

Oliver had been under the impression that his father lost the land in a card game—a version of events supported by the ace. Unfortunately, the true story might be lost to time, given that Sir William was the lone surviving witness.

"It was a fair exchange made in good faith. Just because Dorcas didn't do her duty does not mean Althea can't marry well. I'll be damned if at least one of my daughters doesn't become a lady."

Instinct urged Oliver to leave. To stand, tell the man to sod off, then walk away from the entire mess. In the same situation, his father would have been out the door the minute he saw Dorcas's name on that playing card.

And wasn't that the sticking point? Oliver rubbed at the ache pounding at the base of his skull. When in doubt, he always chose to do the opposite of what his father would have, and that typically placed him on the path of doing the right thing. The honorable thing.

If he walked away, not only would he lose the river and ancestral lands surrounding it as a source of income, but Althea's future wouldn't be one of opportunities. Not when her father admitted to essentially gutting her dowry, then saddling her with debt-ridden properties and a nearly impossible timeline.

In all likelihood, she'd wed another poor bloke, more easily manipulated by her father. Or worse yet, Sir William would bring in a gambling friend with a title and an appreciation for young blond women. Althea, the now-grown girl who'd trailed behind him and Dorcas as they rambled about their estates, would still be a pawn for her father. Instead of marrying Oliver, she'd face some geriatric degenerate gambler.

Only a man without honor would abandon Althea to such a fate. Oliver could, at least, be a friend. He'd care for her, ensure she lacked for nothing. Perhaps in time, some sort of affection might even grow between them.

Oliver sighed, stuffed the ace of spades in his pocket, then placed his hat on his head. "Get me those marriage contracts, Sir William. Please have any wedding expenses sent to me for payment."

As he marched from the house, Oliver did his best to erase the image of Althea's father as he'd made his exit. Sir

William's face wore a smug smile as he'd released a bellowing gust of air. Relief, celebration, or satisfaction?

Whatever it had been, the sound made Oliver's hands clench into fists as he marched through the drizzle toward the Duke of Holland's home in Bloomsbury. He needed a friend and a drink.

Chapter Nine

~~Ask Caro about the dinner party we discussed~~
Pay and file invoices from vendors
~~Ask for help: how to stop these feelings~~

"*I*'ve created a bit of a sticky situation for myself and could benefit from some advice."

Caro and Hattie froze with their hands hovering over the tray of sweet treats as they glanced at each other, then turned their attention to Constance.

"Define *sticky*, darling," Caro said.

"On a scale of running away from the altar, to burying a body, how sticky is this situation?" Hattie laughed when both cousins gaped at her. "What? You're a whirlwind, Connie. It's only a matter of time until we're called on to move a body."

Caro bit into a lemon biscuit and shrugged, clearly not inclined to argue the point. "Should that day come, I fully believe it would be an accident or a crime of passion."

Hattie bobbed her head. "Absolutely. Nothing premeditated."

While they laughed, Constance mustered a smile. It was on the tip of her tongue to ask for clarification. Did they think she wouldn't plot someone's demise due to a lack of murderous urges, or because of an inability to think ahead and stick to a plan?

She suspected it was the latter. Ironic, given her current situation, which resulted from a plan she'd concocted and was seeing through.

Given how uncomfortable Caroline had been in recent weeks, as the end of her pregnancy drew near, it was nice to hear her laugh so freely. Even if it was at Connie's expense.

Besides, her cousins didn't mean any harm with their teasing—Constance believed that to her bones. Hattie and Caroline would never hurt her on purpose. Should she push back on the topic, they'd blink confusedly from their place atop a lifetime of evidence, anecdotes, and amusing stories involving Constance's ever-changing interests, difficulty being punctual, and inability to remember a damn thing unless she wrote it down.

It wasn't worth making a fuss over. Not when anyone who knew her would agree she was a whirlwind. Hell, Connie agreed with them. Because despite the enthusiastic attention she gave some things, other arguably more important items collected dust in dark corners of her brain.

So she forced a laugh. "If I ever accidentally killed someone, I wouldn't need help being rid of the body. I'd probably walk away for a moment, forget what I was doing, then go along my merry way."

Once Caro and Hattie's giggles subsided somewhat, she returned to the matter at hand. "I would welcome your advice, though. You see, there's a man—" Another pause to let her cousins finish their theatrical groans. "I know what it sounds like, but whatever you're thinking is *not* the case, I promise."

"Darling, I'll wish you happy as long as his name isn't James. Hattie, do you remember that summer when everyone she flirted with was named James?" Caro wiped a tear of mirth from her cheek and reached for her cup of tea. "It was impossible to keep them straight. I think she rejected every James between here and Bristol." Straightening on the couch made her wince and press a hand against the side of her belly. A moment later, the discomfort passed, and she sipped her tea as if nothing had happened. "Although it has been a while since you've mentioned a man."

Hattie scrunched her nose. "You're right. I thought she'd sworn off the lot and forgotten to tell us." Like a bug beneath a magnifying glass, Constance squirmed under her cousins' scrutiny. "Connie, you haven't fancied anyone in a while. Why is that?"

Because running away from her own wedding had broken her parents' hearts. Their shared look of disappointment in the church on that awful morning, silently commiserating over their daughter once again flitting away from something—or someone—she'd claimed she wanted. Except this time their embarrassment took place in front of friends and family, and involved the wasted expense of a wedding.

No wonder they didn't trust her with the future of Martin House. After serious thought, Constance decided that morning that she simply needed to try harder. Especially given what was at stake. If she made a schedule and stuck to it, there would be specific times in which she'd address the mind-numbing paperwork side of the business. As an intelligent adult, there was no reason she couldn't commit to a schedule. Then, her parents would see how dependable she was, and she'd never have to leave the only home she'd ever known.

Shoving those worries aside, Constance forced her attention back to their conversation. "I'm not involved with someone."

"You'd like to be," Caro guessed.

"Absolutely not. While I recognize the signs of a budding aw-awareness…" Her tongue stuttered over the word. "I don't want it to grow into a full-blown attraction. We all know how that ends. Besides, he's entirely unsuitable."

"Well now, I'm intrigued." Caro wiggled her eyebrows.

Constance forged on ahead. "Neither of you ever experienced the ups and downs of relationships as I have. You both seem to have this innate ability to nip inconvenient romantic interest in the bud. Whereas I jump in without thinking. I act impetuously, believing in the moment that because my motives and feelings are pure, all will be well." Anxious energy made her stomach churn, and she feared she might vomit as her mind offered up a parade of memories from the many, many times she'd chosen foolishly in the past. "Please, teach me how to dampen this feeling before I act, well, like myself, and let it run away with my head. Again."

Caro shifted on the couch with a wince. "For one thing, I think you're being awfully hard on yourself. As you said, at the time, your intentions were good. To answer your question…I had my reasons for avoiding romantic entanglements and acted accordingly with every man I met until Dorian. He was impossible to ignore, despite being unsuitable and inconvenient, because he was the *right* man. Might I ask, who has caught your attention after so long?"

Constance picked at a dry bit of skin on her cuticle, refusing to look at her friends. "His name isn't important. Although, let the record state, it's not James." When they laughed, she smiled, still avoiding their eyes. "Besides, I'm asking for ways to ensure I never think of him in that way again. I won't let history repeat itself— Can you imagine?"

If she were to give in to those fizzy feelings from Southwyn's study, what followed after would be so horribly familiar.

She'd think of him constantly, obsessing over whether he returned her regard. Then, once she'd charmed her way close to him, she would realize he wasn't what she wanted after all, and she'd look like a fool all over again. Except this time, it would be with an earl, of all things, as well as Dorian's oldest friend.

Mortification rang clear in the sound she made—an almost-laugh that wobbled when she shook her head emphatically. "It would be courting disaster. Besides, there's no one worse matched for him than me." As bitter as the words tasted on her tongue, they were the truth. "Caro, your advice is to remember my reasons for avoiding romance. What say you, Hattie? Any words of wisdom?"

Hattie wrinkled her nose. She resembled one of those little dogs they sometimes spied in Mayfair that wheezed with each breath, whose eyes bulged when they grew excited. As the comparison wasn't terribly flattering to her cousin, Constance kept the thought to herself.

Hattie finally shrugged. "I don't trust men; thus, I don't want one. What Caro said bears repeating. We are different people, Connie. I avoid the fickle beasts entirely. Caro made up perfect men and wrote about them until a real-life man proved to be her own personal hero. You're not like us. You have always been this effervescent, beautiful creature, eagerly sharing your enthusiasm with everyone around you. Until Walter, you craved romance, so you sought it out. If you no longer want a relationship, I understand. However, something you said just now needs addressing."

Hattie held their attention. "You said there's no one worse matched for him than you. And that, my dear, is incorrect. Your generous nature and open heart would be a gift to anyone. If he's too foolish to value that, it's a reflection on him. Not you. Now, if you recognize that he's either unavailable or undesirable as a partner, then you're right to distance your-self. Every time he crosses your mind, tell yourself why he's not right for you, then go do something else."

The kindness and calm confidence with which Hattie spoke soothed parts of Constance that she hadn't realized were tender. "Thank you. That's very helpful. Both of you."

Again, the memory of Lord Southwyn, rumpled and exhausted, sprawling on the carpet of his study rose in her mind. Instead of smiling or sinking into the details of how he'd looked, she silently listed all the reasons she didn't want him. *He's engaged to someone else. He is so stuffy; you gave him a nickname to reflect that.* Of course, he relaxed rather deli-ciously. In fact, it wasn't until he loosened his death grip on manners and propriety that this damned attraction flared to life.

She caught herself, then shook her head to clear it. Clearly, this technique required practice to master. Since seeing Southwyn with his kitten, he'd lingered in her mind the way favorite passages of the books she read over and over again stuck with her, evoking predictable feelings each time. But, like details of a novel faded over time, this would too.

"Just in case, if you see me making an arse of myself around a man, please distract me for my own good." Pluck-ing a tiny cake from the tray, Constance ate it but didn't register the flavor at all. Instead, she counted the number of times she chewed before she might swallow it without risk of choking.

Anything to distract her from the very real possibility of her cousins watching her act the fool in front of Lord South-wyn, then clapping their hands over her mouth before it ran away with her. As usual. She was convinced the direct path between her brain and mouth never touched on whatever part of her housed common sense or self-preservation.

"Is this a new experience for you, darling?" Caro asked.

"What? An impossible attraction?"

"An unrequited attraction." Caro's voice was gentle.

Comprehension dawned. Did that explain it? "Is that why this is so uncomfortable?" She sagged into her chair. "For the first time, I want a man I can't have." Another tiny cake plucked from the tray beside her. This one tasted of raspberry preserves. A positive sign, she acknowledged, as the rest of her brain mulled over Caro's revelation. "That makes me sound a bit like a spoiled brat, doesn't it?"

"Don't interpret it that way." Caro shifted to squeeze Constance's hand.

Hattie leaned in and laid her hand atop both of theirs. "It's not your fault you're rather relentlessly charming and attractive."

They laughed, and Constance welcomed a flood of relief. Asking her cousins for help had definitely been the correct decision. Sometimes, the only way to understand something so close to you was to bring the problem to those you trust. She squeezed their hands in silent gratitude, then let them go.

Hattie said, "For all your flights of fancy and short-lived interests, you have an uncanny ability to stay rooted in reality. You don't reach beyond what it possible, therefore you rarely fail to achieve your desires. Perhaps this is the first time someone beyond that sphere has piqued your interest. New situations, especially emotional ones, are uncomfortable. Unfortunately, my love, discomfort is part of life."

"Hattie is correct, as usual. Since you don't intend to pursue this mystery gentleman, we will be sympathetic ears as you navigate the novel experience of not getting what you want," Caro teased.

"I don't particularly like how this all makes me sound,

but it rings true. And I feel better after telling you about this temporary madness. I'll deal with it as you've advised. What would I do without you two?"

As Caro reached for the teapot from the cart and refilled each of their cups, Hattie protested, "I can get that."

"I'm pregnant, not an invalid." Caro's mild rebuke lost credibility with the grimace she made as she wedged a small pillow behind her back, attempting to find a comfortable position. "Although if this child doesn't stop climbing up under my ribs, I might resign myself to my bedchamber and make everyone wait on me. Lord, I'm ready to carry him or her *outside* my body." At last, she seemed to find a position that didn't exacerbate all the things making her irritable, then returned her focus to Constance. "May I ask you something, darling?"

"Of course." Steam from the tea, bright with notes of citrus, tickled her nose, and Constance took a moment to enjoy the aroma. One benefit of her cousin becoming a duchess was exceptional tea. Life above the bookshop was comfortable, all things considered. But the tea her parents bought couldn't compare to this. Constance took a remarkably short time after Caro's marriage to grow accustomed to such luxuries.

Caro canted her head, studying her. "What is it you find so appealing about this man? If we introduced you to someone else with those qualities, we might give you a quick escape from this discomfort."

Constance grinned. "I do love how we're speaking of him as if he's a blister. If only I could place a plaster over this attraction and ignore it until it's gone."

The question of what she found appealing about Southwyn wasn't one she needed to ponder for long. A warmth began in her chest, warning of how dangerous it could be to speak his virtues aloud, even as she did exactly that. "I know it sounds silly, but when he's messy and unbathed, he smells nice. I want to bury my face in the side of his neck and see where the scent is strongest." Like citrus and herbs, his cologne brought to mind drinking lemonade in an herb garden on a warm day. "When he's not wearing a cravat, there are a few hairs that curl up into that notch at the base of his throat. For some reason, I find those hairs fascinating." She swallowed a mouthful of tea, relishing the comfort of its heat traveling to her belly. "Also, when he's swearing, he makes me laugh. It's like a window into the realest part of him. Getting a peek at the emotions beneath the logic." Her cousins wore expressions she couldn't decipher.

Hattie raised a brow. "When have you seen him in his shirtsleeves, without a cravat?"

"You like the way he curses?" Caro asked, equally bewildered.

Constance grinned. "I realize it's not an attribute we usually value in a man, but he truly has the most creative language. As to his state of undress, that's a long story. Nothing untoward happened, though."

The duchess studied her in a way Connie recognized all too well.

"Caro, you're looking at me like I'm a misbehaving character, or troublesome plot device in one of your books. If you need something to entertain you, perhaps we could choose a date for that small dinner party you agreed to host."

Caro conceded the point with a shrug. "I simply find all this fascinating. That's all. And thank you for the reminder. I'd forgotten."

Constance didn't believe her. Judging by her carefully bland manner, Hattie didn't either. If they knew Caro—and they did—she'd treat this like a character exercise until it made sense. Unfortunately, there was no making sense of

Constance's hopeless attraction to a man so far beyond her status as to be laughable. Especially when she refused to divulge his identity.

Hattie spoke. "What you're saying is, all we need to do is visit the docks, find a foul-mouthed fellow in need of some soap, and you'll be right as rain. Then you can bring him to Caro's dinner and we will all toast the beginning of your relationship and the end of Althea's."

Constance choked on the sip of tea she'd been swallowing and coughed out a sound somewhere between a wheeze and a laugh. It faded swiftly to silence when Dorian entered the room, followed closely by Lord Southwyn.

Chapter Ten

Act nonchalant in his presence
Dinner party at Caro's! Don't forget
Althea: act intoxicated, flirt with the footman

Honor dictates I keep my word—" Lord Southwyn was saying.

"Honor is a cold bedfellow. Let others suffer the consequences of their actions for once, Oliver." Dorian spied his wife, and such clear affection lit his eyes, it nearly hurt to watch. "There you are, love." He glanced around. "Ladies, I didn't know you were here. Good to see you, of course." Surveying the nearly decimated tea cart, he grinned. "I intended to make sure Caro ate something. If she goes too long between meals, she feels unwell. I see you have the matter well in hand."

"Meaning I vomit into random vases, because this child is determined to make me uncomfortable until the very last second," Caro explained cheerfully. "That lovely soup tureen I liked so much will never be the same, I fear." To her husband, she said, "My girls are keeping me company, lest I grow too bored. Cook has me well-fed. Don't worry so much."

Dorian shook his head. "Impossible. It's my responsibility

and privilege to worry over you. I'm sure it was somewhere in the marriage contract." He dropped a kiss on her mouth, then sat beside her.

Constance envied the adoring way the duke teased his wife. When Dorian had been no more than a customer in their bookstore, she'd thought him handsome, if sad. The thick melancholy he'd worn like a cloak back then always made her want to pat him on the head like a child, then offer treats until his outlook brightened.

She peeked at Lord Southwyn, only to catch him looking back at her. They stared for a moment, and something shifted inside her. Or perhaps between them?

Caro addressed him, and he veered his gaze away with a jerk.

"Please forgive my lack of a proper greeting, Oliver. I'm afraid it would take an act of God to heave me off this sofa to do the thing correctly. Would you care to join us?" She waved a hand toward the remaining chair beside Constance.

"Thank you. I can spare a few moments to visit," Southwyn said.

He claimed the chair next to her. Constance tried and failed to ignore how the arm closest to him tingled with awareness. *Nip it in the bud.* Limiting herself to a vaguely polite smile, she asked, "How fares the little prince?"

The corners of his eyes creased in an alarmingly attractive way when he grinned, sending butterflies aloft under her ribs. "Happy to report he's no longer destroying my study. The maids successfully removed the smell from the carpets. The drapes are beyond saving, I'm afraid."

"He's adjusted to the boxes then?"

"With one in nearly every room in the house, yes." Oliver glanced at the others. "Sorry. Althea brought me a cat," he explained.

"A kitten," Constance corrected.

"A hell spawn," he countered, making her laugh.

"A scared kitten, who's clearly been mistreated by men, and therefore had a difficult time trusting you at first."

Lord Southwyn nodded, although she was fairly certain he rolled his eyes. "That's accurate. A sympathetic explanation of his behavior doesn't invalidate his status as hell spawn."

She'd let that go, since she was enjoying this conversation. A conversation she might have with anyone, without a single flirtatious comment. He hadn't admired her cleavage, and she hadn't touched him in a faux innocent manner—not so much as a graze on his arm, she thought smugly. "Is he letting you pet him yet?"

Everyone in the room remained silent, watching the interplay.

"Shockingly, yes. When faced with starvation or eating fresh meat from my hand, he chose to risk my attention without inflicting bloodshed."

"There you have it. The prince decided your touch is better than death."

"A ringing endorsement, indeed," Southwyn drawled. "In all seriousness, though, you saved the day. Prince and I are both indebted to you."

"I am so confused," Caro said from the couch.

"I'm entertained and baffled in equal measure," Hattie interjected.

"Althea gave him a kitten, then left him to his own devices," Dorian said.

"After several days of trying to convince the bloody thing to tolerate me, I sent for the only cat owner of my acquaintance, Miss Martin. She kindly came to call, and saved the situation," Southwyn said.

"Interesting. You must have been in quite a state." Caro's character study expression was back, this time directed at Lord Southwyn, and a wave of foreboding swept over Constance.

"I was indeed," he answered.

"You know what would make me happy, Dorian?" Caro's attention shifted abruptly to her husband. "It's been an age since we've caught up with everyone. Let's arrange a picnic on the heath with all our friends. Something big and packed with everyone we know. Even your mother, if you think she could endure the idea of eating with insects."

Constance bit her lip. Having a huge party, as well as the Silver Dragon—the moniker they'd given the Dowager Duchess of Holland—on hand to witness Althea's attempts at driving Southwyn away had not been the plan.

Dorian shook his head. "Not the heath. I need you close to the house if you go into labor, not rattling about in a carriage. Besides, the weather has been abysmal with this incessant rain."

Caro curled her lip militantly, but Dorian held firm. "If the baby comes while we're out of the house, the only person with any experience in childbirth is my mother. Do you really want her lifting your gown to deliver our child in the mud?"

"Oh God." Caro looked so appalled at the idea, Constance hid a snort behind her hand. Beside her, Southwyn coughed to disguise his own laugh, and she felt a surge of satisfaction at their shared amusement.

"Rather than a picnic, let's host a dinner party. Nothing elaborate or formal. I won't have you tiring yourself out with the details. Let's keep it small. Your family, Althea and Oliver, Mother if she's available," Dorian offered, clearly used to these kinds of negotiations.

A smile flitted around the edge of Caro's mouth, and Connie realized that she'd just witnessed a master at work. Having her husband suggest a dinner party had been the plan all along, the devious woman. Otherwise, it was highly likely the duke's worry over her health would have made him reject the whole idea.

Caro nodded. "I accept your counteroffer, with the condition that if the weather's fine, we move the table to the back garden. If I have to stare at these same rooms for much longer, I'll need Bedlam rather than a nursery."

"Then go for a walk," Hattie suggested. Constance silently agreed, even though her brain had already jumped ahead and connected all the dots.

In their world, pregnancy was a part of life. But in the ton...

"I look as if I could sneeze and give birth on the pavement, so I can't exactly walk in the park without making a fuss. Society refers to this stage of pregnancy as confinement, and they take that word far too literally." Caro's tone turned downright grumpy.

Dorian smiled at the group. "It sounds like we are having a dinner party as soon as possible."

"Hattie and I are available any day after the shop closes," Constance said.

"I'll ask Althea if she has plans. We're committed to an event tonight. Then the schedule is fairly light," Southwyn said.

Caro clapped her hands, then grimaced and pressed a hand to her belly. "Oliver, if you'll send a missive this evening, detailing which evenings work for you and Althea, I'll make invitations. Thank you all, for indulging my need for a distraction."

Especially as the pregnancy caused increasing discomfort, Constance felt guilty for asking her cousin to play hostess. Even if it was only a simple dinner. Of course, if the Silver Dragon joined them, that could make things interesting—as would Caro's crankiness due to growing an entire human inside her.

At least the gathering wouldn't be boring.

Oliver wished, a few days later, that it was possible to categorize people and their actions, as easily as one might within the animal kingdom.

Animals had been a source of endless fascination for his mother. Her interests went beyond the desire to snuggle every cute beast—although that did result in a rather epic row when she'd campaigned to bring home one of the baby kangaroos Queen Charlotte gifted to friends. Not that the Southwyns could claim Queen Charlotte as a close connection. Rather, they were friends of friends, and his mother had glimpsed an opportunity.

No, the late countess had also harbored a scientific mind. Oliver liked to credit his mother for planting the seeds of his logical way of thinking. God knows the inclination hadn't come from his father.

The differences among species, the vast variety within the animal kingdom, had been of particular interest to his mother. When she died right after Oliver's tenth birthday, her most prized possession had been the skull of a gorilla. Macabre as it was, he still had the thing, tucked away on his bookshelves in the study. In fact, he'd had a moment of panic that morning when the skull had somehow migrated off its usual shelf, and onto a side table near the fireplace.

It was a lucky thing the cat hadn't taken a fancy to it and knocked it to the floor. Having a pet was an adjustment.

His father hadn't permitted anything as domestic as pets, but when they were away from Birchwood Court, he'd allowed frequent visits to the Tower menagerie, the Exeter Exchange, and various animal collections around London. Oliver's favorite had been the trips to the Talbot Inn on the Strand to feed the camels.

Those were some of his fondest childhood memories. Mother, cooing over different species, sharing her knowledge with him in hushed tones.

He'd give anything to have her beside him now, using that same quiet confidence to guide him through this dinner party.

Dorian vacillated between hovering protectively over his extremely pregnant duchess and preening with pride when Caro said something particularly witty.

The Dowager Duchess Holland, never an easy woman to decipher, seemed overjoyed at the expected child itself, but only a hair beyond tolerant toward the woman carrying said child. Even this long after the wedding, the dowager appeared determined to shape Caro into a proper duchess.

Which allowed ample opportunity for Caro's cousins to tease and generally poke holes in the illusion of haute ton the dowager desperately attempted to create during what was supposed to be a relaxed family dinner.

For Althea's part, she'd thrown her lot in with the cousins. While not actively poking the bear—in this case, the dowager—Althea was happy to laugh encouragingly at their antics and jest with Miss Martin.

Fascinated, and feeling much like he had as a boy petting a zebra for the first time, Oliver chewed a mouthful of roast beef and listened intently to the conversations whizzing about the table with the speed and accuracy of bullets.

"Your Grace, you simply must eat. The child needs red meat," the dowager was saying.

"If I eat another bite of meat, I *will* cast up my accounts. That, I can promise you." Caro winced for a long moment and held her breath before releasing it slowly. "Someday, I will exact revenge for the way this child is digging its toes into my lungs."

Miss Martin tsked and shook her head in feigned disappointment, and Oliver felt a preemptive shot of amusement at whatever would come out of her mouth next. "I'm not a doctor, but I'm fairly certain your baby isn't floating around inside you, and able to tickle your lungs. Do I need to bring you an anatomy text from the shop? I found the most interesting book last week. The illustrations are incredibly detailed. Especially the reproductive bits."

Dorian closed his eyes while he drank deeply from his wineglass.

The other cousin, Miss McCrae, muttered, "Oh God, must you antagonize her?" and set down her fork with a clatter of metal on china.

Althea's head swiveled to watch Caro's reaction, but her eyes went a bit swimmy. Likely from how much wine she'd consumed.

The duchess glared daggers at her blond cousin, who sat across from Oliver. "This child doesn't tickle. It jabs. It spears my insides with its sharp little knife fingers and toes. And all that is *after* it forcibly ejects everything I eat from my body. I can't wait for you to be with child, Connie. I plan to mock you without mercy while you suffer, and the revenge will be sweet."

Miss Martin grinned. "Luckily, that's a dish best served cold, since I don't have plans to procreate anytime soon."

"Especially not if you insist on running away from the altar," the dowager intoned.

Red blotches colored Miss Martin's cheeks as her smile tightened at the corners. Before she could reply, Caro pointed a finger at her mother-in-law. "No. You won't be vile to my family. I may tease and threaten. You may not."

"That's quite all right, darling," Miss Martin said, then addressed the older woman. "Better to run away and be happy alone, than marry someone who would turn me into a miserable old woman."

Althea raised her glass. "Hear, hear!"

The dowager quirked a silvery eyebrow at Oliver. "Perhaps, Lord Southwyn, your bride is entertaining second thoughts."

Or twenty-second. Miss Martin caught his gaze, and he feared for a moment that she saw too much. Oliver looked away, forcing his attention back to Althea, who held her empty glass out to a footman while flirting rather shamelessly as he refilled her wine. From his place beside her, Oliver had a clear view of her fluttering eyelashes and overheard her quiet comment about how large the servant's hands were, and how...generous...he was with the pour. Subtle, she was not. The footman's cheeks turned pink, and Oliver couldn't help but pity the man as he cast worried glances in his direction.

Jealousy, or any number of other emotions, might have reared their head at her perfectly delivered inuendo. Oliver noted, as if observing himself like an animal behind bars, he felt...nothing.

Ironically, the utter lack of emotion concerned him more than Althea's indiscreet behavior. There were no feelings upon which to apply logic and navigate the awkward moment. Just absolute apathy.

"I've heard rumors of a wedding date this Season but have yet to receive my invitation in the mail," the dowager said.

Oliver offered a smile as false as Miss Martin's had been a second ago. Over the years, Dorian's mother had been generous with him, and he didn't want to offend. But the general rule to surviving any kind of relationship with the dowager was to never let her see your soft underbelly. "No need to worry, Your Grace. I'm positive you're on the guest list and will receive details when a time slot at St. George's becomes available. Althea and I shall contend with the details of our marriage, while you bounce your grandchild on your knee."

Miss McCrae interjected, "I read last year that St. George's sees a thousand weddings per year. Can you imagine? Someone will have to cancel their nuptials or die for Althea to get a wedding date. With all that schedule jostling, how are you supposed to read the banns? Or do you intend to use a license to wed?"

Oliver and Althea looked at one another, as if the other might know the answer to the questions. Finally, he shrugged.

Miss McCrae seemed content to accept that, and continued, "I, for one, don't intend to wed at all. Marriage as an institution isn't beneficial to a woman in the vast majority of situations. Caro is lucky to have a husband who doesn't see her as the weaker party, or merely property he's acquired. Unfortunately, most men aren't so enlightened."

"My incomparable wife would smother me in my sleep if I dared insinuate she was weak in any way," Dorian said with a level of cheer rarely seen when discussing one's own possible demise.

"You know me well," Caro agreed. The same footman who'd been attending Althea moved to remove the duchess's plate, and she thanked him. Oliver couldn't help but note that despite her claims of being full, she'd hardly eaten a thing all night and only sipped at her beverage.

"Of course, you seem like a decent-enough sort, Lord Southwyn," Miss McCrae continued. "Our present company might consist of the last two men in England who don't act like a horse's arse."

Oliver laughed. "Damned by faint praise, but I'll accept it."

"Well, since both of you are off the marriage mart, I needn't feel bad about avoiding the parson's trap for the indefinite future," Miss Martin quipped, and for a brief flash of time, that bright, dimpled smile was aimed at him. Her comment could have been flirtatious, but given the circumstances, it wasn't. Charming, yes. But flirtatious? Absolutely not.

A stab of something twisted in his chest, but before Oliver could examine it with the same distanced fascination his mother had shown her precious gorilla skull, a glass shattered on the floor.

Dorian shot to his feet. "Caro?"

The duchess clutched her stomach as a white ring of tension formed around her pursed lips.

Her cousins sprang to their feet in an instant, but the dowager held out a hand. "Give her space. Don't crowd the woman." Surprising everyone, Dorian's mother pushed the shards of glass aside with her foot, then knelt at Caro's knee. "Breathe," she commanded.

Caro sat still as a statue, her face turning an alarming shade of red.

The dowager slapped her hand on the table, making

everyone jump. "Breathe. Yes, it hurts. But you *must breathe through it.*"

Dorian rubbed his wife's neck, and Caro dropped her chin to her chest as she exhaled slowly. The duke stared at his mother. "Is the baby coming now?"

The dowager nodded. "Yes. Now, are you going to stand there like a ninny, or make yourself useful?"

Chapter Eleven

(List dropped in the shuffle.)

The dowager's gaze never left Caro's face, and Oliver could see he wasn't the only one drawing comfort from the confidence with which the older woman handled the situation. "That's it. You'll do brilliantly as long as you keep breathing. Women have been bringing children into the world since the beginning of time. Now, are these your first labor pains?"

"Her back hurt more than usual today. She mentioned it when we arrived," Miss Martin said. Even though her voice held concern, Oliver appreciated the way she kept a cool head at a time like this.

"Also, she hasn't had an appetite for more than tea since breakfast," Miss McCrae added.

"A few cramps earlier today, but they didn't continue," Caro added, then winced again and let out a low groan.

Dorian finally snapped out of his panic. "We have a plan for this. Caro, keep breathing." He lowered his mouth to her ear, but his words carried in the quiet room. "I adore you. You're brave, and you're strong, and we both know you can do whatever you set your mind to, including this. Now, let's get you to bed."

As the duke gathered his wife in his arms, Miss McCrae pointed to a footman. "You, send for the midwife."

"This isn't some village in the middle of nowhere, girl. Send for the doctor," the dowager argued.

Oliver wanted to cheer when the dark-haired cousin's face turned stony before turning back to the footman. "The duchess, *the mistress of this house*, gave clear instructions on this matter, correct?"

"Yes, Miss McCrae. Her Grace wants the midwife first. We are to only send for the doctor if the midwife is unavailable." The footman refused to look at the dowager, and Oliver couldn't blame him.

"Then you have your orders," Miss McCrae said, then the footman fled the room.

Miss Martin knelt to gather the glass from Caro's broken goblet, and Althea joined her. From where he stood, feeling absolutely useless, Oliver watched two blond heads come together, and heard the low murmur of voices, but couldn't decipher their words.

He detested feeling useless. Oliver motioned to another servant, hovering nearby—"Could we have a broom please, to deal with the glass?"—then joined the women. "Please watch the sharp edges, ladies. One medical emergency per night is my limit. If one of you needs stitches, you'll exceed my emotional resources."

Althea snatched her hands back, but Miss Martin continued plucking glass off the floor, onto a napkin. A second later, she hissed, then sucked her finger.

He'd swear his heart stopped. "How bad is it?"

The flash of her dimple, directed at him for the second time this evening, struck Oliver as nearly obscenely inappropriate, given the circumstances. "No more than a nick."

Thankfully, a maid hurried over with a broom and waved everyone away from the remaining shards on the floor.

"Althea, I'll take you home, then return to stay with Dorian. Miss Martin, I assume you plan to be on hand during the labor?"

"Wild horses couldn't drag me away." Miss Martin brushed her hands on the skirt of her gown, then examined her finger again. Oliver craned his neck to see the cut, but she shot him an exasperated look. "Go. We will be here when you come back."

Miss McCrae appeared at his side and sent him a wry smile. "It sounds like you have your orders as well, milord."

Althea said her goodbyes, then left to retrieve her cloak from the butler.

"Ladies." Oliver bowed. "I'll see you both soon."

At the front door, he took his hat from Hastings, the butler, and waited impatiently as Althea fussed with her cloak until it draped just so over her shoulders. Why was she taking so long, when she knew he was eager to be with Dorian after seeing her home? And he wasn't the only one. Caro's cousins would be right by her side as well. Which reminded him—

"Hastings, please send someone up with a plaster for Miss Martin's finger." Thanking the man, Oliver placed his hand at Althea's back and guided her out into the night.

Sweat dampened Caroline's hairline, while strain pinched the corners of her mouth. Dorian stood by her side holding one hand, stubbornly refusing to leave the room, even after the midwife arrived. Hattie held Caro's other hand.

Constance pulled up a chair beside Hattie's, but without a hand to hold, she found herself picking at her cuticles.

Not long after they got Caro settled in her room, a servant arrived with a plaster for Connie's finger. When asked, they said Lord Southwyn had requested it on her behalf. Now, with nothing to do but wait—and waiting wasn't something nature had equipped her to do comfortably—Constance stared at the small bandage as if it held some secret meaning.

Which was silly. Southwyn was merely being kind.

Tearing her gaze from her finger, she checked on Caro.

"So much of this evening will need to be edited out of the official story we tell this child when they ask about their birth," Caro murmured when her body relaxed after another contraction turned her belly to stone. "I'm sorry about what the Dragon said, Connie. That was uncalled for."

"Push it from your mind, darling. You've much more important things to tend to," Connie reassured her.

"Must we have so many people present, Your Grace? Babes like peace and quiet when they enter the world." The midwife cast a disapproving glower over the room as she pulled items from her leather bag. Constance eyed her askance when the woman poured gin into a small bowl rather than a glass. Then she placed a variety of sharp things into the bowl. A needle. A pair of scissors. A wickedly sharp knife.

Bile lurched up Constance's throat.

Hattie clearly didn't battle squeamishness. "Why gin?"

"'Tis cheaper than whisky. Wounds heal better with a splash of spirits. Makes sense to douse in spirits the things that make wounds, eh?" The woman tied an apron around her waist and sighed. "None of you are leaving. The dowager saw sense and left; why can't you lot?"

Caro's mouth was a flat line as she leveled the midwife with a look. "I've been alone for too many important moments in my life. These are my people, and I will have them beside me when I bring my child into the world."

"Men don't handle this well, Your Grace. Messes with their heads to see their wife's body doing this kind of thing, ye understand."

Dorian's answer barely fell short of a growl. "I'm staying."

And that was that. Constance smirked, knowing it wasn't the first time they'd had this conversation with this particular midwife, or the one before her. In fact, the woman they'd sent for tonight was the third midwife to tend to the duchess during her confinement.

The first had smelled so poorly, she'd literally made Caro vomit.

The second was neat and tidy, but she'd been immovable in her opinions regarding a husband's place during what she called the "women's work" of labor. Having lost her mother during childbirth, Caro was equally insistent on having Dorian stay beside her.

Thus, the current midwife who would deliver the first child of the Duke and Duchess of Holland. The woman's number of successful deliveries far outweighed the alternative. Her overall cleanliness, coupled with the fact that she wasn't afraid to push back a little on certain topics, rather than bowing obsequiously to the couple, cinched their decision to let her attend them.

That matter dealt with, Caro returned to her original statement. "As I was saying," then paused as another contraction gripped her. Her face turned red until Dorian's quiet reminder to breathe made Caro wheeze out a long exhale as she rode the pain. A moment later, she opened her eyes and continued as if nothing had happened. "Tonight wasn't the finest dinner party I've attended or hosted. Oliver was oddly quiet. Althea was quite drunk from what I could tell. And did she really flirt with the footman?"

A knock at the door interrupted. Dorian squeezed his wife's hand. "I'll be back, love."

Hattie nudged Constance with an elbow as soon as the duke left the room.

Connie said, "You both know Althea's behavior was for show. The dowager being here was a potential issue. In the end, Althea decided the potential benefits outweighed any risk. When she and Lord Southwyn left, she was feeling rather put out with his lack of reaction."

Caro raised a brow. "Would you happen to know anything about Oliver's subdued mood tonight?"

Her cousin was far too intelligent for comfort. Blinking innocently, Connie said, "I don't know what you mean."

Hattie grinned, and Caro started to, before her face contorted with pain once more.

Dorian returned and faint sounds from the hall slipped into the bedroom with him. Constance thought she could pick out Lord Southwyn's voice.

Even as she recognized the way her attention sharpened to that sound, she hated it. *Engaged to Althea*, she reminded herself. *Has to be* convinced *to not marry Althea*.

Sent a bandage for my cut, a contrary part of her interjected. This ridiculous attraction served no purpose beyond making her keenly aware of her own failings. Yet she couldn't help the way each sense came alive in his presence once she'd admitted to her fascination. Damn him, and damn her fickle heart.

"Oliver wishes you a quick and easy birth. He'd thought to keep me company, but I sent him home. Told Mother to go to bed as well." The duke laced his fingers with Caro's, then lifted her hand to his lips. Constance didn't miss the way he spent a moment breathing in his wife's scent as he kissed the fine blue lines of lifeblood at her wrist. His voice was rough when he said, "I'd take the pain on myself, if I could."

Caro wound a lock of his wavy hair around one finger, her other hand held securely in his. "Just be here. Don't leave me to do this without you."

The bright, pure love in her cousin's gaze shone so confidently, it made emotion sting behind Connie's eyes. No one in the world deserved that kind of love more than her cousin. The kind of love that could be loud, completely sure of its welcome.

Yet that very thing had never felt more out of reach.

With Dorian back, Connie could step away for a moment. Excusing herself quietly, she slipped out the door, then stood in the hall, gripping the doorknob behind her, unsure what to do next.

Lord Southwyn's rangy form strode away down the hall. She could call out and get his attention, but that seemed a tad dramatic. However, the question became moot when he inexplicably slowed, then stopped. Southwyn stared back toward her. For several heartbeats, no one moved.

His expression was one she couldn't read. It was ludicrous to think she might accurately guess at his mood. With the exception of their conversations about his cat, he'd never been especially emotive around her. Caro's observation that he'd been quiet this evening resonated, and Constance would love to know why.

Releasing her grip on the door, she took one step toward him, then another. After a few seconds, he moved closer as well, until they stopped, a few feet apart.

"Are you leaving already?" Connie realized this was the

first time they'd been alone since that day in his study. His jaw lacked the stubble, and his evening clothes were pristine and tailored to perfection. But his citrus scent was the same. It made her want to bury her nose in the dip where his jaw and neck met. She didn't though, because that would be ridiculous, and if she made a habit of chasing every errant thought, she would probably land in prison for entirely preventable reasons.

"I'll only be a burden on the staff if I stay." The words said one thing, but the way he looked at her made Constance think something else was going on behind those eyes. Whatever his emotions, she knew they weren't frustration, anger, or disdain. She had enough experience with being on the receiving end of those to recognize them.

Knowing what he *wasn't* feeling didn't help her understand what he *was* feeling. Of course, she'd be hard-pressed to narrow her emotions to merely one or two. Uncertainty over what to do or say grappled with an aching sort of awareness because he was *right* there, and they were alone, and blast it but he smelled delicious.

Licking suddenly dry lips, Connie tried to determine the best action to take. Perhaps she should encourage him to stay. Or should she do as planned, and thank him for sending a plaster for her finger?

His gaze shifted to her mouth, and she caught a flash of something all too familiar. Breath snagged in her lungs. Hunger. Or, if not full hunger, at least awareness.

Finally, an emotion she recognized. Her lips curved into a smile, and she leaned closer, seized by the reckless impulse to offer to stay with him in the sitting room—or at least split her time between the bedchamber and sitting area.

Except, he moved away. One step, then another. Slowly. Rather like one would retreat from a wild animal.

Oh. That must not have been hunger she'd seen after all. Embarrassment at how she'd misread the situation turned her cheeks hot.

Holding up her finger with the bandage, Connie offered an excuse for her presence. "I won't delay you any longer. I merely wanted to thank you."

Again, something crossed his face, and she wished she knew him well enough to hazard a guess at what it meant. Dipping his head in acknowledgment, Southwyn turned and continued down the hall without another word.

He didn't look back. Not even once. And she felt like a ninny for lingering outside the door long enough to know that.

Silently castigating herself at her foolishness, Constance returned to the bedroom in time to hear the midwife say, "Right then. Let's take a peek at how the babe is progressing, shall we?"

Morose thoughts could wait. It was time to have a baby.

Chapter Twelve

~~Show him how expensive a wife can be~~
~~Can we replace all the waistcoats? NO?~~
~~Don't forget about Betsy and Georgia's visit~~

This is unacceptable. It's not even Tuesday." Oliver lifted the blanket to stare down at his determinedly rigid cock, then huffed in disgust when the bloody thing refused to listen to reason.

Friday morning dawned with dim light sneaking around the edges of his bedroom curtains, to slip silently between the drapes enclosing his bed.

Not. Tuesday.

At the age of twenty-one, Oliver had realized the only way he'd successfully remain celibate until his wedding night would be to apply the same rules to his personal ministrations that he lived with in other areas of life. There was a time and a place for everything. And when one was a perfectly healthy red-blooded adult with sexual desires and urges, that meant choosing the time and place for indulging said urges.

Namely, the privacy of his bedchamber, every Tuesday.

The choice of a bedchamber should be obvious, given his virgin state. There was no one else with whom he'd lustfully tumble in a drawing room, or some such place.

Tuesdays were typically rather open on his schedule, and it was a neglected day in the grand scheme of things. No one greeted a Tuesday with enthusiasm, except his cock.

Tuesday had been typical, as Tuesdays went. Prince recently started sleeping with him at night, and the only thing noteworthy about last Tuesday was the hard-learned lesson to put the kitten out of the room before causing any kind of rhythmic movement under the covers.

The dreams began on Wednesday.

Dreams where a man who looked like him fisted his hands through tight blond curls, kissed at a deep dimple in a woman's cheek, then swallowed her cries of passion with his open, groaning mouth as he lost himself in her wet center.

He'd awoken painfully aroused, more than a little confused, and blamed the whole thing on the meal he'd enjoyed at Dorian's house the prior evening, moments before Caro decided to give birth instead of serving a dessert course.

Thursday brought more visions of his fingers tangling in blond curls, this time as a plump pink mouth wrapped around his cock. Dream Oliver begged the woman to let him spend in the slick heat between her thighs. She'd complied, then muffled his shout of completion with one lush breast at his mouth.

On Thursday he considered taking matters in hand. However, after years of providing a perfectly adequate schedule for sexual release, he refused to bow to his unruly body now. Instead, he called for a hip bath filled with cold water, and didn't leave the thing until his testicles threatened to become internal organs and his persistent erection calmed down.

Now, morning light turned the empty pillow beside him a shade similar to the dream woman's nipples. Oliver frowned. This last one felt more vivid than the others. His body ached for release. Unlike the previous mornings, this had one notable addition—he'd seen her face.

"What the fuck is Constance Martin doing invading my dreams?" Invading. Seducing. Alternating between dominating and begging.

His sensual dreams often featured blond women. Dorcas was blond. Althea was blond. Without realizing it before now, Oliver acknowledged how he'd been oddly proud of the way his body remained faithful to his intended wife, even while asleep.

The virginity had been a choice, not an accident. A state he eagerly anticipated waving farewell to, and soon. After all, society dictated that his wife would be a virgin on their wedding night, so it seemed fair to join their marriage bed in the same condition. Especially since he'd been in the unique position of knowing who he'd marry, from a young age.

It made indulging himself with someone who wasn't Dorcas—or Althea—a nearly adulterous act. Thankfully, he was a patient man, and he'd remained true to his intended. Out of fairness, if nothing else.

Until Constance bloody Martin showed up in his dreams, making him question if he'd ever actually seen the face of his fantasy lovers before. As his unrepentant arousal made a distinctive mountain beneath the covers, Oliver rubbed a hand over his face. No, he couldn't recall specifically dreaming of Althea or Dorcas.

Just as he couldn't remember awaking with their voice so clearly in his mind. Certainly not the way Miss Martin's throaty moans clung to the last cobwebs of sleep, bringing with them memories of how she'd gasped his name then encouraged him with sensual, explicit words until they climaxed together.

Then, the truly damning part.

They'd laughed. Him, still hard, and Miss Martin with her thighs wrapped around his hips, holding him deep within her, they'd laughed with the kind of familiarity he imagined lovers developed over time. A sort of mutual exclamation of "goodness, we just did that and it felt amazing" translated into wordless sound. Dream Oliver had kept one hand tangled in her hair, the better to keep her close, as he rested his forehead in the crook of her neck. Miss Martin—Constance—smelled faintly of sleep and musky woman, with a faint trace of honeysuckle soap clinging to the slightly damp skin under his face.

In the dream, he'd been content to remain there, with her legs keeping him in place while his cock slowly softened. Breathing her in, enjoying her light laugh and murmured comments against his ear.

Morning arrived with an achingly hard erection, and an even more uncomfortable sensation of exclusion. Like when he'd returned to Dorian's townhouse after seeing Althea to her door the night of the dinner party, and his friend instructed him to go home. Caro was determined to have Dorian by her side for the delivery, so Oliver didn't need to keep him company.

Oliver hadn't commented that a husband didn't typically stay in the room during labor. After all, basic self-preservation instincts advised against arguing with a woman on the cusp of giving birth. But as he'd walked away from their bedchamber, the sound of Miss Martin and Miss McCrae speaking with their cousin made him acutely aware of his place outside a significant moment in his friend's life.

Then, as if that feeling summoned her, he'd sensed rather than heard Miss Martin join him in the hall. Facing one another and saying barely a handful of words should have been awkward, but he didn't remember it that way. For a brief time, she'd included Oliver by seeking him out. While the duke's family tree grew without Oliver there as witness, someone had missed his presence. As devoted as he knew her to be to her cousins, Miss Martin still stepped away from their side to see him. The finger plaster might be a tiny thing, but her thanks made Oliver feel seen.

Of course, that moment when her pink tongue darted out to wet her lips, turning the cupid's bow glossy and slick, his cock had nearly made a fool of him. In an instant, he'd gone thick and heavy, and vaguely lightheaded. Somewhere inside him, a primal urge—something he thought he lacked altogether—flexed its claws, and the feeling had been both exhilarating and fucking terrifying. No wonder Constance Martin haunted his dreams.

"Bloody fucking hell. This is unacceptable." He threw the covers aside. A disgruntled "mew" made him flip the edge back. "Apologies, Prince. Go back to sleep."

And unlike his still-turgid cock, the recently feral kitten did as it was told.

The day loomed before him, a schedule packed to the brim with meetings, objectives, and goals.

"Because it's not Tuesday," Oliver muttered, splashing water on his face, then shaking tooth powder onto a bone handle toothbrush.

At the end of the afternoon, he'd set aside two hours to visit Dorian, Caro, and their new son, Nathaniel. It was the one thing he actually wanted to do today, and part of him wished to cancel everything else, so he could indulge in the novel experience of seeing Dorian and Caroline as parents.

That would be entirely selfish, though, since the duchess would still be spending most of the day resting after the monumental task of bringing a human into the world. Out of respect for the new family, he'd held off this long before visiting.

Miss Martin might be there, helping her cousin. At the fleeting thought, his cock twitched, and he scowled.

Devil only knew what he could do about this new problem. It wasn't as if digging erotic dreams from his brain was possible. Trying to replace Miss Martin's face with Althea's, Oliver attempted to simply rewrite the memory. Recast the dream, like a play. No, wrong blond woman, his inner theater director declared. Make the memory hold Althea's voice, her laugh, and her scent.

Oliver froze, toothbrush in his mouth. What did Althea smell like, exactly? And how did he know with such certainty that Miss Martin used honeysuckle-scented soap?

He made a mental note to sniff his fiancée when he saw her the following evening. They'd promised to attend a ball, and no doubt there'd be plenty of chances to determine what perfume she preferred when he held her in his arms and twirled them around the dance floor.

Rinsing his mouth, he glared at the part of his body that had decided it would allow the front of his breeches to lay flat. Finally.

Padding barefoot into his dressing room, Oliver rang for his valet.

Ten minutes later, his mood darkened further.

Althea had stolen and replaced another waistcoat. Orange in that particular shade shouldn't be possible, much less legal for purchase. This theft forced him to choose a different day's color, further breaking the predictable routine of dressing that had served him well for years. Scheduling such things meant one less decision to make. One thing in his day over which he had complete control.

As he shrugged into his coat, the ace of spades from

Sir William's office caught his eye. Yellowed with age and fraying around the edges, it mocked him from the table on which he'd thrown it. Without overthinking the urge, he shoved the card in his pocket and went downstairs.

Two hours later, Oliver cradled his head in his hands and stared at the tidy stack of invoices.

Modistes. Shoemakers. Milliners—five of them. God, how many different bonnets did one woman need? Lace weavers. A random warehouse with a delivery address near the docks. He wanted to question that one specifically, since the idea of Althea wandering the docks and shopping terrified him. Unthinkable things happened to women at the docks.

Still resting his forehead in one palm, he reviewed the papers. "There's even a cheese monger. Who, pray tell, spends this much on *cheese*?"

It wasn't the expense, although that was enough to make King Midas's eyes water.

It was the fact that no one needed that much cheese. Not even Althea.

Also, the waistcoats. Drinking too much and flirting with the footman at dinner the other night. The damned cat. Perhaps even stranger, the way things moved and resituated themselves around his house. These days, he spent the first few minutes in a room returning items to their proper place.

If Miss Martin was in on the plan—and the longer he considered it, the more obvious that became—it would explain why she moved the inkwell on his desk. Althea was not an unintelligent woman.

All of it was designed to deliberately provoke, annoy, and inconvenience him. Part of Oliver wanted to give them both, Althea especially, a standing ovation. The other part wished he could capitulate and give her what she wanted, even though it wouldn't serve her well in the end.

Althea's feelings on their marriage were quite clear, and God knew he didn't desire an unwilling bride. However, with Sir William's circumstances being what they were, becoming Oliver's countess was the best she could expect.

Without him, Althea would face a father in debtor's prison—or dead from shady moneylenders—no dowry to speak of, and yet another scandal on a family name that wasn't illustrious enough to withstand the stain.

It would be so easy to walk away from the whole situation. Release her from their engagement and allow Sir William to reap the harvest he'd sown with his poor decisions. Yet, a lifetime of memories of a golden-haired, laughing little girl begging him for piggy-back rides refused to let him react as his father would have.

Once upon a time, that little girl trusted him. As had the thirteen-year-old; when heady with her first infatuation, she'd asked Oliver how to get the attention of the boy she fancied.

When Dorcas eloped and Sir William informed Althea she'd fulfill the marriage contract instead, Oliver had witnessed the swift death of her trust.

Obviously, Althea didn't realize how dire the circumstances were. Not when gaining that knowledge required her father to be truthful with her. It seemed like a safe guess to assume Sir William was equally cagey with his family as he'd been with him. Otherwise, Lady Thompson would be making economies, rather than planning a grand spectacle of a wedding.

Which left a few solid truths to cling to. First, he needed to speak with Althea and apprise her of the situation. Preferably before she escalated her current tactics with a visit to Rundle & Bridge and beggared him entirely. Second, he'd reassure her that he would not abandon someone who'd been part of his world for the entirety of his life.

In time, their affection for one another might turn romantic instead of platonic. It could happen. Otherwise, his marriage would be nothing more than a lifetime of Tuesdays.

Oliver drew in a gust of air, forcing calm over the churning thoughts. Restacking the bills, he handed the pile to his secretary. "Pay them."

Constance loved her sister. Of course she did. That they were twins added another layer of intimacy—and conflict. Some, or most, would argue it was impossible to not love Betsy.

A mirror image of Constance on the outside, she too was often described as a pocket Venus. Short, buxom, with wildly curly blond hair and dimples that winked when she smiled. Which was often, because Betsy possessed an even disposition, a methodical mind that didn't betray her at every turn, and the kind of peaceful presence that made others feel lucky to be around her.

It was hell to look like her while being so different in every way that mattered.

Betsy fell in love with Barrister Steven Tilford, married him a few months later, set up a cozy home a couple hours from London, then proceeded to give birth to the most angelic daughter on Earth. A blond cherub with her mother's dimples and both parents' analytical minds, Georgia was impossible not to love. Just like her mother.

Constance might be her mirror image, but in all other ways, they were night and day. Alas, she wasn't the "day" part of the idiom. Her parents would never admit it, but compared to Betsy, Constance must be a disappointment.

Yet, she loved her sister. Loved her niece. Even loved her brother-in-law, although she'd never have chosen him for herself. Steven fit Betsy in the same way Caro and Dorian fit. Like puzzle pieces snapping together, linked for life.

"Aun' Connie," Georgia gently reprimanded.

Constance shook her head. "So sorry, darling. I was wool-gathering." Taking the picture book from Georgia's little fist, she patted her lap and waited as the three-year-old settled in the cradle of her legs. When a pointy elbow dug into her thigh, Constance winced but didn't complain.

"Will I see my cousin soon? Mama's been gone for so long."

"Yes, if Aunt Caro feels he's up to it. Nathaniel is new to the world, moppet. He might be tired after meeting your mama." They waited in the sitting room of the duke and duchess's chambers. Her niece had been watching the closed door to the bedroom since Betsy disappeared inside.

Georgia relaxed against her aunt's chest with the confidence of a child who'd only ever found welcoming arms. Dropping a kiss on the golden head, Connie breathed in. Sunshine, a little sweat, soap, and traces of both her mother's perfume and father's cologne. Connie might never have a family of her own, but she relished being an aunt. However, as time passed, it seemed more likely that Georgia might be the only child who would resemble her.

"Will 'thaniel be my friend? Like Aun' Caro, and Aun' Happy are your friends?"

The day this child learned to say her *t*'s and Hattie stopped being Aun' Happy, Constance would cry. She just knew it.

Smiling, she dropped another kiss on those adorable curls, so much like her own. "I believe you and Nathaniel could be great friends. Cousins are like bonus siblings.

Perhaps someday you'll have brothers or sisters, but Nathaniel will always have been first."

"I wan' a sis'er."

Constance knew it was wicked, but she said, "You should say so to your parents. Often."

The bedroom door opened, and Betsy walked in holding the baby. Caro followed, wearing a loose morning gown.

"Would you like to meet your new cousin, Georgia?" Caro asked. She sat gingerly on the sofa before taking her son from Betsy. Georgia clambered off Constance's lap.

"Careful, darling," Betsy said. "He's quite delicate, remember." She sat beside her daughter, close enough to intervene if the three-year-old grew too excited.

They needn't have worried. As soon as she peeked into the bundle of cloth, Georgia audibly gasped. "How is he so small?"

Betsy chuckled. "You were tiny like that once. And here you are, growing taller and stronger every day. Nathaniel is fragile at the moment, but he won't be for long."

"If you hold very still and follow directions, I'm sure he'd like you to hold him," Caro said, and received a beatific smile from Georgia.

Constance felt her heart twist slightly as she watched them teach the little girl how to support the baby's head. Soon, Nathaniel was cradled on Georgia's lap, who'd instantly fallen in love with him. Caro and Betsy exchanged a sweet, knowing look.

They didn't glance her way, even though Connie probably wore the same expression. Of course, Caro was a mother now, which gave her and Betsy something in common. Something Constance knew nothing of. As Georgia and Nathaniel bonded with murmured words, coos, and grunts, Betsy offered Caro advice about nursing, and discussed nappies and sleep schedules. Connie had nothing to add to the discourse, and she was achingly aware that she might never have a similar conversation with either of them.

Jealousy struck her as too strong a word, but whatever this feeling might be, it wasn't comfortable. It felt a bit like standing outside a bakery, inhaling the delicious smells and admiring how beautiful everything looked through the window. All the while, knowing her pockets were empty.

Soon, Constance would leave this breathtaking home in Bloomsbury, while her sister and niece stayed behind. Caro and Dorian had offered a guest room for the duration of their visit.

Caro and Betsy had never been close. But in this moment, Constance watched them connect in a way that made it seem like they were growing away from her.

"There's a lovely property for sale a short walk from our house," Betsy said with a teasing grin. "Wouldn't it be nice to raise the cousins together?"

Caro laughed quietly. "I can't imagine giving up my perfect little cottage in Kent. That's our oasis for most of the year. I don't think our place is far from yours, though. We should try to see one another more often."

Caro's snug cottage was the opposite of this grand house. A handful of colorfully decorated rooms, with comfortably worn furniture. Not a servant in sight. And more of a home than these marble floors could ever aspire to be. Caro had fallen in love with the property on sight and purchased it with funds she'd earned as an author. That Dorian so readily welcomed a simple, quiet life outside London was one of the things that convinced Connie of the duke's love for her cousin.

Now Betsy would bear witness to their adorable domesticity, when Connie remained hours away. She didn't like how the discomfort of her thoughts chafed against the inherent joy of the moment. How petty and small of her to worry over feeling like an outsider among people who had never done anything but love her. Yes, it might seem as if they'd forgotten she was present. But that problem had an easy solution. Constance scooted her chair closer to them. Caro and Betsy greeted the movement with warm smiles, and the ache she'd been wrestling with eased.

"Georgia, you are doing such an excellent job holding him. I think he appreciates how gentle and calm you are." Connie reached over and stroked a finger over the baby's plump cheek, then brushed the tip of Georgia's nose, eliciting a giggle from the girl. "Well done, darling."

"I love 'thaniel," Georgia whispered. The adults shared a smile. Tension eased from Connie's shoulders when they included her in the moment.

Dorian's low voice rumbled from the hall, and two seconds later, he entered the room. The back of Constance's neck prickled until she glanced back toward the door.

Lord Southwyn stood beside the duke but wasn't staring spellbound at the baby. Instead, he looked between her and Betsy over and over, wearing another expression she couldn't interpret. The mystery was short-lived, because he murmured, "Oh God, there are two of them," in an appalled tone. He studied Betsy for a moment, then shifted his attention to Constance. "One of you needs to speak, so I can hazard a guess as to which is the new one."

Constance bit her tongue against an urge to end his confusion. It wasn't what he'd said, but how he said it. As if there being two of her was such an awful reality. Unfortunately, she'd heard the sentiment more than once over the years. A glance at Betsy showed her sister watching her with a devious glint in her eye.

"You have fifty-fifty odds," Betsy said, with the same chipper lilt she'd used when they'd entertained themselves by switching places in the bookshop. That's how Constance spoke, according to her sister. Although it had always struck her as sounding a bit manic.

Knowing her cue, Constance tried to mimic Betsy's impression. "Do you like those odds?" She almost addressed him by name but caught herself just in time. Betsy wouldn't know who he was, and Connie would *not* be the one to give away the game.

Southwyn narrowed his eyes, studying them both. "You're not inclined to offer me a hint?"

"And ruin my fun?" Betsy and Constance said in unison.

Caro and Dorian laughed, while the sisters shared a grin.

Southwyn took a seat in the nearest chair, then rested his chin in his palm. "There really are two of you," he mused. Perhaps he was growing accustomed to the idea, since he didn't sound nearly as dismayed as a moment ago. Turning to her niece, he asked, "And who might you be, little miss?"

"I'm Georgia, and this is my cousin 'thaniel." Her arms tightened around the baby as if afraid the newcomer would make her give him up.

Southwyn's gentle smile made a sigh stutter in Constance's chest. Damn the man for being so appealing.

"Lovely to meet you, Georgia. Would you please tell me which of these women is your mother?"

"Cheat!" Constance cried.

He grinned, triumph lighting his eyes. "Never mind, Georgia. Your aunt gave herself away." Lord Southwyn dipped his chin toward Betsy. "It's a pleasure to meet you and your daughter. I was unaware Miss Martin had a sister, let alone a twin. The resemblance is remarkable."

Betsy flashed her dimples, amused by the whole interplay.

"I'm Mrs. Tilford. And don't worry about telling us apart. Constance and I may be identical, but our personalities make identifying us easy."

Constance forced a grin. "Yes, if you encounter one of us and she's serene, organized, and holding still, it's Betsy."

On cue, her sister, cousin, and the duke chuckled. As they should, because she spoke the truth. Since one of the laws of the universe decreed that hearing truth would either be painful as hell, or make you laugh, Connie did her best to make them laugh.

The earl, she noticed, didn't crack a smile. Instead, he studied her with a pinch between his eyebrows and merely said, "I see."

What he saw, she didn't know. But she suspected it was more than she wanted him to. Because it might be more than her poor heart could take if a man she wanted, but couldn't have, truly saw her.

Chapter Thirteen

Lady Agatha Darylwrimple, an intimidatingly tall, nearly geriatric leader of the ton, possessed the unique ability to be Oliver's favorite person in the room one moment, and the very devil the next.

Right now, she was the devil. Oliver raised his champagne glass and drank rather than risk saying something he might regret later, once he remembered he actually liked this woman.

Standing shoulder to shoulder with her—literally, as she was an inch taller than him in those heeled slippers—the older lady kept her voice low, and he was grateful for it.

"She is sending a message, and you do not appear to care one whit. Miss Thompson is practically begging for your attention, yet you stand here with all the warmth of a punch table ice sculpture. Will you not give her what she wants?"

As tempting as it was to play at not understanding her meaning, feigning ignorance would be a disservice to them both. "I don't find I'm inclined to, no, because I disagree with your assessment. If she wants my attention, as you say, she could speak to me. Or maybe not dart to the opposite side of the room when I approach, so I might speak with her."

Althea had shut him out entirely. Ignored his requests to call. When he visited uninvited, she refused to see him. She'd even stopped visiting Prince. The only times he laid eyes on his fiancée since she went on her shopping spree were nights like these, when her parents accompanied them. How the hell was he supposed to help her understand their situation if she wouldn't talk to him?

Lady Agatha's sigh lacked subtlety. "Youth does not appreciate passion. Your beautiful fiancée has not sat out a dance all night." She gestured toward the center of the ballroom. Wine sloshed dangerously near the rim of Lady Agatha's glass, although she didn't take notice of it. "Not one of those partners has been you."

"Her dances were spoken for when I asked." Oliver gently removed the glass from her grip to spare her white satin gloves, fully prepared to hold on to it until the conclusion of this lecture.

"And whose fault is that? What kind of man does not ask in advance—especially for the supper dance? Miss Thompson endured that blowhard, Lord Balderdash, for endless courses."

Oliver choked on his laugh. "Lord Baldridge, you mean?"

Lady Agatha shot him a condescending look. "I said what I said. Baldridge is a fool. He could not tell the truth if you held a gun to his head. Yet she sat beside him for a whole meal. Why would you leave her to that fate?" Taking back her wine, she raised an eyebrow and sipped.

Because he hadn't remembered the supper dance until she'd already promised it to someone else. "Althea's the one who agreed to dance with the man." Shaking his head, he groaned. "I'll forever think of him as Lord Balderdash, now. Won't I?"

Lady Agatha's smile was entirely unrepentant but faded

quickly. "Miss Thompson is a lovely young woman and promised to you. Why, when her hen-wit of a mother is speaking of nothing but a grand wedding, does she not assume you will want a set of dances?"

He couldn't resist rolling his eyes. "Althea is enjoying the evening. You're seeing problems when there are none." Even as he said the words, he could taste the lie.

Silver curls quivered when Lady Agatha shook her head. "If you believe that, you are as great a fool as Lord Balderdash. Miss Thompson has flirted outrageously with each of her partners, while pointedly ignoring you. Lord Southwyn, she is perilously close to making a scene."

Draining his glass, Oliver stuffed down a spike of irritation. How much easier it would be for everyone if she caught the attention of a wealthy, titled man who wouldn't care that she came with debts instead of a dowry. Then Oliver could buy the land from her, build the locks in stages as money allowed, and all of them would live happily ever after. "Am I to play the jealous lovesick swain, then? Or the tortured hero? Everyone knows our marriage is an alliance of families. To pretend otherwise would be ridiculous." He held up a hand to stall her interruption. "I care about Althea. We've been in one another's lives as long as she can remember. And I'll be a good husband to her, assuming her mother successfully persuades her down the aisle. But I won't play these childish games. If Althea wants to dance and flirt the night away, so be it. I see no reason to stop her."

"Do you not?" Something akin to disappointment crossed Lady Agatha's face. "I am sorry to hear it, Lord Southwyn. I had hoped for better for you both."

Oliver glanced at Althea, lovely and laughing with someone else, then back at his companion. "I'm not sure what you mean. This is exactly what I expected." His intended wore a different face than a few years ago, but when one married for duty, that didn't matter.

Lady Agatha took his empty glass and placed it with hers next to a vase of lilies atop a short Greek-inspired column. "Have I ever told you about my first marriage?" When he shook his head, she continued. "It was typical of those in our set. A merger of families and lands, like yours. While my husband was not cruel, he was entirely apathetic about me, my happiness, or my needs. Refused to come to Town. Kept me away from my friends and did not care when I cried over the loss. And you know I threw the kind of fit only the young can get away with. If he had not beaten me to it and died in a riding accident, I likely would have expired from boredom, just for a change of scenery."

Lady Agatha grasped Oliver's hands in hers, holding his gaze with a fierceness that caught him by surprise. "Because I was a gently bred young lady, it was exactly what I expected. I did not know any better, but I knew I was lucky the marriage was brief. When Alfred asked for my hand, I did not realize the joy awaiting me. At the time, I chose him because he was *kind*. As a younger son without a title, he was everything my family would have rejected. And he is the best part of my life." Her voice gentled. "To love your spouse is a gift, Lord Southwyn. One I have enjoyed for nearly forty years, and one I hoped you would have with Miss Thompson."

"Love can grow over time," Oliver said, but the phrase felt like reciting sums with his tutor as a child. Something he'd heard so often, he'd memorized, then stored away in a little brain compartment in case he needed it at a future date.

If Lady Agatha was correct, and God knows she often was, then people were watching Althea and making their own assumptions about his relationship—which was none of their bloody business, but he didn't intend to add kindling to the gossip pyre. And, since he wasn't about to charge across the ballroom floor and cut in on her dance, the least he could do was pretend to be infatuated with her.

Oliver fastened his attention on Althea once more, attempting to mimic the way Dorian looked at Caro. The soft expression in Dorian's eyes when he watched his wife do the most mundane tasks. How his mouth curved slightly as he delighted in the smallest things. In fact, Dorian had once gone on for nearly five minutes about the way Caro focused so completely on her writing, that he could stand and observe her for hours, unnoticed, if he wished.

While Oliver didn't understand why Dorian admired the way his wife ignored him in favor of her imaginary friends, he could appreciate that the duke genuinely received joy from the experience.

The way Caro's cousin always seemed to be doing two things at once was far more impressive to his way of thinking. When they'd been on the floor of his study that first week with Prince—unbidden, a smile curved his lips at the memory—Miss Martin had masterfully called him to task while soothing the kitten. He'd be hard-pressed to think of another woman with the same combination of sharp wit and gentle hands, who would have handled the situation with the same blind eye to the casual setting and his state of undress.

"Perhaps there is hope for you yet, lad," Lady Agatha murmured. "As long as you can gaze at her like that, love may grow after all. Ah, I see my Alfred."

Oliver watched her silver hair weave through the throng of people as she made her way toward her husband. Mr. Darylwrimple's face creased into a wide smile at the sight of his wife. He excused himself from the gentlemen he'd been speaking with, then pushed through the crowd to meet Lady

Agatha. Without hesitation, he clasped her hand and led her to the dance floor, as the opening strains of a waltz signaled an opportunity to hold her close in public.

Unexpected longing stole Oliver's air. Someday, when his hair faded to gray, or fell out altogether, what would it be like to greet every opportunity to hold his wife with that kind of enthusiasm? The idea brought a sharp sting, as that primal, instinctual *thing* he'd experienced in Dorian's hallway flexed its claws again. Some part of him, long thought dead, craved what his friends had.

He searched for Althea's pink gown amidst the couples on the dance floor. A familiar man bowed before her, although his name escaped Oliver at the moment. From what he remembered, he was from a good, but not excessively wealthy, family. A younger son. Not even the spare behind the heir, but the fifth or sixth born. Poor man would have to find a way to make his own way in the world, as was the burden of all younger sons.

Yet, the way he regarded Althea was enough to make one believe that young man thought himself the luckiest blighter on the planet. As he—damn, what was his name—pulled Oliver's fiancée close and set them spinning to the music, his face resembled the way Dorian looked at Caro. Like Alfred looked at Agatha.

Glancing about the room, Oliver noted no less than five men watching Althea dance, all wearing expressions of desire or interest. She was, objectively, a lovely woman. In what many considerd the height of her beauty and youth. The ready smile she gave her current partner probably made him feel like the center of her world.

Althea had never looked at Oliver like that. Not once.

Everyone, it seemed, adored the woman he had to marry. Everyone except him.

* * *

"...is that *cheese*?" Constance stared, torn between fascination and shock at the impressive wax-covered wheel Althea dropped on the counter. It must have cost a small fortune. Raising her eyes to Althea's, there was nothing lighthearted in the other woman's demeanor. "Apologies. Is it *sad* cheese?"

That brought a smile from her friend, and made Constance feel like she might be able to help with whatever was bothering her. "Althea, I am going to need more information before I know how to react."

"Are we alone?"

"Hattie is upstairs and might be down any minute. Mum is in the office." Catching up on the account books Connie had procrastinated doing *again,* despite the schedule she'd created. The birth of Nathaniel, followed by Betsy's visit, wreaked havoc on that plan, and she had yet to get back to it. Guilt and self-recrimination spiraled through her, but Constance shoved them aside for the time being. Althea needed her attention right now. "Otherwise, we are alone."

Althea slumped onto the counter, then thumped her head on her folded arms. "I'm sorry about the cheese, but I couldn't think of anywhere else to take it, and it was going to make my clothes smell if I kept it in my armoire. Mother is on a never-ending reducing diet and refuses all rich foods when at home. Father would eat it, then have terrible wind. Besides, there's just *so much of it.*"

Understanding dawned. "Ah, so it's both revenge cheese and guilt cheese. You purchased it and had it billed to the earl?"

Althea raised her head enough to share a miserable pout. "I bought gowns and slippers, and so many hats. More silk stockings than I can wear in a lifetime. I heard of a place near the docks that had a fresh shipment of tea and bought enough for three houses. I was running out of ideas when we passed a cheesemonger on the way home, and I thought, why not?"

Constance lifted the wheel and wheezed from the strain. "This cheese weighs more than a child. How much did it cost Southwyn?" She tried not to laugh, and failed, when Althea winced. "That much?"

"If I told you, your ears would bleed and you'd probably cry. Every time I look at it, I feel sick. I dropped off most of the tea with Roberts this morning, since his employer paid for it. I thought for sure I'd gone too far, but Oliver doesn't appear to care."

"Maybe he appreciates a woman who loves cheese?" The ridiculousness of it all made her laugh again, despite Althea's glare. "It could have been worse. You might have passed Tattersall's on the way home, instead of a cheesemonger."

"Miss Thompson, I thought that was your voice . . . Is that cheese?" Mary Martin asked when she stepped from the office, unwittingly echoing her daughter's inflection.

Which sent the friends into a fit of giggles. "I'm afraid so. I find myself with an excess, so I'm sharing."

Mary smiled broadly and took the wheel from Constance. "We're grateful for your generosity. I'll take this upstairs and leave you girls to enjoy a coze. May I bring you anything? Some tea or biscuits?" After an amused assessment of the bounty in her arms, she added, "Perhaps some toast and cheese?"

Althea's laugh was the polite society tinkle of sound, but Constance's mum had no way of knowing it wasn't genuine.

"Thank you, Mum. We will be fine for a while."

"Then I'll leave you to it. Thank you again, dear."

Once she heard the door to the stairwell close, indicating

her mum had gone up to the flat, Constance turned back to her friend. "He truly didn't balk at the expense?"

"Oliver is impossible!" Althea wailed. "I gave him a feral cat, who, by the way, he treats like a prince, just as the name suggests. I've acted drunk in front of his friends, which somehow didn't embarrass him. I don't think he even noticed when I flirted with Her Grace's footman." Althea ticked off the list on her fingers, voice rising with each item. "Not a word about the waistcoats. At this point I've abandoned subtlety altogether and am moving items in his home into entirely different rooms. Meanwhile, my mother is asking me if I prefer cream- or ecru-colored ribbons in my bridal bouquet, as if there's any bloody difference, and the only thing I want to do is marry Franklin and never hear the name Southwyn again." Althea's heaving chest and flushed cheeks made her appear feverish.

Connie wrapped her into a gentle hug. "Have we considered that the real Southwyn is dead, and we're actually dealing with an automaton?"

Althea snorted into Connie's shoulder, but stayed where she was, accepting the offered comfort. When was the last time her friend had received a hug?

"An automaton would make sense, wouldn't it?" Althea muttered.

Constance wished she could forget the way he'd looked in his shirtsleeves, all lean sinew and bone and coiled strength. Alas, he was a real man. A man who had practically fled when she'd considered flirting with him at Caro's.

Althea shifted away, so Connie let her go. "Tell me about Franklin. You've hardly mentioned him, but having feelings for one man while trying to avoid marrying another has to be wearing on you."

Tears welled in Althea's eyes. "I just finished the most

marvelous novel by Jane Austen. *Emma*; have you read it? The hero says if he loved her less, he could talk about it more. And I've never felt a sentence more deeply in my life."

Connie hadn't read that one yet, but the sentiment sent her hand over her heart. "Goodness, love like that would be glorious, wouldn't it? A love that's too big for words."

Althea nodded, tears spilling over. "I think about Franklin constantly. I want to talk about him all the time. But I fear that if I start, I shall never stop. And not knowing if I will ever call him mine makes the enormity of what I feel terrifying. I even waltzed with him in front of Oliver and still couldn't garner a reaction. Is it too much to ask Oliver to *care*?"

Compassion over her friend's distress nearly had Connie crying too. "Do you want him to be jealous?" She'd thought the point of this plan was to drive the man away, not inspire jealousy.

"No, but it would be nice if he noticed. If we truly are stuck together, can't he muster any level of fondness toward me? Oliver holds stronger opinions on the color of his waistcoats than he does about the woman he's supposed to marry."

"I'm sorry his ambivalence hurts. You deserve to know you're loved, liked, and enjoyed for who you are. Don't doubt it for a moment." Constance might see the appeal of the handsome earl, but that didn't mean she couldn't understand why Althea would want to marry elsewhere. Because while Lord Southwyn wasn't unkind or cruel, he also wasn't a good match for Althea. Not when even his kindness and self-control caused her pain.

"Has Franklin given you any reason to hope that he returns your affections?"

"Not in so many words. But, Connie, if you could see

the way he looks at me. He has to love me too. Finding time alone is nearly impossible, so I haven't asked him outright."

"Then maybe that's how we fight now. We find a way for you to communicate with Franklin, or to get you two alone. Eventually, we will find a way to stop this marriage. Everyone has their limit, and we will discover the earl's. No one will force you to marry. You have my word."

Chapter Fourteen

Simply refuse to cooperate

It still wasn't Tuesday.

Oliver rolled over to bury his face into the pillow. The downy softness muffled his groan as he angled his hip to accommodate an erection that refused to abate. Another groan escaped at the sensation of smooth linens against desperate flesh.

And he was feeling nothing short of desperation. Years of discipline and self-restraint were fraying under a barrage of dreams.

The sheets weren't nearly as soft as Miss Martin's hands had been in his sleep. The warm cocoon he'd made under the covers didn't compare to the imagined heat of her mouth and welcoming, wet body.

Lack of firsthand experience didn't equal lack of imagination. Unfortunately. At this point, being ignorant of what awaited him on his wedding night would have been a relief.

Relief. The word repeated in his mind. Oliver sighed and knew that today would be the day he caved to the demands of his body.

"Prince, you may want to leave, kind sir." The kitten grumbled at him before slipping through the bedcurtains. A moment later, Oliver heard a soft thump as Prince jumped to the floor and padded away.

He rolled over, one hand already smoothing across the head of his cock, where a bead of moisture waited, and he smirked. His cock was weeping in gratitude.

After years of a schedule, there was a routine to this ritual. Certain scenarios or movements affected his pleasure in predictable ways. Most of the time, efficiency was key. After all, this wasn't about making love to a partner. It was executing a biological function. He had no reason to draw things out. Which is why he'd never imagined a specific woman while pursuing release.

However, now that he'd taken himself in hand—despite it being Saturday—it felt like that one action removed the usual rules. Which only confirmed his long-held suspicion that breaking one rule led to anarchy. The newfound instinctual part of him that only woke up when he thought of Miss Martin, stretched lazily, knowing it would finally be heard.

To let himself become motivated by uncontrollable primal urges rather than logic wouldn't be a simple slippery slope. Instead, it would be a runaway coach driven by Hedone herself, racing directly toward chaos. If chaos came in the form of wild blond curls and a laugh that made a room feel more inviting, would that be such a bad thing? Just for a little while.

As his mind ached to slip back into the dream he'd just left, he chose to ignore the potential consequences of loosening his iron control. Constance—he couldn't think of her as Miss Martin when allowing himself this pleasure—smiled in welcome and opened her arms to him. His cock grew impossibly harder as the fantasy took hold.

It wasn't Tuesday, and the woman in his mind had a face. All his rules might be gone for the moment, but this was an isolated incident, he promised himself. Tomorrow would bring control. For now, Oliver took his time exploring Constance within the safe confines of his mind.

Much like the real woman, Dream Constance talked a lot. Delicious words, demands, directions, all interspersed with sounds that would make his cock downright unruly if he ever heard them in real life. After all, his fingers might not know precisely how soft Constance Martin's skin was, and he'd never tasted a single part of her body, but Oliver knew her voice. The sound of her was intimate and familiar as she told him how to best please her.

Oliver's breath sawed in and out of his chest while unintelligible sounds that might have started as words fell from his lips. As his hand stroked and squeezed, Constance murmured in his ear, urging him to enjoy her, to let her enjoy him, to stay in this bed and never leave her. He tried to make it last—another rule he'd break just this once. But God, that voice was too real, and his body too eager after days of denial.

Tension coiled low and hot. In his mind, she clenched around him and they flew off that cliff into pleasure together.

Oliver's limbs were languid as he lay there, staring up at the canopy over his bed. He closed his eyes and sighed. One hand smoothed over the bed beside him. A stab of disappointment when his fingers met nothing but empty sheets alerted him to the action.

"Ridiculous. Absolute madness," he said. It was over. Purged from his body and his brain. Things could return to the way they'd always been.

Except, that damnable part of his anatomy jumped to attention almost two hours later, when the voice from his dream floated down the hall to his breakfast room. Prince's ears swiveled toward the sound, so Oliver knew he wasn't imagining it.

Roberts appeared at the door. "Pardon me, milord. Miss Martin is here to visit Prince."

The butler's gaze settled on the chair beside Oliver's, and his face creased into an indulgent smile.

Oliver glanced down at the kitten sitting on the padded seat. Before him was a small porcelain dish holding a formerly-feral-cat-sized portion of kippers. The tips of Prince's ears were barely visible above the edge of the table.

"Show her in." Oliver motioned for the footman to set one more place setting, just in case Constance—no, Miss Martin—wished to join him. Thoughts of Constance, with her deliciously filthy mouth and soft skin, needed to stay in his bedroom. In the real world, she was Miss Martin, a hard-working bookseller and beloved family member of his best friend.

Oh, but the way his spine arched off the bed this morning from the power of the release she'd inspired—

When Roberts arrived a second time, now with a blonde in tow, Oliver rose. Carefully holding the serviette in front of him in a way he prayed seemed casual, rather than a blatant confession of his burgeoning erection, he tried to forget the things he'd done to this woman in his mind a short time ago.

"Miss Martin. We are enjoying some breakfast. Would you care to join us?" Oliver motioned to the cat in silent explanation for his use of the word *we*.

God, when she smiled, that dimple made it damned near impossible to look away from her mouth. Pink and plump, her lips were the stuff of dreams.

Quite literally, in his case. Oliver gripped the cloth napkin tighter.

A footman placed a teacup beside the dishes and silverware on the other side of Prince. "That's very kind of you, milord. Perhaps I'll join you for a cup of tea, if you don't mind. The sky is gray and spitting mad as usual, and the wet is already finding its way through my boots."

Oliver knew the precise moment she truly took notice of the way Prince sat in his own chair with his own place setting, because her smile transformed into something altogether otherworldly. With a surprised laugh, Miss Martin grinned at Oliver, making warmth creep into his cheeks. Delight shone from her features, turning her blue eyes a shade he had difficulty defining. It wasn't the blue of a summer sky, or the gray-toned blue of the sea. It might be closer to a— "Bloody hell," he muttered. Waxing poetic about her eyes? Who was he becoming?

Realizing he'd sworn aloud, Oliver prepared for her to take him to task about his language.

However, she ignored him entirely and knelt beside Prince's chair. "You've grown used to him, haven't you? Even when that big man curses, you know you're safe." Scratching the cat behind his ear, she peered up at Oliver. "Well done, milord. You've won him over."

Since her position put her directly at crotch level, Oliver resumed his seat and cleared his throat. Unfortunately, no words came to him. In fact, the normally organized and neatly categorized brain he'd cherished all his life was devoid of everything but his recent dreams of her. Instead of answering and embarrassing everyone involved, he gently stroked the soft fur behind Prince's other ear, then smiled when the kitten's purr rumbled between them.

"I'd forgotten what a loud purr he has." Miss Martin shifted to perch on the chair before the extra place setting. Pouring a cup of tea from the pot in front of the cat, she spoke to Prince. "You don't mind if I steal a bit of your tea, do you, my darling?" The cat purred, giving her a slow, adoring blink. "Thank you. That's most generous."

It seemed the two of them could continue in this vein for the foreseeable future, and part of Oliver wanted to let them. Just to hear her converse with a cat and see what topics this unpredictable woman chose to discuss.

"Thank you again for your insight. He's settled in nicely. The servants dote on him."

She pointed at the porcelain dish on the cat's chair. "I don't think the servants are the only ones doting on him. It makes me happy to see how well he's cared for."

"Is that your only reason for calling? To ensure I wasn't abusing the cat?"

She shrugged one shoulder, and it struck him how compact she was. With her halo of curls, large personality, and boisterous way of simply existing, Constance Martin took up more space in his mind than she did at the breakfast table. Slender shoulders, delicate fingers wrapping around the handle of the cup...how had he never realized how petite she was? Generous curves abounded on a small frame. She was a pint-size tornado of a woman. The idiom about a storm in a teapot came to mind, but she embodied the opposite of its meaning. She wasn't a fuss blown out of proportion.

Instead, she was a teacup-size tempest. The most literal interpretation of the words. Small, unpredictable, and the perfect size for his hands. Well, perhaps not his hands specifically. Some other lucky bastard's hands.

But did she know that? Did she realize that any man who caught her fancy should be thanking the bloody stars? Because after meeting her sister and seeing the way Miss Martin accepted teasing from her family, he wasn't so sure. He'd hated the way she'd smiled while comparing herself to her sister and saying nothing positive. Hated it. It made him want to shake every adult in that room who laughed at her expense. Which was a novel experience for Oliver. That nearly overwhelming urge to somehow protect Miss Martin from believing the nonsense she spouted from those plush lips had taken him by surprise. Neither the shaking nor the desire to defend her made any kind of sense, so he'd sat immobile until the subject changed.

"What does that expression on your face mean, milord?"

Oliver then took a bite of eggs that had gone cold. It would be impossible to explain his thoughts without initiating a conversation he couldn't have. Besides, his head was too muddled. God only knew what would come out of his mouth if he tried to speak, so he held his tongue.

"I'm on my way to visit Althea and thought I'd stop and see Prince." A nervous lilt to her words made him think she spoke to fill the awkward silence he'd created, which meant he'd made her uncomfortable. Again, the need to soothe and protect reared its head, and some part of his brain made a note that the urge didn't stem from any part of his groin region.

Which was worrisome. Finding someone attractive was one thing. But this—

"Thank you for the tea. It will fortify me for the rest of the walk."

"No need to walk. I've plenty of room in my carriage and planned to call anyway. Sir William is expecting me." After a second's hesitation, he finished the thought, allowing each word to be a brick in a wall between his troubled thoughts, and the reality of his duty. "I'm picking up the marriage contracts today."

Beside him, Miss Martin went still. Understanding her reaction or asking about her feelings wasn't something he could allow himself to do, however, so Oliver drained his tea, then offered a final scratch on the kitten's head. "You're sure you'll only take tea?" At her nod, he rose. "Then I'll gather my coat and be ready to leave when you are."

If she worried over his odd mood, it wasn't any of his concern. Or at least, that's what he told himself when he left the room, refusing to look back.

Men were the most confounding creatures. Welcoming and offering a woman tea on a drizzly morning one minute, then distant and cold the next. For a short time, Constance had felt a kinship with Southwyn as they sat in the domestic environment of his breakfast table.

The warm welcome had been more than she expected when the impulse to call struck. She'd used the excuse of checking on the kitten, but the reality was that she wanted to see what would happen if they were alone again. Would he be Lord Stuffy Pants, or would she catch another glimpse of the man who'd sprawled on the floor half-dressed and spoken so openly with her?

During the time it took to drink a cup of tea, he'd been the man from his study. If she could, Connie would have spent the whole day at his table, befriending that side of him.

Lord Southwyn had been kind, and even—dare she think it—admiring. Then, quick as a slamming door, he'd changed and shut her out. No instigating action on her part, and God knows she'd examined the conversation in her head from every angle since climbing into his carriage.

It reminded her of that moment in Caro's hallway, when she assumed he wanted to kiss her. Then, as today, he'd coolly dismissed her instead.

Rejection stung, no matter how overt or subtle. Once again, without warning or communication, he'd judged her and found her wanting.

To make matters more confusing, after reverting to the haughty version of himself, Lord Southwyn prioritized her well-being in the carriage. There were warming bricks for her feet, but none for his. A lap blanket for her, while he made do with his oilskin cloak, which gleamed with moisture from the short walk between his door and the carriage.

Rain beaded along the brim of his hat. Constance watched the tiny pool of water overflow the edge of black felt, then drip onto the dark blue velvet seat. He didn't seem to notice.

Once he ensured her comfort, Southwyn turned toward the window and didn't glance at her again.

His profile belonged on a coin, she thought. Carved permanently into a mold, then cast in metal for everyone to admire. Had she such a coin, the face would be smooth from her fingers tracing the lines of his jaw and chin.

Lord Southwyn wasn't a large man, or particularly burly. Compared to her, he was a bit of a giant, but standing next to Dorian, he appeared entirely average. The word made her bite her lip the moment it crossed her mind. No, not average. Bulk didn't matter when his body was so lean and strong, and moved so capably and confidently through a room. Heaven knew how the memory of him in his shirtsleeves always caused a flutter in her core.

Southwyn had the kind of face that would age well, she thought, looking her fill while he ignored her. It was easy to imagine silver hair at his temples and deeper lines around his eyes and mouth. For his sake, Constance hoped those lines came from laughter. Years of laughing might leave a map on his features, and it would be a delightful thing to witness firsthand.

Not that she would be nearby for any of that. Unless, of course, she failed to help Althea, and he married her dear friend. Imagining years in which she tried to maintain a friendship with his wife sent a shudder through her body.

Southwyn's boot nudged the warm brick closer to her toes. She'd have sworn until then that he'd forgotten she was in the carriage.

Warmth seeped through her leather walking boots, as she wiggled her toes. Another kind of warmth, bittersweet from her musings, curled through her chest.

Perhaps she should rethink her cousin's offer to find someone with similar qualities as Southwyn. Staring out the window, Connie pretended interest in the gray rain-smeared scenery and compiled a list of qualities she'd want in such a man.

Someone who cared for the little details of her comfort. A partner who saw to the specifics of daily life would be ideal, she decided. Especially since she often forgot to do some of those simple things for herself. Not that she meant to neglect herself or her surroundings, but when her attention focused elsewhere, everything else slipped her mind entirely. Having a husband who made sure she was warm on a rainy day or checked to be sure she'd remembered to eat before leaving the house would be wonderful.

Loving animals was nonnegotiable. Any person she chose had to like cats especially, and other animals in general. The memory of Prince perched on a chair with his own dish of breakfast kippers made her smile. Even though Southwyn's smile had shuttered and he'd turned cold, he'd still brushed a gentle caress on the kitten's head before leaving the room. Yes, a kind man.

A man who was, at his core, a decent person, who would try to do the right thing. Which caused a question she'd harbored for a while to spill from her lips without thinking.

"Why are you so hell-bent on marrying Althea?"

Either her voice or her words made him jolt and blink,

like she'd woken him from a daydream. His hazel eyes narrowed on her. "I beg your pardon?"

Blast. She should think before speaking. Constance bit her bottom lip. Withdrawing the question now would be gutless. "I know it's presumptuous to ask. But Althea is a friend and we speak openly about the situation, so I know you two aren't a love match. She's been vocal about her reluctance to marry you. Forgive my impertinence, but you don't seem like the kind of man who would force a woman into marriage. So…why?"

Lord Southwyn took his time answering, appearing to consider his words before finally speaking. "One of the reasons I'm visiting in person is to discuss several things with Althea. If she wishes to tell you of our conversation, that is between the two of you. But suffice to say, marrying me is her best chance at a comfortable future. We may not be a love match, but I care for her. I've known her nearly all my life. I hope, once she understands the situation, she might feel favorably toward the match."

Interesting. There may be more afoot than she or Althea realized. Or at least, Southwyn believed that was the case. Constance wondered how her friend would view the engagement after today.

Something dull and tender, like a bruise, settled under her breastbone at the thought of Althea and Lord Southwyn standing in a church, happily making vows to each other. Jealousy tasted bitter in her mouth, but she forced sweet words anyway. "You both deserve happiness. If it is with one another, I wish you well. With time, I hope love will grow between you."

All at once, the warmth from the brick at her feet and the weight of the blanket were too much. Connie tucked her feet to the side and busied her hands by folding the heavy quilt into a lumpy squarish shape. If she focused intently on the task, there'd be no way to fall into the trap of searching Southwyn's face for clues to his thoughts and emotions.

And he couldn't do the same to her, should he be so inclined. If he somehow read her mind and sensed her feelings, she would die. Just die of mortification.

Thankfully, the coach slowed, then stopped. When she looked up, the familiar facade of the Thompson townhouse gleamed white and gray in the damp morning.

A footman opened the door, and she offered a quiet thanks when he helped her to the pavement.

Inside the foyer, the butler hurried toward them. "I beg your pardon, milord, miss. Sir William and Miss Thompson are indisposed. This might not be the best time to call."

As if on cue, the deep roar of Sir William's voice bellowed into the hall when a door opened. "Another word from you and you'll regret it, foolish girl! Now, get out of my sight."

Althea appeared, with a red face and stony expression, slamming the heavy wood door behind her.

Lord Southwyn hurried toward Althea, but Constance stood rooted to the spot. Would her friend want witnesses to this? Wouldn't their presence embarrass her? And what on earth—Southwyn asked the question before she could.

"What's happened?" He grasped Althea's shoulders with so much concern on his face that Constance felt even more like an outsider.

"I told my father in no uncertain terms that I don't want to go through with the engagement."

To his credit, the man she was supposed to meet at the altar merely nodded. "I see. That's what the yelling was about, then. Did he explain about the circumstances with your dowry? Why it's best we move forward? I wish there was a better way to see you settled. I truly do."

Althea shook off his hands. "Oh, he explained everything. No dowry, no choice in the matter. I'm to obey, as always. He doesn't want a daughter; he wants a trained hound." Her eyes met Constance's. "I'm sorry you had to see this, Connie. Might we reschedule our visit for another day? I am not great company at the moment. Besides, I've been sent to my room like a child."

Constance rushed forward and wrapped her in a hug. Under her hands, Althea's frame quaked with emotion, even as she woodenly returned the embrace.

"I am here for whatever you need, darling. Be proud of yourself for your bravery. It sounds like your father was awful."

"I'll visit the shop or get word to you soon. I'm not done with this yet," Althea whispered, then drew away and turned toward the staircase.

"I'll do my best to make you happy, Althea. Please know that. Whatever life we make has to be better than what you just went through, right?" Lord Southwyn stared up at where Althea stood.

"That you're willing to go along with my father's wishes makes you complicit in his bullying. Only, you're quieter about it, and don't call me names." The hurt and anger in Althea's voice made Constance's eyes burn.

Lord Southwyn dropped his chin to his chest. From Constance's vantage point, he seemed to study his hands as his jaw flexed. The confidence she associated with him was nowhere in sight. He offered no arguments or defenses.

Without another word, Althea continued upstairs. Constance glanced around the foyer. The servants had made themselves scarce. Probably for the best that she hadn't had a chance to remove her cloak or bonnet. Now she could slip away without a fuss.

Lord Southwyn, however, still stood with his head bowed. The usually straight line of his shoulders slumped under the weight of his emotions, whatever they were. She wished, fruitless as it might be, that she knew him well enough to guess at his thoughts.

Except, they weren't on the same side of this scuffle, were they? Althea said she'd continue in her efforts, and Constance would help her. Because that's what she'd agreed to do, and that's what a friend would do. Althea needed a friend right now.

Seeing him struggling made her want to reach out and be a friend to him as well. Instead, Constance cleared her throat. "I will leave you to collect the marriage contract, milord. Thank you for the ride. I'll make my own way home."

Chapter Fifteen

~

Find a way to reach Franklin
(did Althea ever tell me his last name?)
Find out who Franklin is
Invoices. Just do them
Answer customer mail
Send another note to Althea asking how she is
(Maybe sixth time's the charm)

"There are customers asking for you," Hattie said from the office doorway.

Constance held up a finger, silently telling her cousin she'd be there in a minute, then gulped tea to wash down the last bite of meat pasty she'd eaten while she worked. Glancing at the clock, she winced. How had it only been an hour since she started the invoices? More time should have passed. Several hours, if not days. Wearily eyeing the stack of papers still awaiting her attention, she silently vowed to return and finish the task, then stood.

After a single hour at the desk, her brain felt like it might melt from her ears, and her eyes burned. How was she going to do this every day for the rest of her life? The books themselves, the customers, designing eye-catching displays? Dealing with them was second nature by this point. But this cramped office, with its endless demands of filing, record-keeping, and writing down every last detail…she had to find a way to thrive here if she was to keep Martin House.

With a heavy heart, she stepped onto the sales floor.

It had been over a week since she'd seen or heard from Althea, so finding her perusing the shelves with Lord South-wyn came as a surprise. The last time she'd been in their presence, Althea had essentially called her fiancé a bully, and he'd silently accepted the accusation. Now they appeared perfectly content in one another's presence. What had she missed?

Several other customers milled about the store. Hattie was busy wrapping a parcel with paper and twine as she spoke with one of their older patrons.

Constance recalled the date, then nodded. Yes, Mrs. McArthur usually visited the shop during the first week of the month. Which meant the parcel contained one new purchase—usually a torrid novel, like those Caro wrote as Blanche Clementine—and three books from their lending library. Smiling a silent greeting at the woman, Constance turned her attention back to the newcomers and dipped a curtsy.

"Lord Southwyn, Althea. This is a pleasure."

"Miss Martin," came the deep greeting. Although she tried to ignore the way his voice affected her, she understood now how Gingersnap must feel each time he arched into her hand when she scratched that one spot on his back. Constance gritted her teeth at how much she liked the sound.

Althea laid one dainty hand on Southwyn's arm and smiled prettily up at him as they exchanged a few quiet words. The way she leaned close made it seem like an intimate moment, and Constance caught herself retreating toward the safety of the office. Irritation at the instinct forced her to still, and she silently berated herself for the surge of jealousy she felt at seeing them together like this.

The self-chastisements would have to wait, however. Because when Lord Southwyn gave her a nod, then wandered deeper into the shop, Althea faced Connie with a vastly different attitude. Like a mask had dropped, her face changed from demure and sweet to intense and a little angry.

"I don't have much time," Althea hissed.

"Is everything all right?" Constance followed her to the side of the store furthest from Southwyn.

"Not at all. Connie, for all intents and purposes, I'm a captive in my own home. Father has done everything short of posting a guard outside my bedroom door. No messages allowed in or out of the house. The only time I leave my room during the day is when Oliver calls to take me somewhere. Mother told everyone I have a knee injury and can't dance at events. One of my parents sits beside me all evening when we're out in society."

This sounded like one of Caro's stories. Minus the entertaining bedroom escapades, unfortunately. "Your father has become the villain we feared. Are you unharmed?"

"He hasn't laid a hand on me, if that's what concerns you. Father prefers to force his will on others—which doesn't leave a mark to incite gossip."

"You say Lord Southwyn escorts you about. So, he knows all this and has done nothing?" Constance shot a look at the man currently examining the lending library section by the front windows. Even with the backdrop of a world drenched in dirty mop water, he stood out to her as something rather brilliant and beautiful. The line of his back seemed tense in this public place. Not the relaxed posture he'd had at the breakfast table when she saw him last.

If he was as culpable as Althea thought, then the man

truly was a wolf in disguise. A small kernel of doubt stopped Connie from loathing the sight he made. His straight posture made her fingers itch to unwind him. To see Southwyn soften and smile for her in his shirtsleeves. Because that version of the earl struck her as honest, somehow. And Honest Southwyn might shed light on the situation. Hadn't he said there were extenuating circumstances to discuss with Althea? The paltry words they'd exchanged within Connie's hearing hadn't been enough to clarify much of anything.

It was hard to comprehend how the suitor Althea described could be one and the same with a man who fed a kitten fresh kippers out of a porcelain dish and ensured Constance's feet had a warm brick during a short carriage ride on a rainy day.

"You heard Oliver just as clearly as I did. He specifically questioned if I knew Father planned to withhold my dowry should I try to marry anyone other than his precious earl. Pretty promises about making me happy count for nothing when he's cooperating with my parents."

Horror held Constance's mouth agape. She'd been so sure he was different. "That's what he was talking about when he asked about your dowry?" She stared back at Southwyn, trying to merge what she knew of him into one image.

"Father is determined to get his way, even at the cost of making me unattractive to other suitors and knowing he ruins any chance I might have at happiness. I told my parents there was someone else I prefer, and this quasi-imprisonment is their response."

Constance swiveled her gaze back to Althea. "You told them about Franklin? I recently realized I don't know any details beyond his first name. Without more, I'm not sure how I can help."

Althea clutched Constance's hands in hers. "I promise I'll

explain everything when we have more time. As to how you can help, I have an idea. During the last dance we shared, before my fabricated injury, Franklin admitted he loves me too. However, I can't write to him, and he can't get near me at events with my parents standing guard."

Constance nodded. "Yes, of course. Do you need me to deliver a letter? Perhaps use the shop's mail system and communicate with him that way?"

"I can't risk putting this debacle in writing and it falling into the wrong hands. Franklin says he loves me, but who knows how he will feel when he learns that I have no dowry and a family threatening to disown me if we wed. We will need to take drastic measures if we're to be together—if he still wants me once he knows of my true circumstances."

Constance grimaced. Promises and romantic declarations, no matter how heartfelt, were fragile things. Having been on the breaking side of those promises, she knew that more than anyone. "What can I do?"

Althea drew in a deep breath, and that was when Constance realized that whatever her friend was about to ask of her, it would be well beyond anything she'd mentally prepared for.

What the devil was Constance Martin doing here? Oliver craned his neck to peer around the dancers lining up as the music began. The damned woman was so short, it was nearly impossible to spy her head amidst everyone's shoulders. Thankfully, even though she'd made a valiant effort to contain her curls in a fashionable coiffure, the sheer mass of her hair added several inches to her height. Rather than looking for her blue eyes, or that distracting dimple, he searched for a puff of blond curls.

Who knew how long it had been since she'd arrived at Lady Bellingham's event, or how long she intended to stay, but her presence at all was highly suspect.

Over the next few excruciatingly long minutes, he tracked her progress around the perimeter of the ballroom by following the male heads turning in one direction. When she stopped on the other side of the dance floor, and he took in the full impact her, he understood why.

Fuck, she was beautiful. She'd been lovely in her simple day gowns and cotton aprons in the bookshop. And he'd seen her in a rather nice gown during that dinner party at Dorian and Caroline's. Neither of those ensembles did her justice.

Coral-pink satin traced her curves and made her skin glow in the light of hundreds of candles overhead. Bountiful breasts pushed against the low neckline of her gown, framed and seemingly barely contained by delicate lace trim designed to draw the eye. As if her natural form wasn't eye-catching enough.

With those wild blond curls pinned high on her head, her unadorned earlobes and neck seemed exceptionally naked, leaving observers little recourse but to imagine this delicious creature *actually* naked. The whole effect made Oliver both ready to pant after her and growl like a dog with a bone at anyone who dared look her way.

And they were looking. Not just because she was stunning, but also because Miss Martin was a new face in a room of people well-known to one another.

She didn't belong here. Not because she didn't fit the part—she did. But because anyone raised in society would know that an unknown beauty walking into a ballroom would be the furthest thing imaginable from being incognito.

Teacup-size tempest that she was, Oliver doubted she'd thought through the unlikelihood of successfully sneaking into an event like this. And she'd definitely sneaked in, because Dorian and Caro weren't in attendance, which was the only potential—albeit, highly unlikely—avenue to getting her hands on an invitation.

Althea once again sat with the dowagers along the wall, due to a weak knee that plagued her lately. Odd that it only flared during the evening, but her mother claimed that resulted from doing too much during the day.

Sir William and Lady Thompson had been more present than usual over the last week. Oliver suspected things were tense in their home, but no one seemed inclined to talk to him about it, even when asked directly. Althea put on a brave face, but he could tell she was still upset over the argument with her father. It appeared she'd resigned herself to the situation, though. With Lady Thompson determined to see them wed at the next available date at St. George's, it was about time they both made peace with the reality in which they found themselves.

Like it or not, she didn't have a dowry to speak of. Only debt-ridden properties of little value and no importance. If she wanted to get out from under her parents' thumbs, becoming his wife was the best option. And Oliver had to do the honorable thing. He couldn't abandon her to live out the consequences of her father's recklessness.

Their open acknowledgment that theirs wasn't a love match but a matter of business and compassion for her circumstances was the only thing salvaging his conscience. Each day passed and the only woman to visit his dreams and the one on his mind when he took himself in hand each morning—twice yesterday—was Constance Martin.

Right this moment, however, the physical pull toward

Althea's friend wrestled with the worry over what would happen when someone realized she didn't belong.

Oliver glanced back toward where Althea sat. Although far from genuine, she kept a smile on her face while listening to the woman beside her. If she knew Miss Martin was in attendance, she'd seek her out, even if only with her eyes. Like he was.

Searching the crowd for Miss Martin and her astounding cleavage, Oliver gritted his teeth when he spied a flash of her coral gown slipping through a door at the edge of the ballroom.

Whatever her reasons for being here, there was a 100 percent chance they'd lead to disaster. Not only for her, but her connection to society, the Duke and Duchess of Holland. Even if Oliver wasn't battling an inconvenient attraction to the woman, he'd intervene to protect his closest friend.

Besides, if some half-drunken randy buck with too much money and too little common sense realized a shopgirl had infiltrated the event, Constance would be in genuine danger, from more than whispers and glares. The idea made his heart race and a cold sweat bloomed on his brow. Having a father like his meant Oliver knew all too well how some men of so-called quality thought of women in general, but especially commoners. They were disposable. During his childhood, their estate cycled through housemaids as quickly as coal and firewood, even before his mother died. After she passed away, things went from bad to worse.

Concern and curiosity compelled his feet across the room to the door through which she'd disappeared.

In the room beyond, there was a distinct lack of the decor their hostess had strewn about the ballroom, and not a servant in sight. The lights were low in an attempt to discourage guests from venturing beyond the event itself.

A faint click echoed from the far wall. Oliver swiveled his head to follow the sound. That had to be another door latch closing behind her. Sure enough, a cleverly camouflaged opening in the wall led to a steep stairwell, then down a short hall. The faint *shushing* of silk drew him around a corner, to a dead end with a single closed door.

This wasn't a rambling promenade. Someone had provided Miss Martin a map of the servant's domain—specifically an area away from the main bustle of the kitchen, where the staff were no doubt rushing to handle a gathering of this size. What purpose did she have for being this deep in the house?

A tremor rocked his hand when he reached for the door-knob. Oliver clenched his fingers in a fist, breathing until the trembling passed. Worry and curiosity, titillation and fear, need and anger—all writhed so violently within him; it was no wonder he shook with it. If he could, he'd climb out of his skin to escape this discombobulation.

Emotion lurked too close to the surface for comfort. Through sheer force of will, Oliver donned reasoning and rationality, like a well-worn coat.

There had to be a purpose for her presence. Dashing toward a hidden corridor and whatever this room contained had been deliberate. Should he leave her in peace?

Had she fled to the gardens, Constance would be vulnerable to the kind of men he'd worried about as he'd watched her go. But here in this barely lit hall, with the event nothing but a distant thrum of muted music and chatter, there were fewer dangers.

There were also fewer reasons to justify her presence. No doubt it all came back to some plot she'd embroiled herself in, beyond what he could imagine. Probably involving an underground spy network of footmen and boot boys. Or— oily unease churned in his gut. A tryst, perhaps.

The logic of William Ockham dictated that the simplest theory was often the correct one. A tryst.

As if to confirm the centuries-old principle, the deep tones of a man's voice drifted through the closed door. Even though it confirmed his suspicion, when Oliver reached for the knob, it wasn't logic compelling him.

Drury Lane would be hard-pressed to set a scene better than the one he found inside. A small lantern sat on a short wooden table, casting meager light on what appeared to be a storeroom. Shelves lined the walls, stocked with metal canisters and glass jars. A copper contraption in the corner that might have been a still. How much cordial did one have to drink to warrant having a still in one's home?

None of that mattered, because as quickly as Oliver took in these details, he noted one thing more important than anything else—Constance's face. Even more damning was the man whose hand hovered near the creamy flesh of her neckline.

The distressed emotions twisting her lovely features told Oliver everything he needed to know. Whatever their reasons for meeting, or the circumstances that brought these two people to this time and place, Constance was not happy to have this man touching her.

Dimly, in a corner of his mind that stood separate from the animalistic rage threatening to overtake him, Oliver recognized the man as the younger son who'd danced with Althea while wearing a besotted expression.

Did Constance know he was wooing her friend as well as her?

It didn't matter. Because whatever had transpired in the moments before Oliver entered the room had clearly made her uncomfortable.

That same reserved area of his mind examined her face.

Blue eyes wide, eyebrows pinched together, mouth open in a silent cry.

In the mental file of memories of her he'd kept, and not realized existed until that instant, she was a lively whirlwind. Chattering, laughing, scolding, teasing, silently contemplating the world, or fidgeting as she tried to hold her tongue. But seeing Constance in pain was alien and...

Absolutely. Unacceptable.

"Unhand her this instant, or so help me God, I'll throw you from the nearest window." Oliver didn't recognize the growl in his voice, but the threat made the couple before him freeze.

"Lord S-Southwyn," the man stuttered. Despite his obvious shock, he didn't move his hand.

Red crept in around the edges of Oliver's vision, and those baser urges flared to life. The sound he made was nearly a roar as he clutched the young man's lapels and flung him away from Constance. She shrieked, then clapped a hand over her mouth.

"I didn't—I don't—" Damnit, what was his name? Sir Wellsley's fourth or fifth son. Anthony? No, Franklin. Maybe it was Franklin. Whatever his name, he seemed prepared to plead for his life, but the words came out choked and disjointed. If Oliver had to guess, it was partly due to panic, and partly from the bruising grip he had on the whelp's neck and shoulder as he dragged him to the door.

They charged out into the hall, which was thankfully free of servants, because Oliver shoved the other man's body against the wall with an echoing thud. "You don't touch her again unless she sends you an engraved invitation. Otherwise, I will end you. Do I make myself clear?"

Wellsley's jerky head movement was as close to a nod as he could manage, since Oliver had pinned him to the wall like a butterfly on a board. The young man fell to the floor in a graceless heap when he let him go.

Oliver returned to the storeroom and Constance, then slammed the door on the sight of Franklin Wellsley. Breath bellowed from him as he examined her. Thoughts of calm fled at the sight of her tears.

"He hurt you."

"My—my gown!"

Oliver's hands shook with the effort it took to slow his movements, lest she feel threatened by his presence. He gently cupped her chin, assessing her features. "Never mind the bloody gown. Where are you hurt?" No scratches or red marks marred her face, although her wet cheeks made him positively feral. Oliver wrenched his attention from the damp trails on her skin to examine her neck, then her shoulders, before running a palm down each arm.

"It's not even mine!" she wailed. "I borrowed it from Althea. Hattie and I took up the hem to make it fit, and now it's ruined."

Confusion hit like ice water on his fiery emotions, making his words rough. "Some scrap of fabric isn't as important as you are."

Constance sniffled, swiping at her cheeks. "But it's the loveliest thing I've ever worn. Or it was, until his cuff link caught on the lace. You scared poor Mr. Wellsley witless when you barged in like some invading horde."

Cuff link? What were his hands doing near her bodice in the first place—which was none of his business, damn it all. Every emotion that had careened through him during the last several minutes—and there were too many to contemplate at the moment—coalesced into something foreign he couldn't name. "I was defending your honor! Would you rather I ignored some man pawing at you?"

She huffed and rolled her eyes, and Oliver couldn't believe the audacity of it. Another step brought their chests together, although he was hardly aware of moving.

"Don't be ridiculous. The only thing in danger was my gown."

"You were in a closed room with a man, at an event you haven't been invited to, and you think you weren't in danger?" The bare flesh of her arms was warm under his hand, then shifted when she gestured toward the lace. However, when he tried to examine the tattered, dangling scrap hanging by a single remaining thread, all he saw were the breasts that had haunted his dreams for weeks. More concerning than the lace was a section of her bodice seam threatening to separate entirely.

"There was no danger, you irritating man!"

"You can't know that," he bellowed.

Ignoring the loud reply, she waved off his concern and focused her attention on her neckline. "Of course I can. I know men." She fingered the scrap of lace. "I might be able to fix this. Replace it with another trim, perhaps."

How had he lived for so many years and never felt this much before? Oliver battled to regain some semblance of his usual calm, but it was damn near impossible in the face of . . . her. If he rephrased, would she listen? "Miss Martin, it's reckless to meet a man alone. Especially at an event you've sneaked into, where you don't have people to help you when you inevitably find trouble."

God help him, her breasts jiggled when she laughed. "Mr. Wellsley doesn't want me."

"Don't be deliberately obtuse. Every man in that room wanted you."

"Not every man," she muttered distractedly, plucking the lace free of its last thread.

A growl wrapped his words. "*Every* man, Constance."

Blue eyes finally lifted to meet his, and held. A distant part of him noted the way they flared wide, then fluttered closed as his mouth covered hers. At the contact, realizing what he'd done, Oliver froze. Was she holding her breath as well? He pulled back, taking in her flushed cheeks, and keenly aware of his drumming pulse, he confessed, "Every single one of them."

Slender hands lifted to frame his face. A second passed between them, in which her gaze searched his before she pulled him down to her mouth again. Just like every one of his dreams, Oliver sank his fingers into those gold curls and gave himself over to the absolute relief of finally kissing her.

There was no time to worry about technique. Not when she met his lips with such enthusiasm, eagerly learning his mouth, as he did hers. Each of his senses hummed with ragged breaths and moans, the pull of clutching fingers, and the heady scent of warm honeysuckle skin.

Her hair seemed to have a mind of its own, wrapping around his fingers as if to tie them together. She fit against him perfectly. Plump breasts to hard chest. When she rose on her tiptoes, the heat of her core met his hardness, and they both whimpered.

Touching her felt as important as breathing. Memorizing the taste of her mouth and eliciting delicious sounds from her became vital. The need to map her shape pounded at him relentlessly, and Oliver caved to the urge. Gently freeing one hand from her hair took a moment, especially when he refused to leave the heaven of her mouth to see what he was doing.

Oliver groaned when his hand finally traveled down her body to the line of her ribs, the dip of a waist, and then the generous curve of her bum. She rose on her toes again, creating another bout of friction between their hips, then gave a cry of relief when he cupped her bottom and lifted her against him to capture more of the alignment both of them sought.

"More." Her demand made Oliver want to beat his chest in satisfaction. Instead, he tasted the bare skin of her neck that had so tormented him from across the ballroom. That voice, exactly as it had been in his dreams, threatened to undo him entirely.

Every breath, every pump of blood through his veins, urged him to comply with whatever she asked for. "Anything," he agreed, far beyond control or reason.

Clothing shifted, exposing the curve of her shoulder. An instinct shook him with the need to sink his teeth into the incredible softness of her and leave evidence of this encounter. To ensure she'd remember his mouth when she looked in the mirror.

Constance tugged her silk bodice until the top of one nipple came into view. The sound she made was one of encouragement, while his was pure desperation.

"Holy fuck," he whispered reverently. Everything within him that was feral and dangerous, rather than coolly logical, ached to bite and suck. One remaining shred of awareness clung to a certainty that should he give in and fully uncover that breast, there'd be no turning back. No stopping. Years of depriving himself of female companionship would be moot, in the face of this particular pair of breasts. *Her* breasts.

At the moment, Oliver couldn't remember why that would be the wrong choice. In fact, the erection pulsing against the fall of his trousers urged him to listen to the needy sounds Constance made and give them both what they wanted. The way her hips pushed against his, grinding through their clothing told him she was as mindless with arousal as he was.

He'd give anything to sink into her heat and lose himself entirely, reality and consequences be damned.

"God, I want you," he said between kisses. How refreshing to admit that truth out loud.

"Need you." Her answer came on breathy gasp as the tempo of her hips increased against his. "Please."

If she wanted him enough to beg, he could not say no. Not when he needed her as urgently as his next breath. Together, they fell against the wall of shelves and he set her bottom on the edge of one sturdy wood plank, intent on reaching for the hem of her gown.

Glass jars rattled at the impact. The sharp sound cut through the haze of desire, creating a tiny opening through which reality returned. Oliver's hips pinned hers to the shelves. Scant few layers of cloth separated his aching cock from the heat pouring from the juncture of her thighs. Blown pupils nearly swallowed that particular shade of Constance blue, and a flush stained her cheeks and chest.

As often as he'd caught himself staring at her lips before, he'd thought he knew their curves. But the sight of them as they were at this moment, plump and reddened from his kiss, would haunt him forever. Blond curls hung in a tangle, escaping her coiffure.

At some point in their wild fumble of limbs, the part of her gown with the damaged seam had given way and now it gaped to show a love bite on the curve of her shoulder, and the dusky rose of an areola peeking above the neckline. She looked rumpled, and *his*.

Except, she wasn't. Neither of them had any business being in this room together, much less kissing with such fervent madness.

Reality was a cruel slap, bullying aside whatever part of him had demanded he ravish this woman five seconds ago.

Miss Constance Martin of Martin House Books might have sneaked into a ton event, but there was no way she could leave the same way she'd entered. Not appearing freshly tumbled and thoroughly debauched—which was his fault.

"Well, fuck," he sighed.

Chapter Sixteen

~~Change the goal entirely~~

J'm glad I searched our emergency location. I believe this is yours." Althea handed Constance her red cloak, which she took gratefully. The army had missed a phenomenal logistical mind in Althea. She'd made backup plans upon contingencies when they laid out their goals for last night's ball. "How did you get home without freezing to death?" Althea asked the question around a mouthful of rye bread. The Thompsons' cook offered them the loaf with fresh butter and thinly sliced ham when Constance arrived as scheduled in Althea's kitchen the day after meeting with Franklin Wellsley.

Cook plunked a pair of ciders next to them, then returned to the wall of ovens. Constance smiled her thanks before gulping a mouthful. Retelling the events of the night before would be difficult. Withholding the details of her interaction with Oliver was never under consideration. Some said confession was good for the soul. After a lifetime of making impulsive decisions and living to regret them, Constance was all too familiar with accepting the inevitable consequences of her choices.

Even when that meant telling Althea about the scorching kiss she'd shared with her friend's fiancé. Recalling the sounds he'd made, the desperate way he'd promised anything she wanted, and the way she'd begged for more sent shame and desire battling in her mind. If the heat from her cheeks was any indication, her face must be alarmingly crimson.

"That map you sketched saved the day. Thank goodness you know the house so well. Choosing the storeroom to meet Mr. Wellsley was a stroke of genius."

"Over the years, I've had to entertain myself in Lady Bellingham's home for hours at a time, while she and my mother visited in her drawing room. I wasn't permitted to join them—probably because they drink a concerning amount of cordial while gossiping about their friends."

"In this instance, your penchant for snooping worked in our favor."

"What I want to know is how you sneaked out of the house, unnoticed, with your gown and hair in such a state. At least your hair should have been in more disarray than usual if Oliver kissed you properly." Althea offered a wicked smile, and Constance thanked the stars for the ten thousandth time during this conversation that her friend didn't feel territorial about her fiancé.

"He insisted I wear his coat to cover my gown. As to the hair, Southwyn helped pin it into some semblance of order. Enough to not draw attention, anyway. Although wearing his coat would certainly warrant a second look." While the memory of how he'd lost control at the first touch of lips had kept her awake long into the night, it was the moments afterward that made her heart twist.

Without prompting, Lord Southwyn had expertly coiled her curls back into place, securing the mass with pins they'd found scattered on the floor. "My mother had curls like this," he'd explained in that deep, quiet voice. "Her hair was dark, so it didn't create the nimbus effect yours does. But I spent many afternoons helping shape her curls into individual spirals like these."

"The rainwater makes the curls particularly soft," she'd said, and he grunted an agreement.

After such fervent kisses, the gentle way he'd taken care of her had been a surprise. Especially when she checked in her mirror at home and spied the purplish marks on her neck and shoulder. That he could be nearly violently passionate one minute, then patiently taming her hair the next was another facet of a man who became a greater enigma the longer she knew him. A man she had no business kissing or wanting.

"I suppose you used the servant's entrance to the garden, then hailed a hack near the mews." Althea drained cider in her mug. "That's what I'd have done."

Nodding an affirmative, Constance took another drink to wet her parched mouth. Her lips were tender against the rim of the glass, and she nearly whimpered. Hours later, her body still bore signs of his conquering in the most delicious, welcome way. God, he'd been nearly feral, and she craved more. Beyond her lust, there remained one important piece of information to share.

"I discovered something else. He didn't know about your parents' restrictions. That he hadn't noticed doesn't speak well of him. But he did not realize your father is keeping such a close eye on you for nefarious purposes." She'd completely forgotten about his role in Althea's life the second he touched her, which was something Connie needed to mull over. What if he'd been the villain actually? How had she not thought of her friend after that first kiss?

Studying Constance with a speculative look, Althea finally nodded. "I believe that. After all, I keep saying he doesn't care enough to pay attention. He likely believes whatever Father told him. All that might not matter in the end, though, because Oliver likes you."

Constance shrugged. "We get along fine, I suppose." She bit into a slice of rye, slathered with thick butter. It was a truth universally acknowledged that swallowing emotions was easier when accompanied by baked goods.

"No, he *likes* you. He wants you. Do you know what this means, Connie?" Althea grinned as she leaned close.

The bread turned to a brick in Connie's throat. Wordlessly, Althea nudged Constance's mug toward her with a finger. A moment later, Constance's wheezed "What?" sounded feeble and a tad desperate.

"This can be our secondary plan, if Franklin takes his affection elsewhere." A shadow crossed her features.

It hadn't been easy to tell Althea's beau about the lack of a dowry. Connie had encouraged him to carefully consider the situation before leaving word of his decision at Martin House. Franklin claimed he didn't need time to answer, but before he'd given a concrete reply, disaster struck. One of his expansive gestures while ranting about Sir William's beastliness resulted in the lace debacle and Oliver barging in.

"As soon as I receive his answer, I'll come to your kitchen as we discussed. If you could have seen how concerned he is for you, you wouldn't feel the need for another plan. That man loves you, dowry or no dowry."

Althea sighed. "I hope love is enough. Just in case, let's focus on you. You enjoyed kissing Oliver last night, correct?"

Constance's face flamed again. And it had just begun to cool, she thought ruefully. "Lord Southwyn is an attractive man. I've always said so. And amusing when he's not striving to be proper."

Althea wrinkled her nose. "Oliver's quite accomplished at playing proper, isn't he? It makes me want to shake him.

Which makes his behavior with you all the more intriguing From what you said, it took one kiss to wake him from tha stodgy personality. Like a fairy tale, but in reverse. It wa the prince who woke up. Or rather, the earl. We can use this."

Constance sobered. "I know I've called him Lord Stuff Pants, but he's a good man, Althea. I won't lead him on o play with his heart. Not even for you."

Her friend squeezed her hand. "I would never ask that And should it come up, feel free to tell him I'm mad fo Mr. Wellsley. He's probably pieced together the truth, anyway. Even if Franklin retreats, I want Oliver to know my heart belongs to another. Maybe the knowledge will give him permission to search elsewhere.

"Because I see how we've been going about this all wrong We don't need to give Oliver a disgust of me. *We need to make him fall in love with you.*"

"You don't understand. I was barely more than an animal." Oliver wasn't sure how clear his words were, given the way he covered his face with his palms.

Dorian must have caught the general idea. "Hardly. I'm not sure many members of the animal kingdom experience lust."

Oliver's mother would have known the answer. That was something she would've found fascinating. Although thinking of his mother at a time like this struck him as odd. Oliver sighed and slumped in the chair he usually claimed in front of the fireplace. "Lust is not part of my usual repertoire."

"I know you've always preferred to keep your private matters, well, private. But surely Connie's not the first woman to get under your skin. Sometimes there's an unexplainable connection." A smile quirked Dorian's mouth as he stared at a set of bookshelves.

Oliver followed his gaze, then thought better of it. Right. The duke and duchess had probably passed an enthusiastically pleasurable time against that bookshelf. If he recalled correctly, the books at hip level on that shelf consisted of mostly poetry. Not his usual fare, so he needn't worry about borrowing a book on which his friend previously shagged his wife. As had been happening since he'd covered Constance in his coat, then shuffled her into his coach last night, images from their time together assailed him.

The memories had literally kept him warm as he'd walked home in the rain, staying in the shadows as his shirt turned transparent. It hadn't been a long walk. Or at least, that's the argument he used when Constance asked if he'd join her in the coach.

Truth was, he knew that way lay madness, and he couldn't fool himself otherwise. After experiencing exactly how quickly things could escalate, Oliver knew his good intentions would dissolve if he climbed into the privacy of a dark, enclosed carriage with her. Especially with her taste lingering on his tongue, while his coat covered her perfect, nearly exposed breasts.

In the time it would take the carriage to traverse Mayfair and jostle through traffic to the Martins' working-class neighborhood of stores, Oliver could have buried himself in her willing heat and found pleasure three times over.

After all, the first time would be fast. There was no avoiding that. Hell, he'd probably lose control the first time she touched his cock, and not make it inside her until he recovered.

Oliver rubbed the back of his neck and tried to think of literally anything else.

Silence filled the room. When he glanced up, Dorian watched him with a shocked expression.

"Oliver, this wasn't your first amorous encounter…"

Rather than answer, he angled his body away from the duke and felt the faint crinkle of paper against his side. The ace, of course. For some reason he'd started carrying it in his pocket, like a talisman, reminding him to stay the course. Or perhaps, reminding him that the only thing keeping him on this course was his determination to act with duty and honor.

Dorian sank into the other chair flanking the fireplace. "Are you a virgin?"

"I've always known who I'll marry. Even if I didn't love Dorcas, or Althea for that matter, I wasn't going to betray that agreement. Besides, you know about my father. I couldn't risk turning into him, Dorian. My conscience is all I have as protection against that fate, so I listen to it."

Dorian stared, apparently fascinated to meet a *Masculum virginalis* in the wild. "How did I not know this about you?"

"You were happily married, then overseas for years. Even after Juliet died, you weren't the kind to go carousing." Instead, they'd attended the theater, visited their estates, and spent long hours reading or talking about nothing. When Dorian spoke of women and needed Oliver to chime in, he'd simply omitted a few bits of information.

"I always assumed you enjoyed discreet liaisons and spared me the details."

Oliver shrugged. "No details to spare, my friend."

"Was that—Oliver, was that your first kiss?" A deep V dug a groove between Dorian's eyebrows, and Oliver had to wonder at the marked concern.

"Third, actually. I kissed a barmaid in the village. She was open to more. The earl was in the room, and made it clear he'd not only had her already but highly recommended the experience. Everyone was watching and laughing, so I ran. That prompted my conscious decision to abstain. How could I return to that pub with Dorcas after paying their barmaid to relieve me of my virginity? I decided, if my fiancée had to wait, there was no reason I shouldn't as well."

"Jesus, Oliver."

"The second kiss was Dorcas. An experiment of sorts, although I didn't realize it at the time. Roughly a month before she eloped, she kissed me. Whatever she was looking for, she didn't find. That, or the experience confirmed I couldn't measure up to the man she wanted."

Dorian shook his head. "Then this incident with Connie was entirely unprecedented. No wonder it's weighing so heavily. May I ask, which part is most worrisome? That you kissed a woman who is not your fiancée? That she's Althea's friend?"

When Oliver winced, Dorian studied him closer. "Or is what's really bothering you that you want to do it again?"

Heat suffused his body and he ran a finger under his collar, feeling a new sympathy for insects under a magnifying glass. He couldn't push aside the truth when stated so directly. "Althea and I are not a love match, so there's not as much guilt in that regard. Especially after Constance explained that she was delivering a message to that man from Althea."

"Interesting. What was the message?"

"She wouldn't say. Having seen the way that Wellsley chap watches her, I can hazard a few guesses."

"I see. Is it their friendship, then?"

"No. Although that makes me a bastard for saying so."

"Then you're kicking yourself for wanting more." A smile teased Dorian's mouth, and Oliver didn't have the energy to call out his friend on such blatant enjoyment of the situation.

"I lost control. Completely lost control. There was no logic or reasoning, or explainable escalation of events. It was just...boom. Like a lit fuse tossed into a barrel of gunpowder. Only far messier."

"Those are called emotions." Dorian was fully smiling now, and Oliver searched halfheartedly for something to throw at his head. "They can be bloody inconvenient and often terrifying, but they're quite literally what makes life worth living."

Rather than argue, Oliver waved away Dorian's sarcasm like a pesky bug. "There's no reasonable explanation for my reaction—and with Constance Martin, of all people. I have to believe it was a one-time occurrence. The...powder keg nature of one encounter isn't reason enough to change my entire future."

"Horseshit. One person can change everything, and you know it. You watched it happen to me—and laughed a few times, if I remember correctly. The issue is, you've never cared before. Didn't you sit in this very chair and tell me about the appalling situation Sir William created and expects you to rescue him from? Even though your future and the financial stability of multiple estates are at risk, your analytical brain remained in charge. Very little emotion. The fact that Connie inspires any reaction at all warrants an examination of your plans."

Speaking of analytical brains, Oliver needed his more than ever. "Help me find a way out of this. That's what I need right now."

"All right. Let's play out each scenario." They'd done this often over the course of their long friendship when one of them faced a difficult decision. "What happens if you cry off from the engagement?"

"Sir William throws a tantrum—which Constance says

is already happening. Althea's knee injury keeping her from dancing? Fabricated. Her parents are only allowing her out of their sight if she's with me. The girl's practically living in her bedchamber. If I don't get her out of there, they'll take away her dowry—if we can call it such a thing—and she's stuck under the thumb of a bully for the rest of her life." After years with the late earl, Oliver couldn't stomach the thought of subjecting her to such an existence. "Oh, and there's a distinct possibility that he'll go to debtor's prison, leaving Althea destitute."

"But you get the girl." Dorian's tone suggested he already knew Oliver wouldn't capitulate so easily.

"If I ruin her dear friend's future, Constance won't want me, and for good reason. Next."

"Sir William won't accept a loan or sell the river instead of marrying off his spawn? You could build your canals and wiggle out of this."

"I've offered. Repeatedly. Besides, if the weather doesn't change and allow us to grow something, I might not have ready cash to make good on an offer should he change his mind."

"You could dower her yourself, although I suppose you run into the same financial issue."

Oliver nodded. "It might take every penny I have to keep my staff and tenants alive if this disastrous growing season continues beyond the year. Have you examined the grocer's bills lately? Prices are already high because of tariffs, and rising because of anticipated shortages."

"Damned, bloody Corn Laws," the duke muttered.

"It's going to be awful, Dorian. No one knows how long this will last, or how widespread shortages will be."

Crops were looking dire as nature proved to be a fickle bitch this year.

"Even if the sun came out tomorrow and we miraculously salvaged our growing season, there's another problem with throwing money at the situation. Imagine Althea's chances at a decent match after the scandal of a broken engagement, Sir William's histrionics and possible stint in prison, then me offering to pay literally anyone else to marry her."

"What's the worst that can happen if you gave in and got Connie out of your system? Assuming, of course, everyone was honest about intentions, et cetera. Hypothetically, of course."

Memories of the heat from her core rubbing against his cock, and that nipple he'd never fully glimpsed, flashed through his mind. Oliver shifted in the chair in a futile effort to relieve the building pressure in his breeches. "In that hypothetical scenario—if I could live with myself and marry Althea after being intimate with Constance—I'd spend the rest of my life desperately wanting to fuck my wife's dearest friend."

Dorian winced. "No matter what, you're spending the rest of your life in that scenario."

Oliver shot him a withering look. "Yes. My choices are either marrying Althea and knowing I've shagged her friend, or marrying Althea and knowing I *want* to shag her friend. Only one of those scenarios leaves me with any honor."

"At some point, emotion has to pair with judgment, as does allowing people to make their own decisions and suffer the consequences. You know what I think? I think you've been able to keep your breeches buttoned all this time because you've never wanted anyone the way you want Connie. That's not living by logic. That's emotional constipation."

Oliver gaped. "Emotional constipation."

Dorian nodded. "Nathaniel didn't have a dirty nappy yesterday. When things finally worked their way loose, it was quite the mess. Obviously, it took Connie to work your emotions loose."

Oliver barked a laugh. "You're comparing my impulse to kiss a woman to a shitty nappy."

"Right, I am. Apologies. Perhaps Caro and I need to leave the house and let the nurse take care of Nathaniel for more than a couple hours at a time."

"I think that would be wise."

"Consider what I said, though. Ponder the spirit of the metaphor, rather than the excrement of it. You're finally feeling something for someone, and that is a good sign." At Oliver's doubtful noise, Dorian sighed. "Would it have been better to have this flood of emotions for Althea? If she returned your affections, then yes. You've had years to develop feelings for her, and she's never affected you like this, so the point is moot. The situation stinks." A devilish glint to his smile assured Oliver that the pun was deliberate.

"Could you please stop?"

"I don't think I can. The puns are rushing out of me. And it's rather satisfying, to tell the truth. Rather like Nathaniel's little grunts when he finally—"

"Caro!" Oliver bellowed toward the door. "Retrieve your husband before I throw him out the nearest window!"

"Thrown out of my own home?" Dorian asked through his laughter.

"We're English. We come from a long history of walking in and taking over, regardless of rightful ownership. Don't tempt me, friend."

Chapter Seventeen

Admit you're in trouble

"Hattie, I feel as if this entire thing slipped from my control, and I don't know how to regain it." Constance's voice broke the relative silence of their bedroom. The house had long-since grown still, her parents having gone to bed over an hour before.

Gingersnap's wheezing snores rose from the bed beside her, where he lay curled in an orange fluffy spiral in the crook of her arm.

Outside their window, London bustled with night noises. Carts on cobblestones, footsteps, and horse hooves making their distinctive clack against pavement. Occasionally a voice rang out in exclamation or laughter laced with drink.

But here in the dark, in the bed she shared with her cousin, they'd been quiet since she'd told Hattie about kissing Lord Southwyn.

Finally, Hattie spoke. "Matters of the heart are rarely within our control. I'm curious though. If you could go back and do it over, what would you do differently?"

The question made Constance furrow her brow. "You mean, what I would erase?"

"Yes. Which of your interactions with Southwyn would you choose to forget? All of them? Only a few?"

Flickers of memory played on the ceiling above her in the dark.

The first time she'd met him, back when Caro and Dorian were falling in love and they'd hunted a man who hurt Dorian's late wife.

How he'd looked standing beside Dorian when Caro walked down the aisle.

Seeing Southwyn in Caro's drawing room, placidly drinking tea and making polite small talk with Althea, appearing to the world like her perfect match.

Every moment of confused disgruntlement he'd tried to disguise when Constance began turning up wherever he was with Althea.

Then, the well-worn memory of that day in his study, when her heart had leapt into her throat with awareness of him.

At the breakfast table with Prince seated like the family member he'd become.

And finally, in that low-lit room at the ball. The way he'd been ready to go to war with Franklin on her behalf. A man who usually appeared so contained that he often seemed cold, had turned frantic with one kiss. Like a tamed beast reverting to its wild nature with the right provocation.

Except, she'd had no idea wildness waited beneath that starched demeanor. Despite the many men who'd courted her, the stolen kisses, and a few sexual interludes with her former fiancé, Constance had never experienced the multitude of emotions that pounded through her during Southwyn's kiss. In those stolen moments, she'd also become a wild thing, all primal instinct and want.

Realization dawned but brought no comfort. "I wouldn't

want to erase a bit of it. Even though it would be easier to forget he exists. Does that make me foolish?"

"Perhaps."

A laugh surprised her. "This would be an excellent time to lie to me, Hattie. Soften the blow, so to speak."

Amusement laced Hattie's voice. "You don't come to me for comforting lies, Connie. You know better."

"I suppose you're right. On all counts, blast it. Life would be simpler if I could just forget Lord Southwyn entirely."

"You can still walk away. Let Althea sort this out herself. It sounds like she's planning a way out with her beau. At the end of the day, it's their life, not yours. You can avoid them entirely, should you decide that's what you want. If they visit the store, I'll serve them. If your heart is at risk—and it sounds like it is—perhaps that's the best path."

Instant denials and counterarguments rose, but Constance bit them back. Hattie was always the voice of truth and reason. Dismissing her insight would be pure folly. "I'll think about it."

A moment later, Hattie said, "I assume the coat I found in your wardrobe belongs to him?"

Connie closed her eyes against the embarrassing thought of Hattie spying the way she'd been sniffing it. He just smelled so damn good. What else was a girl to do in her situation? "Yes. He wrapped me in it, then sent me home. Althea retrieved my cloak for me."

"She really is a sharp one," Hattie commented. "I have to ask. Are you in love with him, Connie?"

Swallowing became an effort, and the resulting gulping would have been comical if it hadn't come from her. As it was, Connie barely managed a quiet "I don't know."

What did she know about such things? After making it all the way to the church on her wedding day, she'd run.

While it was the right decision in the end, before that point, Connie had thought she loved Walter. When doubts rose, she'd pushed them aside, blithely confident in her choice of husband. Until she wasn't.

She realized now, that wasn't love.

Running away from a church where Southwyn awaited her inside was unimaginable.

Before Walter there'd been a long line of interested men whom she'd enjoyed, considered, then ultimately rejected. Just like there were bits and bobs around the house and store from hobbies she'd dived into headfirst, then lost interest in after a while. Yarn from knitting. Paints from the summer she'd taken up watercolors. Easily a dozen books on various topics she'd added to the lending library collection in the store once they no longer tickled her fancy. She'd made the quilt they were under that very minute—they'd used it for three years, even though the edges weren't finished. Mum finally took care of those final touches, since the abandoned project had long since ceased to exist in Constance's brain.

Caro's methodical drive enabled her to write and publish books often enough that her readers stayed enthralled. Hattie was steady, the logical rock of their little trio. She was content to keep her head down and live a quiet life. Constance flitted from one thing to another, like a honeybee gathering nectar. Except, at the end of the day, she had knitting needles and half-finished paintings to show for her efforts, rather than sweet honey.

Tomorrow she might awaken to a world where the Earl of Southwyn no longer had a hold on her affections. Perhaps she'd keep the memories but walk away from this aching desire coiled within her that focused entirely on him. It seemed impossible right now, but she'd thought herself in love before, hadn't she?

Except, a calm sort of certainty coalesced within her when considering the validity of her feelings. That emotional oasis whispered in a quietly confident voice that if given the chance, loving Southwyn would be different.

Oh, God. She might be falling in love with him. Honesty drove her to amend her answer to Hattie's question. "Maybe."

"Whatever I'm paying you lot, it isn't enough." Oliver stood with his hands on his hips, surveying the scullery. A veritable army of maids bustled about, their mobcaps wilting in the humidity of the room. The overall damp stemmed from the giant copper cauldron giving off steam as it boiled a mountain of fabric.

Maxine, the head washerwoman, crossed her arms. Years of exposure to hot water and lye soap had turned the skin up to her elbows red. "An offer of a raise, and the lord of the house wantin' to wash his own sheets. Is this a holiday, milord?" While the jest was genuine, it came with a healthy dose of concern that Oliver might have lost his damn mind.

"I appreciate your willingness to teach me this skill." He watched as a slender maid stirred the copper pot with a sturdy wood paddle as tall as she was.

Maxine's laugh cracked through the air, drawing attention from three other maids before they continued their business. "I'll teach you everything you need, never fear. Better to know how to do a thing, even if you never have to do it again, am I right?"

Rolling his shirtsleeves to the elbow, Oliver nodded. "The purpose of this exercise, summarized quite succinctly."

"It's ready, your lordship." The maid at the kettle lifted the bedding from the boiling water with the paddle, then slapped the sheet onto a nearby surface. Jesus, she really was stronger than she looked.

Maxine passed Oliver a boar-bristle brush, the likes of which he usually associated with grooming horses. "Let's get to work, milord."

Lye soap burned at his palms, as did the temperature of the linen. Oliver held his tongue except to ask questions, and followed Maxine's directions as he scrubbed all evidence of his embarrassing incident from the bedding.

Since losing control so thoroughly in that storeroom with Constance—it seemed disingenuous to think of her as Miss Martin in the privacy of his mind, given what he did to her in that private space—he'd thought it best to return to his previous morning regimen. It felt like Tuesday had been seventy years ago. Today, his body took matters into its own hands, so to speak, and he'd awoken with wet sheets.

He hadn't ejaculated in his sleep since he was a green lad. Without thinking it through, Oliver had sprung from bed, tearing at the bedding until it was a pile on his floor. Using the ewer of water and his shaving soap, he must have resembled Lady Macbeth, with her wails of "out, damned spot" as he'd tried to clean the semen from his sheets and forget the erotic dream that inspired it.

Which might have been enough, until he realized the scented oils from his shaving soap were leaving marks of their own on the fabric. Thus, a morning spent in the scullery with a laundress who now thought him an "odd duck."

He wasn't supposed to overhear that, but with his cheeks burning and every nerve on alert from embarrassment, the whispers in the room might as well have been shouts to his ears.

It was better than the alternative. He'd rather they believe him fancifully indulging in maid's work, like Queen Marie

Antoinette milking cows at Versailles, than they know he'd shot off like a firework in his sleep due to a certain dimpled blonde.

Besides, the laborious task could act as a deterrent to whatever part of his mind created such dreams. Reddened, chapped hands should convince his brain to never put him in this position again. A man could hope.

One inescapable truth lingered as he scrubbed, rinsed, boiled, then pressed the sheets through the rollers of the mangle—things couldn't go on like this. Keeping his hands off his cock clearly wasn't enough to dull the ache of need pounding at him, as his body apparently had its own agenda.

He'd told Dorian that only one version of the future allowed him to act with honor. With each passing day, it grew clearer that there wasn't any honor in marrying Althea when he desperately desired Constance. Even if he kept promises and fulfilled obligations, fantasizing about his wife's friend would make him a shit-stain of a human.

Thanks to Maxine's thorough instruction and chatty nature, Oliver now knew how to remove shit-stains as well as a host of other marks from various fabrics. If only removing offending marks on his conscience was as straightforward.

Two hours later, with hands pink and sensitive from his brief stint as a laundry maid, Oliver sat at his desk. First order of business was to raise the wages of the servants. He'd peeked into the kitchens on the way to his study and had been a little ashamed to see the level of industriousness happening there as well.

They kept his house in order and a score of people fed besides him—all while he worked in this padded chair, in a comfortable room, reading and writing letters and examining account books. Yes, the work he did was important, but it wasn't the backbreaking sort expected of those in his employ.

Constance's imaginary reaction to his morning crossed his mind and he chuckled, shaking his head. No doubt she'd roll her eyes, then tease him about being a soft, pampered lord. She would be proud of him for raising the wages of his servants, though. Somehow, he knew that.

Would she ever feel comfortable as a woman in charge of a house like his? Caro brought changes to the ducal household, and Oliver had seen firsthand the way Dorian dealt differently with people in the working class since falling in love with a bookseller. Maybe witnessing those changes prepared Oliver for this, he thought. If placed in a similar position, Constance would likely rise to the challenge, as Caro had. Somehow, he knew that too, with a steady confidence in her abilities that took him by surprise when he paused to examine it.

Constance, for all her cheerful chatter and vivacious presence, was entirely competent.

Not the stuff of poems, or ballads, but the truth. She was eminently capable and didn't seem to need him or anyone for a blasted thing. Whether blending in at a ball, running a bookshop, or navigating the streets of London alone, Constance didn't wait for assistance.

It left him at loose ends, to be honest. Oliver stared, unseeing at the stack of mail on the corner of his polished wood desktop. Althea hadn't visited since her parents began restricting her movements, so everything was in its place.

What Constance told him about Sir William's treatment of Althea had been circling Oliver's brain like a vulture. The information scavenged the tattered remains of any delusions regarding the kind of fiancé he'd been up until then. He'd been negligent. Uncaring, cold, and aloof to the point of not noticing when his fiancée's parents essentially put her under house arrest.

While he might not be Althea's adoring swain, he did consider himself a friend. Somewhat. Frankly, he'd feel more inclined toward friendliness if he didn't have to marry the woman. Enough commitment to her remained within him to make the thought of causing her harm untenable. Yet he had. Then he'd made it worse.

After Constance's revelations, he'd paid a call on Althea's parents. Sir William told him, in no uncertain terms, that Oliver didn't have any say in Althea's treatment until they married. Since that visit, he'd only seen her with her parents present. By trying to defend her, he'd tightened the collar around her neck.

Althea needed him if she was to have a decent life away from her family.

His mother had needed him as a like-minded companion. Then toward the end, as someone to stand between her and his father's blows.

Constance Martin didn't need him for anything.

He remembered the way a flush pinkened her cheeks and chest as he'd draped his coat around her shoulders and sneaked her out of the ball. The furtive glances they'd shared. How she'd surprised him with a final toe-curling kiss after he bundled her into his carriage. It had been sheer hell to send her home alone. Perhaps she needed him for one thing, he silently amended. But it was something he'd lived without all his life.

Blinking, he adjusted the snug fit of his breeches and got to work. The faster he dealt with estate business, the faster he could puzzle through to a solution that would solve the problem of his pending marriage to the wrong woman. There must be an answer to all this; he just hadn't found it yet.

The hopeful bent of his thoughts lasted until he reached the final letter on his desk. Outside, the day was gray and damp, although not outright raining. He stood at the window and studied the garden beyond the glass.

Each year, Cook and her staff planted a vegetable and herb garden for the household's use. Not that the yield met the need of a house this size, but it contributed.

The view on the other side of the window showed a different landscape than it usually would by this part of summer. Instead of green plants, bursting with potential, the garden was a muddy wasteland. Herbs grew in pots rather than the ground, and Oliver suspected the staff brought them indoors as needed, to save the plants from the miserable onslaught of rain and cold. Even with that intervention, the green bushy things they'd coaxed into existence were nowhere near as large as one would hope.

Lines from the letters he'd just read played out over the bleak scene before him.

I fear the worst, milord. At this rate, even if we're blessed with sunshine every day until October, the yield would be slim. Without the sun, our harvest will be nothing but mud.

Crops are rotting in the ground.

The cost of oats has nearly doubled. We may have to choose between feeding our livestock and feeding our tenants.

Landowners in the area are divided in their response. Some are forgiving rents and providing aid in the form of supplemental food to their tenants. Most are ignoring the situation. Due to our long history, I dare hazard a guess as to which tack you'll take. However, I must warn you. The costs will be dear, indeed. Once we deplete last season's stores, we will need to slaughter livestock for food rather than take them to market.

This damnable weather, a topic Londoners discussed ad nauseam, would cost him far more than a small fortune. Like a runaway horse, his brain calculated rising cost in food, extrapolated that data to overall cash needed to feed and help those who depended on the estates to provide for them, then subtracted the expected income from those properties.

Realization settled like a musket ball in his gut. Sighing, he drew the weathered playing card from his pocket.

On this twelfth day of March, 1787, Lord Southwyn promises his son, Oliver Vincent, in marriage to Dorcas Thompson, daughter of Sir William Thompson.

Running a finger around the edge, he stared at the single pip. One pip. One viable option that served more than his own selfish desires.

Sure, he could follow this burning need for Constance, dower Althea, and browbeat her father into selling him the land and river for his canal system—or he could pour his finances into ensuring the survival of every man, woman, and child relying on the Earl of Southwyn.

In his shoes, Oliver knew what the late earl would choose.

He turned his back on the dreary sight of the garden. A packet of papers caught his eye, and he cursed. The marriage contracts he'd been procrastinating taking to his solicitor.

Well, choosing Constance had been a lovely thought for

the brief moments when it felt possible to awake every day with tight blond curls sprawled across the pillow beside his.

In light of reality and the latest information from his estates, there wasn't really a decision at all. One path remained. One pip. Somehow, he'd quash this ache for Constance. Given enough time, surely her allure would fade as long as he saw her as infrequently as possible, and never alone.

A selfish part of him wished for one more chance to touch her, taste her. To revel in the experience of Constance in all her glory. Knowing for certain it would be the last time meant he'd memorize each sensation in vivid detail. After all, the memories would have to last him a lifetime.

Chapter Eighteen

Stay the course... or not
Maybe just accept reality?
Ask for help

Somewhere in London, a clock struck two right after Constance opened her eyes. Sleep had come in fits and starts because her busy mind wouldn't permit true rest. As she stared into the dark, listening to the rain that never seemed to abate these days, she tried to settle her brain enough to go back to sleep.

When the same distant clock chimed three, she gave up. Hattie didn't stir as Constance slipped from the bed, but Gingersnap opened one eye, grunted, then tucked his head under a paw.

Slippers protected her feet from the chilly floorboards as she donned her warmest wrapper over Southwyn's coat—stopping to indulge in another stiff of his heady citrus and sandalwood scent—then fumbled on the bedside table until she found the iron candleholder. Once in the hall, she lit the candle and crept by her parents' room, carefully avoiding the squeaky boards on her way to the stairs.

Down in the office of her silent bookshop, Connie stoked the fire, lit a lamp, and put the kettle on.

Everything was still. At this time of day, even the streets of London were fairly quiet. She sat at the desk and ran a hand over the scarred and stained wood surface. On the front right-hand corner were initials, carved with a penknife when she'd been about five. As usual, her sister had hissed at her to stop, that they'd get in trouble, and Connie had done it anyway. B&CM. Betsy and Constance Martin. Tracing the lines, she smiled.

This desk, this office, this shop. Home. The only place she'd ever felt entirely safe to be herself. Even when she didn't understand what that was.

She'd always been curious, absorbing knowledge like a sponge from the many books around her. At times, creativity seized her and she easily picked up new skills like knitting, sewing, writing poetry. She'd even made new games to play with her family based on the globe in the map section.

Other times, the number of things to do held her in place, unable to accomplish anything. Not because she didn't understand the importance of the tasks awaiting her attention, but because she understood all too well how important they were. And somehow that knowledge made it impossible to begin.

In this shop, it didn't matter if it was a good or bad day. People who loved her accepted whatever she could give that day. In return, she loved them fiercely.

But this desk? This was where her parents forced her to sit and write endless letters and sums. At times, her mum resorted to bribery to get the work done. Now the desk held papers she needed to somehow conquer if she was going to convince her parents that Martin House would be safe in her hands.

And . . . she didn't think she could do it. Not alone, anyway. Admitting that made her chest expand in a deep breath she didn't realize she needed. Yes, she could take care of the store and keep the home that meant so much to her, but she needed to convince Hattie and Caro to help. Caro might not be in a position to work here anymore, but having her as a partner would open possibilities and resources for the store Constance couldn't provide. And with Caro willing to contribute, it might help Hattie to feel less trapped, knowing she wouldn't be abandoning Connie entirely if she needed to run.

Constance had tried to do it herself. Schedules and lists only went so far, though. While she'd made some progress, if she was being honest, the amount of effort it took to make that small dent wasn't sustainable. Not when it meant pushing equally hard until the day she died.

What a depressing thought.

Pulling the smaller-than-usual stack of paperwork toward her, she examined the top sheet—a reminder to write quarterly payment slips for each of the mail accounts and lending library patrons. She could do that.

But when she put pen to paper, it wasn't the standard request for payment she wrote.

> *What I want:*
> *Martin House*
> *A home where I feel safe*
> *Trustworthy friends*
> *Him*

The last word's letters were smaller, and an ink blotch spread from the tail of the *m*, where her pen had lingered.

> *What I can have:*
> *Friends*
> *Partnership with cousins=Martin House=safe home*

Tears gathered as she stared at that ink blotch. When one fell onto the paper and turned the script into a murky river, it felt oddly fitting.

"Couldn't you sleep?" Hattie's voice, drowsy and rough, came from behind her. "Your kettle's hot. Were you wanting tea?"

Connie swiped at her eyes before her cousin could see the tears. "Yes. Thank you."

The familiar sounds of tea preparation came from behind her, and Connie knew Hattie would give her a few minutes before she pressed.

True to form, it wasn't until the cup appeared at her elbow and Hattie sat down that she spoke. "Any particular reason you decided to do paperwork at three in the morning? Usually, if you're up like this, you're bustling about. You're not like that tonight."

Wordlessly, Connie handed her the list she'd made. A moment later, Hattie murmured, "I see. Can you help me understand what this means, exactly?"

Like a dam breaking, the worries over her parents retiring, losing her home if the store sold, and the things she'd tried in an effort to fix the problems her father foresaw, came pouring out of her. "I need help. If we band together, I'm sure my parents will let us run the store. As much as I hate to admit it, I can't do this alone. This blasted brain of mine doesn't work like yours or Caro's. She actually enjoys recordkeeping. Which makes me think she's sick in the head, but that's another matter entirely. Please, Hat. We work well together. You're much more consistent regarding these office things than I am. If we divide everything up, or if Caro wants to hire a bookkeeper, we could keep Martin House. When my parents move to Kent, one of us will take their room, and we can grow old together. We'll make a grand time of it."

Above the collar of her wrapper, Hattie's throat worked.

Before she could protest, Constance added, "Including Caro means you can leave at any time if you need to. I know you don't want to feel bound to one place."

Hattie's eyes lowered to the cup she held, then the paper. One finger reached out and settled on the list. "What about this?"

Him with the tearful ink spot.

"I think we both know the likelihood of two Martin House girls becoming titled ladies is a bit far-fetched."

A furrow appeared between Hattie's eyebrows. "You're giving up? That's not like you. You're one of the most resilient, determined people I know."

Connie cocked her head. "What?"

"No matter what happens, no matter how hard you struggle with something, you don't give up. Determination. And eventually, you find a way through. That's resilience."

"I suppose I've never viewed it that way. I think I tend to see the struggle rather than the perseverance. Thank you for that."

"You're welcome. Now, are you going to apply that determination to Southwyn?"

Oh, she wanted to. How Connie wished she could stand and declare, like the hero in a book, that no obstacle was large enough to keep her from what she wanted. Alas, reality and logic pointed toward nothing but failure.

The thought sparked a bitter laugh. Southwyn must be rubbing off on her.

"I want him. I don't deny that. And after our little interlude the other night, I think we need to have an honest discussion. The problem is, he's engaged to Althea. Even if they aren't happy about it, her mother is planning a grand society wedding. Unless Althea's beau finds a way for them to be together, the engagement stands."

"Will you call on him this morning?"

Constance nodded. Taking matters into her own hands, marching into Southwyn's home, and telling him to explain exactly where they stood was the right thing to do. "As soon as it's a reasonable hour, yes."

"I'll look after the shop. You take care of this. Get whatever answers you can." Hattie squeezed her shoulder, then stood.

"What about the rest of it? Being an official partner in the shop with me?"

At the bottom of the stairs to their flat, Hattie turned. "If Caro agrees, then so do I."

Connie rose. "And if she doesn't, and it's just us?"

Several seconds passed before Hattie sighed. "I won't be the reason you lose your list, Connie. I suppose I'm willing, no matter what. It will be easier with Caro, though."

Connie charged across the room and threw her arms around her. "Thank you." Tears choked her words. "Thank you."

"I love you. We'll figure out the details when the sun is up. All right?"

Nodding, she let her cousin go back to bed. Gingersnap padded down the stairs, pausing for a pet from Hattie on the way. His inquisitive mew made Connie smile. Like he was asking what he'd missed. "Are you going to keep me company? These payment requests aren't going to make themselves, Mr. Gingersnap."

When the cat flopped on his side in front of the fireplace and gave her a slow blink, Connie returned to the desk, smiling.

"What the hell. It won't hurt anything."

"Nothing except my eyes and your dignity, milord," came his valet's reply.

Oliver laughed as he slipped into the ugly orange waistcoat and pocketed the ace of spades out of habit. Something told him that when the day came to leave the card on his dressing table, he'd know. For now, the ace, like the change in waistcoats, was part of the reality he must accept.

The newspapers at the breakfast table were depressing, so Oliver decided that what he needed was a day to play hermit. He'd sit in his most comfortable chair, wearing this godawful waistcoat, and cuddle his cat while reading a good book.

And that's where Roberts found him, with the unexpected news that Miss Constance Martin had come to call.

She entered a few moments later, cheeks pink from the cold and curls escaping in damp coils around her face. The sight of her was simultaneously a punch to the gut, and a relief.

"Pardon my rudeness in not standing to greet you. I'm trapped by a cat," he explained.

The dimple in her cheek flashed as she drew closer and spied the furry spiral in his lap. "I see that. I bow to the prince's rank. May I sit?" She gestured toward the chaise.

With a small table separating the chaise and his chair, her seat placed her close enough to tantalize the senses, but not as close as he wished she was—on his lap. However, since Prince occupied that space, he said, "Please do."

With anyone else, an awkward silence might have fallen. Except, this was Constance. While his mind raced with myriad things he could say—70 percent of which were not appropriate for mixed company, and the other 30 percent would make him sound like a bumbling youth with his first crush—she jumped right in. He couldn't think of a situation yet in which this woman hadn't found her footing and adapted to her surroundings. A rather marvelous talent, he thought.

"Please excuse my calling uninvited, but I thought we should talk after our encounter the other night. Also, I wanted to return this." She held out a paper-wrapped parcel secured with twine. "It's your coat. Thank you for letting me borrow it, as well as ensuring my safe return home."

She didn't even look nervous. Was this due to her ability to walk into any situation with an air of confidence, or did she have a history of kissing men?

If it was the latter, perhaps she might share some advice on how they should go on from here.

"Why did you kiss me?"

Ah, it was to be the direct approach, then. Having never done this before, he found he didn't have an easy answer. *Because the usual parts of my brain turned off and I became some kind of wild animal obsessed with fucking you.* "I'm not sure."

A quirk of her lips suggested she might be reading into his pause and making accurate assumptions. "Allow me to rephrase the question. Why, Lord Southwyn, did you kiss me as if your very life depended on it? From what I recall, you were hell-bent on defending my honor, nearly made poor Mr. Wellsley piss himself, then proceeded to give me the most erotic kiss in the history of kisses. Or the history of me, anyway."

Oliver's respect for her went up another notch. Exposing her vulnerability in that way was risky. However, that courage called on him to match it in kind. Vulnerability for vulnerability.

"Perhaps most interesting of all was the way you didn't appear surprised at how things were between us. Almost as if you'd known we would be good together. As if you'd spent considerable time thinking about it."

When he cleared his throat, it seemed especially loud in the silent room. Right, then. Vulnerable. Honest. He could do that. "I have spent quite a bit of time wondering about you. About... us. Together."

Satisfaction crept over her face until Constance's smile bordered on smug. "Wanting me, you mean."

He finally met her gaze without looking away. "Yes. I wanted you." *Still want you, you maddening woman.*

Connie raised one eyebrow. "So, you were curious, satisfied that curiosity, and now can move on to other things? I confess, I do that quite often as well. Fixate on one thing, get my fill, then flit off to something else." She leaned toward him, and the skin above her neckline, skin he knew for a fact was velvety smooth, bulged above the top of her gown. Had she left off a fichu purely for his benefit? If so, he wanted to kiss her in gratitude.

Who was he kidding? He wanted to kiss her anyway. What was the question? Oliver blinked and tried to focus on something besides that delicious dip of cleavage.

"Is that common, you think? For a man to search out one last kiss before committing himself for life with another woman?"

Any tension in his breeches wilted at that. "Rather a low blow." His lips pressed into a thin line. "But to answer your question, I'm not."

"Not what?" Her cheerful smile struck him as slightly forced. Maybe she liked talking about his upcoming nuptials as much as he did.

To hell with it. If she was brave enough to ask direct questions, he was brave enough to answer. Besides, he owed her the truth. This might be his only chance to tell her how he felt.

And hadn't he just been wishing the day before to experience her one more time? Well, this was his opportunity. Blowing out a sigh, Oliver let go of his death grip on self-control. "I'm not satisfied. One kiss in a back room at a ball, no matter how earth-shattering it was, could never be enough to satisfy me where you're concerned."

"Oh…" Now she was the one with her breath whooshing out from parted lips. When she grazed her teeth over her bottom lip, he made a pained noise deep in his throat. "I thought you might regret kissing me."

A rueful smile tilted his mouth. "My attraction to you is wildly inconvenient, given that I'm an engaged man."

"To a woman who is actively trying to escape that marriage."

"Have you noticed your penchant for saying uncomfortable things?"

Constance shrugged. "Uncomfortable doesn't mean untrue. Althea doesn't want to marry you. She's in love with Mr. Wellsley."

Brave, sometimes reckless woman. Instead of taking offense, he slowly reached out a hand and brushed his pinky finger over hers.

That was it. Just one finger. But the connection was enough to make his heart jolt in his chest. "I'd speculated about the attachment to Mr. Wellsley. Unfortunately, unless Wellsley has loads of money and a secret title, Sir William will continue to be a tyrant. I've lost more sleep over this situation than you know, and don't see a way out. Sir William is stubborn and vindictive in nature, I'm afraid. I can't leave Althea at his mercy."

As he said the words, which were so familiar after frequently repeating them, he realized something. Like Althea's father, Oliver survived by stubbornly resisting change. Once upon a time, that dogged immovability was something he'd been proud of.

Constance's finger wrapped around his as he drank in the sight of her creamy skin and the determined jut of her chin. How would his life be different if there'd been a place for flexibility in his life? The way she adapted to any setting, be it a bookshop or a ballroom, showed a malleability he admired. Probably because that particular trait was so absent from him.

"You know," he began, lacing the rest of their fingers together and savoring the contact, "for my entire adult life, nearly every decision connects to my father in some way." Constance shifted in her seat, getting comfortable. He loved that. *Yes, please settle in. Even if I can't have more days like this, talking away the hours, let me have a little more time now.*

"He was an absolute bastard, so I act in the opposite way he would in any given situation. As if I'm constantly proving to myself and everyone else that I'm the better man."

"I think you're a good man. Otherwise, you wouldn't have lost sleep over all of this." She squeezed his hand, and he offered a tiny smile in thanks.

"My mother, though. I think you would have liked her. Even though she was scientific and logical, she also laughed freely and butted heads with my father without regard to decorum. She was emotional and followed her gut when it came to matters of the heart. If I'd put thought into which parent should influence my actions the most, I would have picked my mother." Why, then, was she relevant to so few areas of his existence? The thought made his eyebrows pinch together.

Constance reached out a finger and smoothed the line until the furrow relaxed.

"Mother loved animals. Not just for their appeal as companions, but also from a zoological perspective. Pick an animal, and she could list so many facts you'd lose track of them all. Her favorite thing to do was visit menageries and animal collections." Oliver pointed at the gorilla skull on the shelf nearby. "That specimen was her most prized possession. It's from an adult male gorilla. You know why she loved it?" Constance raised an inquiring brow, waiting. "Because it resembles a human skull. She believed animals had more in common with us than we give them credit for. That beneath it all, we are all animals—predator and prey."

"She was a wise woman," Constance mused, staring at the skull.

"Yes, she was. One day, we were petting a young rhinoceros. He was quite tolerant of people. She told me that no matter how docile he might appear, he was still a rhinoceros and wild inside. Without warning, his instincts might react to something and cause harm." Oliver stared down at their joined hands, brushing his thumb over her knuckles. Faint lines scarred her skin, and her cuticles split in several places. They were working hands. Capable fingers. Soft palms. He'd give anything to know how they felt on every inch of his body.

"My father lived by his animal nature and hurt everyone he came in contact with." Meeting her gaze, he confessed, "Until I kissed you, I believed I lacked those primal instincts Mother warned me of. I'm ashamed to admit the lack of what she called an animal nature never worried me. Because those urges would have made the concrete state of my life impossible to maintain."

Constance watched him, content to listen.

"That, in itself, is pretty damned telling, isn't it? Even though it hadn't been conscious, some part of me must have recognized that to stay the course I'd laid out for myself, I had to forgo my father's worst traits, and my mother's finest."

"For those few minutes, when emotion led your actions instead of logic, how did you feel? Did the intensity scare you?" she asked.

"I felt alive in a way I never have before. Free. I didn't know I was capable of such depth of emotion. And now, I am examining the life I've created and all I see is bars. As much as I want to snarl and bite at my circumstances, I can't change course without hurting Althea or causing irreversible damage to the lives of hardworking, honest folks depending on me for their survival."

In his lap, Prince shifted, then stretched awake. With a rumbling sort of greeting, he padded to his feet, then jumped across to the chaise. Oliver smiled as his pet's tiny kitten nose nudged Constance's cheek before he continued on across the back of the chaise, then hopped to the floor.

"I'm so sorry, Constance. Fuck. Whatever this is between us, I want it desperately. Please know that. But having you means hurting innocent people." Looking away from the understanding and disappointment in her eyes was impossible. "I...can't."

Without a word, she stood and walked to his chair, then perched sideways on his lap. Her feet dangled over one of his arms as she tucked her head against his neck. Wrapping his arms around Constance Martin and holding her close felt like the most natural thing in the world.

"I'm sorry too. We could have been happy," she whispered.

The tip of her nose was chilly where it touched the side of his neck. "We would have been so damned happy," he quietly agreed.

One of her hands curled under the ugly orange waistcoat to rest over his heart, and a sigh rattled through him. Painful as it was to hold her like this, the experience was also nearly unbearably perfect. He'd enjoy the moment for as long as it lasted.

A small snore escaped a short while later, and he grinned. She'd fallen asleep, and she snored. What a delightful, intimate thing to know. Careful not to wake her, he picked up the book he'd been reading, and found his place.

Chapter Nineteen

Say goodbye
Go to your favorite novelist for advice

Connie awoke from her unexpected doze with her cheek pressed against a warm, firm shoulder. A puddle of drool darkened his jacket. Embarrassment warred with the need to stretch like Prince had after waking in this same lap. Opening her eyes to Southwyn's angular jaw and an up-close view of his sideburns had been disorienting at first. Individual strands of deep red and black blended into his dark brown hair. The scent of cologne was stronger there, as was his underlying natural smell.

For those few seconds, she had everything. Constance felt safe, cherished, and content—but with a low simmer of desire that would become a conflagration with the tiniest spark.

"Did you enjoy your nap?" The rumble of his voice acted as that spark.

She'd never been simultaneously aroused and dismayed. "I'm so sorry. I didn't mean to fall asleep. I've been awake since two o'clock this morning, and—"

"Constance," he interrupted, cupping the back of her head and meeting her gaze. Hearing her name on his lips made her toes curl. "Please don't apologize. Holding you while you slept is something I never thought I would do outside of my dreams." He touched their foreheads together. "I was able to pretend for a little while that I had you. Thank you."

Under her bottom, something stirred, and they shared an amused look, loaded with awareness.

"Perhaps I should leave before we do something we'll regret," Connie said. Slowly, she cradled his face, then placed a gentle kiss on his lips. A goodbye of sorts, and her heart broke at the contact. After today, they wouldn't speak of this again, or of their passionate encounter in the storeroom.

His expression mirrored her feelings, and she knew he'd received her wordless message. "Farewell, Oliver." It seemed appropriate to use his given name aloud. Just this once.

At the door to the study, she donned her outerwear, then glided a hand over Prince's shiny head.

"It was easier before I knew what this felt like," he said, low enough that she wasn't sure he meant her to hear.

Tears streamed down her face the entire way home, while Constance chastised herself for being ridiculous. After all, it wasn't as if they'd had a real relationship to end.

Why, then, did it feel like she'd lost something precious?

When the sun chased away the clouds an hour later, she begged her father to cover the store, since Hattie had slipped off to places unknown. Owen agreed readily, noting with concern that her red-rimmed eyes would drive away customers.

Gingersnap purred when she slipped the lead over his head and grabbed his basket. While he loved to walk on a leash, there were times when it was unwise to do so on London streets. Even where she was going, in Bloomsbury.

Because when a woman realized she'd fallen in love with a man entirely beyond her reach, then fell asleep in his arms and had the best nap in the history of the world, she needed a sympathetic, nonjudgmental ear. Preferably one who grasped the awful, gut-wrenching beauty of this emotion pushing against the seams of her soul.

Thus, she needed Caroline, the Duchess of Holland—a vicar's daughter and erotic fiction writer who'd thumbed her nose at the ton and snagged herself a duke. If anyone would understand what Constance felt for Lord Southwyn, it would be her cousin.

Except, when Hastings showed her into the drawing room, she found more than Caro.

In the doorway, she hitched Gingersnap's basket deeper into the crook of her arm. "H-hello."

On the sofa sat Caro with Baby Nate and Dorian, as expected. Beside them was Hattie, not expected. As well as Althea and Oliver—definitely not expected. He didn't meet her gaze, although his spine straightened when she spoke. Damn and double damn.

"Connie! What a lovely surprise," Caro said.

Gingersnap mewed a pointed complaint. Releasing the animal to wander gave Connie something to do besides gape at her friends. During those vital seconds she forced a friendly smile. An outward appearance that didn't betray how her mind spun. Had she forgotten they were all meeting today? Wouldn't Oliver have said something if that was the case? And wouldn't she remember an appointment that included him?

Except, Caro said it was a surprise to see her. Ergo, Constance hadn't been invited to whatever this was.

Thoughts raced, searching for an explanation and finding none.

Southwyn still hadn't looked in her direction, while the others glanced around with a distinctly sheepish air. Years of being told she was sensitive and took things too personally stopped Constance from asking outright why they'd excluded her.

Instead, she reverted to her usual carefree chatter. "The sun came out, so Gingersnap and I are taking some air. Are we interrupting anything?"

A chorus of guilty-sounding *no*s confirmed her anxiety. Fine. She could pretend there wasn't anything suspicious about all of this.

Nathaniel slept in his father's arms, wearing the hat she'd knit for him. The wool was remarkably soft, one she'd bought from a lovely woman at the market. Well, Constance began the project, then passed it on to her mum to finish— who'd done an excellent job as expected. The hat fit his adorable little head perfectly.

Dorian smiled at his son before handing him to Constance when she held out her arms and made a silent grabbing motion.

There. Armed with a sleeping infant to provide comfort and something to do with her hands, she turned and realized the only available seat was beside Oliver on the tiny settee.

Althea waved from her chair but didn't seem inclined in the least to move and sit beside her fiancé. But then, Althea wanted to throw Connie and Oliver together as often as possible. If she only knew how little assistance they needed to develop feelings for one another. There was nothing to do but perch next to him and pretend that the last time she'd seen him, they hadn't been closing the book on Althea's hopes.

Constance offered Southwyn a tight-lipped smile as she snuggled Nathaniel close to her chest and sat as far from the earl as possible. Which, she noted with a resigned sigh, wasn't far enough to escape her thrumming awareness of him.

The Hollands had boatloads of money. They could afford larger furniture.

"It must be the day to call on the duke and duchess," Althea chirped. "Oliver arrived a few moments before you. What happy luck."

Constance risked a glance at Southwyn and caught him watching her before he looked away. But not before she noted his closed expression. That ability to lock away emotions behind cool reserve was something she wished she possessed. Especially when she feared her heart bled on her sleeve for everyone to see.

Thankfully, Nathaniel's soft baby snores distracted her from mulling over the effect Oliver—no, Southwyn—had on her feelings. A soft grunt escaped her when Gingersnap landed on her lap with a heavy thud.

"Are you jealous of the baby? Apologies, but you can share me for a few minutes," she told the cat, cradling Nathaniel closer. Goodness, he was such a delightful weight in her arms.

After fleeing her wedding, she'd accepted that Georgia might be the closest she'd get to having a child of her own. Which was a little bittersweet, but fine. After all, she'd never longed intensely for a child, or felt like her life would be somehow incomplete if she wasn't a mother. But right then, she understood women who desired that. Especially when long, strong fingers she knew felt delicious on her skin entered her vision and gently plucked the orange cat from her lap.

"Young man, Nathaniel doesn't need fur up his nose. You can share your mother this one time. Come here." Southwyn placed Gingersnap on his thighs and petted him with a long stroke that made her temperamental cat reconsider the immediate instinct to bolt. When a deep, rumbly purr rattled from Gingersnap, Southwyn exchanged a look with her. He didn't even fully grin—more a quirk of one side of his mouth. That devastatingly imperfect smile.

It was a mere second in time. A minuscule blip in the day everyone else missed entirely. But in that instant, she experienced a flash of what could have been. In another lifetime, when Lord Southwyn was plain Mr. Oliver Vincent and within the realm of possible marriage options. A man who spoke to their pets as if they were people. A man who came alongside and helped. Who would gaze adoringly at the child they'd created. He'd stare at their baby the way Dorian watched Nathaniel. And he'd greet her with kisses and a private, uneven smile he saved just for her. And every morning, she'd wake with her head on his shoulder, as she had this afternoon.

The mirage of another life gripped tight enough to make swallowing a challenge. Constance allowed the time it took for a single deep inhale to enjoy the fantasy, then shoved it aside. "Gingersnap likes you. Not that I'm surprised after you successfully earned Prince's affections."

"Winning over that kitten was impressive," Althea interjected. "Ladies, don't you find it attractive when men are kind to animals?"

Caro and Hattie agreed, while Constance held her tongue and brushed a fingertip over Nathaniel's perfect cheeks.

"Does that mean we need to get a cat?" Dorian asked his wife.

"I've always wanted a dog," Caro said.

"Father keeps hounds in the country. I can send you a puppy the next time there's a litter," Althea offered. Then she grimaced at her watch pin. "Speaking of my father, I should depart for home. My parents' goodwill only extends so far."

Wait, Althea said Southwyn arrived a minute before

Connie. Which meant he and Althea hadn't arrived together. She'd been here first. "How did you manage to escape the house on your own without them?" Constance asked.

"They could hardly say no when I was calling on a duke and duchess. My parents are, if nothing else, eager for connections to the highest levels of the ton." Althea wrinkled her nose in a silent apology to Caro and Dorian. "I lied and told them I wanted to speak to His Grace regarding a wedding gift for Oliver."

Southwyn's face pinched. "I'm so sorry, Althea. I didn't realize they've been restricting your movements. I feel awful for not recognizing what was happening."

Althea's lips thinned to a flat line. "Didn't you find it strange that my turned knee only makes appearances when there's dancing? Or that I haven't been out with my maid running errands or making calls? My parents stay at my side every moment I'm out of our house."

An intriguing muscle at Southwyn's jaw ticked with tension. In fact, tension radiated from every inch of him. Even the cat stopped purring and stared in concern. "I wasn't paying attention. I apologize."

Before she could think better of it, Constance placed a comforting hand on his arm and found it rigid and tight under her fingers. Realizing what she'd done, she jerked away.

"Her father is a villain." Hattie turned to Caro. "Can we kill him in your next book? I think Sir William would make a brilliant character everyone could hate. He'll have to die in a particularly gruesome manner, though. I insist."

"I agree. No insipid poisons or clean shot at dawn." Caro nodded.

"Connie, have I mentioned how terribly fond I am of your cousins?" Althea grinned as she gathered her things. "I really must be going though. Your Graces, thank you for your hospitality. Miss McCrae, it was a pleasure to see you again. Oliver and Constance, I'll be in touch soon." She crossed to the sofa and kissed Connie's cheek, then nodded to Southwyn.

When she'd left, Dorian cleared his throat. "Betsy wrote this week. She mentioned for the second time, apparently, a property near her that's for sale. The owners decided to immigrate to America. They have family there already and, according to gossip, have been considering a move for several years. It's not a lot of land, but a nice house with an established garden plot and orchard. This damnable weather convinced them they won't have a harvest this season, so they're selling now."

Beside her, Southwyn's attitude sobered even more. "My estate managers aren't optimistic about our harvests, either. The situation is growing dire. People are scared. Unfortunately, I expect we'll hear about more farmers choosing to sell or leave and try their luck elsewhere rather than starve."

The bleakness of Southwyn's voice made Constance study his profile. Was this what he'd been referring to when he said he could either have her, or condemn those who depended on him? Their conversation had veered away before she asked for clarification, so she didn't understand the intricacies of the situation. At her side, Constance's hand twitched with the need to comfort him somehow.

"I worry that this may escalate to a famine if Mother Nature doesn't smile on us soon," Southwyn added.

"*Famine* is a terrifying word. Are your people in awful danger, then?" Caro asked.

The duke must have wondered the same thing. "If you need help weathering this season, just say the word."

Southwyn shook his head, but the smile he offered Dorian was halfhearted. "I should be able to meet the

needs of the properties and tenants, but it means making...
sacrifices." The hand on Gingersnap tensed, then resumed
petting. Constance knew, without him saying explicitly, a
relationship with her was one of those things he had to sacri-
fice. Why exactly, she wasn't sure. But it was clear he believed
it to be true.

"If it comes down to my pride or my people, you know I'll
ask for aid," Oliver reassured them.

"I will hold you to that. In the spirit of anticipating hap-
pier times, I'd value your opinion on this property. If the
price is right, you could live a short ride from our cottage. I
might buy it anyway and lease it, even if it's not to you."

"Are you offering to be my landlord?" Oliver laughed,
and the sound was such a welcome thing, Connie couldn't
stop her smile.

"It's an idea." Dorian shrugged. "I thought we'd take a
drive to Kent in a few days and look at it. Caro and I are
dying to get out of the city and check on the cottage."

Caro sighed wistfully. "I would love to go home, even
if just for a short while. Now that Nathan is here and
we're both healthy, perhaps we can start splitting our time
between there and London. Connie, Hattie, do you want to
come along and keep me company? I've never traveled with
an infant and could use a few more hands. Especially if the
men are out tromping through muddy fields."

"You go, Connie. I'll watch the shop," Hattie suggested.

"Yes! It's decided then. Besides, Georgia would love to see
you if we stop and visit Betsy while we're nearby."

Apparently, she was going to Kent soon. Constance
glanced at Southwyn, who shrugged.

"I need to meet with my banker tomorrow and discuss
my options for the estates. But after that, I'm available," he
said.

Dorian stood. "Excellent. Shall we plan on leaving before the week's end? Let's go to my study, so I can show you the letter. I think I have a map of the area somewhere."

Southwyn placed Gingersnap beside Connie and joined his friend. She immediately missed his warmth when the men departed.

Finally, it was just her and her cousins. The memory of how uncomfortable it had been to walk in and see them all gathered without her made Connie hesitant to ask about whatever she'd interrupted.

In her arms, Nathaniel let loose an adorable squeaky grunt, followed by a significantly less cute odor. "Darling, your son needs his nappy changed."

Caro gathered the baby and left.

Turning to Hattie, Constance asked, "What are the chances of you telling me why you were all here without me?"

Hattie widened her eyes in faux innocence. "I have no idea what you mean."

Constance heaved a sigh. Prying information from Hattie was damn near impossible. The woman was a vault—secrets went in and never left her lips unless she decided they served a purpose.

Gingersnap crawled back onto her lap and gazed up at her, satisfied now that she was free of the baby.

Maybe she could finagle a way for Dorian to ride in Southwyn's carriage, while she accompanied Caro and the baby. Then they'd have a couple of hours to talk. "I think I might use the drive to Kent to ask Caro about becoming an official partner at Martin House. Is that all right with you, or would you prefer to be present?"

"Tell her what you told me. Then maybe the three of us could sit down when you return."

Constance agreed, but the awkward gathering she'd stumbled upon when she arrived nagged at her. "Whatever that was you all were doing when I interrupted...should I be concerned?"

Hattie shook her head. "I promise, it's nothing you need to worry over. And you know we'd never deliberately hurt you, right?"

She nodded, since that was the expected answer. "Of course. We wouldn't do anything to cause each other pain." That, at least, she knew to be true. But they were up to something, and she didn't know what.

Chapter Twenty

~~Review tax paperwork preparation with parents~~
~~Mail payment notices to lending library patrons~~
~~Ask Caro about next book release date~~
~~Forward letter from Mr. Wellsley to Althea~~
Bookmarks

Franklin Wellsley was waiting when Oliver returned from visiting Dorian. The young man leaned against the townhome's wall beside the stoop, with one booted foot propped on the house and his hands in his pockets. The picture of relaxed repose, and not at all the panicked man he'd dragged from Constance's cleavage in that dark storeroom.

Wellsley held his hat in one hand and rested with his eyes closed and face lifted to the sky, like a flower seeking out the sun's rays. Peaceful and unencumbered by things like regret, self-recriminations, and begrudging adherence to duty.

Oliver would dearly love to smack him with something. Given the few details he knew about the man's relationship with Althea, it was intriguing that he'd call.

As Oliver drew near, Mr. Wellsley straightened and donned his hat. "Lord Southwyn. May I have a moment of your time?"

This should be interesting. Oliver swept his arm toward the door. "Of course. Come in."

Rather than the study, Oliver headed toward the seldom-used blue drawing room at the front of the house.

The study was his sanctuary, where he stored his broken heart and unfulfilled wishes. Holding Constance in his favorite chair, knowing she felt safe enough to sleep in his presence, had forced him to assess how deep his feelings went. Yes, he desired her. After all, she was all curves and laughter and unruly hair that quivered with every movement. And she moved a lot. Being allowed to hold her while she dreamed, absorbing her honeysuckle scent, and feeling her breath on his neck, had been about more than desire. He loved her.

Sitting beside Constance on Dorian's love seat, without touching her, had been a special kind of torture, and all he'd wanted to do was haul her back with him in time to that morning, when she'd been his for a brief while.

So, no. Oliver wouldn't be opening his study to visitors anytime soon.

"Roberts, will you please bring some refreshments?" Knowing his butler, he'd read the tension in Oliver's shoulders and would ensure there was something stronger than tea on offer.

Sure enough, a moment later, Roberts returned carrying a tray with a decanter and two glasses. "Will you be wanting further refreshments, milord?" Bless him and his priorities.

"Thank you, Roberts. This will be all. Mr. Wellsley, may I pour you a drink?" If nothing else, the manners his mother instilled in him would ensure the younger man didn't walk away from this meeting thinking Oliver a monster. At his nod, Oliver handed him a crystal glass containing a generous splash of amber liquid.

Taking a seat, Oliver rested a booted ankle on his knee and indulged in a bracing swallow. "I assume this call pertains to Althea." Better to dive into the matter than waste each other's time.

Mr. Wellsley's sip became more of a gulp. Dutch courage, perhaps?

"I'm in love with your fiancée." Twin slashes of pink colored Wellsley's cheeks, but he held Oliver's gaze. Interesting. Oliver's estimation of the man went up at the show of bravery.

"Does Miss Thompson know you're here?"

"Not exactly. She'd probably be livid if she knew."

Oliver cocked his head, studying the man. Really, he was becoming more intriguing by the moment. "Why risk her wrath, then?"

"Because it's not an honorable thing, is it? To love another man's bride to be. So, I've come to do the only thing that feels right. I'm here to inform you that, if at all possible, I intend to marry Althea."

He said it in a way that didn't strike Oliver as empty bravado, or an attempt to urge them toward something truly unadvisable like pistols at dawn.

"Is that why you were in that storeroom the other night? Sending a marriage proposal via a third party?"

"Receiving a message from Althea, actually. She wanted to give me the opportunity to run away without feeling yellow-bellied. You see, if we elope, Sir William will withhold her dowry and raise such a fuss, there'll be no escaping the scandal."

Oliver sipped his drink and tried to identify the emotion coursing through him. Not the fiery spikes of anger, or even the inky sticky sensation of jealousy. This was warm, and a bit tentative. Like hope, afraid to bloom after feeling reality's boots too many times before. Because perhaps this young man's courage and honesty could be the sliver of sunshine needed to light their way to a different path. Already, Oliver's brain buzzed with starts and stops as he attempted to imagine a new course of action.

"I assume you're certain of her affections." Constance had told him as much, but he wanted to make sure Althea was being forthright with her beau.

"Yes. That she was so determined to warn of the consequences we'd face if we elope confirms it. Althea wants the best for me, even if it's not her." A smile tilted Wellsley's mouth. Oliver heard the unspoken words. There was no one better than Althea for Franklin Wellsley. And damned if this visit didn't convince Oliver of that.

"You're a younger son, correct? Do you have prospects, or an income to support a wife?"

Wellsley rested his elbows on his knees, cradling the glass between his palms. Light from the window illuminated the whisky swirling in the tumbler but wasn't bright enough to cast the crystal into prisms on the floor. Oliver missed those days when the sun sent rainbows through this room.

When his mind turned back to Wellsley, it was to see the man draining his glass with a tight expression on his face. In matters of his finances, things weren't looking bright, then, if Oliver had to guess.

He allowed the silence to fill the room, and took another taste of his drink. Finally, Wellsley spoke. "I need a year. I'm not just a younger son. I'm the fifth son." Oliver winced in sympathy. "Exactly. I've no patience for the law, haven't the faith for the clergy, and with the war over, there's no place in the army."

That narrowed the usual options significantly.

Unfortunately, twelve months was entirely out of the question, given the complication of Althea's father and his pressing debts. "What would you accomplish with your year, if you had it?"

"I'm interested in estate management. Particularly the latest farming innovations. Rather a shit season in which to find a position, I must say. Everyone is in a panic, and rightly so. However, we've dealt with bad harvests before. I have to believe there will be a need for land stewards in the future. Within a year, I hope to have work that will provide me with a house. It wouldn't be a grand life, but it's honest labor, and stable. I could support Althea."

An idea germinated, and that earlier sprig of hope grew. "Do you know anything about canals and locks?"

Wellsley shrugged. "A bit. My grandfather built one in our county when I was a boy. It was quite the undertaking, but the benefits have been enormous." An eager spark lit his eyes, and he leaned forward. "Two years ago, Mr. Stephenson built an amazing steam locomotive and ran it on the Killingworth Railway. I read that his engine successfully hauled eight coal wagons, weighing thirty tons *uphill*. Just imagine what the combination of canals and tracks could do for England. We might see the transport of goods entirely revolutionized within our lifetime."

Oliver smiled. Young Mr. Wellsley might do just fine with the right resources. If he was eager to learn, and genuinely loved Althea, there might yet be a way out of this damned marriage. Pulling the ace card from his pocket, Oliver ran a thumb over the weathered surface and studied the single pip. If this card was anything as fanciful as a sign, one spade could mean one right path, rather than one logical path forward. They were not always the same.

"Unfortunately, I can't give you a year. However, I have an idea. I'm not comfortable sharing specifics until I know it will work in our favor. It would be cruel to raise your hopes. But I will say, that if we ensure your financial stability, I have no issue with stepping aside so you and Althea can marry. Sir William is another matter altogether."

"We will probably need to elope, which eliminates her dowry. Sir William wants a title for Althea. I'd give her the moon if I could, but I can't make her a lady. Simply being part of a noble house isn't enough for him." Bitterness colored his words.

"I am on your side, Mr. Wellsley." Hope grew a little more as details fell into place in his mind. "I have an appointment with my banker tomorrow and need to visit my solicitor. Hopefully, they will agree that my idea holds water, then you and I can sort the details."

The fates might not be so unkind as to tie Oliver and Althea together when they'd given their hearts elsewhere. The thought was illogical to the point of being whimsical and made him smile. It was just the sort of thing Constance would accept as fact, without blinking. The kind of thing his mother wouldn't have questioned, despite her love of the scientific method.

Oliver focused his attention on his visitor once more, on alert for any sign of insincerity. "You'll love her, provide a safe home for her, and protect her heart with your life?"

Not a wince, a smirk, or even an eye twitch betrayed doubt in Mr. Wellsley. "It would be an honor and a privilege, milord."

Oliver nodded and stood. "Then, Mr. Wellsley, I will be speaking with you soon."

The young man rose, a grin splitting his face. "Lord Southwyn? Thank you for not drawing my cork. In your place, I wouldn't have handled this conversation so civilly."

Oliver cleared his throat. How could he explain the allure

of the mere possibility of having Constance Martin? "Thank you for calling. Let's work together to make a way out of this for both of us."

At the door, Mr. Wellsley looked back. "I'll hear from you soon?"

"You will. I'll call on my solicitor today."

Wellsley's smile was almost childlike with his happiness. God, he was young. Yet probably a few years older than Althea.

Oliver blinked. The highs and lows of the last few hours were aging him like Methuselah.

Two days later, Sir William frowned down at the papers on his desk. "Why would I agree to this?" He plucked one page off the polished wood to wave it in the air. "A trust? I don't think you understand how marriage settlements work, son."

Oliver crossed his legs, resting an ankle on one knee. "When my father died, he left financial chaos in his wake. Not a huge surprise to anyone who knew him." He leveled a scowl at the man who'd been the late earl's closest companion. "The only reason the Southwyn name isn't synonymous with debtor's prison is the trust set aside in my mother's marriage contract. With her death, it passed to me. Father couldn't touch it."

"That whole separate trust nonsense was the bane of his existence. Hated the bloody thing," Sir William grumbled, reading through the text again.

Oliver smiled wryly. "Because it worked as intended, and didn't name my father as the trustee. In the end, that document saved me and the Southwyn holdings. I wouldn't be in a position to support my cat, much less a wife, if not for Mother's family funds."

"You realize, if I sign this, you'll never have your ancestral lands back. Your father sold me those acres with the agreement they'd return to the Southwyn estate eventually. You may be the trustee, but you'll only be managing the property, not owning it."

Oliver shrugged. "As my wife, Althea would own that acreage, then pass it on to our children. It will become part of the Southwyn estate."

Sir William sputtered. "Why not dower her with it? It's the same in the end."

Because the laws of coverture meant everything Althea brought to the marriage, except items set aside as separate estate trusts, would become her husband's. If Sir William deeded the property to Althea now, the property would only remain hers until marriage. However, he was a horse's arse and wouldn't do anything so generous without knowing he'd get something in return. So, the solicitor had drawn up the document to name Oliver as the trustee immediately. Upon her marriage, that property would remain hers, giving her as much control as the law allowed.

Instead of explaining that, Oliver said, "This continues the legacy my mother left, of the Countess of Southwyn being an heiress in her own right." Since discovering how Althea's parents treated her, and the subsequent conversation with Sir William, anger had simmered within Oliver. Now, he let it flare hot, although his voice remained icy. Years of dealing with the late earl had trained him to handle bullies like Sir William.

The concepts were simple. Successfully manipulating a manipulator depended on preparation. Bullying a bully meant being willing to at least appear bigger, stronger, and meaner than them.

Now, Oliver wrapped his words in steel and allowed his

displeasure to show clearly on his face. "Sir William, if you don't sign these documents, I will walk out that door and tell everyone what an utter disaster you've made of your finances. Then, I'll spread the tale of how you and your wife have essentially been imprisoning your daughter. No vendors will extend you credit. Doors will slam in your wife's face all around London. Every creditor will stampede to your door."

The threat hung between them as Sir William's skin turned a rather alarming shade of purple. "How dare you—"

The time had come to be bigger and meaner. Oliver shot to his feet, slamming his hands on the desk. "No, how dare you? How dare you treat your own flesh and blood in this manner? Even when I initially confronted you about your mistreatment, all you cared about was making Althea the Countess of Southwyn. But you underestimated one thing. *No one* treats my countess with anything less than respect. So, here." He shoved the inkwell toward Sir William, who scrambled to catch it before it tumbled into his lap. "Sign the fucking papers and ensure your daughter's future. After this meeting, if I hear one word of you restricting Althea's movements or correspondence, I'll make sure you are persona non grata in every house in London. By the time I'm done sullying your name with the truth of your actions, you won't even be welcome in the rookeries."

Silence fell in the room. Finally, Sir William flipped open the inkwell and picked up his pen. "You've a bit of your father's temper, don't you, son?"

Oliver didn't answer. It was wiser to hold his tongue and allow his heart to calm back into its usual rhythm. Besides, Sir William had it wrong. It wasn't the late earl's temper on display.

Unlike his father, his mother used her position and power to protect others. The last Countess of Southwyn had once thrown rocks at a man who'd been beating his horse in the street. Oliver remembered being scared until he'd seen her determined, warrior-like visage. Later, she explained that if the man had turned violent toward her, their armed footmen would have stepped in. In the end, she'd paid the man for the horse, then brought it back to their stables.

His mother would have applauded today's actions. The late earl would have equally appreciated the cunning way Oliver gathered everything into a leather folio without adding his own signature to the marriage contracts.

Outside, Oliver ducked between the carts and carriages clogging the street. Next, he needed to write several of his managers and find the right position for Wellsley. It wasn't just a vocation the couple needed, but a house and the right environment for them to thrive. Once he secured those necessities, he'd lay out the whole plan to Wellsley. Today's task had been the largest, trickiest piece of the puzzle.

Althea's father had not balked at the deliberately vague language defining the trustee. Sure, Oliver was the trustee for now. Upon her marriage, the document stated that her husband became the trustee. Which meant Althea was now the proud owner of a property she could use to create a lucrative transportation canal if she wished. Not only that, but she'd legally retain control over that property and have a source of income for life—no matter who she married.

Chapter Twenty-One

Lay your cards on the table
Follow your heart. Even if it leads to disaster

Constance suspected a master moved them about, like pieces on an invisible board. Except, the manipulator didn't play chess. No, far worse. They were at the mercy of a novelist.

Lord Southwyn's carriage thumped over a rut in the road, and Connie instinctively braced to anchor herself to the seat. This wasn't the carriage he'd bundled her into after kissing her soundly. This was a traveling carriage, comfortable and luxurious. And she suspected if the roads had not been in their current state from the abysmal weather, it would be a wonderfully smooth ride.

A less cushioned equipage would have left bruises on her bottom.

The duke's carriage—where she was supposed to be right now—had been equally luxe. Between Dorian, Caro, Constance, and Nathaniel in his sleeping basket, there hadn't been room inside for Southwyn as well. Besides, the men reasoned, with two carriages, they'd be free to explore the area around the property and surrounding area without leaving Caro and Constance stranded with an infant.

It had all sounded so terribly logical. She'd never suspected a thing.

Until Caro complained of a headache during their mid-journey stop. The headache had struck rather suddenly, and Connie agreed that Caro looked a bit worn around the edges. Purple smudges shadowed her eyes, and she seemed rather pale, in addition to wincing and shifting occasionally on the seat. When asked if she'd mind moving to the other carriage, so Caro could lie down and rest for the remainder of the drive, Connie hadn't hesitated.

Now, alone with Lord Southwyn for the foreseeable future, she wondered why Dorian hadn't been as concerned about Caro's comfort as one would expect. The man doted on his wife to a nearly ridiculous degree. Usually, the duke would have been brimming over with solutions or demands that they take a room at the inn and allow Caro to nap until she felt better. Instead, he'd nodded sympathetically and said Connie moving to the other carriage sounded like a fine idea.

At times, it was only with reflection that things made sense. Sure, Constance bubbled and smiled through most social situations, but often she'd think back and realize she'd been too chatty, or out of step with the emotions of the others. This was one of those times. As each mile passed, she began to wonder if the meeting she'd interrupted the other day at Caro's had actually been her cousins and Althea devising a way for Connie and Southwyn to be alone together.

Such as inviting them on a road trip to Kent after the weather wreaked havoc on the roads, then fabricating an excuse to put them in a carriage by themselves.

Southwyn was oblivious. In fact, during the brief times she'd seen him today, he looked more cheerful than usual.

Smiling at Constance, drawing her into the conversation, and even touching her hand at the inn—twice.

While she'd never begrudge the man a fine mood, Constance was vexed that his grief over ending their relationship before it began had been so short-lived.

"I hope Caro feels better by the time we arrive at the cottage," Southwyn said.

She pursed her lips. "Oh, I'm sure she will be right as rain by then." Although, if Constance were writing this plot, she'd make sure the young lovers had more than an hour or two in a carriage together. If she were a betting woman, she'd play the odds on arriving at the Hollan home to eat and check on the condition of the cottage, as planned. The day's schedule called for them to head back toward Betsy's house and assess the property for sale. However, Constance expected she'd arrive at the cottage with Southwyn, then learn shortly thereafter that the duke and duchess wouldn't be joining them.

A broken wheel, perhaps? Or claims of one, at any rate.

Constance studied the passing scenery as she pondered. Betsy's home must not be far from the Hollands' current location. If she were to hazard a guess, she predicted they'd stop there. It would be far more comfortable than an inn. Would they stay overnight? How long was she going to be alone with Southwyn?

A glance at the man in question showed him watching her with open curiosity. "What is it?" she asked.

"I don't think you've ever been quiet for this long in my presence."

"I'm thinking. Enjoy the silence. It doesn't happen often," she mused self-deprecatingly.

His handsome face creased into a scowl. "Don't do that."

She blinked. "Do what? Think?"

"Speak of yourself in a negative way. I enjoy your chatter." His annoyance melted into a wry smirk. "Yes, I'm surprised to discover that as well. But it's the truth. I'm usually flummoxed by what comes out of your mouth, and I...like that. A silent Constance Martin is unnerving."

The noise she made might have been a snort, or a weak laugh. Honestly, she didn't know which, as his simple statement so thoroughly stunned her.

"What were you thinking about?" he pressed.

Studying his face, Constance considered how he'd react if she shared her suspicions about their friends playing matchmaker.

"My brain is a hive of activity as usual," she said instead. After all, they'd agreed—although not in so many words— to go back to how things were before their devastating kiss. Past Constance would never discuss such things with him.

Yet, Southwyn was being so kind. Did he still want to return to their previous relationship of mutual tolerance? Could they?

A few days earlier, Franklin Wellsley had visited the bookshop and given her a message for Althea. In short, Franklin loved her friend. Lack of a dowry wouldn't sway his affections, and he was trying to find a way for them to be together.

Assuming Franklin succeeded, did that solve the other problems Southeyn had mentioned, but not explained? Pushing for details now, when they'd already agreed to retreat to their non-romantic corners, felt like begging. *You listed two things as obstacles to us being together, and one of them is taking care of itself. Is that enough? Do you want me now?*

Apparently, she could only beg with his mouth on her body. Memories of the way they'd been together on that one occasion immediately sprang to mind, making the carriage too warm for comfort.

With her focus on the passing scenery, Connie silently wrestled her myriad emotions under control. Cooler air seeped through the glass and felt wonderful on her face, as she leaned against the wall. The movement caused her cloak to fall open, bringing a chill to her overheated skin.

A noise from the other seat in the carriage made her look up. Southwyn's eyes were dark and fixed on the flesh swelling above her neckline. It wasn't even a terribly low neckline, more's the pity. Granted, it was low enough to warrant a fichu, which she'd abandoned an hour earlier after Nathaniel spit up on it.

She nearly laughed aloud as Southwyn's Adam's apple bobbed. He wrenched his attention back to her face with such obvious effort, it was difficult not to preen. It didn't serve anything but her pride, but it was lovely to know she still affected him. Taking pity on his fracturing composure, Connie tried to change the subject.

"Is there a particular reason you're in a better mood today? I would enjoy some pleasant news for a change."

God, the way his gaze slid so hungrily over her made the cold from the windows moot. Southwyn's throat worked again and all at once, she remembered the taste of his skin there. The scent of his cologne filling her senses. The rough abrasion of new beard stubble beneath her tongue, with a hint of salt. How his chest vibrated against her when he spoke.

"My mood? Maybe it's hope you're seeing. There were countless times this week when I considered calling on you." His eyes were bright as he unabashedly drank her in. "I may have found a way for us to discover just how happy we could make one another. But I'm still sorting the details, and I knew you'd want to talk about everything."

"I thought you like hearing me talk, milord." Not only was Wellsley searching for a way to be with Althea, but Southwyn hadn't given up on them after all. Constance' heart felt more buoyant than it had in days as she leaned forward, hoping the light from the window effectively illuminated her cleavage for his viewing pleasure.

She felt his inspection like a caress, brushing her curls—oh God, the escapee hairs were probably twisting about her head like a lion's mane—lingering on the cleft of her breasts, down to the outline of her thighs, and back up.

For once, he didn't hide his appreciation. He didn't appear to be hiding a single thing, in fact. Or maybe he didn't realize his pupils took over that hazel color she loved so much. With his lips slightly open, Southwyn's mouth practically begged for a kiss.

When he matched her posture and rested his elbows on his knees, their faces were mere inches apart. By the time he finished his perusal and met her eyes, she'd nearly forgotten what they were discussing.

Like they had in his study, he reached out his pinky finger and caught hers. And just like the first time, the touch sent a shiver up her arm. His small finger curled, bringing her hand into the cradle of his. Then his thumb caressed a path along the thin skin of her inner wrist. Goose bumps rippled in his wake.

"I realize this requires a leap of faith for you. But I'm asking you to trust me. I'm trying my damndest to take care of Althea without marrying her myself."

Constance swallowed roughly. "I care about Althea. I won't have a relationship with you if you marry her."

Dark lashes cast shadows on his lean face as he watched her intently. "I won't put you in that position. Please trust me."

Strangely, she did. Lord Southwyn might be many

things—logical, sometimes overly cool and emotionally detached—but he'd also proved himself to be the opposite of those very characteristics. Passionate, loose with his language and humor when unconcerned with propriety, and direct with his declarations, like now.

"You want me, Lord Southwyn." Her pulse fluttered like the wings of a hummingbird at her bold statement.

His knees widened, legs bracketing hers, as the toes of his boots flirted with her hem. "I want you, Constance. More every day. You're the only woman I've ever said that to or about. I'm in uncharted water, here."

"Feeling a bit vulnerable?"

A raspy chuckle titillated her senses. "Very. It has never been about not wanting you enough."

"It was about making the decision your father wouldn't," she acknowledged. The tip of her boot nudged up his calf. "I still want you too. Although I'm not clear on what you intend to do about these mutual feelings."

His smile grew wide. Open and unfettered. Constance wished it was possible for him to always have such a smile readily available. Inspiring an expression like that in a man such as him was a heady thing.

So, of course, her natural inclination was to make light of it. "If I were a lady of quality, it would simplify things, don't you think? A maid or chaperone would be watching us, and we'd never have to decide the best way to spend our time."

That smile of his turned wicked, and heat blossomed between her thighs.

"But then, we wouldn't find ourselves in delightful circumstances like these, together in a carriage."

Constance's earlier suspicions returned. This time, she shared them, since they'd clearly abandoned their previous decision to pretend their kisses never happened. "We might find ourselves alone for longer than this drive."

"Why do you say that?" They sat on the edge of their seats, and it amused her to no end to see the way his breathing stuttered when she placed one hand on his knee. The poor man was trying so hard to have a conversation, and she relished making things difficult.

"I may look foolish for this prediction if I'm wrong. But I suspect Dorian and Caro will experience an overnight delay once we reach the cottage."

It was fascinating to watch his analytical brain fight with desire. Oliver cocked his head in thought while the muscles of his thigh jumped under her touch.

"Based on what clues, exactly?" The words came out breathless, as he clenched one hand in his. Her free hand explored freely, sliding high on his leg before sweeping toward his inner thigh. Tempting the earl might be her new favorite pastime.

"Althea wants you to shift your attentions to me, rather than her—"

"Done," he interrupted, making her laugh.

"Plus, my cousins know I've been harboring an irritating attraction toward you for weeks now. Of course, there's also that meeting we interrupted between Althea and my cousins the other day."

"That means Dorian knows about this scheme as well. I went to him for advice after our first kiss."

No matter how much Dorian adored his wife, he wouldn't put his closest friend in a compromising situation without believing it was for the best. Which meant the Duke of Holland fully believed Constance, a bookseller and runaway bride, was a suitable match for the Earl of Southwyn.

What a realization to have, while facing the damnably

attractive man in question. Who, it turned out, was reaching the same conclusion.

"Dorian approves of a romance between us. Otherwise, he'd have warned me away when I told him about the storeroom."

One word struck her as significant. Romance. Not match. Not marriage. Romance.

Disappointment settled in her gut, followed swiftly by self-recrimination.

It was as she'd told Hattie. One bookshop cousin marrying above her station was rare enough. Two of them doing so would be inconceivable.

A rueful laugh built, but she refused to set it free. It would be the height of foolishness to believe, even for a few moments, that an earl—an *earl* of all things—would choose her. A common-born nobody, slightly notorious in one area of London. A shopgirl. A woman who often couldn't keep a thought in her head for longer than five seconds and lived by lists to keep track of basic tasks. Lists with things like *remember to eat today* written on them.

It would be silly to assume any of this meant more than what he said it was—wanting. Lust. Their places in society were so disparate, she couldn't logically expect him to marry her.

Given the reality of the world in which they lived, a romance with the Earl of Southwyn was the most she could enjoy with him.

The inevitable end might hurt beyond measure. It might crush when they eventually said goodbye. Hell, she'd mourned the loss of him after sharing one passionate encounter. Becoming his lover would permanently imprint him on her soul.

Could. Might. Maybe. Constance swallowed down her

dread over something that hadn't happened yet. It was a risk. However, when she recalled the details of her life, she wanted to smile at the memories of this man and how fiercely she'd loved him. How bravely she'd loved him—knowing all the while they wouldn't grow old together.

Hell, perhaps she'd never marry. Constance and her cousins could take over the bookshop when her parents moved closer to Betsy—perfect Betsy, with her beautiful family. Constance could be the spinster aunt with the unflagging energy needed to run a business. The aunt with the unique stories.

It wouldn't be a bad life.

One day she might even fall in love again. Who knew what the future held.

All of this would have been easier if he'd been a passing fancy, like watercolors or quilting.

Instead, it seemed the only way to get past her fascination with Oliver was to throw her whole self into it. Wallow in him happily, and let the rest of the world disappear.

So, she did the only thing that made sense. She kissed him.

Chapter Twenty-Two

Follow your heart, and urge him to follow his

How was the taste of her so familiar, while simultaneously being wildly new? Would it always be like this between them? Oliver pulled Constance across the short span of the carriage to sit beside him, and she came willingly.

Willing was too small a word for it. She was as eager as him. Being on the receiving end of Constance's welcome unleashed emotions he'd never experienced before. Oliver smiled against her mouth and felt her smile in return.

Bubbles of giddiness pushed at his chest. Part of him wanted to roar in triumph. Another part silently thumbed his nose at Dorian's claim that Oliver was emotionally repressed. After all, he'd confessed his desire to the luscious woman in his arms, and this was the result. Not repressed at all.

Constance leaned back, tugging him down with her to the seat.

Logistical complications rose as quickly as his cock. The bench wasn't long enough for them to fully lie down. And God, he wanted to feel her beneath him more than anything. Desperate prayers flew toward heaven that Constance was correct and the Hollands planned to leave them alone.

Bracing himself above her, Oliver's eyes nearly rolled back

in his head when she anchored one leg around his hip and brought him down between her thighs.

The incredible bounty that was this woman spread out like a feast below him. The blue velvet seat acted as the perfect foil for her wild curls. It was enough to make a man wish for some sort of artistic talent, so he could capture her exactly like this. Eyes dark with desire, flushed cheeks, lips plumped and damp from his kisses.

"How long do you think we have until we reach the cottage?" His voice was rougher than he'd ever heard it.

In answer, she offered a wicked smile. "Long enough, I hope."

Wait. Did she want to...now? Here? Sweat broke out on his brow. Shit, he'd have to tell her. Otherwise, she'd have no way to understand the awful showing he'd make of this.

And he would. At least at first. Maybe his enthusiasm would make up for lack of technique. Acutely aware of the way his erection pressed against the fall of his breeches, Oliver cleared his throat. "Constance? You should know something."

She froze. "I'm sorry. Did I misread your intentions?" Red suffused her face as she shifted to sit up.

"No, not at all. God. If I could, I'd keep you in bed for the next week."

She relaxed back on the seat. "Then what is it? If we want to be together like this, I fail to see...oh."

Before she could reach her own conclusion—and God knew she could hop like a rabbit from one disastrous scenario to the next—Oliver gathered his courage.

"I'm a virgin," he said at the same time she asked, "You have the pox, don't you?"

They gaped at one another. "What?" they chimed in unison.

This time, he thumped back on the seat and she sat upright again, blowing a curl off her face.

"How are you a virgin?" Fascination and a healthy dose of disbelief coated her words.

"I've been engaged my whole life. Everyone expected my bride to be a virgin, but not me, which isn't fair. And knowing who I'd marry meant opportunities with other women felt like a betrayal."

Inching closer, Constance gave him the soft and dewy-eyed smile usually reserved for babies and small animals. "You're really the most marvelous man, aren't you? Then, why now? Why me?"

How could she ask that as if it were a real question? He traced a finger over the full curve of her cheek, marveling at her soft skin. "Because, with my conscience clear on the engagement, I can finally admit how desperate I am for you. I can't imagine being with anyone else."

Her hand slipped under his cravat to the opening in his shirt. They both sighed when bare skin met bare skin. "Have you abstained from everything? Wait, I wasn't your first kiss, was I?"

His chuckle ended on a hiss when those clever fingers delved farther under his shirt and found a nipple. "You were my third kiss."

A saucy grin made her eyes light. "Really? What about looking, but not touching? Bawdy houses, and the like."

There must be an invisible string he'd never noticed running between his nipple and his balls, because with every touch, pressure built between his legs. "Do you really want the specifics right now?"

Her smile turned wicked when she lightly pinched his nipple and he gasped. "If I'm going to let you into my body, I think I have the right to ask questions. I'll answer any you have for me. But if you'd rather not discuss specifics, as you say, I can respect that. Especially knowing you don't carry the pox or the clap."

"Am I to gather you aren't a virgin then?" Oliver kept his voice light, lest she think he was somehow passing judgment.

Despite his efforts, her smile froze. "Is that a problem?"

He shook his head. "Not at all. I'm glad one of us knows what they're doing."

The line of her shoulders softened. "My former fiancé and I anticipated the marriage bed. I've kissed plenty of men, but you'll be my second lover."

Shifting to straddle his lap, she clung to his front like a spider monkey. "This is better. Now tell me, Lord Southwyn, if I'm to be your first woman, what do you want from this encounter? You've waited for this, and I'd hate to disappoint you." The question was teasing, but Oliver heard the sincerity behind it.

His hands traced down her spine, then snugged under the lush curve of her bottom. "First of all, stop with the title nonsense. If by some miracle I manage to make you come, it would be awkward as hell for you to yell 'Lord Southwyn' in the heat of passion." As he'd hoped, she laughed. But because she was Constance, she still managed to surprise him.

"Oh, Lord Southwyn! God, yes! Harder, Lord Southwyn!"

Fuck. She was funning with him, but her approximation of a woman in the throes of climax was damned convincing. Oliver shifted under her, trying to make room in uncomfortably tight breeches.

Constance snickered. "Liked that, did you, milord?"

The way her laugh lit her from within made him sigh. "You're so damned beautiful. I'm afraid I'll take one look at you without your clothes, and spill at your feet like a green lad." Honesty was much easier when combined with laughter.

The vulnerable confession inspired another sweet smile from her. "Then you come like a green lad. I'll take that as the compliment it is. Oliver, our time together doesn't end when you finish. After all, you have hands and a mouth." A thumb caressed his lower lip. Her voice turned husky. "And a tongue."

Images raced through his mind. "I've never done anything with these hands or my mouth."

Honeysuckle and her warm breath clouded his senses when she leaned in, whispering between nipping kisses, "Shall I teach you, Oliver? Would you like to learn how to give me pleasure?"

He was firmly in her thrall. A brush of fingertips on the crest of his ear made him shudder. Light kisses across his cheekbone. Innocent touches and seductive words—confounding, surprising, and arousing, like everything else about her.

"Yes. Yes, I want that," he rasped. Oliver's eyes fluttered closed as her mouth explored his ear and neck with feather-light touches that made his toes curl inside his boots.

"By the time we're done, you'll know exactly how to make me keen and beg and scream your name."

He moaned. "Fuck, yes."

It was at that moment the carriage slowed, and the coachman's "whoa, lads" reached them. Oliver thumped his forehead on her shoulder, making her giggle.

"I would never wish ill on them, but I hope our friends stay away all night. Possibly all week." That earned another laugh. Which, from his vantage point, did delightful things to her breasts.

By the time the footman opened the door, they sat on opposite sides of the coach, and he was thanking whatever fickle deity had decided the people of England would need a warm coat in June, because the garment covered his raging erection.

Inside Caro and Dorian's cottage, Constance immediately busied herself building a fire. She was so thoroughly competent for a woman who often reminded him of a honeybee, flitting from one thing to the next.

As she went about being rather marvelous, he inspected the cottage for any signs of problems since the duke and duchess left for London.

Because, with their friends, in theory, arriving any minute, he couldn't take Constance up on her offer to teach him how to make her beg.

Fuck, he needed to think about something else. Oliver imagined dunking himself in an ice bath and walked away from the fascinating temptation that was Constance Martin.

The cottage felt alive with color and texture, and so very different from the ducal townhome. No marble floors or silk-covered walls. Windowsills—dry, despite the weather, thank God—and doorways were painted in shades of crimson, navy, and saffron. Art from their travels adorned the walls, and woven rugs in every color of the rainbow covered the stone floor.

The majority of Dorian and Caro's marriage had been spent on the Continent serving the king during the war. After Waterloo they'd returned to the cottage they referred to as their sanctuary, rather than to London.

Sure, there had been the odd few days in Town. But it soon became clear to those in their inner circle they preferred life here. Oliver glanced around the kitchen. A pantry held a few basic shelf-stable goods. Otherwise, the area was bare. No surprise, since they'd been in London for the final part of Caro's pregnancy.

"Dorian mentioned how challenging it can be to live such wildly different lifestyles. I admit, it was a shock to see the Duke of Holland chopping wood and baking bread, when I last visited," he commented, breaking the silence.

"I've always admired the way they've made their own happiness, even if it isn't conventional. This house has witnessed so much love. You can feel it," Constance said.

She was right. Some indefinable thing made this a home, rather than a house.

The back door off the kitchen remained locked tight, and the floor was dry. Weather hadn't seeped into the house there, either. Good.

The primary bedchamber held a large bed that immediately inspired all sorts of ideas, so Oliver quickly backed away.

The room he usually stayed in for visits was oddly bare. Frowning, Oliver went to the second guest room. That too stood empty, although the walls now showcased a mural, suggesting this would be Nathaniel's bedchamber.

What had happened to the guest beds?

Still pondering that question, he returned to the main room, now noticeably warmer thanks to the fire crackling in the grate. "Did Caro mention she planned to make over the guest rooms?"

Constance looked over her shoulder as she hung her cloak on a peg by the door. "No. They hired a local artist to paint Nate's room, but I don't recall anything about the other bedroom. Why?"

"If they do abandon us here, there's only one bed."

Her laughter rang out, echoing off the exposed timbers of the ceiling.

Confusion prevented him from joining her. "Why is that amusing?"

Still giggling, she explained, "Stranding the couple in a cottage or inn with only one bed is a tried-and-true way to force characters together in romantic novels." Still chuckling, she shook her head. "If there were a way for Caro to expose us to a rain shower first, I'm certain she'd have done so."

Now he was truly baffled. "What does catching our death in the cold have to do with anything?"

Constance's eyes sparkled. "Because we'd have to remove our clothing to get warm and dry. Obviously."

"Of all the days for the damned rain to stay away, it had to pick today," he grumbled good-naturedly.

As if they truly were in a play, someone knocked on the door.

"Right on cue?" he asked.

Constance stifled a laugh when they found a footman wearing the Holland livery on the step. "Pardon the interruption, your lordship. The duke and duchess have stopped for the day but send these for you and Miss Martin."

Refusing to meet Constance's eyes, lest he laugh and confuse the poor servant, Oliver took the folded paper and passed along a small packet wrapped in string with her name on it.

Caro isn't feeling well, so we've stopped at Betsy's home. Your servants will find comfortable lodging in the barn, with ample supplies. If you and Connie need anything, our neighbors will happily help. There should be enough food in the pantry to survive overnight.

We plan to be there by late morning tomorrow.

Love is worth seizing, my friend.

-D.

Handing the note to her, he addressed the footman. "Thank you. Will you be returning to them, or bedding down here with my staff?"

"Plenty of hours of daylight left, so I'll make my way back and be on hand for His Grace. Unless you require my presence, of course."

"I'm sure we'll be fine. But thank you."

The servant nodded. "Will there be a reply?"

Oliver glanced at Constance, who shook her head. "Nothing that should be put into writing, no. I hope the duchess feels better by tomorrow," he said.

As soon as the door closed behind the footman, he turned to her.

She clasped her hands behind her back, pushing her breasts against the neckline of her gown as she swayed playfully from side to side. "Feel free to tell me I was right anytime the urge strikes you."

Oliver leaned against the door and tried not to eye her like a hungry wolf. "You were right. Now, it seems we're all alone in this cozy little cottage in the middle of nowhere."

Her eyes widened comically. "With only one bed! If I'm not careful, I might let my base urges overwhelm decorum. We must find something to do with ourselves to pass the time."

Desire thrummed through him, thick and insistent even as Oliver grinned at her playacting. "You mean, to distract ourselves from temptation? Is this when I'm supposed to nobly offer to sleep on the floor so you may have the bed?"

The undulation of her hips stole his attention as she stepped closer. "I couldn't possibly sleep in that big bed all by myself, knowing you were on the cold stone floor." One of her hands covered his thundering heart. "I'm sure I can trust you to not take advantage of me." Constance grinned cheekily up at him.

"Ah, but can you be trusted to not take advantage of me?" he asked. If she took another step toward him, she'd feel exactly how her playful teasing affected him.

"I'm afraid I may not be able to help myself," Constance murmured, kissing the corner of his mouth.

"Thank fuck for that," he growled and wrapped her in his arms.

Chapter Twenty-Three

~~Drive him mad~~
~~Regret nothing~~

The few times she'd been with Walter, Constance had loved the thrill of skulking about with a man. The possibility of her parents catching her in a lie, or Walter's landlady opening her door and finding them sneaking down the hall to his flat, had sent her pulse racing. However, when it came down to the act itself, she'd struggled to rein in her mind.

Not that Walter noticed. Sure, it had felt nice. If it didn't make a body sing in such a way, sexual intercourse would likely have gone out of style eons ago, and the human race would be extinct. Even as her body enjoyed the experience, Constance's mind wandered. For example, there were fuzzy memories of him on top of her, but she had a vivid recollection of the water stain on his ceiling that looked exactly like the outline of a duck.

Yet something magical happened when Oliver kissed her. Those random thoughts, reminders of things she needed to write down, but would ultimately forget—all of it disappeared, like a snuffed candle. Instead, images of things she wanted to do with him flooded her brain, The smell, sound, taste, and feel of him engulfed the rest of her.

But then Oliver pulled back and narrowed his eyes comically. "What was in the package from your cousin?"

Grinning, she pulled the two items from her pocket. There'd been no note, not that she needed one. A sea sponge with a length of thread attached, and a small vial of vinegar. At his look of confusion, she explained. "Pregnancy prevention. Since she assumed you wouldn't have reason to carry a French letter on your person."

Constance made a mental note to thank Caro the next time she saw her. And that was a reminder she knew she wouldn't forget. No writing it on her list needed.

Oliver paled. "Damn, I hadn't considered that."

Of course he hadn't. After all, he'd abstained for this long. Fearing by-blows was simply not within his sphere of experience.

"Now, didn't I promise to show you how to give me pleasure?"

His smile bordered on feral. "I believe the exact promise was teaching me how to make you beg and scream my name."

Under her skirts, slick heat dampened her inner thighs. "First step." She nipped the hard point of his chin, breathing in the sharp citrus scent of his cologne, and pressed her body against his. "Strip. Let me see you." One hand brushed against the hardness tenting his breeches.

Urgent noises escaped his throat as he threw his coat to the floor, followed by his cravat. During the spare seconds it took for Oliver to whip the linen shirt over his head, he acted as if it caused physical pain to not touch her.

But oh, the glorious relief of having all that skin at her fingertips. Constance nearly purred at the feel of him. Smooth and warm, with the occasional abrasion of wiry hair interrupting the gentle curves of muscle and bone. Oliver's build was lean like a greyhound, all tightly coiled power.

When her fingers traced a line low across his belly, dipping into the waistband of his breeches, the muscles in his abdomen rippled in her wake.

Oliver gasped and wrapped his fingers around her wrist. "I was not exaggerating when I warned I'd finish quickly. I'd rather not do so inside my clothing."

Fevered ideas of ways to explore him, of teaching him how to please her, turned Connie's core molten. She'd never thought of a man finding his pleasure as an exceptionally arousing image. Given how that confession affected her pulse, the idea of Oliver in the throes of passion was enough to make her lightheaded.

"We should accept that you'll finish quickly this first time. As long as we both know that, there's no embarrassment. I'm feeling rather smug that a brush of my fingertips is enough to make you warn me." Constance tugged her hand free and backed away. "Do you think watching me will have the same effect as my touch?"

The way his chest heaved with each labored inhale was its own answer. That breathing stopped altogether when she stepped out of her gown, then unfastened her short stays.

"Oliver, if I take off my chemise and you faint from lack of air, I will tease you about it *forever*. Do I make myself clear?"

His gasp for air sounded especially loud and they both laughed. With quick, clumsy movements, he braced himself on the door and attempted to remove his boots, muttering curses when the impressive tent of his erection got in his way as he bent.

Knowing Oliver wanted her as desperately as she wanted him gave her a euphoric feeling. When he finally approached her, wearing a look hot enough to set fire to her last piece of clothing, Constance was amazed her chemise didn't turn to a pile of ash.

Vague memories of shyly disrobing in front of Walter fel
like recollections from another woman. In the face of Oliver's
blatant admiration, Connie knew she could dance naked
before him and never doubt his appreciation for what he saw

And wasn't that a lovely thing. The realization felt both
deliciously scandalous and absolutely safe at the same time.

"May I?" he asked, fingering the ribbon securing the
neckline of her undergarment.

"You may do whatever you wish, milord." At his disgruntled expression, she dimpled up at him. "I mean, Oliver. You
may do whatever you wish, Oliver."

"I wish…to finally see you naked." He pulled the bow
loose, shifting the fabric until the chemise gaped over her
shoulders. "I've dreamed of you for weeks now, only to wake
hard and aching. That's when I knew I wanted you. You've
haunted my bedchamber every morning. I'm scared I'll wake
up and discover this is all an exceptionally vivid dream."

Constance pressed her thighs together, trying to alleviate
the building ache at her center. When he finally touched her
there, he'd find a slick and warm welcome. "Not a dream.
I'm curious about the accuracy of your imagination, though."
A shrug of her shoulders, and the thin chemise drifted to the
ground.

"Jesus holy fuck," he breathed.

She couldn't help it. Constance laughed, even though it
sent all her wobbly bits jiggling with abandon. Still giggling,
she looped her hands behind his neck and relished the hot
press of his torso against hers. "Do you know when I realized
I was attracted to you?"

Oliver's eyes were a bit unfocused as his hands explored
her back, then down her bum, not missing an inch. The noise
he made was vague, but agreeable, so Connie continued.

"When you swore at your kitten that first day in your

study. You were unwashed and exhausted, and your language was atrocious. That's when I knew I wanted you."

At that he gave her a disbelieving grin. "You're a strange woman, Constance Martin."

Yes, but I'm yours, for as long as I can keep you. "Then you've a predilection for strange women."

"I've a predilection for you. Specifically, your breasts."

She grinned, then gasped when he weighed them in his hands, squeezing her nipples between his fingers. Goodness, he gazed at her as if she were a dessert fit for the king's table.

"When we kissed that first time, I wanted to tear that seam on your gown the rest of the way and finally see these beauties. I didn't, because I knew if I did, that would be it for me. I'd have fucked you against those shelves and never come up for air. The hostess would have found us the next day with my cock inside you and my face buried in your cleavage."

A snort escaped and Constance slapped a palm over her mouth. "What a picture you paint."

"And now you know how I anticipate greeting the morning." He kissed her dimple, then the side of her neck.

More intimate than a waltz, they danced backward one step at a time toward the bedroom, murmuring and laughing softly.

The quilt was cool on her skin when he laid her down on the bed, then crawled over her, and rested on his elbows. Face abruptly serious after their playful banter, Oliver said, "I'm glad it's you."

Constance bit back declarations and promises of forever. Instead, she cradled his cheek and said, "There's no place I'd rather be." Tingles skittered up her arm when he kissed her palm and held her gaze. "Now please, for the love of all that's holy, take off your breeches. Otherwise, I won't be responsible for the condition of your clothing."

He laughed deep and low, and she felt it like a brush between her legs.

When a fully naked Oliver rejoined her on the bed, Constance reached for him with greedy arms.

"Swear to everything, if I wake up in the next few seconds, I'm going to tear my bed apart with my bare hands."

Constance pushed him onto his back, then nipped and licked down his neck, to his chest, and lower, where a line of dark hair pointed directly toward his stiff cock.

After a single lick from base to tip, he bellowed. When she continued, his raspy growl repeated, "Fuck, Connie. Oh God. Fuck."

Everything disappeared from her mind except Oliver. The taste of him. The delighted look he gave her when she slipped his wet length through her cleavage and held her breasts tightly around him, creating a channel with her flicking tongue at the end. He shouted her name when he finished quickly, as predicted.

The dazed way he watched her while he caught his breath made Connie feel like the most accomplished lover in history. Which, given the many erotic novels she'd read over the years, she might be, she thought smugly.

"Now, show me how to make you come. I'll be hard and ready again in short order," Oliver said.

Her belly quivered at his wickedly intent expression. "Let the lessons begin."

Oliver was a quick study, bless him. And lord, his mouth. Not just the way he tormented her nipples so deliciously, but the things he said. Filthy confessions of desire, murmured in her ears, affected her as thoroughly as his fingers slipping into the slickness between her thighs.

It was impossible not to feel a bit lost to arousal, when his words of praise filled the room, making her feel like a goddess. What began as gentle instructions of *there, like that*, and *please don't stop* grew into a full conversation as they explored one another.

"I love the taste of you. So sweet and hot. I'd feast all night, but I can't wait to sink my cock into you." The vibration of his words rumbled against her sensitive flesh as he held her thighs open to his kiss the way she'd shown him.

"Please, Oliver. I need you." Constance arched against his hands, nearly mindless after climaxing twice during their so-called lesson.

"Once more," he urged, before wrapping his lips around the stiff bundle of nerves at the top of her folds. "Come in my mouth one more time. Then I'll fill this gorgeous pussy until we both can't see straight."

"Greedy man." Her teasing dissolved into a moan. Within moments, another wave crested within her, leaving Constance gasping and boneless.

Then he was there, filling her vision. "Yes?" he asked simply.

Constance nodded, suddenly eager, when seconds earlier she'd have sworn on a mountain of holy objects she'd be incapable of movement for at least ten minutes.

They saw to the vinegar-soaked sponge, then Oliver was finally at her entrance. After taking so much time to learn what the other liked amidst their heated confessions of need and lust, letting him into her body felt nearly painfully intimate.

For the first time since she'd removed her clothing, Oliver didn't speak. Instead, he stared into her eyes, refusing to look away.

When his words returned, they were sweet. Still riddled with swear words but equally peppered with her name and declarations that she was everything he wanted. Perfect in every way. That he couldn't get enough of her. That nothing had ever felt better than her body, and he never wanted to leave.

Constance absorbed the praise, reveling in the beautiful way they fit together. Even though reality predicted that she'd live to regret it, she gave herself permission to believe every word. For the moment, they were true. And she refused to miss a single moment of loving him.

Oliver awoke the next morning with his cheek pressed against one of Constance's breasts, and frankly, waking up any other way would pale in comparison. For the rest of his life, this was how he wanted to greet the day. Soft, warm flesh that smelled of well-loved woman and honeysuckle, with a dark rosy nipple close enough to lick. "And it's not even Tuesday." His voice was gravelly with sleep.

"Hmm?"

Refusing to move from his spot, Oliver rolled his eyes up to meet hers. Sleepy deep blue, and so satisfied, it made him want to pound his chest like his mother's precious gorilla.

"Nothing. Just content." It didn't take a high intellect to know she'd tease him about his Tuesday limitations. However, she'd probably feel terribly smug to know thoughts of her had left his self-imposed restrictions in tatters. Fuck it, he'd tell her. "Actually, I said it wasn't Tuesday. I'm in bed with you, cuddling the most spectacular breasts in all of England, and it's not even Tuesday."

Her eyes closed on a wince. "Is this a conversation I'll need tea to understand?"

Grinning, he gave in to temptation and drew that fascinating nipple into his mouth, then released it with a pop, and stared in awe as the darker skin around the peak tightened. Breasts really were the most remarkable things. "I realized about a decade ago that if I was to remain a virgin, I'd need rules. Things I could and could not do to stay in control."

"Since, unlike women, you don't have the judgment of society as a whole to keep you in line." Curiosity cleared the sleep from her eyes, and he was thrilled to learn that her intellect woke up with her.

"Exactly. So, Tuesday mornings were my time to masturbate."

Light brown eyebrows, shot through with the same blond of her wild curls, met over the bridge of her nose. "Once a week? You masturbated once a week?"

"On Tuesdays, yes."

She blinked, and those delightful lips parted, although she didn't say anything for a long moment. "I'm not sure if I should applaud your self-control or use this as evidence that you're daft. I share a bed with my cousin, and before that, two cousins, and before *that*, my sister. And I still manage to masturbate more often than once a week."

His cock, which had been hard as a pike since the moment he awoke, jerked against the sheet. "I'm adding watching you masturbate to the list of things I want to experience. If you're comfortable with the idea, of course."

Constance stretched her arms overhead, arching her back and shifting her soft breasts beneath his cheek. "I believe that could be arranged." She rolled to face him, which led to a second or two of pouting on his part when his pillows moved.

Amusement lit her face. Seeing her sleepy, mussed, and enjoying him—even though he wasn't doing anything special—struck him as so terribly *right*, he forgot to breathe for a moment. "Do you have any idea how beautiful you are?"

Gold-tipped lashes fluttered closed, hiding her expressive eyes from him. Hiding her. And that wouldn't do. Oliver sank one hand into her curls and kissed her the way he'd dreamt of kissing her every morning. Hard and possessive. Within seconds, eager hands clutched at him, as demanding of him as he was toward her. Constance murmured a gasped *please* between kisses, before he slid deep.

The noises she made, her restless movements as they urged one another closer to that peak, the delicious extravagance of her soft curves—it was so uniquely Constance. Oliver couldn't imagine wanting someone else. It didn't matter that a few months ago he hadn't been ready to love her. Hell, a month ago he'd been determined to keep this gnawing need contained to fantasies.

To have her now, beneath him, welcoming him between lush thighs, was more than he'd ever expected to have. Those feelings he'd been collecting, suppressing, refusing to examine, burst from their tidy little mental boxes. "I love you. I've never loved anyone before, but I love you, Connie."

Her eyes closed and her mouth opened around a cry of pleasure. Oliver couldn't resist sucking that sensitive place where her neck met her shoulder. As she shuddered and squeezed him tight, he kept his relentless pace, chasing his own orgasm.

It wasn't until later, when they'd dressed and welcomed Dorian and Caro home, that Oliver realized she hadn't said she loved him too.

Chapter Twenty-Four

~

Talk to Caro about Martin House

He was a dunderhead of the first order. Oliver tended to make a decision, then stick to it, no matter what. Sometimes because his initial choice was the correct one, and sometimes out of sheer stubbornness. Before now, he hadn't encountered many moments of regret regarding his lack of experience in love.

This, however, was one of those times. Would a man who'd fallen in and out of love with multiple partners recognize the ideal time to confess his love to a woman? Because clearly, he'd fumbled that spectacularly. Oliver made a huff of disgust at the paper on his lap desk, when another bump in the road made the letters scrawl over the page. Not that he was writing the right words anyway.

After visiting the property they'd come to see, today's travel back to London mirrored yesterday's initial caravan. Dorian, Caro, little Nate, and Constance were in one carriage, and he followed in the other. Had he expected Constance to join him today, and had he been anticipating more time with her on the road? Yes. Unequivocally yes. To his surprise, she'd joined her cousin outside the cottage this morning, leaving him wondering where things had gone wrong.

Damn it all, but he just didn't have the right words. Everything he wanted to write sounded needy, or insecure, or too gruff, or cold and unfeeling. Ideally, he'd love to make this missive as simple as possible, with a short list of options for answers, thus removing all those pesky emotions from the situation.

Do you love me too?
A) Yes, marry me!
B) Maybe. Perhaps more sex will provide clarity.
C) No. You're a disappointment as a lover. Go to hell.

She'd chosen to not ride with him back to Town, after sharing the best night and morning of his life. Not knowing what to do about it was tearing him up.

Slipping the paper into the lap desk, he slammed the lid closed and tossed the whole thing onto the seat beside him. Could he ask for clarification at the inn, when they stopped to change horses? If he couldn't find a private moment with her, was he doomed to stew and fidget all the way to London? Either way, he needed to learn what he'd done wrong, so he could castigate himself accurately for the rest of his bloody life. Was he expected to read into her decision to ride with Caro, and draw a conclusion from that?

Unfortunately, if the only data available was someone not saying "I love you" back, followed by them choosing alternative transportation home, the obvious answer didn't give him much hope. But—and the enormity of that *but* couldn't be overstated—this was *her*.

A rueful smile crooked his lips when he considered how drastically Constance's reasoning for this morning might differ from his. If he could somehow walk through that woman's brain, he imagined it would resemble a cluttered office, packed with haphazard stacks of interesting facts from random books and piles of unexpectedly practical skills. All interspersed with half-finished artwork and topped with a rock she'd kept because it resembled a frog. And the entire office would be run by seven squirrels and three mice subsisting on nothing but tea and iced lemon biscuits.

Oliver's real-life workspace, on the other hand, was orderly and laid out so precisely that Althea successfully ruffled his peace by shifting items to the left by four inches.

They were vastly different people, and that was one reason he loved her. However, those differences meant that anything related to Constance Martin would be, by default, entirely new territory for him—which made him indecisive. Because that was the effect chaos had on the world. Indecision, and wandering about scratching one's head, muttering "How did *that* get there?"

Like now, when he'd laid his heart at her feet, only to have it ignored, and he didn't know what to do.

His father would throw up his hands, mutter about fickle women, then stomp off and get drunk. Obviously, Oliver wasn't going to do that—although he wasn't ruling out a large whisky at the end of the day. If his mother were here, she'd urge him to ask for answers. After all, he'd fallen in love with Constance, baffling as she often was, for good reason. This wouldn't be the last time she left him wondering which direction was up.

Thankfully, buildings flashed by the window, more frequently by the second. Which meant they'd stop at the inn soon. Calm settled over Oliver, knowing he'd speak with her in a few minutes.

When the carriages rolled into the inn yard, Oliver hopped down before a footman could reach his door, then waved away the Hollands' servant and opened their door

himself. Dorian's surprise turned into a smirk when he saw
Oliver.

"My love, why don't we go inside and see if there are any
private dining rooms available. I believe Oliver wants a few
moments with Connie." The duke hefted Nate's traveling
basket and climbed down.

Caro sent Oliver an encouraging smile when he offered a
steadying hand from the carriage.

"Thank you. We'll join you shortly," he murmured, then
turned toward the one person remaining. "Constance, I need
a word."

Her obvious surprise at his request baffled him, but
she took his hand and didn't drop it when she reached the
ground.

"Not to be indelicate, but do you need to use the facilities,
or can you walk with me a while?" he asked. "Since we left
the cottage, I've been wallowing in questions only you can
answer. I'm tired of my thoughts and need to hear yours."

Her gaze darted toward the inn. "I do need to... but perhaps I could ride in your carriage the rest of the way to London? We'll discuss whatever's on your mind, then."

Oliver gave a nod, content with her assurance that they'd
speak soon. "Of course."

That relief sustained him through the hour they spent
in a private dining room at the inn. By the time he helped
her into his carriage, then waved off Dorian's, he was only
slightly twitchy with impatience.

When the coachman told the horses to "drive on," Oliver
spoke, as if the words were a breath he'd been holding. "I
don't know what to do, or what to think. All of this is new,
and I'm afraid I've already somehow made a hash of things.
Whatever it is, I need you to tell me, so I can fix it."

"Oliver... what are you talking about?" He had to give

her credit; she appeared calm and collected, until you noticed the way her fingers fussed with the edge of her cloak.

"I told you I love you, then you rode in the other carriage. I don't know what that means."

Her laugh sounded forced, and he thought he might vomit, then die from humiliation.

"Men say things in the heat of the moment. Don't think I'll hold you to that declaration."

Oh God, he'd read all this correctly, hadn't he? She didn't return his regard, and she regretted what they'd done. Oliver leaned back against the seat, scrambling for the cool reserve he'd clung to for so many years. That would be his only defense against whatever came next.

"I rode with Caro because I needed to ask her about partnering with me and Hattie at the shop. I'd planned to speak with her about it while you and Dorian looked at that house, but we spent the time visiting Betsy. Given the choice between begging my cousin to go into business with me, and playing with my niece, Georgia will win every time. Besides, this way, Dorian joined the conversation as well."

That...wasn't what he expected. Oliver blinked and allowed the defensive reserve he'd erected to slip. "The bookshop?"

"My parents want to retire. It's been a journey for me to accept that I can't run Martin House on my own. However, with Hattie willing to share the work, and Caro's influence and purse strings, we'll make a compelling argument toward convincing my parents the shop will be secure in our hands."

Oliver rubbed a palm over his hair. As suspected, everything happening inside her brain was beyond what he'd considered. "I would like to hear more about the future of the shop, and your role in that. Before that, might we please address the first thing you said? About not believing my feelings are honest?"

Hang it, he needed to touch her. Oliver transferred to her bench and took her hand. When she interlaced her fingers to his, something inside him calmed.

"Oliver, our lovemaking was…magical. I'd even call it combustible. But it would be easy to confuse your first orgasm at someone else's hand—or other body part—with abiding devotion," she explained patiently.

"I agree with all of that." She stiffened beside him and he wanted to growl in frustration. "Except I knew I loved you when you fell asleep on my lap in my study. If I told you too soon, I'm sorry. All of this is new to me. I've never been in love before, or had a relationship I actually wanted. I'll make mistakes, but I promise you can trust me."

Watching belief dawn across her face was a beautiful thing. Constance whispered, "You already knew you loved me? So, you were in earnest?"

"Of course I did. And then I panicked when you didn't respond."

Quick as a blink, she shifted from soft and wondering, to argumentative. Constance threw one hand in the air and huffed, "Oliver, you were literally inside of me, on the verge of an orgasm. Everyone knows to not believe anything a man says under those circumstances."

His mouth covered hers in a hard kiss designed to take her by surprise, then released her. "Let me make one thing clear," he growled. "When I say I love you, I mean it. It doesn't matter where we are, or what is happening around us. If I'm fucking you, or yelling and angry as a wet cat, or talking in my sleep, I still love you. I adore every maddening inch of you, in any circumstance."

She kissed him this time, and he instantly turned greedy

for more. After a morning spent wondering if he'd ever taste her again, desperation lurked too close to the surface to control himself. It was that deep primal instinct only she brought out that had him gathering her skirt toward her hips, then urging her to straddle him.

Within seconds, Constance unbuttoned his breeches, and he was home. His shout of relief was muffled against her chest, and he could die happily, just like that. "God, I love you," he groaned.

Oliver lifted his gaze to hold hers, then sank his fingers into her hair. "You are everything I want. Do you believe me?"

Constance nodded, biting her lower lip as her eyes fluttered closed.

"Open your eyes. Tell me. I need to hear it." One hand clutched her hip, pinning her on his cock.

"I believe you," she gasped. Oliver canted his pelvis to hit a spot within her heat that had made her scream the night before. "I love you too."

The need to hear more fought with his desire to feel her unravel around him. "Tell me," he asked again.

"I love you. I crave you. Oh, God, keep doing that."

The noises she made when he did as requested made his balls tighten.

Pressing their faces close, she panted above him and held herself still, while he kept flexing to hit that same place deep inside over and over. "I love how much you care about everyone around you. I still don't understand the myriad things you say prevent us from being together, but you can explain when you're not doing—*God, that.*"

"Later. I'll explain later." And he kept doing *that*.

Constance rocked on him in small shifts that made his eyes roll back in his head. But he couldn't black out from pleasure, or dive into oblivion quite yet, because he'd asked his girl to talk, and she was doing exactly that, soothing insecurities while making him mad with desire.

"I love that you're feral, with a filthy mouth underneath all that control."

"Do you?" He moved aside her bodice until one gorgeous breast plumped over the top so Oliver could worship it the way it deserved. Flutters began massaging his cock. She was close.

"Every time I see you, I get wet," Constance confessed, bringing his peak closer with the admission.

He released her nipple with a pop, then bit her bottom lip. "Now I'm going to wonder if you're slick every time we meet. Tell me," he growled, feeling his orgasm nearing. "What gets wet for me? What do you call it? Your pussy?" A thrust. "Cunt?" Another thrust, and her walls clenched in earnest around him.

"Whatever we call it, it's yours," she managed before flinging her head back and riding out her pleasure.

It killed him to do it, but Oliver withdrew right before he spilled inside her.

They cuddled with her on his lap, just as they had in his study. Unlike that day, Connie's body felt loose from their lovemaking, and Oliver looked deliciously rumpled.

His hand caressed her leg in lazy strokes. The sensation was so lovely, sleep pulled at her limbs. If she gave in, she'd miss this precious time. So she asked, "Can you explain the weather and the tenants? I want to understand."

And he did. He told her about the plans he'd made to build a canal on his ancestral property that would help not only his estate, but also the surrounding area. Except, the land was part of Althea's dowry. The vibration of his voice rumbled against her body as he laid out how he'd considered dowering Althea himself but couldn't because of the expense involved with sourcing food in an increasingly dire situation. By the time he finished, her heart ached for all the worries he carried.

"I'm so sorry," she said.

"As it stands, it might be years before the estates recover. When we get home, I'm hoping to have letters from a few of my managers waiting for me. If everything works out, I'd like to present Althea with the plan I've devised before sharing the details with anyone else."

Since it was Althea's future at stake, it seemed right that she learn the intricacies first. Especially if it meant only waiting a few days more, Connie would be patient.

She nodded. "After the engagement ends, what do you want your future to be like?"

He tightened his arms around her. "This. I want this, and to know everyone depending on me is fed and safe. The rest is open for discussion. What do you imagine our future looking like?"

Our future. Hope forced a crack in yesterday's conviction to love him well, but only for a short time. "With Caro and Dorian becoming partners in the shop, we should be able to convince my parents to leave us Martin House. Caro offered to buy it outright if they need the funds to retire. While we will all be equal partners, the day-to-day operations would fall to me and Hattie."

"May I ask if there'll be time for us, when you take on running the business?"

A hesitant note in the question made her reach up and kiss the corner of his mouth. "There will always be time for you, Oliver." His lips relaxed somewhat. "I don't want a boring life, you see. Being busy doesn't bother me."

"What else do you want? Do you imagine marrying one day? Children?"

"If that's where life takes me, then yes. But anyone in my neighborhood will tell you I've already run from one wedding. I don't know if I'd want to plan another."

"What about a mad dash for the border in the middle of the night, rather than a church and wedding breakfast? That's the opposite of boring."

She grinned. "You have the right idea."

"What happened the first time? When you ran away."

How strange to think they'd said I love you, before explaining these important points of their lives. The things he'd dealt with to free himself of the betrothal. Her reasons for ending her engagement at the last possible second.

Constance sank deeper against his chest. "Walter is a cloth merchant. At first, he seemed perfect in every way, which should have been my first clue that I wasn't seeing him clearly." Oliver's chuckle made her smile. "The courtship was short, and I ran headlong into planning the wedding. Our real problems began when he was traveling to the coast to meet with suppliers and said he might not return in time for the wedding."

"When you say suppliers, you mean…"

"Smugglers, yes. Not the kind of delivery you can reschedule. I suggested we change the church date, then turn his trip into a sort of wedding trip. We fought. He wasn't fair or kind when we argued."

His arms tensed into iron bands, until Constance ran a soothing hand down his chest. "He didn't lay a hand on me. You needn't hurt the man in my defense, Oliver."

A soft kiss landed on her head. "Go on, then."

"What killed the relationship was realizing he never intended for me to join him on those adventures. He expected me to be home, doing wifely things, like making his meals, and birthing his babies, while he went off to court danger and consort with ruffians. I tried to resign myself to that. It's what women do, after all. In the end, I couldn't go through with it. Hattie and Caro hustled me out of that church and we ran."

Silence fell between them. For a few moments, there was only the rattle of coach wheels, thunder of hooves, jingling horse harnesses, and his heart thumping steadily at her ear.

"I hate that you've had to make difficult decisions. But I'm intensely grateful that this Walter character is an arse."

She laughed, and Oliver dipped his head for a lingering kiss.

Chapter Twenty-Five

If at first you don't succeed, escalate the situation

Not only were there letters from two estates waiting when he returned home, but a notice from Gerard Bellmore, his solicitor. Althea's deed and trust had been recorded and filed. Oliver couldn't stop smiling.

Prince rubbed against his hand, insisting on more pets to make up for Oliver's absence. One hand scratched the cat's ears while the other dashed off a summons to Mr. Wellsley.

Roberts knocked on the study door. "Milord, Mr. Wellsley is here. He says the matter is urgent."

"Perfect. Send him in." Oliver slapped the lid of his silver inkwell closed, and it gave a satisfying *thwap*. Standing, he stretched to loosen the aches from spending so long in a carriage. Other muscles he hadn't known he possessed made themselves known, but the ways he and Constance had earned each twinge and pang left him feeling smug as hell.

Franklin Wellsley's face was set in grim lines when he entered a moment later.

Oliver rounded his desk. "What's wrong?"

"I'm not sure what to do. I couldn't think of anywhere else to go."

Oliver gestured toward the chairs and chaise near the

fireplace. "Take a seat. We can figure it out together. I just finished writing you to ask for a meeting, so your timing is excellent."

Mr. Wellsley's shoulders relaxed. Giving his guest time to gather his thoughts, Oliver knelt by the fire and added another log, then poked at the embers until flames once again leapt merrily in the grate.

"Now. Tell me what's happened."

"Sir William and Lady Thompson secured a time at the church for next week. According to gossip, Miss Braithmore cried off from Lord Landry. Althea is desperate. I'm hoping you have news about your idea."

Oliver grimaced. A week? Finalizing those papers had happened at the last minute. They didn't have long to figure out how exactly he and Althea would miss that wedding date. "Then it's best we decide on our next steps. A desperate Althea could be ruinous."

Mr. Wellsley visibly gulped. "Interesting word choice. She's determined to ruin herself publicly and force her father to let us wed."

"Which leaves her bearing the brunt of the scandal. How do you feel about that idea?" Letting Althea seem like a jilt didn't appeal to him.

"I love her. I'll marry her under any circumstances. I worry that this throws too much mud on her. She might regret that later." The younger man looked pained. "At the same time, so much of her anger stems from how she's been controlled, with no choices."

A glow grew in Oliver's chest the longer he listened. Mr. Wellsley truly did love and respect Althea. "Everyone might assume you were forced to marry because of the scandal, rather than out of genuine affection."

"We'd know the truth. That's what matters."

"All right. Before you two decide what you'll do, there's a second option. You're familiar with the idea of a separate estate trust in marriage contracts?"

Mr. Wellsley nodded. "Of course. Pin money, or family wealth set aside for a woman's children."

"I convinced Sir William to deed Althea a tract of land he'd intended as part of her dowry. That land is now in a trust. I'm currently named as the trustee, but when she marries, her spouse becomes the trustee. The documents don't specifically name her husband, so legally, it can be you. Everything is filed with the government and official. Sir William can't take it back."

Oliver returned to his desk and gathered the letter from the solicitor, his copy of the trust, a map of Birchwood Court's surrounding area, and the engineering plans. Althea's determination to cause chaos in his life seemed to have truly died, because each item was where he'd left it.

From now on, the title of Head Chaos Coordinator belonged to Constance. With a spring in his step, he brought the stack to Wellsley. "The land includes a river dividing my estate from the Thompsons'. I intended to turn the river into a canal."

Unrolling the paper on the low table between them, Oliver pointed at various areas of interest on the map. "This orchard is large enough to produce goods for a family, with a decent leftover crop to sell at market. Or you could clear it and build an office or shelter for the canal workers. There's space for a house here—nothing too grand, but a nice-size cottage. However, it's on the Thompsons' side of the river." They exchanged a grimace. "A canal would connect our farmers and artisans with larger markets to the east and south."

Wellsley leaned in and examined the papers. "I can't

imagine how much building an undertaking of this size will cost."

Oliver nodded. "With this year's harvest looking so grim, the canal system is not an immediate solution. I'd like to partner with you both on this venture. Even still, we will need investors, and that could take years. In the meantime, I'm prepared to offer you a position working with a land steward at my property in Cornwall. You would have a salary, a cottage on the estate, and an escape from the scandal all this will cause. Also, Dorcas lives nearby."

A frown crossed Wellsley's face. "That sounds wonderful. But even with her sister nearby, will Althea be happy in Cornwall?"

That his first concern was for her happiness confirmed she'd be well loved. Oliver remembered a much younger Althea running barefoot through the estates, climbing trees, and playing in the dirt. Once upon a time, she'd loved the country and cried when they went to London. Even after she could take part in the Season, she complained about missing rural life.

In short, beneath her polished exterior, Althea Thompson was a bit of a hoyden.

"I think so, but don't take my word for it. Ask her. Since Sir William is a horse's arse, I doubt he's told her about any of this. Would you like to do the honors? Take the papers to her so she can examine them for herself. With this in place, she doesn't need to resort to a publicly compromising situation."

Wellsley grinned. "I don't know how I can ever repay you. This is more than I thought possible."

"Just be kind to my childhood friend. Ensure she laughs every day."

"You have my word as a gentleman," Wellsley promised.

That should have been the end of it. Althea could have

eloped to Scotland, then moved on to Cornwall. Except, she didn't.

I should know better than try to predict anything with these women. If Constance was Head Chaos Coordinator, Althea could be Assistant Chaos Instigator, because she stormed into his study an hour later, waving the sheaf of papers. An amused Wellsley followed at her heels. "Oliver, you wonderful man!"

At least she liked him again, Oliver thought when she hugged him.

Althea pulled back with a serious expression. "I still want to cause a fuss and compromise myself."

Oliver's gaze went heavenward. "Why, for the love of God, when you have a perfectly reasonable, logical, and legally sound way to quietly elope?"

Wellsley wrapped an arm around her shoulders. "You might think me mad, but I'm inclined to agree with the idea." Seeing Oliver's face, he urged, "Hear her out."

"If we make our attachment public, Father can't make up his own version of events. After the way he's treated us, don't you want everyone to see what he's really like? Think about it. Even if Franklin and I slink off into the night, you're still here, facing the scandal. That isn't fair to you. Creating a spectacle lets us have some control over what people say. Besides, for the last three years, I've been a pawn in everyone else's game. I want to control the way this ends. Father doesn't get his precious title, and Mother doesn't get her society wedding."

They were valid points, much as it pained him to admit it. But two glaring problems needed addressing. "I don't want you taking on the majority of blame, Althea. Also, when we eventually build this project *literally right beside* your father's land, if his temper hasn't cooled, he will be unbearable."

Althea shrugged. "He'll always be an arse. If he's still angry, I'll take delight in inflicting the mess and noise of construction on him. Becoming wildly successful will be even sweeter."

Oliver considered her, feeling his smile grow. "Have I ever told you what an interesting woman you've grown to be?" Arguing with Althea was as successful as pissing into the wind, so he threw up his hands in defeat. "Fine. You two put on a show. Serve Sir William a generous helping of consequences. If we can't avoid a scandal, we might as well use it to your advantage. However, I can't in good conscience let people frame you as a jilt. If you're willing to share your moment of victory, I have a request."

By the time they left, his good mood was back in force. For once, he and Althea were not only intent on the same objective, but also in agreement about how to go about it.

Which meant he needed to visit Lord Bixby, London's most notorious purveyor of personal information. If the society sharks wanted to swarm at the scent of blood in the water, Oliver would need a shark of his own.

Lord Bixby lived in a tidy, if sparsely decorated townhome in a genteel area of London. A housekeeper opened the door at Oliver's knock, then escorted him through a warren of hallways and identical doors, keys jangling from the chatelaine at her waist.

Gold-shot burgundy silk covering the walls had faded with time. Darker squares and rectangles showed where art had once hung. The Bixby barony came with a mountain of accumulated debt that grew as the family mausoleum filled.

The current baron had thus far managed to tread water

and stay afloat, but he'd made his motives clear to anyone who cared to pay attention. Lord Bixby had younger sisters, and the man was determined to see them married. Not only well, but happily. Not an easy feat when their dowries were pitifully small.

Essentially, Bixby bartered information for entrée to the best society events.

"His lordship will be with you shortly," the housekeeper said.

"Thank you." Oliver sent her a respectful bow.

Lord Bixby didn't keep him waiting. "Southwyn. This is a surprise." His tone offered no clues as to whether he considered the surprise a happy one. He likely didn't know if Oliver calling for the first time ever was a reason to celebrate, or duck and cover.

"Thank you for seeing me, Lord Bixby. May I beg a few minutes of your time?"

His host motioned to a sofa, upholstered in faded blue damask. Like almost everything else in the house, the furniture was old, but of good quality.

Oliver clasped his hands together until his knuckles shone white. So much depended on this. If Constance wasn't happy with what he planned, he'd be a laughingstock. But asking her about it would ruin the surprise, and he wanted to give her what she wanted—the opposite of a boring life.

"Something is going to happen. Everyone in the ton will be talking about it. That's deliberate. While I understand what the people involved intend to gain from the chatter, I want to lessen the negative impact on them."

Bixby's eyes gleamed. "Well, well, well. You come bearing gifts, don't you, Lord Southwyn? May I ask what you expect in exchange for this information?"

"Your help in guiding the conversation, as it were. I give

you two pieces of information. The ton will pick apart one like vultures. The other, only you will know. I need you to spread that story far and wide. Offer something juicier, so to speak."

Lord Bixby crossed his legs in a graceful movement that struck Oliver as nearly theatrical. "So, I'll receive two nuggets of information—one of which is an exclusive morsel—and all I have to do is talk about it? You may not fully understand the concept of bargaining, milord." An amused smirk made him appear younger than usual.

"How so?"

"Usually, you give me something in exchange for something else. It sounds like, in this instance, I get everything."

Oliver smiled, even though his heart galloped at a breakneck pace. This whole madcap plan fell outside his realm of experience. But that was the point. Wasn't this what heroes in romantic novels did? He'd read a few of Blanche Clementine, or rather Caro's, books. The hero made a public, grand gesture before they lived happily ever after.

Still, it wasn't a comfortable thing. Decades spent walking that narrow road of honor and unobjectionable behavior made putting his heart on his sleeve difficult. Constance was well beyond what society consider an appropriate countess. Despite that, Oliver had no doubt she'd be perfect for the role. She cared. She was adaptable, intelligent, and already had the Duke and Duchess of Holland in her corner.

What scared him was not knowing if she'd think this grand gesture came too soon. He wasn't the impulsive sort. But she was, and he hoped she'd see his heart in this, as well as welcome the chance to lessen Althea's scandal. Oliver's gut told him she'd think it a great romp and a wonderful story to tell their children one day. The tension in his neck eased, imagining the way she'd eventually spin the tale.

"Your cooperation in spreading the counter-story is my only request. No need to suppress the other gossip. Merely add to it. Are we in agreement?"

The baron chuckled. "I see no reason we wouldn't be."

Oliver nodded, feeling resolute. Down in the depths of hell, he hoped his father wailed over Oliver throwing everything at the feet of one woman. And his mother? She'd applaud how fiercely he loved Constance.

"Right, then. Day after tomorrow, the Forsyths will host their annual soiree. During that evening, Miss Althea Thompson will be compromised by someone who is decidedly not me."

Bixby's eyebrows lifted to nearly meet his hairline.

No going back now. "When that happens, I need you to counter the story with the rest of the truth. No only do I wish them well, but I'm in love with a bookseller and intend to elope with her that same night."

Bixby laughed aloud. "Is there something in the brandy you're sharing with Holland? You've both lost your heads over booksellers."

"When you meet my new countess, you'll understand. She's sunshine and chaos, and leaves smiles in her wake."

"Jesus, you are a goner, aren't you?"

Openly talking about marrying Constance was a unique kind of relief. "Yes, I am. Now let's hope she'll agree to have me."

A knock sounded at the door, and Bixby called for them to enter. A maid appeared, pushing a cart bearing a teapot and a small decanter. Equipped for every eventuality.

His host thanked the maid, then poured a finger of amber liquid into two glasses.

"In that case, let's drink to your upcoming nuptials." Lord Bixby handed Oliver a tumbler, then raised his own. "May you and your bookseller enjoy many years of happiness. And may Miss Thompson find love elsewhere."

Oliver grinned. "I'll drink to that."

Despite the run-down air of the man's house, his brandy was exceptionally smooth as it rolled down Oliver's throat, leaving a mellow trail of heat in its wake.

Chapter Twenty-Six

*If you're silly enough to fall in love,
don't forget your friends*

Constance nibbled at a dry cuticle, then forced herself to stop and return to work. Creating a new display would keep her hands busy. And lord knew she needed busy. Nervous energy hummed under her skin.

The prior evening, the cousins and Dorian sat down with her parents to discuss the future of Martin House. Owen and Mary listened intently and asked seemingly endless questions. After two hours, everyone was in agreement.

Dorian and Caro would purchase the store once Connie's parents were ready to live closer to Betsy. The cousins decided they'd equally share ownership of the shop, as well as the responsibility for major decisions. Since Caro's role as Blanche Clementine, mother, and Duchess of Holland took a considerable amount of her time, they'd add a staff member to take over the bookkeeping.

Connie's relief at that particular item in the discussion had been acute.

At her parents' insistence, everyone agreed to one stipulation. If Hattie or Connie chose to move on at any point in the future, they'd hire someone to take their place in the day-to-day running of things, without risking their share of ownership. Owen didn't want anyone to feel trapped. Regardless, Martin House stayed in the family and would be there for the next generation.

Which meant Constance never needed to leave the safety of her home. She couldn't have dreamed of a better outcome, yet her happiness lacked something. Oliver hadn't been there to celebrate with her, and she'd felt the loss deeply.

Which was ridiculous. After all, they'd only declared their feelings days before. Her heart, however, insisted this achievement—becoming a business-owner-to-be—was one she needed to share with him.

Except, she hadn't heard from him since their return from Kent. Last night, unable to sleep, she'd written a long missive, sharing the details of the meeting and telling him how much she wished he'd been there. However, Oliver sent no reply to her life-changing news, and waiting for one grated on her last nerve.

Waiting was the worst thing in the world and you couldn't convince Connie otherwise.

It took a while to gather the books for a display, but once she had, things came together quickly. The store offered a variety of titles explaining the finer points of skills like spinning wool, knitting, and needlepoint. Thanks to her collection of abandoned hobbies, she had plenty of bits and pieces of half-finished projects to incorporate as examples.

The goal was to inspire people to touch a variety of handcrafts, then find a book and learn how to make their own—and hopefully finish them. The result was colorful, visually interesting, and would have made Constance smile if she wasn't so busy overthinking her life.

Two days, plus today. Almost three days, really. Not a peep from Oliver. Every time she thought about it, which was every four minutes—give or take fifteen seconds—anxiety grew until she wanted to climb out of her skin. Noises struck against her ears. Her shoes pinched across the top of her foot, and no amount of wiggling or loosening them helped.

On top of her general discomfort in her own body, the contents of Althea's last missive nagged at her. The note had been waiting for her when she returned from Kent, and all requests for more information had been ignored.

> *Connie,*
>
> *Franklin and I decided it is time to take drastic measures.*
> *Thank you for everything you've done thus far in this matchbreaking attempt.*
> *You've been the best of friends to me. Girls before earls, forever!*
> *(For me, anyway. You can keep your earl)*
>
> *Althea*

For once, Connie didn't know her friend's intentions, and Althea's silence during the days since didn't reassure her.

Why wouldn't anyone write her back?

Planning for the meeting with her parents took most of yesterday, as the cousins haggled over details between customers. Caro and Baby Nate spent the whole day in the shop. There hadn't been a free second to call on either Althea or Oliver. Not when the future of her home and income were at stake.

Normally, two days without contact with a man or a friend wouldn't be remarkable. That was before their night together, when Oliver asked her to trust him to end his engagement. Now, Althea was doing God-only-knew-what, and Connie feared that might somehow undo Oliver's efforts. Because even though they both worked toward a common goal, *no one was talking to anyone else.*

Constance shared these concerns regarding Althea's unknown scheme in that missive to Oliver. Even that hadn't warranted an answer.

Pain pushed at her temples. Connie leaned on the table and tried to breathe deeply. The alternative was to cry from overwhelmed frustration. *Everything is happening at once. The good things feel a little too huge, and the bad things are entirely out of my control. I hate this.*

One question in her swarming sea of thoughts gave her pause. When it came to Althea's vague message, did she worry more about Oliver's work unraveling, or Althea's plan failing? Surprisingly, the answer came immediately. Oliver.

At the end of the day, her friend had Wellsley and enough brash determination to run from the church if it came to that. Whatever Oliver's method, she suspected it had involved considerable time and effort to develop and execute. If Althea's impetuousness blew him off course somehow, Constance would be vexed on his behalf.

At what point was she allowed to storm into his house and demand an explanation to why he hadn't answered her message? The watch brooch pinned to her apron read six twenty-nine. *Damnit, Oliver. You have until eight o'clock to either write or show up. Then I'm done waiting. I can't stand here and do nothing.*

As if summoned by her call for something to do, Caro charged through the door, sending the shop bell jingling merrily.

Constance attempted a welcoming smile, but she needn't have bothered. Caro's face was thunderous, with pinched lips and her chin drawn in a mutinous point. Without a word of greeting, her cousin slapped a sheet of heavy cardstock atop a book of lace patterns.

"Are there customers here?"

Connie shook her head. "It's been quiet for the last quarter hour."

"Good. Because that son of a—"

"I'll be upstairs if you need me, ladies!" her father interrupted from the office, and Constance genuinely laughed for the first time all day.

Pink splashes of color warmed Caro's cheeks. "Apologies! I love you, Uncle Owen!" she called.

The sound of his chuckle reached them on the sales floor, followed by the click of a closing door. Within moments, floorboards creaked overhead.

Caro continued, "As I was saying, that bastard Southwyn has a lot to answer for. Dorian is appalled and worried, but I'm absolutely murderous."

"What's happened?" Dread coiled like a spring, ready to explode in her chest. She eyed Caro's paper as if it were a viper.

Sir William Thompson
requests the pleasure of your company at the marriage
of his daughter
Althea
to
The Right Hon'ble. The Earl of Southwyn
Tuesday, June 18th, 1816
At eleven o'clock St. George's Hanover Square

Tuesday. A choking sound rattled nearby, and it took a moment for Constance to realize she was the one making it.

Oliver had asked her to trust him. Pinpoints of pain flared in her palms as fingernails dug into her flesh. This must be why Althea and Wellsley were escalating their own plan.

"Breathe, Connie. Inhale. Good girl. Now, slowly let it out. No, slowly. That's right." Caro's voice sounded like it came from far away, through a tunnel. "Here, darling. Sit down. Inhale again. Now, gradually let it out. Bit by bit. Good, there's color in your cheeks now."

Caro's worried face came into focus when Constance blinked. "He's getting married in a little over a week." But... he'd promised he wasn't marrying Althea—that he'd handle it. And he'd been so adorably awkward and vulnerable while explaining the personal significance of Tuesdays.

Constance was no longer worried or sad. Indignation pulsed through her veins and angry ripples under her skin made small hairs on her arms stand on end. It wouldn't surprise her if a wind came out of nowhere, and her skirts whirled around her legs like an evil witch in a fairy tale.

Oliver Vincent, Earl of bloody Southwyn, had better be prepared to explain himself.

Constance shoved to her feet, then wavered for a second when the world wobbled at the abrupt movement. "He said he had it sorted. *He said he loved me.*"

If the plan had been for him to bolt from the altar, he would have said as much. It wasn't as if the topic hadn't come up in their discussions already.

Caro looked ready to go to war on her behalf. "Shall I put up the closed sign?"

"Yes. I'll tell my parents we're leaving." Constance pulled her cloak from the peg on the wall and shoved the nearest bonnet onto her head. Opening the door to the stairwell, she bellowed, "I have to close early. Caro and I need to go kill a man."

There was a beat of silence before she heard her father say, "I knew there'd be a body someday." Then meant for their ears, he yelled, "Don't get caught. We love you."

Her mother's voice joined the conversation. "Would you girls like some biscuits to take with you? You shouldn't commit violence on an empty stomach."

On cue, her belly gurgled. "Um, yes please," Constance called meekly, and smiled when her father's chuckle drifted down the stairwell. A moment later, her mum appeared with a tin.

"Here you go, my love." She kissed Connie's cheek. "I don't know what is happening, but if you find yourself in trouble, use your connection to Dorian. Having a duke in the family helps almost any legal situation."

Mary Martin, pragmatist baker.

"Thank you, Mum. I love you."

As Constance turned to leave, a small rectangle caught her eye. She groaned, sending up a futile prayer for sanity. "Bloody hell." She snatched the paper off the counter—the note she'd written Oliver, then apparently forgot to send—and stormed toward the front door. Holding up the tin, she announced, "We have biscuits. And I think I forgot to eat today."

Caro cheered. "Aunt Mary is my hero. Eat in the carriage, then we will go ruin Oliver's day. Where's Hattie?"

"Visiting Widow Fellsworth. She should finish soon."

Outside, Connie jiggled the key in the door, willing the lock to do its damned job.

Caro paced in front of the window. "Hurry up!"

"I'm trying! The lock sticks. You know that," Connie grumbled.

"Uncle Owen still hasn't fixed—is that my husband?"

A carriage bearing the ducal crest barreled toward them, the coachman yelling "outta the way" at anyone unwise

enough to linger in his path. The women plastered themselves against the shop window, narrowly avoiding a wave of
water and muck from the wheels.

Dorian opened the door and hopped down before his
horses came to a complete stop. "Thank God, I caught you.
This arrived after you left." He thrust a missive toward his
wife. "I don't know what is going on, but it had better involve
Oliver walking away a free man."

Constance read the contents over Caro's shoulder.

Your Graces,

*Oliver and I request your presence in the Forsyth
library at 9:30 tonight.*

Althea Thompson

"What the devil?" Constance asked no one in particular.

"We need to find Oliver. His damned misplaced sense of
duty will cost his entire future at this rate. Vague, dramatic
notes might work in your novels, Caro love, but this whole
situation makes me peevish." Dorian handed them up into
the coach, then directed Caro's servants to return home with
her carriage. When he returned, he was still muttering about
having heart palpitations. "Wait, where's Hattie?"

"Tutoring a widow's children down the road. We hoped
to pluck her off the street," Caro said.

He stuck his head out the window. "I see her!" With an
order to his coachman to intercept the last member of their
party, the carriage rolled into the street, then slowed a few
moments later.

Connie threw open the door. "Get in, wench. We're off to
make a grown man cry."

* * *

Oliver thanked his valet, running a hand down the front of his most comfortable traveling coat. He wore the ridiculous pink and lime-green waistcoat, for two reasons. First, in hopes that it would make Constance smile. And second, as a symbol of his willingness to bend and accept chaos into his life.

Heartbeats thumped in his ears in a tattoo. *Thump thump.* Breathe. *Thump thump.* Leave the ace of spades on the table. Slip his mother's ring into his pocket. *Thump thump.* Downstairs.

And so on, until he arrived at the dark windows of Martin House.

"Shall I wait here, milord? It appears the place has closed for the night." The coachman's voice reached him through the open window.

Oliver murmured a curse. He'd never called on Connie before. Sure, he'd visited the shop. But with the storefront closed, he didn't know how to access the family quarters. Did he bang on the door like a debt collector, and make a spectacle of himself? Was that how he wanted to introduce himself to her parents in this new role of potential son-in-law? He could see it now. *Sorry for scaring a year off your life. I'm here to convince your daughter to marry me.*

"Drive through the alley. There might be a door to their private residence."

"As you wish." The coachman clicked to the horses, and they were moving again.

Behind the store, all was wet and gray with soot and grime. Doors dotted the back of the brick and stone buildings, but few held identifying markings.

Disappointment gripped him. This might ruin his plan for tonight, but at least Althea and Wellsley could still leave. He'd return tomorrow, and he could follow with Connie immediately after, if she agreed. Surely there'd be a way to meet Althea on the road somewhere. Yes, the plan could adapt. Adaptability went hand in hand with spontaneity, after all.

Even though this new plan made sense, it didn't feel right.

Constance had put so much time and effort into helping Althea convince him to search elsewhere for a wife. Well, here he was.

The women hadn't given up, and he wouldn't either. Oliver jumped out of the carriage. "I'm going to knock on doors. Wait here."

At the first door, he met a local solicitor. Very polite man, although bewildered to find an earl wearing an ugly waistcoat on his doorstep after dark.

No one answered door number two.

Door number three opened, and Owen Martin greeted him with equal parts worry and confusion.

"I apologize for disturbing you, Mr. Martin. I'm not sure you remember me, but I'm a friend of Constance's. The Duke of Holland introduced us a few years ago. May I speak with her?"

Holding his gaze, Mr. Martin called over his shoulder. "Mary, do we know who Caro and Connie went after?"

A woman's voice replied, faint but discernible. "They didn't say. Why? Is there actually a body?"

Well, that was concerning.

Mr. Martin lowered his voice. "Son, if you're the one my daughter shot out of here to deal with, I'm going to give you some friendly advice. Either grovel or run. Good luck to you."

The door closed in Oliver's face, leaving him in the dark alley once more. What the hell just happened? Why were Caro and Constance angry?

Back at the carriage, he told his coachman, "Bloomsbury. Duke of Holland's residence."

Unfortunately, Hastings, the Holland butler, didn't have happy news. "I apologize, milord. Their Graces are currently not home. They left separately, both in quite a state."

"Damn. Nothing is going as expected tonight." Oliver ran a hand through his hair and bit back a growl. "Are they planning to attend the Forsyth soiree?"

"Yes, milord."

Returning once more to the carriage, Oliver grumbled to his coachman. "The Forsyths' on Hill Street." He'd intended to propose to Connie back at the shop while Althea and Wellsley made their scene at the Forsyth event. They'd agreed to meet at eleven o'clock in the mews behind the pub on Hill Street, then leave Town from there.

Except, Constance wasn't home. She was with Caro, and God only knew where Dorian had rushed off to. If he'd be at the Forsyths', Oliver would track him down and work backward from there to find Constance.

Who…might be angry with him, although he wasn't sure why. Whatever it was, Constance's mood warranted her father doing everything short of reading last rites over Oliver on their doorstep.

Whatever was wrong, they'd talk it over as they had in his carriage on the way back from Kent. That one trip out of Town had entirely reshaped Oliver's idea of what he wanted for his future. One morning of waking up beside Constance, and everything in him sat up, begging, *more of this, for the rest of my life*. To make that possible, the last two days had been frantic, without a moment to himself. Preparing Wellsley for his new position, coordinating with Althea and her beau in planning their elopement as well as his, filled every hour.

When she heard about all he'd done, Constance would probably tease him about painstakingly arranging an event most people did impulsively. Among a dozen other things, he'd needed to visit Gerard Bellmore for more marriage documents.

Someone needed to protect Constance's future. Especially since she hoped to hold equal ownership in Martin House. What she did with that share was up to her, but he wanted Constance to retain the right to make that decision. Because although he craved becoming one with her in the "making the beast with two backs" sense, under law she'd cease to exist as a separate person once they wed. He couldn't imagine Constance disappearing, even if it was only in the legal sense. Thus, another trust. Another pile of legal paperwork from his poor solicitor, although he left these for her to file when they wed.

Since Althea and Wellsley were bound for Scotland, he and Constance would be too. Then, all that dimpled sunshine and teasing laughter would be part of his days forever. Assuming she accepted his proposal, of course. Nerves turned his stomach a bit touchy at that thought.

Oliver searched for his usual calm as the coach's wheels clattered over cobblestones. It would do him no favors to walk into the Forsyths' with every worry parading across his face, especially as he hadn't dressed with a soiree in mind. Oliver ruefully examined his most weathered, and therefore comfortable, boots. Appearing in traveling garb was the least scandalous sin he'd planned for this evening, so his attire wasn't worth worrying over.

As the London streets passed by in seemingly endless blocks of stone or brick houses and businesses tacked one on the end of the next, that familiar reserve settled over him. The buildings changed, growing larger and finer.

Architectural nods to the classical lines of Rome crept over the marble structures transforming the facades into things of beauty rather than shelters designed purely for durability.

Sharp, wet night air filled the carriage. Misting rain peppered his face, but Oliver didn't close the window. The cold was bracing, like dunking one's head in a frigid stream.

So he heard the Forsyths' house before he saw it. Coaches lined Hill Street off Berkeley Square, inching forward as they waited their turn to belch their passengers at the Forsyths' door. Outside, the pavement teemed with finely dressed members of the ton brave enough to subject their evening clothes to the night's drizzle. Gas lamps lined the street, causing yellow circles of illumination to spark off the jewels encircling necks and winking from artfully styled curls.

Patrons at the Coach and Horse lingered with pints in hand outside the pub doors, watching the hubbub, as if the people were animals in a zoo.

"I'll walk the rest of the way," Oliver called to his driver. Donning his hat, he joined the mass of London's elite. Nodding and smiling greetings at the others walking toward the brightly lit house, he ignored their curious stares at his clothing. Patting his pocket for the outline of the ring, he tried to appear unruffled.

Grand gestures were nerve-racking. Novels never mentioned that part.

Chapter Twenty-Seven

*Be willing to go as far as it takes to get
what you want*

To give credit where it was due, Roberts appeared genuinely baffled when he informed them that the earl was not at home. Of course, when faced with three incensed women and a duke demanding entry, it would be understandable if the man prevaricated a little.

Caro braced her hands on her hips. "Are you quite sure? Is he not receiving visitors, or has he physically left the premises?"

"Left the premises for the evening, Your Grace," Roberts replied with a deferential nod.

"Do you know where he's gone?" Hattie pressed.

The butler's eyes shifted away. "As I am not his lordship's personal secretary, I have no way of knowing, miss."

A blatant lie. Servants were the eyes and ears of a house. Rather than quibble, Constance stepped down to the pavement. "Maybe we should ask the woman he's marrying where to find him tonight." Was that anger and bitterness in her voice? Undoubtably. To think, not long ago, she'd stood in her shop and thought the last few days had been overwhelming.

Every second since proved how much louder and out of control the world could feel. Constance clenched her fists and tried to breathe through the cloying sensation of everything being altogether too much to take in.

"We'll determine our next step in the carriage," Dorian suggested.

"I can't believe there are actual invitations to this farce," Hattie groused, settling back on the seat she'd vacated moments before.

"Wedding invitations are a step too far. We all agree on that," Caro fumed.

"All right. What do we know? Althea's message said to be in the Forsyths' library," Dorian said.

"She sent me a message several days ago saying she and Mr. Wellsley had concocted a plan. No specifics," Connie said.

"And we know Althea will do anything to avoid marrying Southwyn." Hattie leaned toward Constance and squinted in the dark. "Connie, love? I want you to take a deep lungful of air. You're pale as a sheet and look like a spooked horse. Caro, Connie's overwhelmed."

Removing her cloak, Hattie handed it to Constance. "Wrap this tight around you if it will help. Close your eyes and ignore us. We will find our friends and get you where you need to be."

Constance took the garment, because arguing that she was fine would be futile and a blatant falsehood. Huddled in the corner of the carriage with Hattie's cloak covering her head, she closed her eyes and focused on the rumble of carriage wheels beneath her.

Several minutes passed before Connie felt slightly more in control of herself. From far away, snippets of conversation reached her.

Caro said, "Dorian and I planned to attend the Forsyths' soiree this evening anyway. In light of the invitation, I think it would be cruel to send everyone back to the shop and ask you to wait for word. Althea wants Dorian somewhere at nine thirty? She'll get all of us." Then, her cousin called, presumably to their coachman. "Home, please."

"All of us? I can't go to a fancy ton event." Hattie didn't sound pleased. "I'll be thrown out onto the street."

Constance smiled in her dark cocoon. Caro would never let anything happen to Hattie.

"I'd like to see them try," Dorian growled.

Neither would Dorian, Connie thought. As for her, this wouldn't be the first ton event she sneaked into. Tonight, she'd have the added protection of a duke and duchess.

"We have plenty of time to tack up the hem on a gown for Connie, and I know I have a few that will fit you, Hattie," Caro said, sounding genuinely excited. "It will be just like those nights when we'd sit and alter clothes for Connie's many, many, many outings with men."

Constance nearly laughed when Hattie added a dry "so many men."

That's when she knew she could emerge from her cloak cocoon. As usual, her cousins were Connie's anchor in any situation. Slowly removing the woolen buffer from the world she'd needed for a short time, she handed Hattie her cloak with a quiet "thank you."

Without the layers of sharp sensations, her mind was clear enough to make sense of her thoughts once more.

Doubts crept in. What if Oliver had changed his mind, or realized he couldn't keep the promises he'd made to her?

An ache in her jaw told her she'd been clenching her teeth. Connie rubbed at the pain and tried to follow those thoughts to a conclusion.

If Oliver wanted to marry Althea after all, he'd need to tell her himself. She deserved that much. Not to learn about it from an—admittedly beautiful—wedding invitation.

That wasn't even meant for her.

In a week, she'd have read about their marriage in the *Times*, assuming Althea hadn't told her first.

Why *hadn't* Althea specifically mentioned the invitations in her missive? Or that her mother had secured a date at the church? Why had she written to Dorian requesting his presence tonight, instead of Constance?

Checking her watch brooch, Connie sighed. Each question would have an answer in a little over two hours. Not soon enough.

Waiting was awful.

Arriving at an event in a timely manner made for a boring evening. Especially when you'd never planned to show up in the first place. Oliver prowled through the game room, filled with tables, chairs, and cards with betting tokens laid out for the guests. He explored hallways to see which rooms were open, downed two flutes of champagne as he wandered the conversation area and assessed every new face entering through the door, searching for Dorian. Glancing at his pocket watch, Oliver stifled a groan.

How had it only been three-quarters of an hour? *Hell and damnation. I'm supposed to be kissing Constance right now.*

If he remembered correctly, Althea and Wellsley planned their scene for 9:30. Surely he'd find Dorian before then and still have time to track down Constance—provided Caro knew his intended's whereabouts.

Circling back to the game room, Oliver dodged a flower

swinging free from its moorings. The Forsyths clearly underwent some expense for the decor this evening. Garlands and ribbons draped off everything.

Would this be his last annual Forsyth soiree? If Constance married him, would they live quietly away from society, or would they face the lions together? He rather hoped they'd stare down the ton, if only to see Constance work her charm on everyone, then watch them fall under her thrall. Like it or not, by this time next year, the best of them would adore her too.

Imagining her by his side next year, flashing that dimple at people she counted as friends, made him smile to himself.

London nobility didn't stand a chance against that dimple.

Mr. Wellsley entered the room and hurried over when he spotted Oliver. "Southwyn? Didn't expect you to be here. Is everything, uh, going well this evening?" Wellsley wiggled his eyebrows suggestively, and Oliver nearly laughed. England's army had not lost a master of espionage when it failed to snatch Franklin Wellsley into its ranks.

"I'm trying to find her. She's with her cousin, the Duchess of Holland. Since the Hollands are attending tonight, here I am. Hopefully, they'll help me track her down before eleven, and all will be well."

"They'll be here. Althea thought we needed someone high-ranking to witness everything and dispel any doubters. Who better than a duke? She sent a message telling them when and where to meet." Worry pinched his face. "But if you're here now, who's going to be *you know where, you know when*, with *you know what*?"

"My coachman returned home and will be in place with the right equipage at the agreed-upon time." Anticipating the next question, Oliver hastened to add, "When Dorian arrives and I find out where Constance is, I'll take a hack. All will be well. You focus on your part."

Over Wellsley's shoulder, Oliver spied Lord Bixby arriving with his sisters. Catching his eye, Oliver gave Bixby a nod, which the man returned with a raised eyebrow, as if to ask "are you certain?" Oliver nodded once more. Yes. He was sure.

Bixby and his sisters melted into the crowd. Before Oliver could look away from where they'd stood, another party entered the room. Constance stood in the doorway, flanked by her cousins and Dorian, who'd positioned themselves like her royal guard. Air rushed from his lungs. She was just so...everything. She was everything.

Everything except *supposed to be here*. "At least this simplifies the schedule."

Wellsley followed his gaze.

"Good, His Grace is here with...oh. Miss Martin? Now? When you haven't—"

"Quite. The woman between Constance and Her Grace is their cousin, Miss Hattie McCrae. Remember that name and face. They're inseparable. If they've accepted Althea into their pack as an honorary cousin, you do not want to cross Miss McCrae."

"That's good, right? That Althea has such close friends?"

"It's wonderful, unless you land on the wrong side of them. Those women would kill for each other."

Wellsley nodded seriously, and Oliver suspected if there'd been paper at hand, he'd be taking earnest notes. "Since you're all here, will you be in the library?"

"Assuming I'm not busy pleading my case with Constance, yes. I'll play my part."

"Plead your case? Do you think you'll need to beg?"

Oliver grunted. "Perhaps. When I visited Martin House, there'd been some kind of uproar earlier. Her father wished me luck. Said I should be prepared to either grovel or run. You might witness the wrath of the cousins firsthand."

Wellsley winced in sympathy. "What did you do, Southwyn?"

"Damned if I know."

Chapter Twenty-Eight

Remember: girls before earls

Hattie's face had gone pale the instant their carriage arrived at the Forsyths', and the pinched lines around her mouth deepened with each passing moment. Crowded inside the house with a swarm of guests, her wide eyes looked haunted. "How does one become used to this?"

Caro placed a comforting hand on her arm. "Believe it or not, you will grow more comfortable the more you're out in society."

Constance stood on her tiptoes, attempting to see over the shoulders of everyone in front of her. After taking several minutes alone in a quiet room at Caro's house, she was feeling more like herself. A lifetime of experience taught her that she could stumble over that tipping point into fully overwhelmed again if she wasn't careful tonight.

"Pretend you belong, and most won't question you," Caro told Hattie.

"If anyone does question us, we will smile and apologize for forgetting their name, then say we enjoyed meeting them last month," Connie said.

"Thank God I'll never need to do this again," Hattie muttered. "Repeated exposure will not be necessary."

Dorian brought them back to the task at hand. "The house is filling fast, but I don't see Althea or Oliver. With this crush, we could stay all night and not find them." He checked his pocket watch. "We're meeting in the library in one hour. If we're separated, assemble there."

"We should split up and search for them." Caro linked her arm through her husband's.

"I'll stay here," Hattie said, still resembling prey in a room full of predators.

Constance stepped to her side and waved the others on. Helping Hattie feel comfortable served a secondary purpose of giving Connie something constructive to do. "You two go. We'll meet you in the library if we don't cross paths sooner."

Forcing herself to stand tall—or as tall as her petite stature allowed—she gently straightened the lace along the low, square edge of Hattie's neckline. "Look at us. We're beautiful. We blend in perfectly. Pretend we belong and no one will throw us out." Searching the room, she spied a clock on the fireplace mantel. "We have fifty-seven minutes to find Althea and the man I may or may not strangle before the end of the night."

"Since we don't know where the library is, let's scout the terrain and time how long it takes to get there," Hattie said.

"I adore your tactical mind, darling. That's something you share with Oliver."

"Speaking of Southwyn…When we see him, do you know what you'll say?" Hattie remained close to her side as they wove through the press of bodies.

"I hope something brilliant and witty will occur to me in the moment. Right now, all of this"—Connie gestured vaguely to her head—"is a muddle."

A thought made her pull Hattie to a stop. "I hope you don't think I'm creating reasons to push him away. This isn't like what happened with Walter. I adore Oliver, but I still think I deserve answers to why he didn't warn me they'd set a wedding date. If he'd considered my feelings at all, he would have shared that information and reassured me there was still an escape route for them to get out of this."

"Of course you deserve answers. Granted, your situation is unique. Due to the odd nature of your circumstances, he should be even more transparent with you about what is happening."

"All right. I didn't want you to think I'm flitting away, like he's an abandoned quilting project, or some such nonsense. I want him. I also want to rail at him over what his silence during these last few days has put me through this evening."

Hattie scowled. "Connie, loving Southwyn and wanting to occasionally wring his neck for being as communicative as a rock are not mutually exclusive. Whether you two are destined for wedlock, or merely enjoying each other for a short time, communication must be honest and consistent."

Constance nibbled her bottom lip. "Not that it excuses his silence, but I wrote him about our meeting with my parents and warned that Althea is up to something. I've been annoyed all day because he never replied, but *I forgot to send it*. And now I can't help wondering how long it will be before things like that make a logical, centered man like him realize I'm utterly daft at times."

Hattie, with hands on hips, scowled. "You're the most confident woman I know. Where is this self-doubt coming from?"

A nearly hysterical laugh bubbled from Constance as her eyes burned. God, she would *not* make an utter cake of herself in public and cry simply because she couldn't handle her own ricocheting thoughts. "Confident? Hattie, I question everything, most of all myself. You and Caro are my dearest friends, *and* family. Still, I wonder what you think during moments like tonight, when I needed to burrow under your cloak. I dread what would happen if you two ever realize exactly how messy it is inside my head. Would you stop loving me, or decide you don't trust me with Martin House? Everyone thinks I'm feckless, but I truly am doing my best. And even my best efforts lead to things like hiding under my cousin's cloak, or walking around in a huff because I never received a reply to a missive *I forgot to send*. What need does an earl have for someone like me? If Betsy were available, she'd be a much better match for him. They could be calm and rational together and build a perfectly serene life." *But would Besty appreciate the way he unraveled behind closed doors?* She thought not. That part of him belonged to Constance, and she wouldn't share. Not even in her unhinged emotional ramblings.

Hattie tugged her toward the relative privacy of the room's edge. "When you give your heart, you're doggedly faithful. Southwyn is damned lucky to have earned your regard. No one is a more loyal friend or goes so far above and beyond expectations. This whole madcap escapade with Althea is the perfect example. Who else would be her—what did she call it? Matchbreaker? Connie, your mind might feel like a jumbled, inhospitable place at times. And I hate that you have to live with that. But I promise, those of us who love you are lucky to do so."

As Hattie squeezed Constance's hands, a sliver of that lifelong crack in her heart, from which all these painful words leaked out, began to heal. "Thank you, darling. I wish I could see myself as you do."

"I do too. Because you're such a beauty. Inside and out. We love you exactly as you are, even when that means you need to hide away for a few minutes under my cloak and breathe. I hope, in time, you'll come to appreciate the gift your unique way of thinking can be. Because we already have."

Constance threw her arms around her cousin in an impulsive hug. "Thank you," she whispered. After a moment, she added, "You really don't think I'm Inconstant Constance?"

"Never. You've bravely searched for the right person to love, instead of settling. If that's Oliver, you'll stand by him with the same strength and loyalty you show me and Caro, and now Althea."

The reminder made her jerk back. "Althea! What time is it?"

They craned their necks, trying to see the clock on the mantel, but it was too far away. A man stopped beside them and withdrew his pocket watch. "It is quarter till the hour, ladies."

"Thank you," Constance said.

He nodded but didn't move on. In fact, he stepped closer and lowered his voice. "Please forgive me, but I couldn't help overhearing."

Hattie stiffened and gave him a withering glare. The newcomer stood several inches taller than Hattie and had a face made remarkable only by a scar at the corner of his mouth that pulled his lip slightly out of symmetry.

"This is a private conversation, sir." Hattie's voice could have frosted glass.

He offered a small bow, appearing shamefaced. "Lord Bixby at your service."

"Bixby?" Hattie repeated, exchanging a shocked look with Connie. This was the man who'd unknowingly provided hours of entertainment as they read the scandal sheets.

"Indeed. Again, I apologize most profusely. I heard nothing except your friend inquire about the time, and the name

Althea, which I assume refers to Miss Althea Thompson."
He bit at that scarred bottom lip, and despite the way Hattie
had appeared ready to breathe fire moments before, Constance caught her cousin watching the movement with reluctant fascination.

"From your tone, I assumed you already heard what people are saying. Miss Thompson will need her friends now
more than ever," Lord Bixby said.

"I'm not sure to what you're referring, milord," Hattie
gritted out.

He openly assessed her now, that scarred mouth tilting in
a subtle grin. "You're wise enough to protect your friend and
not reveal what you know. Admirable, but ultimately useless. Soon enough everyone will hear about Southwyn jilting
her because he's in love with another woman." Lord Bixby
leaned closer, but Constance noticed he didn't lower his
voice. "And we understand how the ton works. They'll be all
aflutter because not only is he throwing over a lovely woman
like Miss Thompson, but he's doing so for a commoner. She's
a bookseller, of all things. First the Duke of Holland, now
the Earl of Southwyn."

Despite her frayed emotions, Constance's reserves of sarcasm ran deep. "Oh no." Her patently false dismay made
Hattie smirk. "Well-read women are infiltrating the ton?
What is England coming to when such a thing is possible
within the hallowed halls of Mayfair?"

Outwardly, she seemed flippant, but her damned brain
spun with new questions. How did the ton already know
about their affair? Would being involved with her—publicly
choosing Constance over someone suitable like Althea—
cause irrevocable damage to Oliver's place in society?

In forty-two minutes, according to Lord Bixby's time-
piece, Althea planned something that would send more

tongues wagging. Or, was this part of what Oliver had prepared for?

Hattie clamped a hand around Lord Bixby's biceps. "Who told you such scurrilous gossip? You're going to point them out to me, then I expect you to keep what you heard to yourself."

Lord Bixby looked both startled and amused, as if Hattie were a kitten who'd surprised him by hissing instead of purring. "On whose orders?"

Her cousin, bless her, who kept her head in nearly any situation, reached the end of her patience. White shone at her knuckles as she squeezed and stepped close enough that her nose nearly touched his chin. A hint of Scotland laced her words like the subtle peaty undertones of good whisky. The accent was a remnant from her childhood, and something she'd actively tried to lose since moving to England. That it made an appearance now was indicative of exactly how close she danced to the edge of her temper.

"On whose orders, you ask? Hattie McCrae, cousin to the bookseller in question, and friend of Miss Thompson. If your loose lips cause either of them so much as a wince, you will live to regret it."

Lord Bixby's chuckle put him in genuine danger, and the foolish man either didn't know or didn't care. "What, no empty death threats?"

Hattie's smile turned calculating. Anticipatory. "I'm not a killer. But I *am* a woman prepared to hunt down the next man who hurts one of mine, then dismantle his world piece by piece, and laugh as I bring him low." She jerked him around to face the room. "Now, show me who told you." Hattie glanced at Constance. "Try to find the others and keep an eye on the clock—you can't be late."

"Right. Girls before earls. I'll be there."

Hattie's lips twitched at the quip, then flattened before focusing once more on the man in her grip. Lord Bixby smirked at something behind Connie and allowed Hattie to lead him away.

"Constance, my love, I've been searching for you all over London, and here you are." Oliver's voice flowed over her senses like warm honey, magically soothing some of her frazzled nerves.

When she spun to face him, his welcoming smile faded. In an instant, he looked ready to fight dragons on her behalf. Oh, this man. "Have you been crying? I saw you enter, then lost you in the crowd. What's happened?" Strong fingers gently swept under her eyes, then fell to trail down her bare arms.

Constance took a steadying breath and her senses filled with…him. Oliver must have applied cologne right before leaving the house, because the top notes of sandalwood hadn't yet faded enough to allow the citrus undertones their moment to shine.

His dark hair needed a trim. A tuft stuck up where he'd run his fingers through it. For some reason he hadn't dressed in evening attire, and he wore one of those godawful waistcoats they'd sneaked into his wardrobe. Tonight, his angular jaw was freshly shaved, which brought to mind the area of beard burn high on her inner thigh that had yet to fade.

There were probably men present who were taller, or broader, or more classically handsome. But this was the one who made her pulse race while soothing her rough edges.

"Today has been emotional." Rather than the witty retorts she'd hoped would come to her in the moment, Constance said the first thing that came to mind. Which she'd always done with him, from that first meeting. Something about Oliver had always allowed her to be comfortable being her verbally impulsive, unvarnished self. And he'd still fallen in love with her.

"When I left the shop, I wanted to thrash you, milord. You have things to answer for."

Concern etched his features. "Perhaps we could speak somewhere more private and you can tell me what I've done?"

After her conversation with Hattie, she felt slightly freer from the emotional muck of insecurities. Her typical humor asserted itself. "Does our hostess happen to have a spare storeroom?"

His grin flashed white teeth and made a fan from the creases of his eyes. "Would you settle for a music room? The Forsyths have closed theirs to visitors, but it's just down the hall. We could sneak in and no one would notice."

That was another reason she loved him that others might not understand. This logical, dutiful man would bend rules to be alone with her. Oliver's willingness to soften his rigid control meant more to her than a love letter or posy of flowers.

"Lead on." She tucked a hand in the crook of his elbow. "Although I must warn you, I have somewhere to be in—what time is it?" He pulled out a pocket watch and showed her the mother-of-pearl clockface. "Thirty-four minutes."

The hum of conversation and laughter grew when they stepped into a room filled with tables and guests playing games of chance.

"The amount they'll lose at these tables would probably feed my entire neighborhood for a year," Connie commented in a low tone.

Oliver leaned closer. "It's enough to turn your stomach if you consider it for longer than a few seconds." Disgust colored his words. "My father was a gambler. That's one vice you never need to worry about me embracing."

A ripple of conversations followed them through the crowed as more guests realized the Earl of Southwyn escorted an unfamiliar woman rather than his fiancée. The heavy weight of everyone's stares poked between her shoulder blades. Part of Connie wanted to spin around, throw her hands in the air dramatically, and say, *Yes, I'm the lowly bookseller who's compelled the Earl of Southwyn to jilt Althea Thompson. Look upon my common-born charms and be...* Amazed? Impressed? Constance laughed quietly at her own ridiculousness. *Look upon my common-born charms and be as confused as I am* felt more accurate.

Soon enough, the sounds of the event faded when they turned several corners and found a dimly lit corridor. Only half the wall sconces glowed in a subtle signal of unwelcome. Oliver stopped, then opened a door, and motioned for her to enter first.

Chapter Twenty-Nine

~

Demand, without apology, the things you need

Inside, the room was still and dark. Silvery moonlight trailed through a window, tracing black shapes of furniture, a piano, and a harp.

Oliver laid his hand at the small of her back as he shut the door behind him.

Silence solved nothing, and he seemed to be waiting for her to speak. "Caro received an invitation to your wedding today and brought it to the shop."

"What? Oh, shit," Oliver groaned. In the moonlight, she could barely make out the way he spun away from her and put his hands on his head.

"My reaction was more verbose, but yes. To add insult to injury, your wedding is on a Tuesday. A *Tuesday,* Oliver! You toss off on Tuesdays, and we both know it."

An entirely inappropriate snort of laughter came from his direction. "Toss off? How do you know that term?"

Constance rolled her eyes, even though he couldn't see her exasperation. "Please. I'm not some pampered society princess. Toss off, Box the Jesuit, Frig. It all means the same thing."

"Holy fuck, I adore you, Constance Martin. But a

Tuesday? You imagined the most atrocious scenarios, I'm sure. I would too, if I held a bloody wedding invitation."

"For an instant, yes. It was a flash, but in that moment, it felt possible you'd changed your mind about marrying Althea and hadn't told me. Or that it had all been a ruse, and you'd lied to me in a deeply personal way."

"You thought I lied to get you into bed?" Shock and hurt colored his voice, but she refused to feel guilty about the fears she'd harbored for a few terrible heartbeats.

"We spent the night together, returned home, then you disappeared. No messages. Nothing. Mind you, I didn't suspect you of villainy for long, but seeing your wedding date—*a Tuesday, Oliver*—in black and white felt like a physical blow. I didn't know what to believe. For all I knew, you might have fabricated your inexperience and have actually had scores of lovers. Since you're quite good in bed, the theory holds weight."

"Only you could so thoroughly insult and flatter me in the same sentence."

He wrapped an arm around her waist. In the low light of the room, the shape of him was no more than an inky blot, so she was grateful for the connection of his touch.

"Lady Thompson chose a date, but I didn't think to ask what it was. I'd just received word that my scheme to get out of the engagement had worked, so it didn't signify. No one mentioned details about the invitations, or delivering them." The brush of his sigh caressed her face. "I was so intent on finalizing details to escape, it didn't occur to me that you might hear about the wedding date. I'm so sorry, my love." Gentle kisses dusted her cheek, then over her eyelids. "I hate knowing I gave you reason to doubt me. Even if it was only for a second."

Which was all well and good but didn't answer the

real question at hand. Constance threaded her fingers into the hair near his nape, then tugged to look him in the eye as much as possible in the dark room. "Where've you been for the last few days, Oliver? You said you loved me, then disappeared. Some reassurance that you weren't regretting everything we did in Kent wouldn't have been remiss."

"I could never regret anything about you."

Even if his explanation showed areas from which they could learn to do better, she trusted he'd accept that lesson. They both would. So, this discussion was vital.

"You're not marrying her?"

"Not if the king himself held a gun to my head. I'm not marrying Althea Thompson."

The last of her worry quieted at his reassurance. When he dove in for their first real kiss of the night, Connie relaxed her grip on his hair.

Patiently, he teased the seam of her lips until she opened for him. Oliver's relieved groan sent shimmers of desire waking through her. Within seconds, he'd hardened against her belly. Long fingers grasped her hip, holding her against his arousal.

However, even though she believed all would be well, Connie still asked for what she needed. "Answer the question, Oliver. Where were you? Don't take advantage of my inability to focus," she chided between kisses.

Oliver's low chuckle made her warm all over. "Am I distracting? Is my desire to pin you against this door and sink into your delicious body scrambling your wits, my love?" His lips grazed her jaw. "Allow me to account for everything that's happened since you last rode my cock and screamed my name."

He clasped her bum and lifted her until their hips were flush. With a spin and a step, the unyielding wood of the door met her back, and she grinned against his mouth.

"First, Franklin Wellsley paid me a visit."

Connie wrapped her legs around his waist, bringing the hard length of him more intimately against her core.

Oliver's words were rough, but he continued, between kisses. "No matter what, I wasn't marrying Althea. I asked you to trust me because some details weren't finalized yet." He felt along her calf until he found her hem. Pushing her gown up her leg, Oliver paused to trace a satin garter ribbon. Cool air brushed her bare thigh. "You're so damned soft."

"Focus, Oliver," she teased. "Everything is final now?"

"Yes, thank God." When those fingers continued toward her core, she stopped him with one hand.

"Days of silence, while I waited to learn what you've done. Explain." Every wicked impulse came out to play during these intimate moments with him. While Oliver's hand stayed where she'd stopped it, Connie dipped one finger into her slick heat.

He went still, then shuddered when she painted her liquid arousal across his lower lip. "You promised me a full accounting, and I expect one," she taunted playfully.

"Fuck, you're brutal." He licked his lips, then dropped a groaning kiss against her palm. Constance ran the pads of her fingers over the planes of the face she loved so well, trying to memorize him by touch alone.

"Thanks to some vague language on legal documents, I tricked Sir William into giving Althea the land by the river, separate from a dowry."

She froze. "The river? But what about your canal?"

The kiss he offered to soothe her dismay was gentle. "And now it belongs to Althea and Wellsley. I'm going to be a partner in the canal, but the primary income is theirs. Until it's built, he'll work with the steward at my estate in Cornwall, so Althea can be near her sister. They'll elope tonight to Scotland, then go straight to their new home."

A swell of love made her eyes go misty. Constance framed his cheeks with her palms and poured every ounce of admiration for him into her next kiss. "You're a good man, Oliver Vincent."

"What I am, is yours." Oliver clutched the top of her thigh, with his thumb achingly close to her molten center. Constance moved his hand to where she wanted it, and they groaned in unison.

"Connie, love. Fuck, you're wet."

Her answer was an inarticulate needy sound. But Oliver was, if nothing else, an equal match to her devious teasing. She'd demanded an explanation for his silence since their return to London. Even as his fingers explored her slick heat, he continued to speak—albeit with a shaking voice.

"Before they leave, Althea will expose Sir William as the bully he is and make it clear that she's chosen Wellsley. But we both know people might still place blame on her." His words ended in a moan as she fumbled with the front placket of his breeches, then gripped his cock.

"People always talk. What will you do about it?" Constance nocked his erection at her entrance, but he held himself there, letting the anticipation build to a nearly painful degree.

"I gave the biggest gossipmonger in London a juicier morsel." Oliver slowly sank into her, inciting a moan at the delicious stretch. "Hell, speaking of juicy..."

So Oliver had been the one to tell Bixby of their affair.

Connie's laugh made her clench around him and stole his senses momentarily. "What did you tell him?"

"I'm in love with a bookseller who stole my heart and rearranged my perfectly ordered world into chaos." Thrusts punctuated his words. "Chaos. You're a tiny teacup-size tempest who upended all my plans, and I fucking adore you for it. And now everyone will know I'm mad for you."

"I love you too. God, Oliver." Each push of their bodies coming together inched her higher against the door and closer to bliss.

The delicious movements slowed and she nearly whimpered. "I'll never tire of hearing that." His voice was a rasp in the dark. "I asked for blind faith, and you gave it to me. You really do love me."

"Except for that minute when I wanted to kill you."

"When you're holding my bloody wedding invitation, you're right to question me. But then what did you do? You asked for an explanation. Thank you."

"I only demand answers if I love you. Otherwise, I'd be off in a field dancing naked under the moon and asking the fates to curse you with genital lice for the rest of your life."

Oliver rested his forehead against her shoulder. "If I'm ever fool enough to think I can predict what will come out of your mouth next, you'll prove me wrong within seconds."

She grinned, running gentle fingers through his hair. "As I recall, you like my chatter."

He met her gaze. Now that her vision had adapted to the darkness, it was easier to make out his features. "I love your chatter. The way your brain works is a constant delight. So many thoughts, so many words. I don't care if you're speaking them, singing them, or screaming them. I'm here to listen."

After that, she had to kiss him again. A loving, sweet kiss that immediately raged out of control. Oliver pinned her to the door with another deep thrust. "Say it again for me."

A wide, joyful grin made her cheeks ache as she leaned her head against the wood, relishing how they moved together. "I love you, Oliver. I'm yours."

"Mine. And I'm yours."

Tension built in her muscles, tightening for that final flight into climax. "And you're mine," she repeated.

"Always. Now. Forever." His breath grew choppy and the words came out strained as his pace turned nearly frantic.

Oliver vowing to be hers forever pushed Constance to the edge. As her orgasm overtook her, she dimly heard Oliver say, "Marry me. Please, love," before his own peak claimed him.

She carefully stood on knees like jelly and struggled to gather her wits. "Did you just propose marriage?"

Oliver collapsed against the door beside her, gasping for air. He rolled his head and met her grin with his own.

"Why do you always wait for an orgasm to blurt out life-changing declarations?"

In the dark, she could barely make out his wink, but it still sent a frisson of heat through her. God, he was handsome. An amalgamation of parts that created exactly what she wanted. What she needed.

"I'll take your critique under advisement," he said.

Languid warmth filled her limbs, and for the first time all day her brain was nearly calm. "I think your cock might be magic." She motioned toward her head. "All the noise is quiet."

"Then marry me for your own well-being. Magical penises must be good for your health."

She snorted, enjoying the peace of being right where she wanted to be.

"You laugh, but I'm quite serious." Clothing rustled in the dark. A second later, he grasped her hand, then traced her ring finger to the tip. The cool press of metal nudged at her finger, and she gasped.

"Oliver?"

"I stopped by the shop to do this earlier, but you'd already left with Caro. Constance, I have two questions for you. First, will you marry me?"

She didn't need a second to contemplate her answer. "Yes. Absolutely."

A ring slipped onto her finger, and Constance thought she might burst from joy.

"Second question—and keep in mind, you may say no. Will you elope with me tonight? We can leave with Althea and Wellsley for Scotland."

Constance pulled him into another kiss. "I'll marry you any time, any day. Including tonight."

At that moment, two things happened. A clock somewhere in the room struck the half hour, and Constance remembered she was supposed to be in the library. "Girls before earls! Damnit!"

Oliver, bless him, didn't ask questions. He hurriedly set himself to rights while Constance did the same.

A peek down the hall in each direction proved there weren't witnesses to their exit. When the hallway spilled into the more populated rooms, they stopped to take in the sight before them.

As if a wave went through the crowd, each table of guests paused what they were doing, listened to the chatter at the table beside them, then stood. A few truly committed gamblers stayed where they were, grumbling as others abandoned the games.

"It's happened," Constance whispered. "We need to get to the library."

He gave her a speculative glance. "Are you ready to set the ton on its ear, Countess?"

Countess? That will take some getting used to. "At least it won't be boring."

Thirty

The crowd at the double doors of the library parted for Oliver like the Red Sea before Moses.

Acutely aware of the many eyes on them, he focused on the only one who mattered, right beside him. Blue eyes, wide with nerves, held his gaze as Connie's grip on his arm tightened. Guests closed in around them, so reassuring Connie with words was impossible without being overheard. Instead, he raised one brow in a silent question. *Are you sure?*

She raised her chin, then gave a subtle nod. Hopefully she also heard the reassurance in his gaze. *We're in this together. I'm right here.*

In the library, Oliver barely managed to turn his laugh into a cough. Giving credit where it was due, Althea and Franklin had taken pains to set the perfect scene.

Some elements were merely set dressing, as if the whole thing were on a stage. They'd removed Wellsley's coat. Unlike Oliver's coat, which had been in a heap on the floor the morning after he and Connie fell on each other like ravenous wolves, Wellsley's draped artfully over the back of a chair. There'd been an effort to muss his hair, but the pièce de résistance was Althea.

Althea understood the finer points of weaponizing her appearance for maximum impact. Not an inch of gown lay out of place. Which didn't matter one whit with her hair tumbling down her back in long blond waves.

While he'd known she was intelligent, with a tactical mind, Oliver had to clench his free hand so he wouldn't accidently applaud. The goal for this evening was to make a spectacle, and she'd succeeded.

First on the scene appeared to have been Connie's cousins and Dorian, with the ladies assigned their own roles. The duke joined Oliver, sending him the silent support of a shoulder bump.

Miss McCrae's lips pinched in a convincing approximation of distress as she fluttered around Althea, making a grand show of "putting her to rights," thus cleverly creating the illusion of misconduct.

A tug on Althea's bodice made onlookers think her bodice needed adjusting. After ensuring that everyone had witnessed the fuss required to restore Althea's modesty, Miss McCrae set about gathering hairpins from the floor, announcing each one, lest any bystanders miss the way pins had been flung about in the heat of the moment.

Caro's exclamations were so loud, stableboys in the mews could probably hear every word. "Oh, Althea! What have you done? There is no way you can marry Lord Southwyn now! Will you do the honorable thing and wed her?" Caro dropped the faux concern to level an intense scowl at Althea's beau until he nodded.

At Oliver's side, Dorian whispered, "I'm happy she's a writer, because she's a terrible actress."

Oliver covered a snicker and hoped the result was an attitude appropriate to the situation. Stepping forward, flanked by Constance and the duke, Oliver sent a silent wish out to the universe that he'd say and do the right thing. Because later, when everyone shared details with their friends and picked through memories for things they'd initially overlooked, he didn't want his actions to counter Althea's goal.

"Mr. Wellsley, is it your wish to marry Althea? To love her for all your days?" Oliver asked.

"Yes, milord."

Oliver turned to Althea. "And Althea, do you love him as deeply and want him as your husband?"

Her smile glowed as she clasped Wellsley's hand. "I do."

The exchange was oddly reminiscent of wedding vows, but it felt right. Whispers from the crowd behind him grew, swelling to a shocked hiss of disapproval. Dorian sent a quelling glare at the assembled onlookers.

"Althea and Mr. Wellsley, I wish you both a lifetime of wedded bliss." Oliver gave them a shallow bow. "And I hope you'll return the sentiment, as Miss Martin has just agreed to make me the happiest of men."

This elicited genuine gasps from everyone. Constance's cousins rushed to hug her, and her beaming smile was one he'd remember until his last moment on earth.

"Darling, congratulations!" Caro wiped away happy tears.

Miss McCrae's response was more reserved, but no less earnest. "He's a lucky man, Connie love."

Dorian clapped him on the back. "Congratulations, friend. You've chosen well. Welcome to the family."

Oliver brought him into a hug. "Thank you."

As soon as Connie's cousins stepped away Dorian joined them. The three stood by, seeming quite pleased with themselves.

Constance reached for Oliver's hand. Joy nearly leveled

him at the way she so naturally threaded her fingers with his. Even their hands fit. As he'd told her moments ago, locked together in passion—he was hers, and she was his. The crowd's murmurs surged again.

Not wanting to steal Althea's thunder, Oliver tore his eyes from the stunning woman who'd agreed to be his bride. "If Sir William and Lady Thompson had been willing to listen to our wishes, we could have both been happily married weeks ago."

Althea welcomed the conversational volley with a faux grimace. "Unfortunately, my father cares more for refilling the depleted family coffers, than the happiness of others. When I told him I love Franklin, he put me under guard and denied me a dowry unless I married you, Lord Southwyn. He's a villain of the highest order and I'm ashamed to share his blood."

Since she'd brought up the rocky Thompson family finances, Oliver filled in a few missing facts. "Having seen the marriage contracts, I don't think you'd want the dowry anyway. Sir William is deep in dun territory. Excluding the river land, of course, the properties in your dowry are acting as collateral to violent moneylenders. That's why he pushed for us to marry this season. He dodged debtor's prison by paying his taxes with money borrowed from cent-percenters, then planned to pass along the debts—and threats—to me."

Althea's eyes went wide, but she regained her composure quickly. "That's appalling!" She glanced around at the gathered guests. "You're all witnesses to Lord Southwyn and myself joyfully ending our engagement and following our hearts elsewhere."

Constance spoke up. "So, if you received a wedding invitation today, feel free to use it as kindling."

Again, Althea's jaw dropped in surprise. "Oh dear. Mother wasn't supposed to send those until tomorrow."

Wellsley placed a soothing kiss on the side of her head, but Oliver could tell the information had distressed Althea.

"Since I hardly expect Sir William or Lady Thompson to be as happy about this development as we are, you're also all witnesses to something else." Mr. Wellsley waved Oliver over, inviting him to play the final part they'd put in place a mere hour earlier. Oliver and Constance joined the other couple, then turned to face the guests.

"Thus far, our luck has held and Althea's parents are not part of our merry group. When they arrive, please inform them she is safe and soon to be married. Because my new co-conspirator and I"—Oliver sent a friendly wink toward Wellsley—"are wasting no time in making off with our brides. Farewell."

Wellsley tugged a giggling Althea toward a set of glass doors on the far side of the room. Oliver wrapped an arm around Constance's waist and followed, but her cousins stopped their progress for one more goodbye.

The duchess was pink faced and smiling widely as she wrapped her arms around Constance, then kissed Oliver's cheek. "Be good to my cousin. Love her well."

He held her dark gaze and nodded. "I promise."

Dorian leaned in. "I'll explain to Mary and Owen. They'll want to welcome you to the family properly when you return."

"Tell Mr. Martin I chose to grovel." At his friend's raised brow, Oliver grinned. "He'll understand. And please apologize because I didn't ask for his blessing. I intended to when I called earlier, then everything fell apart."

Miss McCrae was next. "Lord Bixby told me what you did. If Connie had said no, you would have looked like a fool in front of everyone. I respect that. So, I'll echo Caro and tell you to cherish her. Or else."

Oliver studied her expression and was grateful Connie had this fierce friend on her side. "I believe you, because you're a rather terrifying woman, Miss McCrae. I assure you, I'll love and protect Constance with my last breath."

The firm line of her jaw softened. "You may call me Hattie," she said, then stepped aside.

"You weren't kidding," Wellsley hissed to Oliver, while staring in awe at Hattie.

Behind them, a gasp broke the rapt attention of the guests, followed by the distinctive sound of Sir William's bellow.

Before Oliver could do more than calculate the length of time it would take to get through the doors, across the garden to the street, and then the pub, Lady Agatha Darylwrimple's voice carried above the din. "Carry on, Lord Southwyn. I am proud of you, boy!" Then she said, in a far less friendly tone, "Sir William, I believe your wife requires some smelling salts. I am sure our hostess can provide them if you are unprepared. No, you may not enter this room. Tend to your wife."

"Who is that?" Constance whispered.

Oliver searched the room and spied the older woman standing between them and Althea's parents. "A friend. I'll introduce you at another time, but I think you'll like her. And I suspect she'll adore you."

Franklin held open the doors to the terrace.

"Come along, we need to leave." Althea made a shooing gesture. Since her parents' arrival, her happy glow was fading to anxiety.

Wellsley led them through the dark garden, where hedges and topiaries loomed like mythical beasts in the night. Oliver wrapped his arm around Constance's shoulders to ward off the night's chill as they hurried down Hill Street, toward the glowing lights of the Coach and Horses pub and his traveling coach.

"Connie, the invitation," Althea wailed. "You poor dear. That must have been quite a blow."

Constance didn't prevaricate yet wasn't unkind. Oliver loved that about her. "For a few moments, Oliver's life was in danger. However, he'd asked for my trust, and your annoyingly vague message gave me hope for a better outcome."

"In we go." Oliver ushered them into the coach. "Extra cloaks and blankets are on the seats. There should be warming bricks for your feet. If you think of anything else you need or forgot to pack, please let me know and we will get it when we stop at the inn tonight."

Althea and her soon-to-be husband settled onto one seat. Oliver handed Constance into the coach, then called up to his coachman. "All is well?"

"Aye, milord. We'll join the other coach shortly, transfer baggage, then get out of London before stopping for the night."

"Good man." Oliver climbed in beside Constance, humming with satisfaction. "Excellent work, everyone."

Althea giggled. "Yes, excellent work, Connie. You are the best matchbreaker a friend could ask for."

Oliver glanced between the women. "Matchbreaker?"

"I needed help making your life uncomfortable, so you'd see we wouldn't suit. Constance was perfect. In more ways than one, obviously." Althea's smile was smug.

Constance grinned, then leaned her head on his shoulder. Such a simple, trusting gesture. He dropped a kiss on the wild curls trying to escape their hairpins.

"If you ask very nicely, I'll show you our matchbreaking list. Perhaps we should frame it and hang it somewhere," Constance said.

"We'll put it in the dressing room, next to my horrible waistcoats." Oliver ran a hand over the pink and green one he wore. "Though I admit, I'm growing fond of this one."

"You needed more chaos in your life." She dimpled up at him.

Gazing down at the face he'd wake up to every day for the rest of his days, Oliver couldn't imagine a future more perfect. "I needed more Constance in my life."

Epilogue

~~Live happily ever after~~

One year later

When one possessed an army of staff and deep pockets, it was impressive what could be accomplished in a day.

Owen and Mary Martin had long since adopted dazed expressions and simply stepped out of Connie's path. The look was familiar. Her husband wore it on a regular basis.

Two of the men they'd hired for the day carried a wooden crate marked with a swipe of orange paint and paused in front of where Connie stood, unpacking dishes into a cupboard.

Color coding the boxes had been Caro's contribution to the move. After a quick consultation with her master list, Constance directed, "World history and geography. Second bookcase on your left, in this next room."

Two more sweaty-faced men approached bearing a crate with a green paint stripe as Connie closed the cupboard and moved on to a stack of table lines. "Primary bedchamber." When they hesitated, she realized they were newly arrived and didn't know the lay of the land yet. "East side of the house. With the view of the orchard, not the smaller room looking out on the road. That one is the guest bedroom."

Through the wide doorway to the main living area, Constance checked to ensure the men with the crate of history texts had found their destination. Hattie greeted their arrival by wielding a crowbar for the boxes and grumbling something about "too many bloody books."

"Don't let Owen hear you say that. It's sacrilege in this family," Oliver commented on his way through the room, carrying a dining chair in each hand. He stopped beside Connie and pressed a quick kiss to the side of her head. "You're a marvel, teacup," he murmured, using his favorite pet name for her, then continued on his way.

The affectionate words hugged Connie as they always did. His tempest in a teacup. A tiny storm, perfectly sized to warm his hands.

"Constance!" Betsy yelled.

Connie stepped toward her. "What is it?"

"Blue curtains. Parents', or the guest room?" Her sister stood in the main living area, holding a bundle of cloth. Oliver stepped out of the dining room, now empty-handed.

One of the men Constance had just sent on their way stumbled and nearly dropped his box. He gawked at the sisters.

Oliver grinned. "I initially had the same reaction, lads. This is Mrs. Tilford." He motioned toward Betsy, then pointed at Connie. "The one giving orders is mine, Lady Southwyn."

"Blimey," the man said.

Dorian's voice carried from the front door. "Beds are here! Connie, are there any changes to where they go?"

"No, continue as planned," she called back.

Betsy grinned at the men holding the crate. "We're easy enough to tell apart once you know us. Constance is the one capable of juggling five tasks at once." Returning her focus to her sister, she held up the fabric in silent question.

The last year had brought several honest discussions between Connie and her sister, and their relationship continued to improve.

"Blue goes in the nursery. The guest room is yellow, and our parents' room is green, like the paint stripe on their boxes."

This property was larger than her parents had anticipated, but their plans for the future hadn't taken into consideration a duke and an earl. Maintaining such a house wasn't too much, as it came with the help of a general man of work and a housekeeper. The couple lived in a caretaker's cottage behind the small orchard and garden plot.

In fact, this was the house Betsy had encouraged Dorian to look into, which led to Connie and Oliver's night in the cottage. Unbeknownst to Constance, her husband and the duke had purchased the property together, hired the caretaker and housekeeper, then kept the whole thing a secret until Owen and Mary began actively planning their retirement. When pressed, Dorian admitted he'd paid the lion's share of the purchase price and justified it as gratitude for the Martins giving Caro a safe home when she needed one.

Constance got misty-eyed whenever she recalled the way her parents reacted to their gift from the men who loved their girls. Regardless of actual place on the family tree, Owen and Mary considered Hattie and Caro to be their girls as fully as the twins.

As promised, Betsy lived a short walk away through the

village, with a convenient, although small, bookshop along the route.

Echoing voices and footsteps gradually grew muffled throughout the day as the house filled with furniture, rugs, drapes, and books. So many books.

Georgia's screeching giggles and Nate's young laugh pierced the air occasionally from where they played in the nursery.

By the time the sun dipped its hat in farewell and sank below the horizon, the house felt like a home, and Connie relished the weary satisfaction of a job well done.

She and Oliver were staying in the guest room, which her mum was having a grand laugh over referring to as the yellow room.

It wasn't terribly yellow yet, but that would come.

"My love, you have that expression on your face again. What are you thinking?" Oliver closed the bedroom door.

"I'm trying to remember where we put the wallpaper Mum chose for this room. She and Betsy plan to begin papering this week. We didn't leave it at home, did we?" When she turned around as if she meant to find it right then, he stayed her with a hand.

"Tomorrow. Wallpaper can wait. I haven't had a moment alone with you all day, and if I don't kiss you properly, I'll go stark raving insane." His mouth met hers and settled in for a deep taste. All thoughts of wallpaper or to-do lists disappeared.

Oliver had a way of kissing her as if the contact provided him relief on a soul-deep level. There was never a moment when she worried that his mind wandered, as hers sometimes did. Every time, he treated kissing her like an experience he relished.

The bed caught them as they fell, pushing a laugh of pure happiness from Connie at the sight of his wide grin above her. It didn't matter if their coupling was frantic or leisurely, the feeling of connection was the same. She couldn't imagine living without it.

So, when he whispered, "Hello, wife," against her lips, she gave herself over to loving him. He tasted of the slightly sweet cider from their meal, and that unique flavor she'd come to identify as simply Oliver.

During their first year of marriage, so much had become wonderfully normal. His taste, the scent of his sweat after a long bout of lovemaking, the way Oliver always made sure she had tea before getting his own cup.

Oliver leaned away to whip his shirt off, and Connie made short work of removing her clothing. Wearing nothing but her stockings and garter ribbons, she posed prettily, resting on her elbows as she took in the sight of him.

Then laughed, because when he saw her bare breasts, he stopped and appreciated them. Every. Single. Time.

There were some things she was learning that were delightfully predictable.

Although they'd come together so many times since eloping in a flurry of scandalized whispers, she had yet to take this part for granted.

This man, bare-chested and unable to tear his eyes off her as he fumbled with the buttons on his breeches. His focus made her core slick in anticipation. Love and lust and a deeper need filled his gaze.

The way he looked at her made it impossible for Constance to doubt herself, her appeal, or her welcome. And that was perhaps the most freeing thing of all. She only needed to be herself.

Oliver Vincent adored her as much as she adored him, and the truth of that had sunk deep into her bones.

He shucked his breeches to the floor, cursing when he realized he'd forgotten to remove his boots. Constance giggled at his flustered state. Rather than help, she chose to torment him while he untangled himself from clothing and leather.

With a lazy finger, Connie explored the plump flesh between her thighs. Her finger came away wet with evidence of her desire.

Oliver lost track of what he was doing. "Witch," he groaned.

"I'm waiting," she sang.

"Seems like you're starting without me, vixen," he grunted, struggling to remove his other boot.

Naked at last, Oliver crawled up her body, then sucked her finger into his mouth. Hungry eyes met hers before he smiled wickedly and reversed course.

"Your parents are down the hall." Throwing her legs over his shoulders, he settled into one of his favorite positions, and Connie's core clenched in anticipation. He placed an open-mouthed kiss high on her inner thigh. "Shall we have a competition, you and I?" A long, lazy lick along the seam of her sex made her whimper. "The one who makes the least noise, wins."

Devilish lips closed around the nub at the top of her slit, and Constance groped blindly for the nearest pillow to muffle her cries. Her husband was far too good at this for her to have any hope of winning the game, otherwise.

She still lost.

Later, they lay intertwined as their breathing slowed and that delightful shimmering sensation hummed through her body. Usually, Connie's brain went quiet after making love. Tonight, the thoughts drifted lazily by.

With her parents retiring, there'd be changes at Martin House. This visit to move Owen and Mary into their new home had been the first time Constance and Hattie left their newest employee, a widow named Whitney Parker, in charge of the shop without a family member available for emergencies. Mrs. Parker was scarily competent, remaining cool under pressure. The cousins weren't worried about leaving her alone.

Hattie loved the idea of living alone and was bursting with ideas of ways to make the flat more to her taste. Between her mum and her cousin, Connie suspected she'd master hanging wallpaper by the end of the summer.

Discovering how to be a countess and a business owner in the day-to-day running of things was ongoing, but exciting and full of possibilities. Navigating the ton sometimes felt like dancing barefoot through a snake pit, but she'd found several kindred spirits in unexpected places. As Oliver predicted, Lady Agatha Darylwrimple was a complete delight and stalwart friend.

Someone with less energy, or a more retiring personality, might find the variety of roles daunting, but the novelty appealed to her.

Oliver and Franklin had begun the arduous process of finding investors for their canal and hoped to break ground in the new year, shortly after the arrival of Althea's first child.

The thoughts floated by, like clouds in the sky. Until one made her snicker. Oliver's noise of inquiry wasn't quite a word, but, nonetheless, communicated effectively.

"Oliver... it's Tuesday."

"Ah, teacup, are you wanting a show? Maybe a five

minute frig?" His laugh rumbled, deep and low from his chest in that way she adored. Constance snorted against his shoulder as he wrapped his arms tighter around her.

One thing was clear: they'd spend the rest of their lives laughing together.

Life with Oliver would never be boring.

Author's Note

ADHD (attention deficit hyperactivity disorder) symptoms were documented for the first time in 1798 by the Scottish physician Sir Alexander Crichton. He described it as "the incapacity of attending with a necessary degree of constancy to any one object." It would be over a hundred years (1970s to be exact) before the first female ADHD cases would go on record. Official study of women and ADHD wouldn't happen until 2002. *2002, people.* Some of us drive cars older than that.

Like so many of my neuro-spicy sisters, I grew up being told I was smart but needed to apply myself. In social situations, I was either the life of the party or entirely overwhelmed and needed to sit in a quiet room with no one touching me. Random facts about niche topics were my specialty, but I couldn't remember if I had homework. Hobbies were things to deep dive into, then abandon entirely. Time management was a myth. Building healthy habits was impossible if it meant stepping outside my routine—except, I hated routines, because boredom was the devil… Also, I totally needed routines. Sideways glances or offhand comments were taken personally 100 percent of the time. Healthful sleep habits? What were those? Songs played on a loop in my head constantly. I'd forget to eat for days at a time.

I was diagnosed with ADHD at the age of twenty-seven, and it was a total lightbulb moment.

Because female ADHD symptoms tend to be far more internal, there's a domino effect. We often also deal with depression, anxiety, poor self-esteem, impulsive spending, emotional dysregulation, forming romantic attachments too deeply/quickly, substance abuse, eating disorders, and burnout...all while doing our damndest to meet society's unrealistic expectations for feminine beauty and behavior. Tragically, women with ADHD have a significantly higher likelihood of attempting suicide and/or developing self-harm habits.

I've said more than once that people love the idea of dating the Manic Pixie Dream Girl, but no one is prepared for the reality of living with her.

Which brings us to this book. Constance is my first ADHD heroine, although her story takes place during a period when diagnosis would have been impossible for her. A woman in Regency England would have had all of the struggle, but without any hope of an explanation.

Back in 1816, the Year Without Summer, our girl Constance would have recognized that she was different but wouldn't have the medical or social framework to understand why. These days we have Google and multiple medication options. Women like Constance weren't so lucky.

And if you're unfamiliar with the Year Without Summer, it's a fascinating topic. TLDR: volcano went boom, whole world went brrrrr, plants went nope. It was bad.

Also, if you're like me (and our girl, Constance), and deep dives into random historical topics are your jam, a key plot point in this story came together thanks to a fabulous paper by Allison Anna Tait at the University of Richmond School of Law. *The Beginning of the End of Coverture: A Reappraisal of the Married Woman's Separate Estate* gave me the "so *that's* how he's getting out of this" moment. Allison, wherever you are, I owe you a drink.

Happy reading, friends.

About the Author

Bethany Bennett grew up in a small fishing village in Alaska, where required life skills included cold-water survival, along with several other subjects that are utterly useless for a romance writer. Eventually settling in the Northwest with her real-life hero and two children, she enjoys mountain views from the comfort of her sofa, wearing a tremendous amount of flannel, and drinking more coffee than her doctor deems wise.

You can learn more at:
  Website: BethanyBennettAuthor.com
  Facebook.com/BethanyBennettHistoricalRomance
  Instagram, Threads: @BethanyWritesKissingBooks

Get swept away by Forever's historical romances!

Rebellious Heroines x Forbidden Love

HOT EARL SUMMER
by Erica Ridley

Nothing will stop Elizabeth Wynchester from seeing justice done. But when her next mission drops her at the Earl of Densmore's castle, she isn't prepared to be locked inside! And her trusty sword cannot protect her heart from the handsome rogue guarding the keep.

When Stephen Lenox agreed to impersonate the earl, he didn't expect him to vanish. Nor could he predict the arrival of his new blade-wielding bodyguard. She'll share his bed until their adventure concludes. Unless he can convince her to surrender her heart…

DUCHESS MATERIAL
by Emily Sullivan

Phoebe Atkinson is what society might call unconventional. Instead of marrying well and taking her place in society, she chose to be a schoolteacher. But when her pupil goes missing, she has only one option: to beg the Duke of Ellis for help.

William Margrave never expected to inherit a dukedom, but he's determined to act the part. Phoebe might not be duchess material, but as they fall further into the mystery, William discovers that he never got over his childhood crush on her.

Witty Banter x Murder Mystery

LADY CHARLOTTE ALWAYS GETS HER MAN
by Violet Marsh

Lady Charlotte Lovett has been promised to a man who, rumor has it, killed his previous two wives. To get out of this engagement, Charlotte will need to prove that Viscount Hawley is as sinister as she thinks. And the person who would know best is his very own brother.

Dr. Matthew Talbot is the exact opposite of his sibling—scholarly, shy, and shunned by society. But as he and Lady Charlotte grow closer to each other, they are also getting closer to a dangerous confrontation with Hawley.

A GOVERNESS'S GUIDE TO PASSION AND PERIL
by Manda Collins

When governess Jane Halliwell's employer is murdered, the former heiress is forced back into the world of the ton—and made to work with the lord who broke her heart.

Lord Adrian Fielding never noticed Jane when they were younger, so her icy demeanor confounds him—as does his desire to melt the tensions between them. But first he must find his mentor's murderer and ensure Jane's safety when she insists on joining the investigation. With a vicious killer circling, will it be too late for their chance at forever?

Find more book recommendations from Forever on social media @ReadForeverPub and at Read-Forever.com